Advance Praise for *The Wayward Moon*

"Weizman brings 9th-Century Babylonia to life so vividly that you can almost smell the jasmine and taste the date cakes."

Maggie Anton
Author of the *Rashi's Daughters* trilogy and *Rav Hisda's Daughter*

"In her debut novel, Toronto-born Weizman, who now lives in Israel and is founder and editor of the Ilanot Review, explores Islamic history through crises confronted by women. The action in the story—and there's lots of it—takes place in the ninth century, mostly in what is now Iraq. The first-person narrator, 17-year-old Rahel Bat Yair, is the daughter of a Jewish physician in Sura, south of Baghdad. Her mother died giving birth to Rahel, and her father raised and educated her. He arranges her marriage and accepts a position as advisor to the governor; the latter action enrages an anti-Semitic member of the governor's entourage, leading to a bloody confrontation in which the doctor is killed and Rahel slays the murderer. She flees and her subsequent exciting adventures, from a stint in a monastery to an ill-fated love affair, occupy the rest of the book. She eventually finds her way back to the Jewish community in the Galilee area and writes her story. This melodrama holds the reader's interest as the strong-willed Rahel weathers this series of disasters."

Publishers Weekly

"Janice Weizman's *The Wayward Moon* introduces readers to a strong, memorable female character who manages to outwit the cruel turns of fate in her life in the 9th century in Iraq. This is a welcome departure from the many novels about European Jewish life. Rahel, the main character, takes the reader on a journey into the lives of Moslems, Christians, and Jews who lived in the area around Baghdad and the land between the Tigris and Euphrates Rivers. The novel is filled with details about the people who made up the population of this part of the world and the place of Jews and women in general in it."

Past president, Association of J
Owner, Off the S

"By blending skillful historical research with excellent storytelling, and psychological insight with adventure, Janice Weizman has fashioned a compelling tale of hope lost and regained. *The Wayward Moon* is a remarkable debut."

Joseph Kertes
Dean, School of Creative and Performing Arts
Humber College, Toronto, Ontario
Award-winning author of *Gratitude*

"Janice Weizman takes us on a captivating journey of a young woman's self-discovery. Rahel becomes the reluctant master of her own fate with the opportunity to determine her life's path. And yet we are left to wonder whether anyone really has the freedom to choose one's destiny. With Weizman's meticulous attention to mood and language, we are transported to an ancient time and place that is both fascinating and vivid. This is a beautiful adventure that unravels with delicate precision."

Kathy Kacer
Award-winning author of *Restitution: A Family's
Fight for Their Heritage Lost in the Holocaust*

THE WAYWARD MOON

Janice Weizman

THE WAYWARD MOON

JANICE WEIZMAN

Yotzeret Publishing
St. Paul MN

The tzaddi logo is a registered trademark of Yotzeret Publishing, Inc.

Cover photo © 2012 by iStockphoto.com/Angela Oakes

Grateful acknowledgment is made to the following for permission to reprint previously published material:

>   M.A. Recordings: Translated excerpts from *Splendour of Al-Andalus* by Calamus. Translated text copyright © 1999 by M.A. Recordings. Reprinted with persmission of M.A. Recordings. www.marecordings.com.

>   Catholic University of America Press: *Discourses Against Judaizing Christians* by John Chrysostom. Copyright © 2012. Reproduced with permission of Catholic University of America Press in the format Tradebook via Copyright Clearance Center.

Publisher's Cataloging-in-Publication data

Weizman, Janice.
    The wayward moon / Janice Weizman.
    p. cm.
    ISBN 978-1-59287-101-8
1. Islamic Empire –History --750-1258 --Fiction. 2. Jews --Iraq --History –Fiction. 3. Women --Middle East --History --Fiction. 4. Jewish women --Iraq --History --To 1500. 4. Historic fiction. I. Title.

PS3623.E4621 W29 2012
813/.6 --dc23   2012944249

For Pino

"All journeys have secret destinations
of which the traveler is unaware."

—Martin Buber

"To attain any assured knowledge about the soul
is one of the most difficult things in the world."

—Aristotle, *On the Soul*

PROLOGUE

Buqei'a, Galilee, 894

The grave was like an open wound in the rocky face of the mountain. Cold drops of rain lashed at the faces of mourners as they huddled together against the winds, the men in long cloaks, and women wrapped in their heaviest shawls. *Blessed is He beyond any blessing and praise and consolation that are uttered in the world. Now say: Amen.* "Amen," the crowd had cried sorrowfully with them, and Yair reflected that his mother, a humble woman who had lived out her days in a remote corner of the Galilee, had nonetheless left a mark on the world.

After the funeral, and for the entire seven days of the *shivah*, the house was filled with people from Buqei'a and the villages beyond. And when he had torn his robe and taken his place on the floor beside his elder brother Yehuda, the men of the village had embraced him and murmured, "Praise God you arrived in time to part with her; when you return to your studies in Sura, it will be with an untroubled heart."

There was a strange solace in the ancient rites and customs. To stand in prayer three times a day in a quorum of men who accompanied them as they chanted psalms. To receive the relatives and neighbors he had known all his life, simple God-fearing men and women who would take his hands in theirs and utter tearful blessings and words of praise, for her and for their entire family. To sit in the evenings with his brother and sisters, recalling her charitable works and her pure heart, so that when he rose from the seven days of mourning, it was with a sense that the book of her life might be respectfully closed.

IT WAS ON the last evening of the shivah, when the grief that pervaded the house had begun to lift, that Ruth, the eldest of Yair's four sisters, came looking for him in the room behind the kitchen where the men sat in mourning. As she entered, they turned their eyes from her, and she knelt down to her brother and whispered, "Yehuda wants to speak with you. He's waiting in her bedchamber." Though Ruth was already a grandmother herself, it was she who had cared for their mother in her infirmity. The task had taken its toll; his sister's once brilliant green eyes seemed tired, and her legendary fair hair had begun to turn gray.

Yair pulled himself up, made his way through the kitchen where the village women were preparing dinner for the mourners, and slipped behind the heavy woolen curtain that set the sleeping quarters apart from the rest of the house. Yehuda was sitting on the bare bed, the one where their parents had slept for thirty years, and his mother had slept alone for ten more. A lamp flickered from its niche in the wall, and in its dim light, Yair saw that his brother clasped a tightly rolled scroll.

Yehuda looked up at him. Over the course of the week, he had received all who had come to pay their respects with the staid, dignified grace of a community elder. But now, alone in the room where their mother had died, he seemed to embody the bewilderment of a child betrayed. "Come here," he said quietly.

"What is it?"

Yehuda motioned with his eyes toward the curtain and Yair pulled it shut. "I've found something. Something terrible. I haven't spoken of it to anyone, but I cannot remain alone with it any longer."

Yair glanced at the bare straw mattress as though he expected to see his mother lying there, infirm, but with eyes still alert, still wise. "Tell me."

"On the morning that the burial society came for the body," he began in a voice just above a whisper, "they instructed me to burn her bedding. I was collecting the blankets when the bed came away from the wall, and I noticed that one of the stones looked odd, as if it were not set in place." Yair watched as his brother rose and moved the bed from the wall, exposing the section that was normally concealed. He then knelt down and pulled out a stone, which tumbled cleanly into his hand.

Yair stared at the gaping hole, perplexed. "It appears that this house has secrets."

"More than anyone could imagine," Yehuda replied in a hoarse whisper. He sat himself heavily on the bed and took the thick roll of parchment in his hand. "This is what I found hidden behind the stone."

The scroll was cracked and dry; clearly it had lain in the wall for many years. "What is written there?" Yair asked uneasily.

"The night I found it, I took it to my study and told Tziporah that I was not to be disturbed. The reading was difficult. Rolled up it looks small, but it's written in a minuscule hand. I read it through without eating or drinking or speaking with anyone. That was one week ago, the night of the funeral. Since that night, I've thought of nothing else."

"For the entire week you've kept this to yourself? Who wrote it?"

Yehuda looked away, to the thin, ragged mat on the dirt floor of the room. "She did."

"Who she?" Yair waited for a response, but he was met with silence. "But that's impossible! She couldn't even read, let alone write!"

"There are many things that we didn't know about her. And now, having read this, I can only wonder if any of us ever knew her at all. There are things here . . . things that have stunned me to my core. Unutterable things. If the tales this manuscript reveals ever became public knowledge, they would tarnish her name, and ours, forever. My first instinct after reading it was to burn it."

"Burn it? You would burn her words?"

"Yes! I wanted to destroy it, so that it would vanish from the face of the earth as surely as she has. And yet . . ." he shook his head, "I find that I can't bring myself to do it without the consent of at least one other man." He met Yair's astounded gaze with a hard stare. "And naturally, my brother, that man could only be you. It is you, of all of us, who's been blessed with father's keen mind and mother's wisdom. And after all," he added with a bitter grin, "you were her favorite."

"Don't be a fool. Mother had no favorite."

"Yair, we are no longer children. She's dead and gone, and there is no need to conceal what we've always known in our hearts. From the day you were six years old and the elders brought you home from the synagogue declaring that you had the mind of a scholar, she took it upon herself to make sure that you would one day go to Sura. The lessons, the rabbis she brought from Tiberius and Aleppo, the coins she saved—it was all so that you would one day study with sages. You were her greatest hope, Yair. Her most solemn prayer. The day we received word that you had been accepted at the yeshiva in Sura, she could barely speak from joy." Yehuda shook his head in a gesture of confusion and sadness. "God willing, your righteousness and brilliance in study will redeem the transgressions of her youth."

"Transgressions? What transgressions?" But again Yehuda was silent.

Yair's eyes moved from the tightly rolled scroll to the place in the wall where it had lain in waiting for who knew how long. "Are you certain that no one else has seen this?"

"No one," Yair replied as he handed the scroll to his brother, "and no one else will. Only you and I will ever know of its existence."

Yair unrolled a little and examined the crudely formed script. "What language is this?"

Yehuda allowed himself a smile. "Let's see if your love of books will prove itself useful."

Yair held the scroll to the lamp. "Is this Syriac? She could write in the language of the Christians?" He looked up at his brother in amazement. "How is that even possible?"

"I'm afraid that you're about to discover many things that will surprise you."

But Yair was no longer listening. He unfurled the scroll and read out, *I, Rahel Bat Yair, was born in the city of Sura, which lies on the western bank of the river Euphrates in the land of Bavel, where the great houses of learning shine their light.* "Sura?" he cried. "But how can that be? She always told us that she was from some remote village!"

Yair rose and put a heavy hand on his brother's shoulder. "Tomorrow morning we will return to her grave. We will recite psalms and pray that her soul finds peace for all eternity, and my prayers will be as fervent as anyone's. But I can't remain alone with all that this manuscript contains. I cannot be the sole bearer of this burden. Time is short and a judgment must be made. Read all that is written here, and when you finish, send for me. Immediately."

FLIGHT

Buqei'a, Galilee, March 851

I Rahel Bat Yair, was born in the city of Sura, which lies on the western bank of the river Euphrates in the land of *Bavel*, where the great houses of learning shine their light. As I write these words, I can only wonder who will read them. Are you, honorable reader, a woman? I doubt that you are, and so as I record my tale, I will imagine that I address a man. But am I to envision one man, or many? Regrettably, I cannot know, and so I will speak as only a book is able, as if to a multitude of strangers, even though each man will hear my tale with his mind and heart alone.

Although I mastered, in the course of my misadventures, the skill of writing, I believed that I would never again have reason to take a pen in my hand. Here in these mountains, only scholars and scribes make use of reed pens and parchment, and obviously I am neither. Yet I've managed, by wits and guile, to obtain instruments of writing, and now, as I sit by lamplight at my table, my hand trembles; for I am about to record the true events of my life, those that are plain to me and those that remain a mystery, in all their horror and their wonder.

THOSE WHO'VE PASSED their lives amongst barren hills and goat droppings can't imagine life in a city. They know nothing of palaces and gardens built by men dreaming of symmetry and harmony, of light and shadow and color. They've never wandered, dizzy with the intoxication of abundance, through the restless alleyways of a market. What can they know of a market? They, whose tables are ruled by the whims of nature, can scarcely imagine a place where pistachio nuts and apricots from the East are displayed alongside melons and dates from the South, and where the scents of cumin and coriander, fenugreek and saffron mingle in the air like unruly children. And of things that delight women—perfumes, scented oils, soft silks, and glittering stones—they know nothing at all. Here in the mountains, the women are ignorant of such indulgences.

It happens, of course, that these unfortunates travel to Tiberius, or Tyre, or even Damascus, which some try, pitifully, to compare with Baghdad. But these cities are tired; like sick, old men, their glory is behind them, and the ruins left by the Romans and their Christian children make these cities sad. Their buildings are crumbling, the public squares are dusty and somber, and the people walk with heavy steps, as though resigned to the fact that their day has passed.

To see real splendor, one must venture east, to cities blessed with culture and learning, where the tables of book shops are emptied before their owners can replenish what they've sold, and men argue in the streets over which of the sciences is most useful. Poets compose works for the sole purpose of delighting their listeners; singers and musicians practice their art in parks under the shade of flowering trees. Architects design fountains and public squares, academies and hospitals, each trying to outdo the other in grandeur and beauty. Prosperous merchants build villas, and then fill them with carpets and draperies, tapestries and chests of polished wood inlaid with ivory. Their vessels and bowls are wrought by artisans, and their beds are filled with the softest of duck feathers.

And this too must be said: the Jews of Bavel—of Sura, Pumbedita, Basra, Kufa and Baghdad—by virtue of dwelling in such cultured places, are themselves superior in culture, in learning, and in refinement to other Jews of the world. There is nothing surprising about this. Were not the Euphrates and Tigris the two rivers that flowed from the Garden of Eden? Was Abraham, the father of all Jews, not born beyond the river Euphrates? And now, when the holy places of *Eretz Yisrael* are homes to snakes and jackals, and the only Jews remaining are shepherds and farmers, is it any wonder that it was the Jews of Bavel who have set down God's laws in the *Talmud*

Bavli, which maintains its authority to this very day? Likewise, it is the heads of Bavel's great *yeshivot*, Sura and Pumbedita, who appoint judges and scribes to serve in all the places where Jews dwell. It is they who decide which sinners deserve to be exiled from the house of the God-fearing, and who may return. And it is to Sura and Pumbedita that the Seventy Scholars come, each spring and each autumn, to debate burning questions and fine points of law at the *Kallot* gatherings.

As a girl in Sura, I was unaware that I was living in paradise. I had to be driven from my home, to traverse deserts and mountains, to sleep under many skies and live amongst people of every sort, before I could know what I had lost.

And I lost it all. Suddenly, without warning. In less time than it takes for a pot of water to boil.

ROSES AND JASMINE sprang from shapely clay pots in our courtyard. The door to our home was framed by two date palms that curved downward, as if in a gesture of humility. Inside the house, the walls were hung with woven tapestries, and our floors adorned with soft carpets swirling with images of flowers and birds. The back of our house opened onto a green garden where, under skies bright with stars, my father and I would sit on warm nights, drinking mint tea and speaking of every subject under the sun. But on this night, his mood was sober. For a long while we sat in silence as he gazed at me with wistful eyes. When he finally spoke, he said he had something important to tell me.

But I already knew what he was going to say.

It was *Adar*, the month of the spring *Kallah*, when the Assembly of the Seventy Scholars convenes at the yeshiva in Sura to debate queries sent by Jews from every corner of the Caliphate. The inns and markets were filled with learned disciples and promising students, and whenever I went out into the street, I would steal furtive glimpses of their sprouting beards and bright turbans, thrilled and terrified that one of them might soon be my husband.

Since childhood, I had viewed the young brides, older girls who had suddenly become women, with envy and longing. I yearned for the day when I would don an embroidered gown and veil, and how, with eyes made beautiful with khol and lips painted red, my new relatives would hang necklaces of gold around my neck and sing me wedding songs. In time, the brides were no longer older girls, but girls of my own age, and lately, to my great dismay, girls even younger than myself. Many of my childhood friends were already raising their children, and the women of Sura had begun to regard me with pity and concern.

There was only one reason for my prolonged maidenhood, and that was my father. From the time I first bled, I had begged him to find a groom for me, but he had always refused, insisting that no girl should enter into marriage before the age of seventeen. When I protested, he would try to frighten me with stories of the birth ordeals of young mothers. For he was a physician, and he had seen countless girls endure grave complications, which often, as in my own mother's case, led to their deaths on the birthing chair. But now, when my seventeenth birthday had arrived and I was practically an old maid, he had finally decided to make inquiries among the scholars attending the Kallah.

"As we agreed," he began, "I've made it known that my daughter is now of marriageable age." I tried to keep my expression serious, even as my feet tapped a dance under my robe. "Two days ago, Rabbi Elhanan sought me out. He told me of a young man who might be a suitable candidate for you." He paused, and with great effort I willed myself to sit still while he poured the tea. "Hiyya Bar Raban of Basra is attending the Kallah with his three sons. The older two are married, and word has it that he's looking for a bride for his youngest, a youth by the name of Asher. Rabbi Elhanan knows the family well, and can vouch for their good name and honorable status. He arranged for me to meet with the father and son."

My feet froze. "And so you've met them?" I managed to ask.

"This morning. In Rabbi Elhanan's library." He broke into a maddening smile. "They're fine people, and I'm sure that Bar Raban's son will be to your liking."

I drew a long breath to calm my racing heart. "Tell me everything about him! I want to know every detail!"

He laughed. "There's little to tell. "They're carpet merchants. They have a workshop in the market of Basra, where they employ twenty weavers. The two older sons help run the business, but the youngest has shown great promise as a scholar, so much so that he has been invited to stay on and study under the tutelage of Rav Yanai. Bar Raban has consented to the offer and will provide full financial support, on condition that the boy marries."

"A scholar," I murmured, clasping my hands together like a gleeful child. "Is he very clever?"

He considered my question. "It's hard to say. During the meeting he barely said a word. But he seems likeable enough, modest, and respectful of his father."

As he spoke, I envisioned a pale, timid youth, and thought of Shalmai, the baker's son, his face spotted with skin ailments, and his voice croaking like a frog's. "What does he look like?"

"He is in good health."

"Is he handsome? How tall is he? What color are his eyes?"

"Charm is deceitful and beauty is vain," he replied, quoting one of his favorite sayings. "But you'll be able to judge for yourself tomorrow evening, when Hiyya Bar Raban and his son pay us a visit."

"Tomorrow?" I cried. "But I'm not ready. It will take days for me to prepare. Maybe even weeks!"

"There's no need for any preparation," he said, chuckling. "You couldn't be more charming than you are right now. On the contrary, it is they who ought to concern themselves with winning *your* favor."

I shook my head. "Impossible. How can I observe him when I know that he is observing me?"

"It is a delicate matter," he agreed, "but I can't make this decision in your place. First impressions are the most telling, though. Watch him carefully; take note of everything he does and says, and we'll discuss our findings afterward."

Such a reply was typical of my father. Though he spoiled me as a parent spoils his only child, he was constantly inventing new trials for me.

All that night, my mind burned as if in fever. A thousand imaginings flashed through my thoughts as I tried to conjure up an image of the boy who would be my husband. When I rose the next morning, my mind was overflowing with all of the preparations I needed to make. Nevertheless, I headed straight for my father's study, where I knew I would find him engrossed in his reading.

Though he had trained as a physician, the breadth of my father's knowledge and his love of inquiry reached far beyond the limits of his medical texts. It was his habit to rise early each morning in order to read from the books and scrolls that he exchanged with his more learned patients. And indeed, though his study served as an office for receiving patients, his desk was that of a scholar. It was laden with parchment scrolls, blackened pens, a brass inkpot, and a pile of volumes in Arabic, Greek, Syriac, and Aramaic. "It's cruel to keep me in this. . . this ignorance," I protested as I dropped into the chair opposite his. "You have to tell me more!"

"But if I do that, how will you form your own opinion?" He grinned, amused. "Give the poor man a chance to present himself in his own fashion. Only then will you be able to appraise him fairly." I watched as he reached out and selected an apple from the bowl of fruit on his desk. Taking his dagger in hand, he sliced the apple in two and offered me one of its halves, which I refused with an anxious shake of my head.

For a moment I tried to envision it: how I would sit at my father's side, and he at his father's side. How I would avoid staring at him, even as I yearned to study him as my father studied his medical diagrams. Though I was well used to receiving my father's patients, and even exchanging pleasantries with them, I could scarcely imagine actually conversing with this boy. "How can I possibly appraise him? I know almost nothing about young men."

He tapped his right temple. "Intuition. Or rather, intuition and intellect; one must use both." He tilted his head thoughtfully and remarked, "Just now I was reading the end of a remarkable Greek drama. The main character is a girl of your own age. She's on the threshold of her marriage, just like you are. And like you, she has little experience of life. But her intuition and intellect are sharp, and these give her the will to take a stand, and to see that stand to its end."

I sighed, letting my eyes wander over his desk. "Is that the book?"

He closed the cover and turned it to face me. "Let's see if you can read the title."

My father had tried to educate me, far more than is normal for girls. I've always attributed this to my being his only child, when surely he would have preferred a boy. Rather than accepting my limitations, however, he chose to ignore nature and teach me reading and writing, not only in the Aramaic that we spoke at home, but also in Hebrew, so that I would be able to read from the bible, some Arabic, and also a little Greek. I leaned over the book and slowly, with difficulty, I sounded out the Greek letters. "*An-ti-go-ne*. Antigone. What does it mean?"

"It's the heroine's name."

"And what happens to this Antigone?"

He smiled as if, in spite of myself, I had passed a test. "There! Do you see, Rahel? That's exactly my point. I've given you only a brief description of the work, and already you want to know more. You can sense that it might appeal to you. But this is not the time to speak of books." He frowned as he rose from his chair. "Matters of great importance are before us. This evening you will meet the man who may become your husband. You will be busy from morning to night, first with your wedding, and then with your new life as a married woman. But a day will come when you'll recall this conversation, and then, when the opportunity falls into our hands like a ripe fruit, we shall speak of Antigone again.

"And now," he sighed as he selected two small vials from the medicine cupboard, "I'm afraid that we both have many things to attend to. I've promised Ben Simon that I would visit his ailing father today, and Hadija, the astrologer's pregnant wife, is in bed with fever. They live on the other side of town, but if I go on horseback, I should be home well before sundown."

AT THE TOWN baths, I instructed the attendants to scent the water with myrrh and sandalwood, and to wash my hair with the powder of crushed lotus leaves. Later, before the long mirror in my bed chamber, I slipped into my white dress and tied a blue sash around my hips. "Say nothing," Shafiqa, our servant woman, advised me as she combed out my hair and fixed it back with a pearl comb. "A well-bred girl holds her tongue in the company of men. And remember to avoid their eyes. There is nothing as appealing in a girl as bashfulness. Of course, if they speak to you, or ask you a question, you must answer sweetly. But take care not to let your eyes linger on the boy; you don't want them to think you a harlot."

When she was done, she beheld me from top to bottom and broke into a joyful song that the Muslim women sing at weddings. And then she took my hands in her own and squeezed them tightly. "Promise to keep a secret?" I nodded excitedly, and she reached into her apron, drew out a small cloth pouch, loosened the drawstring and withdrew a blackened gold necklace strung with a delicately carved *hamsa* pendant.

"It's beautiful!" I cried.

"This," she told me solemnly, "was your mother's. It's a proper hamsa, to keep the demons far away, and protect you wherever you go. Your father means to give it to you tonight if an engagement is announced. He told me to polish it until it gleams."

A strange chill came over me, almost as if she, the stranger who bore me, was standing by my side. I reached out to touch the tiny gold hand and whispered, "This was hers?"

"She wore it the day she went before the rabbi to marry your father. He's kept it for you for seventeen years."

I opened the clasp to try it on, but just as I was about to fasten it around my neck, my father's footsteps sounded in the courtyard. He called for her, and as she rushed out, I thrust the necklace into her hand. But I lingered behind, staring at the girl who looked back at me in the mirror.

WHEN MY FATHER was a young child, one quarter of the residents of his native city of Basra perished in a fever epidemic. Both of my grandparents were among the victims, and my father, an only child, was sent to Sura to be raised by his father's brother, an eccentric young man by the name of Hannanya Bar-Ashi. This Bar-Ashi was reputedly kindhearted and generous, but also headstrong and impulsive. For seven years my father enjoyed a charmed childhood, until his uncle became utterly infatuated with a Karaite woman. In a fit of passion, Bar-Ashi sold all his possessions, sent my father to live with his grandfather Eliahu, and followed the woman to the far-off city of Tiflis.

Bar-Ashi's grandfather Eliahu owned a book shop in the market in Sura. Appalled at his great-grandson's lack of education, he wasted no time hiring teachers to school him: Hebrew for *Torah* and *Gemara*, Arabic for contracts and business, mathematics for calculations. When the old man passed on, my father was still a youth, alone in the world, but endowed with an inheritance large enough to allow him to secure an apprenticeship in medicine with one of the renowned physicians of Sura.

Though he had neither the benefit of a respected family name, nor helpful connections to advance him, my father was blessed with a keen diagnostic ability, a congenial manner, and a talent for discretion. His reputation as a gifted physician soon spread, and his name did not escape the notice of the wealthy and powerful. Not surprisingly, a day came when the governor of the city sent emissaries asking if he was willing to take on an official role as his advisor.

My father had no taste for power and the intrigue that comes with it, and would have rejected the offer outright had he not received a visit from the elders of the community. They approached him after prayers one evening, urging that he agree to the governor's request. "Since Ben Abbaye fell ill last fall, there are no longer any Jews in the governor's office," my father explained to me. "They've asked that I accept the position for the sake of the community."

Yet the situation was a delicate one, for the governor had in his entourage a distant cousin, the eldest son of the Qaddi of Sura, by the name of Abu Said. It was well known that this man, a devout Muslim, was one of those poisoned with a strange, unrelenting hatred of Jews. Though the elders of the community enjoyed good relations with the governor, the Jews of Sura were wary of provoking Abu Said in any way.

My father was still deliberating when, late one evening, he was surprised by a visit from Mudar Al Bahri, the governor's brother-in-law and personal secretary. He arrived unaccompanied, and my father himself ushered him into his study, where we had begun a game of chess. "I apologize for calling at such an hour," Al Bahri began, "but the governor has asked me to speak with you discreetly."

I bid the secretary good night and took my leave, but curiosity made me slip out to the back garden and listen, crouched under the window, to what he had come to say.

". . . the governor has little patience for the endless line of incompetents and freeloaders being forced upon him," I heard Al Bahri tell my father. "He seeks the council of a man who's concerned with more than filling his own pockets."

"This is indeed a great honor," my father replied cautiously, "yet there are members of his retinue who would be extremely dismayed to have me in their presence."

"Abu Said is a greedy, conniving fool. The governor finds him insufferable."

"But he is not without influence. Last week I saw him leaving the police offices with the commander of the *Shutra*."

"Then it is all the more important for you to have access to the governor's ear."

My father was silent for a moment. "I need to think it over."

"By all means, consider the offer carfully, but make your decision quickly. The governor wants to avoid the spread of half-truths and rumors. The sooner we make your appointment official, the better."

After that night, Al Bahri's words sat heavily in my father's mind and it seemed to me that he was inclined to refuse the position. But several days later, while returning on horseback from a visit to a patient in a nearby town, a chance meeting changed my father's thinking. As he rode into the town square, he came upon Abu Said and his friends walking home from evening prayers. Although Jews were not officially allowed to own or ride horses, special permits were granted to men who, like my father, employed them in the service of Muslims. On that evening, however, the sight of my father sitting atop his horse enraged Abu Said, and he called out, right there in the town square, "Will you look at that! The Jew Ben Shmuel rides a horse! The *Shurut Omar* clearly states that the *djimi* are forbidden to ride horses."

Shouts of agreement rang out from Abu Said's companions. But a Muslim patient of my father's, who happened to be crossing the square, called out loudly, "But Abu Said, sir, how are we to understand your sudden concern? Ben Shmuel's horse has never troubled you before."

Laughter rang out from the crowd that had gathered around them, but Abu Said answered back, "There are many things that are not as they should be, many sights to which our eyes have been blind. It is a shame and an insult that a Jew should rule over us. Have any of you heard the rumor that the Jew Ben Shmuel has his eye on the governor's office? If there is even the smallest bit of truth to it, no Muslim should sleep in peace."

"The only one not sleeping in peace is you," the patient cried, "because the Governor prefers the council of a wise man to that of a fool."

More laughter ensued, but my father rode off before the situation could get any worse. By the time he arrived home, he had made his decision. When Al Bahri paid us a visit two nights later, my father gave his agreement to accept the position.

How shall I tell of what came next? The course of a life can change in the time it takes a pot of water to boil.

When Abu Said burst into our house, I was about to perfume my wrists with rose water. As I drew the delicate glass stick from the vial, it occurred to me that Asher Bar Raban might not like the smell of roses. Iyad, our gardener, had told to me that not everyone did.

It was then, at that exact moment, that I heard a shout from the front room. I put down the vial and ran out to the hallway. My father stood in the entrance of our home, and not ten paces from him, eyes flaming with the crazed gaze of a madman, was Abu Said. Although he was not a large man, the sight of him, panting and fuming with fury, was terrible. In his right hand he held a dagger.

"No believer will consent to this treachery," he cried. "Do you hear me, Ben Shmuel? You will renounce the appointment, or suffer the consequences!"

"I will renounce nothing," I heard my father reply sharply. "The governor himself has personally requested that I take on the position."

"We will not be ruled by a Jew because of one foolish heretic!" he screamed.

"I advise you to watch your tongue, Abu Said."

"What's that, Ben Shmuel? You threaten me?"

"If you know what's best, you'll turn around and leave this house at once."

Perhaps if my father had not been a proud man, events would have unfolded differently. Perhaps if he had agreed to renounce the appointment, or even say that he would reconsider the matter, Abu Said would have been satisfied. On the other hand, it is possible that nothing would have appeased him, for he had brought his dagger, and the notion of murder had taken root in his heart.

"Honored sir," Shafiqa cried, falling at his feet. "Please go home. Your father, in his great wisdom, will fix everything."

But Shafiqa's words only fed his rage. "You!" he roared. "You, who were once a good Muslim woman, shame yourself by working in the home of a Jew. Don't you know your rightful place? Where is your self-respect? This man should be *our* servant!"

Somehow, my father remained unmoved by Abu Said's hysteria. "This is your last chance," he warned. "Leave now, and we will both forget your childish outburst. Go home to your father. The Qaddi will be very distressed if word of your behavior reaches his ears."

"Allahu Akbar!" he screamed out, and in a mad rage, charged up to my father and plunged the dagger into his heart. Shafiqa let out a shrill wail. I ran to my father and fell to the floor, where he lay crumpled and moaning, a bright red stain of blood spreading rapidly over his robe. "Run!" he groaned. "Run to the study, close the door and move my desk to block it."

"No!" I screamed as I tried to lift his shoulders. "Don't close your eyes."

But his eyes fluttered shut, and with his last remaining strength he pulled me to him and whispered, "I'm dying. Save yourself."

I looked up and saw Abu Said's face, contorted with insane ecstasy, his hand still holding the dagger, wet with blood. I jumped up, dashed to the study, shut the door, and flattened myself against the wall.

Abu Said's steps were heavy. I heard the study door open, and I slid behind it. "Where did you go, you little snake," he muttered. "I saw you run in here. Do you think you can escape me now?" I was paralyzed beyond reason. It could only have been pure animal instinct that made my eyes dart around the room like a terrified animal until they fell on my father's desk where, alongside the bowl of fruit, lay the knife my father had used that morning. I reached out to grab it, but my trembling fingers pushed it to the floor, where it landed with a low thud. Abu Said swung around, his face shining with madness. In the space of an instant I swooped down and retrieved it. His eyes flashed just as they had in the moment before he stabbed my father. *"Allahu Akbar!"* he cried, lunging toward me.

With a terrible howl, I raised my right hand and plunged the knife into his neck. Blood spilled from the wound onto his robe. I watched in horror as his fingers slowly released the knife, which fell to the floor and spun around in frenzied circles. Shafiqa ran into the room screaming hysterically, while Abu Said gasped and writhed like a fish pulled from the river. He staggered forward several steps, then fell to the floor. It was a gruesome sight, and I too began to scream.

Like a crazed choir, we screamed in unison. But while I felt myself to be on the very brink of madness, Shafiqa, by the grace of God, recovered herself. She held me in a tight embrace, as if she could see the powers of madness beckoning me to fall into abandon. "My daughter, you must run and hide," she whispered as she stroked my hair. "When word of this gets out, Abu Said's family will surely avenge his death." Somehow, the steady tone of her voice calmed me enough to hear her words and know that all she was saying was true. It was only a matter of time until Abu Said's relatives came looking for me. Revenge would be demanded and taken, long before I could plead my story to a judge. The only way for me to stay alive was to flee.

Shafiqa ran out of the room and returned seconds later holding items of my father's clothing. "You must dress in the clothes of a man." I glanced down and screamed again. My white dress was splattered with blood. The sight was so horrible that I could scarcely move. Shafiqa pulled my dress off, raised my arms, and wrapped an old headscarf of hers around me, flattening my chest like a boy's. She put my father's tunic over my head, and his pants around my ankles, and his rider's boots by my feet. Still stunned, I stepped out of my girl's slippers, slipped my arms and legs into the clothing, and donned the boots. In the meantime, Shafiqa had found one of my father's turbans. She gathered up my hair, stuffed it into the turban, and fixed it tightly on my head. Stepping back as if to appraise her work, she shook her head and muttered, "God willing, you might just pass for a boy."

I stared at her blankly, barely comprehending what was happening, and what was about to happen. She grabbed the cloth bag that she used when she went to market, and ran to the kitchen. Seconds later, she hung it across my flat chest.

I remember how she embraced me, then put her strong, rough hands on my shoulders. "You must run, my daughter. Run toward the date groves that grow along the road into town. I have no words of advice to give you. May God watch over you, as He watched over the holy followers of the Prophet in their flight from Mecca to Medina. I will tell Abu Said's men that you ran off in the direction of the river, but remember, you run to the date groves. Allah protect you, child." With that, she pushed me out the door.

Evening was falling. I flew through the darkening streets of Sura, the only streets I had ever known, and into the date groves that grow by the road that leads out of the city. I ran as the deer runs when she is escaping the tiger: blindly, with but one thought in her head. And when I reached the groves, I made my way through the labyrinth of their tall, jagged trunks until, breathless and exhausted, I collapsed at the foot of a low, sheltering palm tree.

THE EARTH WAS cold and damp, and as I stared up through the canopy of palm fronds, I couldn't fathom how I came to be lying there. But when I sat up and saw Shafiqa's bag lying open at my feet, a great wail rose up in my throat, and memory rushed over me like a flood. My heart failed to beat, as if it had forgotten how to breathe. I struck my head against the tree again and again, oblivious to the bleeding, until I collapsed, empty and exhausted. I lay like that for hours, lacking all will to move.

How much time had passed? I no longer cared. When I woke the next morning, Shafiqa's bag still lay at my feet. I stared at it for half a day, too weak and indifferent to open it, and eventually I drifted back to sleep. But the next time I woke, a great hunger came upon me, so that, with my dwindling strength, I sat myself up and pulled the bag to my side. Shafiqa had packed me a wool blanket, a clean tunic, a loaf of bread, a handful of dried dates, several cooked chicken legs wrapped in a cloth, a water flask, and the entire batch of sesame cakes that Shafiqa had prepared for the meeting with Hiyya and Asher Bar Raban. At the bottom of the bag I spotted, to my horror, the knife with which I had stabbed Abu Said. Somehow in those chaotic minutes before my flight, she had managed to wipe his blood from the blade.

I took the knife in my hand and stared at the blade; to drive it into my own heart would only take an instant. It might be days before they found my body, and when they did, I would be buried in the far section of the cemetery, together with the Jews who have committed the gravest and most shameful of sins. But that seemed a laughable price to pay for the chance of escaping the wretched existence that would now be mine.

It is said that suicides are an outrage to God, but truly, it was He who had betrayed me. I had seen funerals where even as the mourners fell to their knees begging to join the dead in their graves, the rabbis chanted prayers proclaiming how the ways of God are a mystery to men, and that God, in His infinite wisdom, has written out a fate for each of us. This explanation had always sounded reasonable to me, but now it seemed like a pitiful excuse for what was nothing but treachery and cruelty. Why had He chosen this wretched fate for me? Why was I lying here on the cold earth when the other girls of Sura were safe at home in their beds?

As I gazed at the knife, there was only one thought that prevented me from doing away with myself; if I died, there would be no one left to mourn my father because, only I, as his sole relative, could perform the rituals of mourning. There would be no shivah for my father, no stream of friends to comfort me, no one to make a tear for me in my clothing, no weeping neighbors to sit at my side. Nonetheless, if I could find the strength to wait out the seven days of mourning, I could at least recite the psalms I knew and pray for his soul. And then, when the seven days passed, I would leave this world satisfied that I had fulfilled all of my filial obligations. It was this final obligation that made me lower the knife and make a small tear in the collar of my tunic. His tunic.

For five days I sat under the fig tree, reciting prayers for my father's soul, and weeping over all that had befallen me. I was in a place outside time and outside of the world, a great gaping emptiness which must resemble the hell where sinners endure their eternal punishments. Again and again, I relived the events that had expelled me from my life. I saw Abu Said, charging at my father like a beast. I saw my father crumple to the floor, the blood spreading over his shirt like a river of wine. Then I saw Abu Said, his hand raised, about to plunge his dagger, still wet with my father's blood, into my heart. Where had I found the courage to stab him? Even if I live to be one hundred and twenty, I'll never know.

But it was the nights that were most fearsome. From my bed on the hardened mud floor, I would gaze up at the distant moon. I would listen to the rustling of leaves and the trembling of branches, as visions of my newly made enemies, enemies who would not rest until I were stone dead, came alive. For hours I would shake with cold and terror until, exhausted, I dropped off to sleep. Later, at the hour when the forest stilled and the stars hid themselves in the black sky, I felt my father's presence hovering close. And then, on the very brink of madness, I imagined that I was back in my bed chamber, with yellow sunlight falling on the soft carpet by my bed, and the sound of our neighbor Elisheva singing as she hung her laundry to dry on her roof opposite my window.

I would wake, damp and shivering, to a gray and empty sky. And then I would take the knife in my hand and gaze at it with longing. Each evening, as the light faded from the sky, I would put a date seed at the foot of the tree, so as to mark another day. When there were finally seven seeds, I knew that I had fulfilled my obligation, and that I was free to leave this world forever. Instead, in my exhaustion, I lay the knife down by my side and fell into the deepest sleep I had ever known.

Like all of the nights before, I met my father in my dreams. As he came near, I held out the knife as if to tell him that I would soon be joining him. But he, with the slow, certain movements of people in dreams, pried the knife from my hand and cast it aside. *No!* I wailed. I sank to the ground, howling as if wounded by a sharp, unbearable pain, but this neither alarmed nor surprised him. He merely nodded as if to say that he knew; he knew what this would mean, just as he knew everything that was going to happen to me. And then he turned and walked away. *You can't go!* I screamed. *You can't leave me here alone.* And then a terrible darkness came over me and I fell away.

When I awoke, the sun was high in the sky, and the trembling leaves of the palm trees were touched with gold. My head was throbbing and I no longer knew what was a dream and what was real.

I reached for my bag, pulled out the clean tunic, and exchanged it for the torn, mud-stained garment of mourning I had worn for the past seven days. The knife lay hot and gleaming beside me, but I refused its promise of solace, and packed it far into the bottom of the bag.

And then, as mournfully as Adam and Eve left Eden for the misery of this world, I tied the turban tightly around my head, rose to my feet, and hobbled out to the road.

I had gone only a short way when I heard the voices of men calling out to each other. I looked up and saw that I had come upon an orchard of apple trees. The men were hidden by the branches, but their ladders revealed exactly where they were. For the first time in my life, I deliberated whether it would be better to beg or to steal. Begging came more naturally. My hunger was so urgent that I nearly forgot to take on the voice and speech of a boy. "*As-salaam alaykum*," I called out weakly.

"Morning of light," a voice called back. But still I couldn't see anyone.

"Could you spare a few apples for a poor traveler?" I asked, speaking the words like one who is no longer certain what they mean.

"Open your bag, son," the voice said with a laugh. Hesitantly, I approached the trees. "If you don't open your bag, you'll have to catch them in your hands." I took the bag from my shoulder and held it open under them. And then, as if in a game, they tossed the apples in, one by one, until it was full.

"God bless you," I called out as I took a fruit in my hands. "May God grant you great prosperity, and good health to you and to all of your family," I cried, like the beggar women at the city gates.

"Wait. Are you hungry?" one of them called.

"Yes."

"Wait there a minute."

Like an angel of mercy, he descended the ladder, opened a straw basket under the tree, and took out a piece of barley bread with cheese baked on it. "My wife wants to fatten me up, so she packed me some extras," he explained. "You take it. I'm fat enough as it is."

I stared blankly.

"Go ahead. Take it." I reached out and took the bread, and could not keep myself from biting off a piece. He watched me, amused, and asked, "Where are you off to, my son?"

"I . . . I'm on my way to my cousin's house," I blurted out, realizing that from this moment on, all that I spoke would have to be a lie. Not wanting to say more, I thanked him again and started down the road, devouring the bread as I went.

But the cheese was salty, and the water in my flask was gone. I knew that the road out of Sura runs parallel to the river, and so I made my way through the growth of weeds and wet leaves until I found the water's edge. I filled my flask, and then, as if sealing the decision to continue along the strange and terrible path that God had set out for me, I knelt down and washed the dust from my face and hands.

I couldn't return to Sura. Abu Said's family would not rest until I was dead, and I feared for the safety of any family who would offer me shelter. Though I racked my brain, I managed to conjure up only one plan. My father's uncle, Hannanya Bar-Ashi, had long ago gone to Tiflis in the footsteps of a Karaite woman. I once asked my father where this Tiflis was, and he explained that if one were to start at the great Tigris, and then follow it northward, one would reach the city of Mosul. From there, one only had to continue traveling north, following the road faithfully until, after a few weeks, one would come to the town of Tiflis.

I was thinking that if I could somehow get to this Hannanya Bar-Ashi, he might take pity on me and welcome me into his house. Perhaps in time he would even supply a modest dowry, and find me a local boy to marry so that I might live as a respectable woman.

The very idea that I, who had scarcely set foot out of Sura, who had never given a moment's thought to matters of food or shelter, who had, since the day of my birth, basked in the warm light of my father's esteemed name, would now have to travel roads and highways relying on nothing but my miserable wits, would have been laughable had it not been so horrific.

I couldn't imagine how in the world I might make such a journey. But if I was to go on living this wretched life of mine, I had no choice but to try.

SLAVERY

I was as a creature split into two: one half a sentry, the other the crazed prisoner in his charge. The prisoner's hand clasped a dagger, and only the vigilance of the sentry could keep her from driving it into her heart.

As I walked along the road, I was constantly bursting into tears, not only because of the terrible events that had destroyed my life, but also because of the outrageous hardships I had to suffer. Within half a day my feet were sore and blistered from walking in my father's boots. But even worse was the problem of finding food. I saw now that if I had to depend on what remained of last season's unpicked fruit, I would wither within a matter of days. On the second day, I spotted half a loaf of bread by the side of the road. It was grey with dirt and dust but not yet hardened. Though the notion of putting such a thing in my mouth disgusted me, I had been hungry long enough to know that I couldn't afford the luxury of refusing it. As I picked off the dirty crust, I realized that if I wanted to eat, I would have to resort to means that just a few days earlier I would have associated with beggars and criminals.

I knew nothing at all of the world outside Sura, and everyone I passed—the traveling merchants, the wagon drivers, the bands of singing soldiers, the families returning from the markets, even the impoverished Sufis who owned nothing but a walking staff and wooden bowl—evoked a cold panic. Who could say if a friendly demeanor was not in fact the mask of a heartless criminal who would kill a man for nothing more than his robes? And worst of all was the distressing fact that underneath my father's clothes, I was not a man at all. This secret gave me no peace; whenever I thought I heard the approach of a traveler or caravan, I would run off the road and hide myself.

These were the circumstances when, on the morning of the third day, I heard the sound of galloping horses approaching. I quickly ran into some bushes at the side of the road, and from my hiding place, watched two horsemen speed by as if in a race. The road ahead curved sharply, and as they passed, I wondered if they were skilled enough to make the turn without slowing down. Sure enough, a few seconds later I heard the squeals of the horses accompanied by a rider's howl of pain. My first instinct was to remain hidden, but I was suddenly struck with a vision of my father, kneeling over a patient as he examined his limbs for broken bones. I well knew that if the rider had indeed broken something, then his situation was dire; without medical attention, a fall from a moving horse could render a man lame or even paralyzed.

"Mustapha," I heard a cry through the trees. "Can you move your leg?"

It could only have been the image of my father and the boy that caused me to burst into the road and scream, "No! The leg must not be moved!"

Both men turned to see who had spoken. From the similarity of their features, I guessed that they were brothers, close in age, and only a few years older than I was. Their fine clothes and manicured beards suggested that they were from a good city family. Now, with their two sets of distressed eyes gazing at me as if I were a spirit of the forest, I regretted my outburst. But it was too late, and so I tried to muster my father's authoritative manner when treating the sick. "I saw you fall," I told them, remembering to use my boy's voice. "My father was a physician, and if he were here now, he would probably say that the leg might be broken. And that if it is, then it should be set in a splint."

The two stared for a moment, unsure what to make of me. The injured one squeezed his eyes shut and groaned, "I swear Hassan, this pain is going to finish me."

Hassan glanced at his brother helplessly, and then at me and asked, "Do you know what to do?"

As if propelled by a strange force, I knelt down, and disregarding Mustapha's grunts of pain, carefully pulled up his pant leg, exposing the knee. I recalled that the first thing to look for is a break in the bone, and so I moved my hand gently along the leg. Just below the knee, I felt how the line of the bone had been severed in two. Though the break had not pierced through the skin, the leg was clearly fractured. My instinct was to scream, but somehow I kept my wits about me, nodded thoughtfully, and told them, "I saw my father attend to many injuries like this one. From what I can tell, it seems that the leg could be fractured, but luckily, the skin isn't broken, so that you don't have to worry about infection."

"Fractured?" Mustapha moaned and grasped his brother's hand. "Hassan, save me! It feels as though my leg is going to fall off!"

Hassan threw up his hands in despair. "We're hours away from any city or town," he cried, and it will take Mother all afternoon to catch up with us." He spun around, gave me a quick, worried glance from head to toe, and said, "You say you're the son of a physician?"

I nodded.

"You said something before about a splint. Can you perform such a procedure?"

I had never set a splint in my life, and I was wary of attempting one now. But I reasoned that any splint, no matter how primitive, would probably be better than none. "I can try," I told him. "But you'll have to help me."

"What do you need?"

"The leg has to be tied down and held in place. The best thing would be a piece of wood. But if you can break a strong branch from a tree, it might work."

Hassan took a knife from his belt, ran into a cluster of trees, and began to cut into a long branch. "And I'll need some cloth," I said, "in order to tie the leg." He ran to his horse and opened one of the many sacks that were tied to his saddle. He returned with a colorful robe, and I instructed him to tear it into long strips. Then, recalling what my father had done, I told him to hold Mustapha's leg to the branch so that I could tie them together. But before Hassan even put his hands on his brother, Mustapha began to yelp. "You have to ignore his cries," I told him. "The leg needs to be supported to prevent more damage. And Mustapha, you keep very still. Once we tie up your leg, you might even feel some relief."

After bracing himself and muttering a quick prayer, Hassan held his brother's leg to the tree branch while I fastened them with four strong knots. "You should see a real physician as soon as possible,"

I said to Mustapha. "Until then, the leg must not be moved." Hassan and I leaned Mustapha against a nearby tree. His face was still contorted from the pain, and I recalled that on the second shelf of my father's medicine cabinet there was a vial of some pungent potion which brought on drowsiness and dulled aches, but that vial was as far from me as the stars.

Mustapha closed his eyes and nodded. Now that the splint was set, I could not quite believe what I had done. "Thank God you were here," Hassan was saying. "To meet a man with medical knowledge on these roads is nothing less than a miracle." I too thought that a miracle had occurred, namely that these men had not yet seen through my disguise.

"Most honorable sir," he addressed me. "I am Hassan Ibn Amin, and my unfortunate brother is Mustapha. And now you must tell us your name so that we can exalt you in our prayers."

"My name is Ibrahim," I told him, thinking of the story of how Abraham offered food and drink to the angels who came to his tent.

"Ibrahim. You are as noble as your name," Hassan remarked solemnly. "Are you traveling to Baghdad?"

I was deliberating what to tell him when he continued, "We're on our way to meet our father in Baghdad. My cousin is getting married. My mother and sisters are traveling behind us. They'll be here soon." He looked up and glanced at Mustapha, and then down the road. "My parents will reward you well for what you've done for us."

"There's no need for any reward." I shrugged modestly. But I could not keep from eyeing the packs of food bulging in the saddle bags. "Except perhaps for a spare portion of bread, if you have one," I heard myself say.

"A spare portion of bread? You'll share in all our provisions!"

Before my watering eyes, Hassan rummaged through the sacks and took out several bags and a blanket. He opened the blanket on the ground and proceeded to lay out a meal of roasted chicken legs, bread, dates, and pistachio nuts. Hunger rose up in me like a storm, banishing every thought from my head, and only the greatest restraint kept me from pouncing on the food. The notion that the meat was not ritually slaughtered crossed my mind, but I am no holy woman, and I decided that after all the suffering God had rained on me, He would forgive my transgression. As I helped myself to a chicken leg, I told myself to eat slowly and modestly, but my efforts must have been inadequate, for Mustapha, injured as he was, observed me with apologetic grin. "Praise God your appetite is healthy. If only we had more to offer you."

Mortified, I smiled weakly and replied, "My provisions were stolen, and for several days I've eaten nothing but fruit and nuts."

"Only fruit and nuts!" Hassan exclaimed. "My poor man! When my mother catches up with us, you'll have a proper meal. Now tell me, Ibrahim, where is it that you come from, and where are you headed?"

The question confused me, for I hadn't yet composed a ready lie. "I come from Pumbedita," I stammered, "and I'm on my way up north, to visit my father's uncle."

"North? Where in the North?"

"He lives in a village just north of Mosul."

"But in the meantime you'll travel with us, at least as far as Baghdad."

I tried to keep an even expression as I weighed the idea. Never before had I needed to make a decision like this one, and I scarcely knew what would be worse: to join these men, who might at any moment see through my disguise, or to continue to walk the roads alone, exhausted, and hungry. "Why do you hesitate?" He frowned, insulted. "Do us the honor of joining us and, *insha'Allah*, the journey will be safe and pleasant."

I glanced from Hassan's grinning face to Mustapha, stoically suppressing whatever agony he felt. In the end, it was their fine clothes and honorable demeanor that tilted the scales in my mind. "Allah's blessings upon you," I replied with just the right note of humility. "I accept your offer."

"Excellent," said Hassan triumphantly. "That will solve the problem of Mustapha's horse."

I smiled, trying to mask my confusion. "What do you mean?"

"You see, Ibrahim, sir, my father intends to sell these two horses in Baghdad, and he has charged us with the task of riding them to my grandfather's house in the city. But Mustapha cannot ride in this condition."

"Of course he can't. But perhaps your servant can ride in Mustapha's place."

"Unfortunately, that's impossible. Our servant Malik must chaperone our mother and sisters, who are riding in the wagon. Other than me, you're the only person in our party capable of riding Mustapha's horse."

"Oh, no," I exclaimed. "No, no, no. Forgive me, but I can't help you. You see, I can't ride a horse. I've never ridden one in my life."

Hassan smiled as if I were a silly child. "That doesn't matter. It will be a while before Malik arrives with the wagon; you have plenty of time to practice."

I shook my head. "I cannot learn to ride these highways in just one day. It is impossible. And just think—if I fall, as Mustapha did, then you'll have two invalids to care for."

"Ibrahim, you protest like a woman," Mustapha groaned. "Any man can learn to ride."

Hassan motioned for me to approach the horse. "You're in luck." He grinned. "Amber's temperament is usually calm."

CALM OR NOT, as I sat high above the safety of solid ground, it occurred to me that as a woman in disguise, as a Jew, as a person who had scarcely ridden a donkey, no good could come of this. But Hassan was determined to make a horseman of me. "Riding a horse isn't difficult," he insisted. "But it does demand a certain amount of attention. You must be as one with the animal. Communicate with her as you would to a young child. Use your reins to give clear instructions. Let her know that you are pleased when she does what you say."

"But what if she tries to throw me?"

"What a girl you are." He laughed. "You are her master. Master. Do you know what that means? It means that Amber is here to do your bidding. Give her your commands by way of the reins. When you pull on them, she'll slow and stop. When you tap her flank with your heel, she'll go. Just don't confuse her; if you don't confuse her, she'll be your best friend. Now give her a kick." I made a weak attempt. "Harder."

I tried again and Amber broke into a trot. Though I sat stiff and frozen in the saddle, it wasn't as frightening as I expected. I rode back and forth down the road a few times until Hassan motioned for me to approach. "You'll be fine," he insisted, "but try to accustom yourself to Amber's movements. And don't forget, you need to constantly survey your surroundings. Envision yourself and the horse as one, as if you're the head and she is the body."

With each trip down the road, I dared to kick Amber with greater force. Before I knew it, we were galloping. The sensation of speed and the wide view of the open landscape both terrified and thrilled me, and after a short time I forgot not only my fear, but also the despair that had accompanied me from the moment I fled my home. After I had ridden up and down the road several times, Hassan and his horse appeared at my side. "Now I ask you," he said with a smile, "is this not a pleasant way to travel?"

I nodded, embarrassed by the fuss I had made.

He glanced up at the sky. "It's time for our midday prayers. Let's go back to pray with Mustapha." As we rode up to Mustapha's tree, Hassan swung one leg over his horse and dismounted in an elegant hop. I attempted the same, but could only land with great clumsiness on all fours. Mustapha laughed, but it came out like a choked grunt.

"He's a born horseman," Hassan declared.

"Though I am still perfecting my dismount," I added with a grin.

"That doesn't matter," Mustapha groaned, and pointed to the sky.

"That's why we had to interrupt Ibrahim's practice," Hassan nodded. He opened one of his sacks and drew out two prayer mats. "Ibrahim, do you not have a mat?"

"No. Unfortunately not," I said, hoping that this excuse would be sufficient reason not to join them.

"Then you must use Mustapha's. In any case, he cannot prostrate himself." Though alarmed, I knew better than to refuse the opportunity to pray. For such a refusal would surely arouse more suspicion than even the most blundering imitation. I graciously accepted the mat, unfurled it under the tree beside Hassan, got down on my knees and waited for them to begin.

Mustapha shut his eyes and recited his prayers as he sat leaning against the tree. Hassan lowered himself to his mat and began to recite in a voice a little above a whisper. I tried to imitate him as closely as possible. Is the God of the Muslims the same as the God of the Jews? I reasoned that since God sees all and knows all, He would surely understand what I had to do, and if it angered Him, well, He had only Himself to blame for this folly. I tried to recite a psalm that I remembered from the volume I would often read on the Sabbath, but the posture and movements of Hassan's prayer required so much attention that I could barely remember the words.

I was greatly relieved when Hassan finally rose and rolled up his prayer mat, but the relief was short-lived, for as I stood up, a sharp branch of the tree caught my turban. I tried to free myself but the turban was quickly unraveling in my hand. I cried out in panic, and as Hassan and Mustapha watched my hair fell free, they too let out a shriek. It was Hassan who spoke first. "Well, you certainly had us fooled!"

I laughed nervously, trying to diffuse the strangeness of the situation. "I didn't set out to trick you," I told them sheepishly. "I'm sure you can understand—I don't dare travel without this disguise."

I prayed that my explanation, which betrayed only a small measure of my actual predicament, would satisfy them. "Where is your family?" Mustapha asked with newfound suspicion.

To hear this simple question from the mouth of a stranger came as a fresh shock. Now, for the first time, I saw it clearly; to be a girl without a father, or at least a brother, was to be as a lone flower in the field, defenseless against any creature who might trample it. I regretted now that I had mentioned an uncle in the North; a father in Baghdad would have been far more useful. But it was too late to change my story, and so I murmured, "I've already told you that I have an uncle north of Mosul."

The brothers exchanged glances, and after a long moment, Hassan said, "When we get to Baghdad we'll arrange safe transportation for the remainder of your journey."

"May God reward your kindness," I replied, but in my heart I knew that I could no longer put my trust in them.

It was at that moment that we heard the sound of approaching travelers. In the distance, a boy of about fourteen or fifteen was riding a donkey hitched to a wagon. "They've arrived," Mustapha cried, but Hassan was still regarding me uneasily. "My sister, forgive me, but I must ask that you keep your true identity hidden; your men's garments are not proper for a respectable woman."

I promised to honor his request, and I quickly gathered up my hair and stuffed it under the turban while Hassan ran ahead to meet his family. "Praise God that you have arrived safely," he exclaimed as he helped his mother out of the wagon. She was clearly weary from the long hours in the wagon, and her fine robes and headscarf were streaked with brown wrinkles of dust. As she embraced Hassan, she caught sight of her other son, sitting sprawled against a tree.

"Mustapha," she cried, breaking free of Hassan's embrace and running to Mustapha's side. "What has happened to you?"

"It's nothing, mother. A minor fall."

She dropped to her knees and stared at the splint in horror. "And what is this? What have you done to your leg?"

"It is called a splint. It will support my leg until we get to the city. Luckily, Allah saw fit to send us this boy, Ibrahim, whose father is a physician. He knew what to do in order to prevent further injury."

She glanced up at me. "May Allah shower on you all of His blessings. Are you traveling alone, my son?"

I was about to reply, when Hassan cut in: "Indeed he is, and I've asked him to join us for the remainder of our journey to Baghdad."

Her easy acceptance of the lie brought on a fresh flood of panic. I had succeeded in fooling the brothers, but surely a fellow female would see through my disguise, for a boy is not only his clothing, but also his speech, his mannerisms and gestures. Now, for example, my place would normally have been with Hassan's sisters. I almost went to join them as they instructed their servant woman in preparing refreshements, but Hassan, who seemed to read my thoughts, shot me a sharp glance that reminded me who I was supposed to be, and so, odd as it felt to me, I went to sit beside Hassan.

"PRAISE BE TO Allah, who put such an angel in your path," Hassan's mother said as she handed me a cup of tea and a sesame sweet. I bowed my head as well-bred boys do.

When the last of the tea was gone, Hassan rose and indicated for me to follow. "Ibrahim and I will start out now. *Insha'Allah*, we'll meet again at the old fig tree that stands down the road from the Well of the Devout." Hassan and Malik helped Mustapha onto the wagon. When they were done, Hassan kissed his mother goodbye, and motioned for me to follow him to the horses.

God be with me, I muttered to myself as I mounted Mustapha's horse. We rode off, slowly at first, but soon speeding up to a steady gallop. Our task, Hassan had explained, was to look out for dangerous or suspicious characters, for the way to Baghdad was known to be full of thieves and criminals, and indeed, Hassan rode with his knife ready in his belt.

The ride demanded all of my concentration. Muscles previously unknown to me soon grew sore, and my hands burned on the reins. Yet these discomforts seemed a small price for the thrill of traversing such great distances in so short a time.

Later in the day, Hassan motioned for me to halt beside a cluster of date palms. "This spot is a well-known prayer site for travelers," he explained. As I dismounted, my thighs felt as weak as wet leaves. I had returned Mustapha's prayer mat, but Hassan insisted that I use his, and again, I followed his movements, praying that I would not pay dearly for the foolishness of traveling alone with a strange man. When I rose, I noticed that a traveler had arrived and set down his mat not far from us. Though he was about to kneel in prayer, I could tell that he had been staring at me. "Did you notice anything odd about the man beside us?" I asked Hassan as we walked back to the horses. "He didn't take his eyes off of me."

"He must have been looking at your turban," Hassan said, laughing. I put my hand to my head and felt that my hair had come loose, so that much of it hung long down my back. "You'll have to be more careful if you want to keep up your disguise," he warned me.

We set out again and as the sun was beginning its descent, we spotted the designated fig tree. Hassan knew the area well, and I followed him to a nearby stream, where we washed the dust from our faces and led the horses to drink. The remainder of the family reached us some time later. Once again, Malik built a fire, and the serving woman prepared a meal of flatbread and salted meat. Night came, and blankets were unpacked and spread on the ground. The girls fell asleep first, and after a final cup of herb tea, Hassan and I parted for the night. But I was unaccustomed to making my bed beside so many strangers, and so I set my blanket far from them, behind a dense bush. Dizzy with exhaustion, I fell asleep immediately.

The next part of my story is difficult to tell, and in truth, I have tried to banish it from memory. But even if the mind manages to trick itself, the body remembers all.

Alas, while I slept, I heard nothing, and when I awoke, it was too late. It was the traveler, the one I had seen when we stopped to pray earlier that day. He appeared at my side like a stealthy night animal, and suddenly, I was on my back and he was on top of me, pinning my hands over my head. "I knew there was something strange about you," he whispered gruffly in my ear. His heavy breath smelled like a dung hole, and through I writhed so as to break free of him, I could barely move. "You thought that you could fool old Kubani. Now you just stay quiet, and maybe I won't kill you." While one hand continued to hold down my arms, he used the other raise my tunic, and then to pull off my leggings. I tried to call out, but he put a knife to my throat, and I knew that he was going to do the act that men and women do. As he forced my legs apart with his knee, my eyes filled with tears, and my mouth with soundless screams. I tried not to pay attention to the rough scratch of his hands, or the piercing pain of invasion, searing and foreign, and vile to the point of nausea.

Struggle was useless, and though Hassan and his family were so close, it seemed like no one was going to come to my rescue. I did not think during these sickening moments of anything but death, a blessed end to this torture, perhaps only seconds away. I prayed for it to come quickly and cease this unspeakable torment. For surely whatever awaited me in the next world could not have been more terrible than what I had endured in this one. And so I surrendered to my fate and prayed that the scoundrel would kill me when he was done.

Such were my thoughts when suddenly, I felt my attacker collapse on me with his entire weight and slowly release my arms. I struggled to get out from under him, and found that he made no effort to restrain me. Stunned and battered, I fell back to the ground.

"My sister," I heard a voice whisper. It was Hassan. With what seemed like superhuman strength, he bent down and rolled the corpse off me. Then he knelt and whispered, "I've killed him; I stabbed the filthy cur and sent him straight to Hell. Wait here and I'll be back in a moment."

Numb with pain and shock, I forced myself to sit up. I felt a drop rolling down my leg, and as I wiped it with my finger, I quickly pulled my tunic down, thankful that the night had shielded the sight of me from Hassan's eyes. Suddenly, I began to retch. I leaned to one side and vomited in sharp and violent heaves. A short while later Hassan returned with a fresh pair of pants. "Go to the stream," he whispered. "Wash yourself and change your clothing. I'll move this carcass out of the way. When you return, we'll perform our morning prayers together." He held out his hand to me, and still stunned, I took hold of it as he pulled me up. He handed me the pants, and I walked off, dazed, in the direction of the stream. My legs moved stiffly, like wooden sticks, and every step brought on a fresh, searing pain. I began sobbing, quietly at first, and then in great torrents. My tears ran down my cheeks and onto my dirty tunic, but I couldn't stop.

Hassan must have heard me. Clutching his prayer mat, he came to me and said: "My sister, that's enough. Your attacker is dead, and I have restored your honor. That son of a dog will rot in Hell. He held a knife to you, didn't he, that scoundrel. I may have even saved your life."

"But I wanted to die!" I wailed and sank to the ground. "My life is nothing but misery, and I have no strength to live it." Even as I tried to stifle myself, I couldn't stop crying, for I was certain that I would never overcome this disgrace.

Hassan didn't reply. Although he had vanquished my attacker, he was powerless in the face of my devastation. "It's very important that you wash," he said finally. "You must go and do it now." Though I could scarcely think, something urgent in his tone impelled me to go down to the water and do as he said. I did not join him in prayer, but merely sat at a distance from him and wept quietly into the earth.

When he was done praying, dawn had broken, and the horizon glowed with a pale orange light. Hassan came to me and said, "We will forget this night. We'll put it behind us, and never speak of it. I'll wake the others and get us something to eat, and then we'll ride out together. But we must leave soon; who knows when that son of a dog's people will come looking for him." He knelt down and put his hand on my shoulder. "You stay here. I'll tell my mother that you're preparing for the journey."

I had no appetite for food, but Hassan insisted that I eat the bread and cheese he brought back. My body ached and burned, and I could not see how, with all I had suffered, I could endure another day of riding. Yet I understood that I had little choice. Limping and sweating and cursing under my breath, I climbed atop Amber. I willed myself to ignore the fiery pains of the day and night before, and feel only the rush of the wind flying in my face.

I BURNED WITH anguish at the notion that I was no longer an innocent girl but a violated woman. The act had been horrible, disgusting, shameful, and dirty. Now that I knew what had previously been a vague mystery, I felt pity for all married women, forced to suffer this disgrace. I swore then that I would never willingly lie with a man.

As the morning wore on, the despair in my heart grew darker. My father had let me know that he wanted me to carry on living, but that was before this. Did I need any more proof that God had abandoned me? Or worse than abandoned me? He had ruined me and betrayed me. Again I tried to recount every wrong I had ever done. Was I a greater sinner than any of the girls in Sura? Surely no act of laziness or gossip could ever justify such suffering. It seemed as if, for some unfathomable reason, all the forces of the world had decided to destroy me.

The next time Hassan brought our horses to a halt and walked off to relieve himself, I reached into my bag and drew out the knife. I raised the weapon, pointed it towards my heart and closed my eyes. I wanted to devour the knife, to give myself over to the beckoning relief of death. I imagined my body falling to the ground, the last of my miserable life extinguished for good. *Just one thrust*, the voice in my head whispered. *One sharp twist and this cursed life of suffering will be over.* Suddenly I felt someone grab me from behind. Hassan twisted my arm behind my back until, fearing that he would break it, I dropped the knife. "Let me go, you scoundrel!" I screamed, thrashing against him like a wild animal. "I cannot stand even one more second of this wretched life!"

But he refused to release me. For some reason he actually cared whether I lived or died. "You crazy, crazy girl," he cried. "Have you forgotten that a Muslim is forbidden to take his own life? Would you sin against Allah and suffer for all eternity?" He threw me to the ground, where I remained, devoid of all will to move. "My sister," I heard him say, the calm returning to his voice, "I want to remind you of a story. Do you remember Hagar, mother of Ismail?"

I groaned feebly.

"Do you remember how Sarah told Ibrahim to cast Hagar and her son Ismail out to the desert, and Ibrahim followed her command?"

I wished that I could simply fall asleep as I was, never to wake again. But Hassan was excitedly recalling the story. "Hagar and Ismail wandered for days, and as their food and water ran out, they grew weaker and weaker, until finally, Ismail could not go on. Hagar laid him under a bush, and in her despair, she called out to Allah for help. And Allah, the Almighty, heard her cries, and provided her with the means to save him. Do you understand, my sister? Allah heard her cries, and just as He promised Ibrahim, he made a great nation of Ismail, our nation. You too must sustain your faith in God."

His words seemed empty and meaningless, yet somehow, for the moment, the urge to do away with myself had passed. "And now, I want you to listen carefully to me. You must put what happened yesterday behind you. Lock it in a chest of iron, and throw away the key. I have exacted the ultimate revenge. Your honor is restored."

"Honor?" I cried. "I have no honor!"

"Hold your tongue," he said. "Are you so ungrateful? Your attacker has paid for his deed with his life. That alone should be a comfort to you. I, for one, am grateful that Allah granted me the wits to act as I did. Just as I am grateful that he allowed me to save you from the disgrace of suicide."

"Oh Hassan," I wailed, "I am as a man who is given a gift that he can no longer use."

"Your suffering has blinded you. But I'm certain that a day will come when you'll think back on today with thankfulness." I regarded him incredulously; it seemed to me that it was he who was blind. "And now, we must continue our journey. My father is expecting us tomorrow afternoon, and we still have a great distance to cover."

That night after the evening meal, I found myself observing Hassan's sisters as if for the first time. During the day they veiled themselves, solely on account of my presence, and I avoided looking at them. But now, when night covered us all, I could watch them without causing offense. The elder one poured tea for us all, and I wished it were possible for me to speak with her, if only to engage in the comforting, idle talk of girls. Yet the gulf between us remained unbridgeable, not only because of my disguise, but also because I had seen the dark underside of the world, while she, pure and innocent, remained happily unaware of all she had.

That evening, I managed to behave naturally, but when everyone lay down to sleep, the recollection of the previous night came upon me with the power of a demon. Though I had placed my blanket beside the others, and I knew that Hassan and Malik were taking turns watching over us, I was sick with the memory of the terrible thing that had happened. Now, in midst of the dark night, I could again smell his stench and feel the sweat of his body against my own. I fought the urge to cry out and the instinct to vomit again. I had promised Hassan to forget all that had happened, and so I wept soundlessly, my mind whirling with a thousand fears. What would become of me now? How could I ever marry when I could not stand the touch of a man? And now that I was no longer a virgin, what sort of man would want me? I had heard stories of pious Christian women who went to live in remote places, never to marry. Perhaps such a place existed for Jewish girls as well. For hours, sleep evaded me. *Lock it in a box of iron, and throw away the key*, Hassan had told me. It was easy for him to utter these words, but to obey them seemed all but impossible.

We rose at dawn, and only the thought of Hassan's concern for me gave me the strength to mount the horse and follow him. Yet once we were riding, a strange lull of contentment came over me. The air was sweet with the scent of spring wildflowers, and the sun shone warm on my back. "Have you ever been to Baghdad?" Hassan asked as we pulled off the road to an open well.

I shook my head. "I know it only from the descriptions of the storytellers of Sura." According to their tales, Baghdad was the most magnificent city in the world. Its mosques, gardens, towers, and canals were the grandest to be seen, and the Round City, with its numerous palaces and towers, was an incomparable wonder of the world, which easily could have rivaled the ancient Hanging Gardens. Naturally, we remained skeptical. Is it not the task of storytellers to describe things in a way that takes you far from the troubles of your courtyard to places of greater wonder than you could ever conceive?

As we approached the city, we were soon caught up in an endless flow of donkeys, camels, wagons, horses, and wayfarers all jostling against each other like twigs swept along a river. The curses of the wagon drivers flew up and mixed with the cries of the money changers and the songs of the food and drink vendors. From atop my horse I gazed down on this carnival with a mixture of trepidation and wonder. Never before had I seen so many converge on one place. And the multitudes were not of one tribe or region, but of a hundred different races and tongues. I struggled to keep Amber close behind Hassan's horse, a task that became increasingly difficult as she too was distracted by the commotion around us.

Just as riding was becoming impossible, Hassan dismounted his horse and led him to the side of the road. "We've arrived," he announced, pointing to a crowded, noisy inn, the sort of place a respectable woman would never think to enter. "Let's go in and have some fun." Shouts and rough laughter rang from the open windows, and in the corner of the courtyard, two men were wrestling, surrounded by a crowd of cheering onlookers. We gave the horses to the stable boy, but as we approached the doors of the inn, I stopped in my tracks and seized his arm. "I can't go in there," I told him.

He glared at me in exasperation. "No one will know who you are. No one will care. The people of Baghdad are not the gossips of your village."

"I can't!" I insisted again.

"It's your cowardly behavior that attracts attention," he replied, and before I could think further, he grabbed me by the arm, pulled me inside, led me to a table, and sat me down. A nimble serving boy appeared, and Hassan asked for two bowls of soup and a plate of bread. I sat stiffly, wishing the ground beneath my cushion might open and swallow me whole. But by the time the boy returned with our meal, hunger overcame my distress. I tore off a chunk of bread and dipped it in my soup, taking pains not to drip on my already filthy tunic. But as I brought the bread to my lips, I could not help but turn to Hassan and ask in a low voice, "Am I eating like a woman?"

I meant the question in earnest, but he just laughed as if I had told a clever joke. In the meantime, a storyteller had taken his place on a stool in the center of the room and began to recount an old tale about a servant who outsmarts his master. Everyone surely knew it, but the crowd that gathered around him listened eagerly as if hearing it for the first time. Hassan too turned to listen, and soon we were so engrossed in the servant's antics that we didn't notice when Hassan's father came through the door and made his way to our table.

He was about the same age as my own father. His graying beard was neatly clipped and, as befits a jeweler, his pinky was adorned with a thick gold ring. After their embraces, Hassan introduced me to his father as "the noble Ibrahim," a farcical title which made me wince. "*Salaam Alechum*," he greeted me, his eyes darting about the room as he sat himself down. "Where's Mustapha?"

Hassan relayed the story of Mustapha's injury and my assistance to them. "Ibrahim was like an angel from heaven," he told his father. "Even though he claimed never to have ridden a horse, he took Mustapha's place on the saddle and rode Amber all the way to Baghdad."

Hassan's father placed a heavy hand on my shoulder and said, "Allah be praised for sending you at my sons' hour of need."

Though mortified at his touch, I bowed graciously and replied, "I did nothing more than anyone with a little knowledge would do." The serving boy glanced over at us, and Hassan's father motioned for him to bring another portion. "What is your business in the city? Do you need a place to spend the night? If you do, I would be honored to host you in the home of my brother."

"Of course he'll stay with us," Hassan answered, and he leaned over and whispered something to his father, who nodded in agreement.

Though I was not at all sure that I ought to accept this invitation, I nonetheless bowed and murmured, "May Allah reward your kindness."

"If anyone's kindness should be rewarded," Hassan's father replied with a glance to his son, "it is your own." And then he reached into his purse, drew out a small cloth pouch, and placed it on the table. "Perhaps my son mentioned that I am a dealer in precious stones. Please accept this small gift as a token of my gratitude."

I stared dumbly at the pouch. "Go on, open it." Hassan poked me. I reached for the pouch hesitantly, loosened the string, and let its contents fall into my open palm. To my astonishment, I beheld a man's gold ring set with a sparkling green stone.

"It is an emerald," Hassan's father explained. "When you step outside, you'll see how beautifully it catches the light of the sun."

I couldn't help but gasp at the fortune that had literately fallen into my lap. The ring already felt warm in my hand; it was like a genie endowed with the power to set my life right again. It could buy a place in a caravan going to Tiflis. It could provide me with a dowry.

And it could win me a respectable husband who would rescue me from this life of endless suffering. Yet thrilling as these plans were, I knew better than to take the ring immediately. "You are far too generous," I told Hassan's father, shaking my head. "I cannot accept such a gift." I refused easily, for I knew that no matter what I said, he would not take it back.

"Sir! Please don't insult me like this. This ring is well-deserved, and it is yours." I was about to protest again when he turned to his son and said, "And now, I must send you on a small errand. Your aunt is preparing a feast for your arrival. But she's threatened that none of us will be allowed through the door if we fail to return without a vial of saffron from Nidal." He reached for his money purse, drew out some coins and gave them to Hassan. "Go and buy what she needs. I'll wait here for your mother and the rest."

Hassan rose and I moved to follow him. His father glanced at the ring on the table. "I'll keep it for you until you return."

I was about to protest again, but Hassan called to me, "Ibrahim. Don't you want to see the markets of Baghdad?" He was weaving his way around the tables, and I jumped up after him, afraid that I might lose him before we even set out. In my haste, I forgot my bag, but Hassan's father noticed and ran out to catch me before we disappeared into the teeming streets.

"Try not to get lost," Hassan warned me. "This neighborhood is like a maze, and if we become separated, you might never find your way out." I needed no more warning than this, and as he wound his way through the streets and alleys, I kept my eyes fixed on his cloak and turban. Following him grew even more difficult when we reached the market, for the shops of Baghdad put those of Sura to shame. Every trinket stall and cosmetic table cried out for my attention. The flower stalls beckoned me with their startling arrangements and heady scents. And a Parsi woman standing before a stand of scarves brighter than peacock feathers almost made me lose sight of him. Never in my life had I seen such abundance. It was as though all of the world's riches were spread out before me.

Hassan led me into the heart of the market, down narrow alleys that opened onto bright squares filled with food stalls. We passed through long rows of olive vendors, cheese makers, bread ovens, and date dealers, and ducked around the dark, scented oil shops where the air was thick and sweet. Hassan maneuvered his way through all of these with such single-mindedness that when he finally stopped at the threshold of a large spice shop and announced, "This is the place," I could only nod breathlessly. "Nidal's is one of the oldest spice shops in Baghdad," he explained, as we stood before a sea of colored powders and dried herbs. I looked among the sacks for my favorite, cinnamon, which Shafiqa often used to flavor not only cakes and deserts, but also stews and stuffed vegetables.

"That cinnamon arrived just yesterday," a smooth voice behind me said. "It is so fresh that if you touch a piece with the tip of your finger, you'll carry its fragrance for hours." I spun around to find a wiry shop assistant with a crooked smile holding out a red-brown chip in his hand. I was tempted to test his claim, but without money in my pocket, I didn't dare.

"Actually, I'm looking for some saffron," Hassan told him. "Show me your finest; it is for my aunt, and if she's not satisfied, she'll send me to another shop next time."

"Ah, but that would be a mistake, sir. Our merchants search out the best saffron harvests in all Kashmir. I swear on my mother's eyes that the threads plucked in the morning are on their way to Baghdad that same afternoon." We followed him to a table where the choicest herbs were displayed in glass jars. "Saffron is the prince of spices, for the most refined of tastes," he said melodiously as he opened the jar, and, using a pair of silver tweezers, plucked out a delicate red thread, which he placed in Hassan's open palm.

While Hassan examined the saffron, I looked out at the alleyway. Two veiled woman in fine robes walked past, and I followed them with my eyes. They stopped a little further on, at the entrance to a fabric shop where bright bales of material stood on display. "I'm just going to look in one of the shops," I told Hassan. "I'll only be a minute." He nodded, and I skipped out, feeling for a brief moment like the old Rahel who wore the robes of a girl.

I could see now that the women were a mother and daughter. The younger of the two lowered her veil and held a swatch of green silk to her face, so as to see how it complemented the tone of her skin. As I moved among the fabrics, a wave of bitterness rose in me, for I could not help thinking that instead of hiding in men's clothes,

I should have been sewing a wedding dress. I picked up a bale of indigo-colored silk with small flowers embroidered in silver thread, and I held it against my face. Yes. The indigo would be perfect for me. And with my long, dark hair, I would look as beautiful as a courtesan. I tugged back my turban a little and drew out a few wisps of hair. The sight of my dark locks on the blue material delighted me, and without thinking, I carelessly pulled out a little more, causing the turban to come loose and fall to the floor. I glanced anxiously around the shop. Luckily the merchant was busy with the mother and daughter, and the alley was empty of people.

Sadly, I gazed at the silk in my hand. I envisioned myself the lady of a grand house who spent her days entertaining other fine ladies. And in the evening when the ladies were gone, I would uncover my head and dine in the company of my husband. I ran my fingers through my hair. How lovely I would appear to him. And to my servants, who would comb my hair each evening before I retired to my soft bed.

These were my imaginings when suddenly I heard a voice that made the blood stand still in my veins. I raised my eyes and there, at the shop directly across the way, stood Hamid, one of Abu Said's older brothers.

Our eyes met and he gazed at me, troubled, for this was not the first time we had stood face to face. Hamid had made several discreet visits to our house in order to consult my father about an unpleasant skin ailment, which he hoped could be cured before his upcoming marriage to the daughter of a palace official from Baghdad. I knew this because my father had charged me with mixing Hamid's medicines and ointments.

Now he stared at me, his face still cloudy with confusion. I prayed that he would fail to recognize me, but when I saw his eyes narrow and his features harden, I knew that he had found me out. As he bolted toward the shop, I dropped the bale of fabric and whispered fiercely to the owner, "I need to get out of here fast! Is there another exit?" He motioned for me to follow him and led me to a small door at the back of the shop. Dashing out into the alley, I cursed my vanity. Like a fool, I had forgotten my turban in the shop.

I tore through the market, blindly pushing my way through the crowds. I flew by food stalls and juice vendors, the butcher's alley, the blacksmith's quarter, and several public squares where street entertainers clamored for my attention and fortune tellers cried out that dressing in men's clothes would bring me bad luck. I prayed that I was fast enough to escape Hamid, yet each time I turned around, I saw that I was still in his sights. Finally, at the point of exhaustion, I turned off a narrow alley which opened onto a large, enclosed court-yard. It appeared that I had reached a dead end. Panting as I stopped to catch my breath, I spied a group of girls about my age standing together at the opposite end of the yard.

I glanced over my shoulder and saw that Hamid had just turned into the courtyard. If I tried to run back into the market, he would surely see me. The only thing left to do was to blend into the group of girls. I dashed to them, fell in behind where they were standing, and bent down a little. If my plan worked, he would soon turn and go back to the market. I crouched low and peered out from between the girls. To my dismay, he stood with the crowd of men who had gathered nearby.

Still breathless, I wiped the sweat from my face and glanced up at the girls who were concealing me. They had round faces with wide cheekbones. Their eyes were as round as coins, their hair hung thin and straight, and their skin was pale, as if they never saw the sun. But strangest of all was the fact that they seemed oblivious to my presence. Though they spoke in an unfamiliar language, it was clear that they were terribly distraught. Some were weeping, while others seemed to be comforting the weepers. And then, to my horror, I saw that all of the girls were joined to one another by a long rope knotted at their wrists.

Suddenly, I felt someone clutch the neck of my robe and yank me up. "Trying to hide, are you?" He laughed. And then he circled my waist and lifted me into the air. "Hey Tariq, it looks like we've picked up a little extra merchandise." In a moment of horror I realized my mistake; I had run straight into a slave market. Still, I remembered Hamid, and that he might still be searching me out amongst the crowd. "Kasim, you scoundrel," a booming voice called out. "Get over here. Now!" I was dropped abruptly to the ground where I remained, stunned and trembling.

In the marketplace in Sura, there is a corner where men and women from foreign lands are sold, as readily as any merchandise. But I had always avoided that corner, and had little concern for the fates of those being bought and sold. Now, I watched astounded as

Kasim untied the wrist of one of the girls and dragged her off to a low podium where a finely-attired merchant was inviting the crowd to come and have a look at her. When she cried out in protest, Kasim gave her sharp kick in the shins. Several men approached the girl and begin to examine her, touching her hair and squeezing the muscles in her arms and legs. Soon one of them came forward, paid the merchant a few coins, and led the girl away even as she cried out to her friends.

The spectacle was more horrible than a nightmare. I wanted only to break out and flee, but I dared not move. I closed my eyes and ears to the terrible scenes playing out before me. And then, I felt a tight grip on my own wrist. I struggled to free myself, and kicked at my captor's legs, but he merely gripped my arm and forced me toward the crowd of buyers. It was at that moment, just as I was about to scream, that I spotted Hamid. The harsh cry of his voice burst upon the square like a bolt of lightning. "There you are! That girl is a murderer! Half of Sura is hunting her down for the murder of my honorable brother." My blood froze; I was done for.

But then I felt a second hand encircle my other arm. "I'll take her," I heard a deep voice say. I swung my head around and looked up. I was in the grasp of a tall, scowling man, the glare of the sun blurring all of his features, except for a thin, silver hoop earring dangling from his left ear. He stood a head taller than the beady-eyed merchants that surrounded him, and his bare head was shaved as bald as a stone. "What's her price?"

The merchant looked me over quickly and grinned to himself, the grin of a man who finds a gold coin in the gutter. He knew I was not his, but nonetheless cried out, "Fifty gold pieces."

"Done," the voice agreed, and handed him a money purse. Stupefied, I watched as the money changed hands.

"Give her to me! I will have my revenge," Hamid screamed, his eyes glaring, his fist shaking with rage.

I glanced to my right at the stranger gripping my arm, and then to my left at Hamid, who was glaring like a fierce dog waiting to tear me to pieces. I understood nothing except that if anyone in the world could save me, it was the bald man whose fingers encircled my arm as if it were a thin twig.

"I'm afraid that you are mistaken," my captor replied calmly. "This is the slave girl of Omar Alharazi. She's been paid for, and now she's coming with me."

"Give her to me now! We will not rest until justice is done!"

"Sir," he answered, this time in a more threatening tone. "If there is a question regarding this girl, I suggest you take it up with Omar Alharazi, her lawful owner."

The small crowd that had quickly gathered around us laughed heartily. "I'll hunt you down, Rahel! I won't rest until my brother's blood is avenged," Hamid cried, red with rage, as I was led by the arm to a horse-drawn wagon. "Climb up here," the bald man commanded. Before I knew what was happening, he had tied my wrist to a large iron ring on the floor of the wagon. "You're worth money now." He grinned. "We can't have you running away."

For a second, I thought of Hassan, who was probably scouring the market in search of me. But nonetheless, the notion of running away was far from my mind. With Hamid shaking his fist at me as we rode off, I could not help but feel gratitude toward this odd character. Now he was staring at me with a wide, idiotic grin. "So it's Rahel, is it? Well, you can call me Salim."

I shook my head. "Oh, no! He must have confused me with someone else." I scoured my brain for another name, but there was only one Muslim name I could think of. "My name is Shafiqa."

"Shafiqa," he repeated and shrugged his shoulders "Makes no difference to me." He looked at me again and laughed to himself. "And who was that fool who was saying all those ugly things about you? You don't look like much of a murderer to me."

Somehow, I was able to put a hand on my heart and reply, "I've never seen that man in my life."

"Just as I reckoned. And it's a good thing too." He chuckled again. "Lady Suraya wouldn't take a slave who's wanted for murder."

Now that we had left the market, I saw no reason to continue this farce. "Sir," I addressed him, "I thank you for your help, and wish you all of Allah's blessings. And now, if you could stop here and release me from this wagon, I'm sure I can make my way on my own."

But Salim shook his head and laughed. "You have been bought, girl, and that makes you a slave. If you want to buy back your freedom, tell your father to return the 50 gold pieces Omar Alharazi paid for you."

I looked at him incredulously. "But I was not for sale. I . . . I am not a slave!"

He spun around and looked at me as if considering my appearance for the first time. "Then why were you standing with the slave girls?" He smiled a slow, wicked smile. "You have no father, do you, girl? You live in the streets!"

"How dare you!" I cried. "My brother Hassan was with me just now! At this very moment he is looking all over the market for me, and when he finds me, he will have you seized and thrown in jail for this treachery!"

He looked me over as if trying to decide whether to believe me. "Ha!" he exclaimed, and spat on the ground in a neat plunk. "We'll see about that. First let him come looking. All I know is that Omar Alharazi has put down good money for you. He'll become a slave himself before he allows himself to be cheated by a whoring slave trader."

The situation seemed so outrageous that I decided against further argument. "Where are you taking me?" I asked him, forcing boldness into my voice.

"Didn't you hear what I said in the market? You've been sold to Omar Alharazi, the silk merchant. A slave has many uses, but you're destined for the kitchen. Azzah is too far gone to do the heavy work, and Zahiya can't do it all herself." As he spoke I tried to loosen the knot that held my wrist, but he had tied it in such a way that my efforts only made it tighter. Finally I gave up and decided to wait for the right moment to escape.

WE HAD LEFT the central part of the city, and were now in a newer neighborhood where the din of the market had faded to a distant hum, and the air was fragrant and cool. Grand villas, surrounded by flowering trees and gardens, hid behind high stone walls. I tried, from atop the wagon, to glimpse the beautiful homes amongst the trees. Though Sura too had a neighborhood of fine houses, they would have stood ashamed beside the splendor and elegance we were passing. We turned onto a path that led up to an imposing villa surrounded by a thick stone wall. Though my heart was beating hard with fear, I was also curious to see what it might look like on the inside. Salim directed the horse around to the back and stopped in front of a stable. Grasping my arm in the same firm hold he had used in the market, he guided me into a large kitchen courtyard. Even before we entered, I could hear the sound of a woman singing, her voice tremulous with enacted suffering. "*You stole my heart, you stole my soul, and now I languish in the prison of your love.*"

"Zahiya," he called out. "I have a surprise for you. Come on out and have a look."

"No, you come in here. I'm busy with the fish."

The voice was musical, but with an odd lilt to it. My arm still captive, I was dragged into the inner kitchen and deposited in the center of the room. "Here she is—a young one, just like you asked for."

I gazed at the tall, large-boned woman, with skin as dark as a brown date, and a shock of frizzy hair bursting out of her headscarf. I could not help but stare at her, for I had never met a black-complexioned woman. She stood at a large table in the center of the kitchen, a plate of pink-eyed fish on one side of her, and a second plate of cleaned fillets on the other. She lowered the fish she was holding, wiped her hands on a wet rag, folded her arms across her chest and circled me, her mouth set in scowl. "Are you a boy or a girl?" she demanded, her accent so peculiar that I had to suppress a smile. I said nothing, for I could see no reason to give this slave an explanation. Her indignant eyes moved from me to him. "Where did you find her?"

Salim frowned. "You ask too many questions, Zahiya. If I were a kitchen slave, I wouldn't ask anything. I would just thank Allah that He saw fit to send me some help." Zahiya shot him a type of look that a mother gives her foolish son. "She was right there, lined up with the slave girls in the market. She wasn't wailing like the others, and I figured that's the sign of a hard-working girl."

"You figured! Have you gone blind? Can't you tell a local girl from a foreign slave? We'll just see what you figure when her father comes around looking for her, and Alharazi takes what he paid for her from your wages, and makes *you* take Azzah's place in the kitchen."

He shook his head. "No father's going to come for her. This girl's an orphan; nobody's coming to look for her." He glanced at me knowingly. "In fact, I think we're doing her a favor, giving a nice home to a poor street urchin."

I was about to protest this outrageous insult, but I held my tongue. Zahiya looked me over and sighed. "What's your name?"

"She calls herself Shafiqa," Salim answered.

"Shafiqa," Zahiya repeated. "Well, Shafiqa, you had better get to work. And you," she commanded Salim, "you go get Lady Suraya. We'll see what she makes of this."

Salim glared, but like a sulky, obedient dog, he went off to do as she said. "I don't know who you are," she said to me once we were alone, "but I can tell you one thing: It's better to be a slave in a fine house than a whore in the street. Do you understand what I'm telling you? It's better to be scrubbing pots and grinding grain than giving a good time to all the scum of Baghdad."

I found myself nodding. "I don't know who you are, but I can tell you, this is your lucky day. Ever since Azzah got herself pregnant, she doesn't do the work of half a girl. First she was throwing up every time Salim brought in a carcass, and then she was falling asleep over the wash basin, and now she cries that it's bad luck for a pregnant woman to hold a knife. Who ever heard such idiocy? She's just lazy. I know what it is to be pregnant. I scrubbed pots until the day Fadi was born! It's just your luck that her baby's father is keeping an eye on her. Of course a man like Karim would never disown his own child!"

My eyes darted around the kitchen. Scrubbing pots? Grinding grain? I had to escape this madness, and fast. "Now, you go wash up and then we'll trade those rags of yours for a clean robe so you'll look half-decent for Lady Suraya. The path out back leads straight to the well, but you can use the basin behind the oven. There's a bathhouse at the far side of the garden for all of us slaves and servants. The men go one night, the women go the next. Tonight's the men's night, so you'll have to wait for tomorrow." She motioned with her hand as if pushing me out the door. "Now go, before Lady Suraya gets here."

The courtyard led out to a garden of the sort described by storytellers. Tall shade trees grew among the stone paths, and flowering plants and bushes enhanced the air with color and fragrance. A handsome well stood in its center, and delicate wrought iron benches were set in the most beautiful spots. The entire yard was enclosed by a high stone wall, over which, far in the distance, I could make out the towers and minarets of the city.

I looked around for a latrine, but seeing none, I squatted down behind a bush and relieved myself. At the basin I found a jar filled with water. I drank deeply, letting the entire contents spill over my face and neck. Then I dried myself with my robe, and looked out on the darkening horizon. The sky was streaked with a fiery splash of orange across its deep blue. My legs trembled with the urge to run.

I imagined Hassan searching for me in the market. I imagined the dark streets, the markets closing for the night, the rush of people, each hurrying back to his home. And then, as if they were right before me, I saw the repulsive men with greedy eyes, who would tempt me with the promise of food and shelter, only to use me like a whore, declare themselves my master and sell me for profit.

It was then, at that very moment that a new, horrible understanding bore down on me, turning my legs to lead and filling my heart with horror. The sky itself seemed to be collapsing; I couldn't move. I could barely breathe. Zahiya, whose words I had dismissed as utter nonsense, had seen my true situation simply and clearly; I could be a slave, or I could be a whore. A lone girl on the streets of Baghdad was as a full purse beckoning to a thief. "Shafiqa, you still out there?" Zahiya's voice shot through the garden. "You better get yourself in here. Now!"

She was holding a slave's tunic of coarse fabric, leggings, and a headscarf, examining them in a way that reminded me of how the women of Sura check their children's clothes for lice. "Slower than a princess, but dirty as a street girl," she remarked, thrusting the garments into my arms. "Go out back into the storeroom and change. We'll give those rags of yours to the chamber maids." My clothes were indeed fit for the rag pile. But when I stood in the storeroom, my father's tunic in one hand and the slave's garment in the other, I couldn't bring myself to complete the exchange. A shudder of anguish seared through me. "What's going on in there?" Zahiya cried angrily, her shrieking jolting me out of my stupor. I threw on the tunic and changed my leggings. The headscarf smelled of oil and onions, but nonetheless, I tied it over my tangled, dirty hair.

And then, as I was about to go back in, I caught sight of my bag, the embroidered one that Shafiqa had given me, lying on the floor. I ran to the bag and embraced it as if finding a familiar face, for it was now my sole possession remaining from my lost life. The fabric was worn and mud-stained, and a small hole had opened in the lining, but I couldn't bear the thought of it being used as rag to clear the filth of others. I scanned the storeroom for a hiding place, and my eyes fell upon a giant sack of dried beans standing in the corner. As if hiding a valuable treasure, I stuffed the bag deep down behind it.

Never before had I seen such a kitchen, big enough for a palace, and filled with enough foodstuffs to feed the Jews of Sura for several weeks. On the far wall, a large wooden cupboard stood open to reveal sacks of rice, grains, and ground barley flour. The wall adjacent to the cupboard was covered in blackened pots and pans of all sizes, and clay jugs of olive oil were set in the corner amongst straw baskets filled with apples, dates, garlic, cabbage, and onions. Opposite me, a wide shelf was laden with mortars, pestles, knives, and all types of cooking utensils, while the shelf beneath it held small clay pots filled with powders, dried herbs, and rose petals. Though the kitchen still smelled of fish, the bones and scales had been cleared away and the table was filled with bowls: one containing sliced lemons, one olives, another mint leaves, a fourth held some freshly ground spice, and a fifth was brimming with small half-circles of celery.

I was thinking of Shafiqa, and what she would say if she were to behold such abundance, when Salim strode in, followed by two women, clearly a mother and daughter. It was not only their moon-shaped faces and abundant figures that betrayed their relation, but also their robes, which were of the same fine silk, and the identical way that their hair was pinned under their shawls. Yet what caught my gaze was the small, pearl-studded comb that held the long tresses of the daughter's hair. For it was identical to *my* pearl comb, the one I wanted to wear to my meeting with Asher Bar Raban. That comb, more than anything else, sent a pang of despair through me that made me want to fall upon her and snatch it. But I quickly dispelled this foolish urge and regained my wits.

Both women looked at me with the cool, superior gaze of a mistress on her slave. Yet behind the smugness, I saw something else— a prudence, a hint of caution that tempered the haughtiness. The mother in particular regarded me carefully, and I knew that she was trying to ascertain whether, as Salim had no doubt informed her, I had no father or family at all. "I am Lady Suraya," she began grandly, "and this is my daughter, Lila. What's your name?" she asked.

"Shafiqa."

"Shafiqa," she repeated. She crossed her arms and circled me, regarding me from all directions. "Salim says that there was a man in the market who called you by another name. A name that is rarely given to Muslim girls, but is often heard among the Jews."

I looked squarely her in the eye. "My name is Shafiqa."

Lady Suraya nodded with satisfaction, as though all doubts about my circumstances were now resolved. "Well, Shafiqa, if you do your work diligently and remember your place, then I can assure you, you will never know hunger, never lack proper clothing, and will sleep each night with a roof above your head. You will enjoy the protection of our estate, and share in the honor and good name that Allah has granted us. However, if we find your skills inadequate, your behavior disrespectful, or your morals lacking, you will be delivered to the merchant from whom you were purchased. Do I make myself clear?"

Though her tone infuriated me, I nodded blankly.

"Good. In matters of the kitchen, this household has the highest standards. We host many important guests, and the food that is prepared in this kitchen is a crucial part of Omar Alharazi's hospitality. Have you any experience in cooking?"

"A little."

Her face clouded. "Only a little? Ah well, cooking is a skill that a girl can master in no time. And you have Zahiya to instruct you."

"I'll teach her everything I know," Zahiya said.

"Good. The sooner Shafiqa learns our tastes and habits, the better. She pointed to a tray of hollowed out vegetables that had somehow escaped my notice. "Is this for the *mahshi*? Karim wants everything to be ready before the scholars come tonight."

"Don't you worry, Lady Suraya. If this girl here turns out to be worth what you paid for her, then things are going to be very different around here from now on."

"*Insha'Allah*, she won't disappoint you." Lady Suraya turned to me. "Shafiqa, Lila and I wish you good luck. May Allah see fit to grant you success."

I stared after the women as they went out, their long robes trailing behind them. "Now you had better get to work so that Lady

Suraya doesn't send you back to the market," Zahiya said in her peculiar lilt as she handed me a cutting board and a knife. She pointed
to a pile of garlic cloves and scowled. "How fast can you chop, girl?"

I tried to recall Shafiqa's method of preparing garlic. Did she first
slice the cloves and then remove the peel, or did she first remove the
peel and then chop? Zahiya watched my attempts and shook her
head. "Idiot!" She smacked my head. "It's done like this." She took
a piece of garlic, chopped off the end and rubbed it between two
fingers. In seconds, the peel loosened and fell away. "Now you do
the rest of these, just like I showed you, while I start the barley." She
scooped out a cup of barley from a large sack, poured it onto a tray,
and then ran her fingers through the grains, scanning them for anything that moved. "This barley that Salim brought is full of weevils,"
she grumbled.

I couldn't help but grimace, for all I knew of barley was the fluffy,
steaming dishes Shafiqa set before me on our table. "Now you listen
to me. I've worked here since I was eight years old, and you just got
here, so you had better listen to what I have to tell you. As long as
you work hard and don't do anything foolish, Lady Suraya will like
you, and if she likes you, everyone else in the house will take her
example and like you too." Zahiya leaned across the table, as if to
share an important secret. "Let me tell you about how things go in
this house. The only reason you're sitting here now is that Azzah got
herself pregnant and had to go home to her mother."

Azzah. Zahiya had mentioned that name before, but I had been
in such a state of confusion that I didn't hear what she had said about
her. "Pregnant?" I asked uneasily. "She's married?"

"Of course not. But everyone knows that it was Karim. Lady
Suraya's son."

"Her son?"

"Uh huh. You see Omar Alharazi has two wives. Lady Suraya, the
one who was in here just now, is the older. She is his third cousin
and the mother of his oldest son, Karim, the father of Azzah's baby.
When you see Karim, you'll know right away that he's Lady Suraya's.
He is big, and strong as an ox, with a face to match. After Karim, Allah saw fit to give Suraya four more children, two of them daughters,
and two more sons. The oldest daughter is Lila, the one you just met
now."

I tried to follow what she was saying, but the casual way that she spoke about what Karim had done to Azzah seemed almost more shocking than the deed itself. I wished that I could go someplace quiet and be alone, just fall asleep and forget everything that was happening to me, and then wake when my head was fresh and clear.

"Lady Suraya wears only robes of the finest quality," Zahiya was informing me. "Her husband gets the fabric from the men he sends to the East. And she loves gold and precious stones; if you see something shining and glittering, it's probably Lady Suraya's fingers. Of course, as the mother of Omar Alharazi's eldest son, she's as proud as a queen. And that wouldn't be such a sorry a thing, if not for Omar Alharazi's second wife, Lady Nur. Now she's a *real* princess."

I looked up for a second, but my hand continued to work, causing me to make a small, painful cut in my index finger. "Stupid knife!" I swore under my breath as I brought my finger to my lips.

"Why do you curse the knife when it is the cook who is the fool?" She laughed heartily in a way that made me want to smack her. But I held my anger and looked down at the pile of garlic before me. Zahiya took this as a sign that she could resume her tale.

"Omar Alharazi took her for a second wife only five years after he married Lady Suraya. Five years; that's not long at all. But maybe it couldn't be helped. You see, when Omar Alharazi was a boy, he would join his father on his long trips to buy silk in the East. That was where Omar Alharzi learned the secrets of silk: how to tell good cloth from bad, how to bring it all the way across the desert, and how to set a price just high enough for the fancy ladies of Baghdad. He and his father would return a few months later in a caravan loaded with the best silk and cotton to be had. Now Omar Alharazi is no fool; he listened well to his father, so that by the time he got to be a young man, he knew the business well enough to make the journey on his own. Ah. There's one." Zahiya stopped to pick out an insect, crushed it between her fingers, and let it fall to the floor.

"Now, Omar Alharazi had a friend, Jalal, who lived in one of the faraway cities of the east. Whenever he traveled, he would sojourn with Jalal's family. And this Jalal had a sister, Nur, who was known to be the most beautiful girl in the province. It was no wonder that when Omar Alharazi saw her walking in the garden one day, he immediately fell in love with her and asked her father for her hand." Zahiya sighed happily, as if she herself had witnessed their courtship.

"Now, when Omar Alharazi brought his new bride home to Baghdad, Lady Suraya's face froze into an ugly pout." Zahiya showed me the pout on her own face, a look so comical that I burst out laughing. "It's not funny," Zahiya said. "Not at all. I tell you, if it had been me in Lady Suraya's place, I would have been just as mad. But I ask you, are the ways of Allah not mysterious? As fate would have it, Lady Nur had troubles of her own, troubles that brought a smile back to Lady Suraya's face. You see, in spite of all of Nur's blessings, Allah put a curse on her womb, and she lost every baby Allah thought to give her."

Zahiya sighed. "Poor Lady Nur. And all the while she had to endure Lady Suraya's gloating, until finally came a day when Allah took pity on her, and she gave birth to Omar Alharazi's second son, Khalil. Well, you can just imagine the feasting and celebrating that went on. Omar Alharazi bought Lady Nur a necklace studded with sapphires and rubies, and everyone thought that the curse had been lifted, and that Khalil would soon have many brothers. But it was not to be. The birth was a difficult one. The midwife managed to save Lady Nur's life, but her womb was spent, and Allah ruled that Lady Nur would bear no more children."

"How terrible!" I cried, caught up in the tale in spite of myself.

You would think that this might lessen Omar Alharazi's affection for Lady Nur," she continued, "but I know that she is still his favorite."

"Then it is true love," I said knowingly.

"Indeed it is. And when you meet her, you will immediately see why. Lady Nur's nature is refined and pleasing. Although the years have passed, she's kept the beauty of her youth. Khalil has inherited his fine face from her, and whenever I look into his eyes, the eyes of a prince, I am reminded of his mother when she first came to Baghdad. Of course, since he went to study in Basra, we only see him when he comes home for holidays." At the mention of Basra, I froze for a moment, for it immediately called up an image of my father. If he were to see me here, in the guise of a slave, he would surely think he had gone mad. Zahiya rose abruptly and sniffed the air. "I had better check on the fire."

There was something swift and efficient about her movements that made me feel heavy and slow. A minute later she returned with a plate of fish, steaming with the scent of celery and coriander. "I say there's nothing worse than a hungry cook." She grinned. "You just try this." She put a piece of the fish on a plate and fed me a bite. I can't say if it was because I had not eaten cooked food in many days, or because it was hot and well-spiced, but to me, that fish seemed the tastiest dish that I had ever eaten.

Perhaps she hoped that the food would replenish my energy, but rather than invigorate me, it only made me want to sleep. Zahiya chatted on, recounting anecdotes about the various family members, but I could barely follow what she was saying. As she spoke, she assigned me simple tasks, such that without my noticing, I not only chopped a sack full of garlic cloves, but also shelled a pile of pistachio nuts, and ground the coriander leaves into a dark green paste with the mortar and pestle. But by the time the coriander was done, my eyes were closing. "Are you tired already?" she asked disapprovingly.

"It's been a long day for me," I told her, thinking that I had endured more twists of fate in this one day than most experience over the course of an entire lifetime. "When do we retire?"

"Retire? Ha! We retire when the work is done." I yawned, so as to suggest that I might need to retire before the work was done. She glared, exasperated, but then broke into a sly smile. "Why don't we make a little bargain? You go to bed now, and next time, when I need a rest, you can fill in for me."

At that moment, I would have agreed to anything she said. Zahiya showed me to her quarters, a small, windowless room just off the kitchen. Two straw mattresses lay rolled up in a corner, and a small shelf was set into the wall. It held a hand mirror with a long crack through its glass, a clay cup, two blankets, and a neatly folded slave's tunic. These, I realized, must have been Zahiya's only possessions. "Most of the slaves sleep in the servants' quarters on the other side of the house," she told me, "but Lady Suraya likes the kitchen staff to sleep in here so that we don't wake up the rest of the house when we start work in the morning." With a sharp flick of her wrist she unfurled the second mattress and set it down across from her own. I stared at the thin, dusty mattress on the dirt floor. The room was obviously nothing more than an old storeroom, yet at that moment, it appeared as luxurious as a palace. "Don't you forget how good I've been to you today," she warned me. "And if I happen to snore, don't you dare wake me!"

I nodded as I drifted off to sleep, thinking that the snores of a slave woman were a small price to pay for a mattress under a roof.

"Are you still in bed, princess?" Rough hands were shaking me, and I opened my eyes to see Zahiya's scowling face. "We've got a household to feed here. Get yourself up!" For a moment, I thought I was having a horrible dream. "You heard me, Shafiqa! Get up! Now!" My sleep had been deep and dreamless, and I wanted nothing more than to close my eyes and forget where I was. "Are you coming or do I have get Salim to haul you in here?" Zahiya hollered again, and, ignoring the iron stiffness in my every muscle, I forced myself to rise.

I found her in the courtyard, poking at the fire, a boy of about eight or nine by her side. *"The stars in the sky, the light of the moon, the song of the nightingale high in the trees——"* When she caught sight of me, Zahiya stopped her singing. "You see Fadi? That's lazy Shafiqa. She's going to take Azzah's place. But if she doesn't shape up and get working, she's going right back to the street. Shafiqa, this is my boy Fadi. He's just running out to fetch water. That's his job, every morning." I stared at him, puzzled, for his skin was several shades lighter than his mother's and where her jaw was round, his jutted out sharply. Knowing what I did about Azzah, I could only wonder who his father was.

"Where is his father?" I asked innocently.

"My father is Omar Alharazi," Fadi called out. Though he was clearly proud of his pedigree, I felt my own heart sink in my chest. It was obvious that the men of this house thought nothing of forcing themselves on their slaves. With a sudden feeling of horror, I recalled Shafiqa telling me that according to Islamic law, slaves were permitted to their masters. Fear rose in me like a storm. I had to escape, to run back to the city, to be any place but here.

"You were like a tired, old donkey this morning. You had better change your ways fast, girl. I don't want to have to tell Lady Suraya that Salim brought her a lazy slave. If she hears anything like that, she'll have Salim take you right back to the market." She grabbed my hands, examined them and shook her head. "Just like I thought; these hands have never seen a millstone!"

She smacked my head playfully. "Well, they'll see one soon enough. Have you eaten?" I shook my head. "There's a little leftover bread in the basket on the table. You go grab a piece, and then I'll show you how to work the stones."

While I was still chewing on the stale bread, Zahiya led me into the storeroom, opened a sack of dried barley, and spooned some into a straw basket. I followed her out to the back courtyard, where she knelt down on a dusty cushion by the millstone, which was similar in size to the one Shafiqa used at home. I had, of course, watched Shafiqa as her sturdy, calloused hands grasped the wooden handle to move the round, flat upper stone in circles over the larger bottom stone. Shafiqa's hands were strong, and within several minutes she was able to grind as much flour as we needed for our daily bread. Now Zahiya poured a handful of grain into the hole in the center of the top stone. "Go ahead. Let's see you do it." I put both hands on the handle and threw all of my weight into the task of moving the upper stone over the lower one. "Harder. Push it harder," she said. "It will take you all day if you push it like a worm."

I gripped the handle harder and managed to complete the rotation. "I . . . this work is for a much stronger person."

"A much stronger person?" She rolled her big eyes. "Ha! The problem is that the person who has to grind the flour is you. Now you sit here and get it done. Fast!" With that, she threw up her hands and went back inside.

A powerful urge to run out of the courtyard and out the back door came over me and then shrunk back. Why did I remain there, sitting by the millstones? Even now, it's difficult for me to answer that question. I only know that when I imagined climbing the high walls of the garden and finding my way out to the road, I was filled with a fear even greater than my fear of what awaited me as a slave. That morning, as I sat in the clothes of a slave under the hot spring sun, I knew only that I had found the promise of a meal and a roof over my head. And that God had not given me the strength to live without these things.

And so I threw my weight into the grinding, and very soon, a fine white powder began to spill out from between the stones. My hands grew red and blistered, and by the time I finished grinding all that Zahiya had given me, I wanted nothing but to sit for the rest of the day with my hands in a bowl of cold water. But when I went in to tell

Zahiya that I had finished, she handed me a large, round sieve, and sent me out to sift what I had ground, and then regrind the grains that were not yet turned to powder. The process had to be repeated several times, so that after half a morning's work, I had produced only one bowl of clean flour.

Later on, when the bread was baking and Zahiya was showing me how to arrange a plate of fruit to serve in the women's quarters, I heard a melodious voice greet us. "Morning of light, to both of you."

She was tall in stature, her frame even leaner than my own. Her face was long, but her features were fine and even, and her soft brown eyes were shaped like perfect almonds. Her dark hair hung down her back in a styled braid, and her face was framed by a wispy scarf of yellow silk. As she approached me, her face opened into a gracious smile. "Hello Shafiqa. I'm Lady Nur. I would have come yesterday evening, but I had to entertain the wives of some palace officials from Samara. I hope you found your first night here comfortable."

Something in her tone made me want to please her. "It's been a long time since I had such a restful sleep."

"I am glad to hear it. It is said that food is tastier if there's contentment in the heart of the cook." *She is clever*, I thought to myself. *She knows how to bring out what is best in a person.* "Lady Suraya told me that Salim found you in the slave market in the city. Where is your family?"

"I have no family."

"Yes." She nodded thoughtfully. "I see how it might suit you to remain here. We shall see what comes of it. Perhaps this arrangement will prove beneficial for all." Her face brightened as she turned again to Zahiya. "Last night, a friend of Khalil's from his travels came to see us," she told her excitedly. "He has brought word from Khalil; we are to expect him home in six months."

Zahiya sang out a cry of joy and embraced her. "May Allah bring him home safely."

"*Insha'Allah*," Lady Nur sighed. "Just yesterday, your Fadi was telling me that before he left, Khalil promised to carve him a wooden tiger." Her long fingers picked a date from the fruit plate and took a delicate bite. "Shafiqa, have you met Fadi?"

"He was in here this morning."

She nodded in approval. "And who else?"

"Only Lady Suraya and Lila."

"Just them? But you must meet the rest of the family. Zahiya, prepare a tray with tea and refreshments for Omar Alharazi. I'll show Shafiqa to his office." Lady Nur sent me to wash the flour from my hands and the dust from my face. When I returned, Zahiya put a tray in my hands, which was laden with a silver tea pot, a platter of date cakes, and two exquisite glass cups.

As I followed behind Lady Nur, I was astounded by the size and resplendence of the house. From the kitchen we came out into a bright central courtyard; it was a large, perfect square, whose stone walls were adorned with a band of blue and green ceramic tiles, and framed by four elegant palm trees. Vines of jasmine and red rose clung to the sides of the enclosure, sweetening the air with their scents, and in the center, a real fountain, just like the one in the center of Sura, gurgled out playful streams of water. From here, the house broke off into two distinct wings: the women's quarters on the left, and the men's to the right. The two sections were mirror images of each other. Both contained an inner courtyard, ornamented with the same blue and green tiles, and graced by colorful flowers, which seem to spring from their ceramic jars. Numerous chambers, framed by arched doorways, opened off these courtyards, and I could see chambermaids taking up the bed sheets to be aired, polishing mirrors, and scrubbing the floors.

The notion that people lived in such splendor astounded me. As we passed through the men's quarters, Lady Nur slowed her steps. "Now you will meet Omar Alharazi and his oldest son Karim." We entered an arched doorway into a spacious room adorned with handsome wall tapestries and thick carpets. Two men dressed in fine robes the color of dark wine were sitting on low sofas, each with a writing desk in his lap. The younger had the same round face and heavy build as Lady Suraya, but the elder's appearance was somehow more refined. He appeared to be in the midst of a calculation. On the desk in front of them, two piles of gold pieces were arranged in neat stacks.

"Morning of light," Nur greeted them.

The elder, whom I took to be Omar Alharazi, looked up and smiled at the sight of her. "Come in my dear. Karim and I were just making an account of this month's earnings. But this isn't all of it. *Insha'Allah*, Karim and I will meet tomorrow with Ibn Talal at the palace. I expect that he'll meet our price." Then he noticed me standing with the tray at his wife's side. "Is this the slave that Salim brought home yesterday?" He nodded for me to put the tray down beside them. I set it down and stepped back.

"Her name is Shafiqa," Lady Nur told him.

Though I lowered my eyes, I could feel the men's gazes sweeping over me like a cold wind. "Shafiqa," he repeated, smiling in a way that made me wish I were veiled. "Since I've taken Latif to help out in the shop, things have been running less than smoothly here at home. Instruct her in all matters relating to the reception of guests, so that she can help the serving staff at parties and gatherings." He glanced up at Lady Nur. "When Khalil returns home, there'll be no need to make use of slaves in the shop."

Karim's face took on a troubled look. "I don't know that we can expect much from Khalil," he remarked. "He's never cared for real work, only for long debates with his teachers and hours of staring into books. A scholar like him isn't suited for business."

But this only brought a smile to Omar Alharazi's lips. "If Khalil is to be a scholar, so be it. Did the Prophet not urge us to acquire knowledge?"

Lady Nur smiled with pleasure and turned to me. "Shafiqa, you may pour the tea."

Who cannot pour a glass of tea? I feared only that I would break one of their beautiful glasses, but somehow I managed to complete the act without any mishaps.

Omar Alharazi nodded with satisfaction and took a long sip. Now that he had taken his eyes from me, I finally ventured to look at him. His face was pleasing, but his nose and jaw had a sharpness that struck me as too harsh to be attractive. And then I remembered that this man, Omar Alharazi, was the father of Zahiya's son, just as Karim was the father of the child that would soon be born to my predecessor. This knowledge, and the casualness with which it was acknowledged, cast a dark shadow over the loveliness of the house.

ONE HUNDRED TIMES in a day I would think of escape, and one hundred times I would remind myself that I had nowhere in the world to go. Much of the time I was in a state of semi-exhaustion. My day began before the sun rose, when I had to rouse myself to grind grain for the household's bread, and it ended long after sunset, when the pots were scrubbed and the fine ceramic plates on which the family dined were washed and stacked away. My hands grew rough and my blisters soon turned to calluses. The skin of my arms became dry and red, and my hair, no matter how I washed it, reeked of smoke and oil.

My days were filled with the dullest, most tedious chores. Each morning, I would stand at the big wooden table in the center of the kitchen, where Zahiya would set out bundles of coriander, parsley, mint, celery, and garlic to be finely chopped. "Useless girl!" she would scream as she inspected my work. "You don't know anything! The celery should be no bigger than . . . than an ant," and she would squash any unfortunate ants she spotted scurrying across the table.

Beets, carrots, zucchini, turnip, cauliflower, kohlrabi, and cabbage had to be marinated in a mixture of garlic, vinegar, salt, cardamom, and lemon, and preserved in sealed jars. Apples, figs, grapes, oranges, pears, and carrots had to peeled, sliced, cooked, and spiced. Yogurt had to be made from goat's milk, and when Salim slaughtered and skinned a lamb, it was I who had to clean its bloody carcass.

I could feel my existence submerging into the tides of the Alharazi household; their troubles, their concerns, their joys and their sorrows were slowly overtaking my own. But late at night, after the pots were washed, the kitchen floors scrubbed, the lentils set to soak and the dough mixed and set to rise, I would go out to the garden, sit under the stars, and remember my old life. What had become of Asher, the boy who was to be my fiancé? What was Shafiqa doing at this moment? And where was my father now? Could it be that he was watching me, even as my thoughts were with him? Or was he merely lying stiff and cold in the ground, in the cemetery where the Jews of Sura bury their dead?

Because I spent much of my time within the confines of the kitchen and its rear courtyard, many days passed before I fully understood the workings of the Alharazi home. But I soon saw that it was the kitchen itself that set the pace and the rhythm of all that went on within its walls.

In the morning hours, Fadi and Lady Suraya's younger children would come asking for sesame cakes and bread dipped in olive oil. Later in the day, any men who had remained in the house would partake of lunch in their quarters, after which they usually retired for the afternoon. It was during these quiet hours that Zahiya and I prepared the dishes Lady Nur and Lady Suraya required for the evening. If someone in the family was entertaining guests or having a party, the cooking would often take up the remainder of the day.

Sometimes in the afternoon, we would receive a visit from Lila and her younger sister, Amal. They would burst in, laughing about some incident or secret plan, and as we worked, they would recount new rumors and tell stories about their relatives and friends. These visits were almost unbearable for me. I would note their colorful robes, their pretty headscarves, their soft hands, and their fine sandals with an envy that burned me from inside. Whenever Lila wore her hair pinned up in her pearl comb, I avoided looking at her.

The women of the house observed strict rules concerning their behavior in company. Whenever male guests were present, they were expected to veil their faces, so that only their eyes were visible. They were not, under any circumstances, to be found alone with any man who was not a relative, and whenever they were in the presence of a man, they were to lower their gaze and assume a modest demeanor, regardless of how they sneered behind their veils.

I, on the other hand, as a slave, often had to appear before male guests barefaced and exposed to their unabashed stares. For Omar Alharazi was what my father would have called a man of culture, and he loved nothing better than to host gatherings where fellow merchants and business partners mixed with scholars, poets, men of the sciences, and students of religious learning. As I moved amongst the men, setting out platters of food and pitchers of drink, I wished that I too could hide myself from their gaze under the cover of a veil. Never, as the daughter of Yair Ben Shmuel, did I imagine that I might one day fall so low as to wait on others. The first time that I was called to serve at such an evening, I fled the minute I set out the refreshments so that no one would see my tears.

Very soon, however, I realized that these gatherings were as a two-sided coin, for they offered me a glimpse of the most noble of pastimes. After setting out refreshments, I would move silently to the back of the room and listen to learned men impart something of their knowledge to audiences of avid listeners. For a few brief moments, my mind was not distracted by the chopping of vegetables or the cleaning of pots, but caught up in the words of men of the world who spoke of astronomy, alchemy, botany, or the fine points of Islamic law.

Though I understood little of what was said, I occasionally heard names that were familiar to me. The first time I heard a translator of Greek speak of Galen, I recalled my father's leather-bound volume lying open on the table in his study. I listened closely to the speaker, struggling to follow his every word. After his talk, as I carried the empty trays and bowls back to the kitchen, I walked ponderously, as if returning from a visit to my old life in Sura.

These meetings with men of learning often evoked sudden, vivid recollections of my father. It happened, for example, when I witnessed a talk given by Rafik Ibn Faruk, a renowned scholar of Islam who had gained a large following of students at the *Harbiah* Mosque. Karim was among the many who attended his lectures on Friday mornings. After attending several sermons, he asked Ibn Faruk to come and speak in the Alharazi home. All the men of the house, including the male servants, were invited to join the guests so as to partake in his teachings.

As always, the gathering took place in the meeting room in the men's quarters. While the men took their places on soft carpets and cushions, I was sent in to serve refreshments. The topic of Ibn Faruk's talk was the nature of Allah and the question of free will. "The Muslim believes that Allah is all-knowing, all-powerful, limitless in time, and in all the universe," he told his rapt listeners. "He knows who among us is righteous, and who will sin, even before the sin is committed. And He knows the punishment that awaits the sinner."

At this, one of Karim's friends raised his hand to ask a question. "Esteemed teacher," he addressed the scholar, "forgive my audacity, but it seems that your words are harsh. Do you mean to suggest that a man has no way of averting the fate intended for him? Do you claim that Allah might create a man with the sole purpose that he will sin, and then receive punishment for that very sin?"

Everyone turned to Ibn Faruk for his answer. "Only Allah knows the reason for everything that exists in the universe, for He has created all, including the sinner and the infidel. No man can fathom the ways of the Almighty. The believer must place his trust in Allah's wisdom." He paused for a moment, and then continued gravely, "There are some, like the blasphemous *Mu'tazila*, who claim that the will of Allah can be explained by means of human logic. These misguided souls—may Allah show them His true path—profess that each man alone is responsible for his own actions. But in this they are guilty of heresy, for they imply that Allah's power is limited, and that man has the capacity to shape the will of Allah."

Ibn Faruk continued in this vein, but my thoughts had flown off, not only in space, but in time. I'm walking through the market in Sura with Miriam, the water carrier's daughter. We're walking arm in arm, and as we pass into the street of the perfume merchants, the air smells like rose water and jasmine. A merchant holds out a small vial of scented oil and beckons me to approach. I want to go to him, to see a drop glisten on my wrist, and inhale its warm smell. But Miriam pulls me away, to a stall that shimmers with glass rings, bracelets, and beads, all set out on a piece of bright red cloth. The afternoon sun makes the glass sparkle as if it's dusted with golden powder. Enchanted, I reach out, pick up a bangle of golden green, and let it slither down my arm. And then, from the corner of my eye, I see Miriam's hand snatch a small blue ring and thread it into the pocket of her dress. "Would the young lady like to buy that bracelet?" the merchant asks.

I shake my head and quickly slide the bracelet off my hand and onto the table. As Miriam pulls me away, I whisper, "Don't be a fool. Go put it back. Now. Before he notices."

"Don't you be a fool," she hisses in my ear. "That scoundrel must have a thousand rings like this one. He'll never miss it, and I'll finally know how it feels to wear something beautiful."

Later that night, I recounted the incident to my father. "It's true," I insisted. "That merchant has a thousand rings and she has none. It isn't fair that some people can buy a whole stand of jewelry, while people like Miriam can't afford even one piece. And anyway," I added, "he won't even notice that it's gone."

The moon was almost full that night. We were sitting out in the garden, and the sky was so light that I could see the reflective expression on my father's face. "Our faith," he began, "teaches us that God has endowed each of us with free will. It is this privilege that raises us from the base instincts of the animals, yet it has left us with a difficult problem, which has confounded even the sharpest minds, both in antiquity, and in our own time. In the face of this freedom, how are we to know if we have chosen the path of righteousness?"

I CANNOT GIVE an accurate rendering of my time in the Alharazi house without speaking of what has always been my most hideous secret, my greatest shame. For it is well known that female slaves are permitted to their masters. The act is never considered a crime, and is readily condoned by all, even by the very wives of the men who take slaves to their beds.

As a slave in the Alharazi household, I was not excluded from this practice.

The first time, Karim sought me out as I knelt by the wash basin. He dragged me into the storeroom and before I knew what was happening, he had spun me around and entered me in the manner of copulating dogs. He was done quickly, and in mere seconds, he withdrew himself and grunted into his own hand. With a smirk of satisfaction, he left me as one leaves a latrine, stopping to wash his wet hand in the basin. I was too astounded to speak. My mind found it impossible to contain what had happened. I opened my mouth to cry out, but what emerged was a muffled wail.

There was no one to turn to, for his actions were the natural right of a master. In the long months that followed, Karim would use me in this way regularly, seeking me out when I was at work in the back courtyard, or accosting me as I passed through the men's quarters. It was always from behind, always with swift, sharp movements and a precise withdrawing at the crucial moment. Sometimes he would move his hands under my robe, kneading my body as if I were a pillow. I would close my eyes and imagine that I was somewhere else, anywhere else, and before I knew it, it was over. Yet it was never *really* over. The horror of it was a dark shadow that haunted my every waking moment.

I sometimes imagined killing him with a dagger, as I had killed my father's murderer, and Hassan had killed the first man who ruined me. But I understood that to kill him would be a death sentence. With every new moon, I would wait for the first signs of blood, thankful in my misery that Karim had no wish to father any more slave children.

During the day, by virtue of some hidden source of spirit, I managed to go about my chores. It was only late at night, when I would walk out into the garden and gaze up at the traitorous stars, that I would allow myself to weep over the nightmare that my life had become. In those first weeks of my enslavement, I would remember the person I once was, and then sink to the ground in tears of shame. But I soon learned that there is no end to the humiliations a woman can suffer, and in time, even when she has sunk as low as a whore, the sun will still rise and set, the moon will wax and wane, and the world will be what it is.

AT THE END of the summer, when the days grew shorter and the air grew sweet with the scent of ripe dates, I remembered that the New Year and the fast of Yom Kippur would soon be upon the Jews. Each night when I would go out to the garden, I would look up the moon and try to calculate the correct date. From the age of twelve, Yom Kippur was a day of fasting for me. I would spend the day in the women's section of the synagogue, praying that God would write my name in the book of life. I imagined His sure hand, recording each name and its singular fate in a heavy leather-bound book, just like those in my father's study. My prayers then had been fervent and full of faith, but now, when the days of my life were dedicated to the service of others and my body was ravaged like a burnt field, I saw no reason to ask God to keep me from harm. The teaching of the rabbis seemed like hollow words, empty promises that were more like wishes than truth.

One evening several weeks after Yom Kippur, Lady Nur burst into the kitchen, her eyes bright with joy. "Zahiya, Shafiqa," she cried. "We've received wonderful news. Ibn Yusef came to us this afternoon. He has just arrived from Basra, and he says that Khalil rides in a caravan only several days behind his own." Zahiya broke out into trills of delight, and we both embraced her, for what slave does not take pleasure in the happiness of her mistress?

Not only Lady Nur, but the entire household awaited Kahlil's arrival. The children prepared gifts for him, and Lila composed a poem about how sorely he had been missed, expressing thanks to Allah for his safe return. I wished that I too could enjoy the celebratory mood, but what I really felt in my heart was a dark dread, for there was no reason to hope that this Khalil would refrain from using me as his brother did.

The Alharazi home saw many festive gatherings, but it was clear, both from the amounts of food we were preparing and the complexity of the dishes chosen, that the celebrations in honor of Khalil's return were going to be especially grand. In the days leading up to the party, Zahiya and I prepared exotic specialties even as we cooked the daily meals. The work seemed endless, and although the chambermaids were sent to the kitchen to lend a hand, we would fall onto our beds each night in a state of utter exhaustion.

In spite of the joyful atmosphere that pervaded the household, I developed a resentment of Khalil, not only because his arrival meant endless toil, but also because I could not see why a mere boy deserved so lavish a welcome. Yet my disdain was tinged with curiosity. One afternoon, as Zahiya and I rolled out pastry for meat pies stuffed with gazelle, a dish that was said to be one of Kalil's favorites, I asked her, "What is it about Khalil that makes everyone adore him so much?"

"Ah, my daughter, there is only one explanation: that boy was born under the most favorable of constellations. Even as a child, whenever he walked into the kitchen it was like the sun coming out after the rain."

"Why is that?" I snapped. "Is he amusing? Clever? Fine-looking?" But Zahiya had just tossed some chopped onions into a pot of hot oil, and my voice was lost in their crackle and hiss.

I WAS IN the back courtyard washing plates piled high with the greasy remains of the fish Zahiya had cooked for lunch, when a high-pitched cry rang through the house. By the time I reached the kitchen, the cry had turned to a trill of joy. "Allah be praised! He's home!" Zahiya shouted, and ran out to join the rest of the family members who were pouring into the central courtyard. I tried to wash the smell from my hands, but I knew that no matter how I tried, I would still be a grimy kitchen slave, the lowest of lowly servants.

At first I could not see him, for he was surrounded by his family, who wanted only to embrace him, to grasp his hands and touch his face. But as a servant escorted him through the garden to the bath house, I caught a brief glimpse. He looked tired, and his robe was brown with dust, but his expression was full of gladness, the gladness of home. From out of nowhere, a terrible mixture of envy and anger rose up in me. I didn't want to see him, to pretend that his homecoming was a joyous occasion for me. As I returned to the stinking dishes in the wash basin, my heart filled with bitterness.

Nonetheless, when a servant called for us to bring out refreshments, I was glad of the chance to go to the men's quarters where the family had gathered. Dressed in a clean, white robe, his long dark hair still wet from bathing, Khalil sat between his mother and his father on a soft, high cushion, while his family gazed upon him with adoring eyes. I set the tray down before him and joined the servants at the back of the room. "Did you meet many fine people?" Lila asked excitedly.

He took a moment to consider the question. "Of course I did," he replied, "but not in the sense that you mean." Everyone chuckled at this, but he continued in earnest. "Men from every corner of *Dar al Islam* come to study in the mosques of Basra. And though each may be of a different station, we are all considered equals. The poorest of paupers may sit beside men of great wealth and power, yet each is judged solely by the piety of his heart and the qualities of his mind. Those who excel sit closest to the teacher, regardless of their influence or connections. My teacher was the son of a street sweeper, but his knowledge of *Qur'an* and *Hadith* is so vast that everyone competes for the honor of studying in his circle."

Lady Nur gazed rapturously at her son. "Tell us about your companions."

At this, Khalil broke into a smile, the likes of which I had never seen before. His eyes crinkled at the corners, as if his mind had been warmed by the fondest of memories. "I spent most of my time with Ali and Jafar. On the surface of it, we couldn't have been more different. Ali is the son of a tile painter from Samarqand, and Jafar is a legal scholar from the *Hijaz*. We all boarded at the same inn, but what really brought us together was that we all sought out the Mu'tazila. At first I went to hear them only out of curiosity, but I immediately saw that if one only takes the time to listen to their arguments, one comes to understand that anything, even the very existence of God, can be explained according to the tenets of logic and reason." Khalil glanced at his father, who was nodding approvingly. "In the morn-

ings, we would go to the mosque to study in the *Halka,* and then in
the afternoons, we would meet in the homes of the city's Mu'tazila
scholars so as to study translations of Greek texts."

"Greek texts?" Karim sneered. "What for?"

Karim's scornful tone cut through the joyful mood of the room.
Everyone shifted in their cushions as they looked first at Karim, then
at Khalil. I too found myself staring at the two, enthralled by the
enmity behind their words. "My dear brother," Khalil replied, "any
of the *Ulama* will agree that our use of the wisdom of other peoples,
be they Greek, Roman, Persian, or Hindi, has only served to glorify
the name of Islam." I saw now how clever he was, how skilled in the
art of rhetoric. But Karim, brute that he was, would not relent, and
the two went on sparing like warriors in a ring.

"The name of Islam needs no assistance."

"Only a fool shuts his mind to the knowledge of the past. In Basra, we read mathematics and astronomy, alchemy and philosophy. It
was as if we were uncovering a buried treasure."

"Philosophy? Ibn Faruk says that only one who despises Islam
finds interest in the words of the Greek pagans."

"What are you afraid of? Rather than dismiss what we don't understand, we should study and explore it. Only then can we know
what of their knowledge may be useful to us."

"There is no such knowledge. The Qur'an embodies all we need."

"The Mu'tazila would agree. Yet you must have heard of the
brilliance of the *Mutakalimun,* who defend Islam in debates against
Christian priests. By studying the works on logic and rhetoric they've
achieved amazing victories. Those who witness them often leave the
faith of their birth and convert to Islam."

"It may be that there are a few who serve the Umma by winning
religious debates," Karim conceded, "but as for the rest of us, I say
that rather than read the words of infidels, we would do far better to
immerse ourselves in the teachings of Islam."

Though Karim and Khalil had kept their disagreement civil, the
room was fraught with tension. Lady Nur turned to her son, took
his hand in her own and said, "Light of my eyes, you've only just
returned. Why trouble yourself with these arguments now? There
will be plenty of time for talk of your studies." Though Lady Nur's
efforts at reconciliation served to end the discussion, they also con-

firmed that with Khalil's return, rivalry and dissent had come into the Alharazi home.

I didn't expect that Khalil would take much interest in the kitchen, yet the very next morning, he appeared in the doorway, gazing at the sight of Zahiya and me rolling out dough for bread.

"Zahiya, my sweetheart," he exclaimed. "You have no idea how much I have missed you. When all of the others would pine for their mother's dishes, I told them that nothing in this world compares to the perfection of Zahiya's cooking."

No compliment could have pleased her more. Zahiya eyes filled with tears as she dried her hands on her tunic and gave Khalil a hug, which he returned with obvious affection. He turned to address me, as if we had known each other for years. "Do you know that this woman practically raised me? When I was a small child, I would spend hours in the kitchen, probably more than I spent with my own mother."

"Light of my eyes," she replied joyfully, "when you were a boy, you were too busy for the kitchen. If you weren't making magic potions, or climbing on the roofs, or carving sticks into swords, or—"

"Not true! It was Karim who was always carving swords!" he insisted and then grinned. "I preferred daggers. But who is this?" he asked, turning his attention to me. "Have they brought you some help? Where is Azzah? I haven't seen her anywhere."

"Praise be to Allah, Azzah had to return to her mother. Shafiqa here is the only reason I'm still standing on these two poor feet." She was about to tell him her troubles, but just then Fadi burst into the kitchen crying that the bread she had left in the oven had burned and caught fire. She ran out after him, leaving me alone with Khalil.

"Shafiqa," he repeated, studying me with a look that betrayed not lechery, as I had feared, but curiosity. "My mother spoke of you. She said that Salim found you in the market—in dire circumstances."

I didn't know how best to answer him, so I looked away like the bashful slave I had become.

"He told her that you were running from a man who called you by another name." He paused and watched my face for a response. "A Jewish name." I pursed my lips and said nothing. "I told her that she must be mistaken. The Qur'an discourages the use of Jewish slaves, and in any case, the Jews always redeem their own."

I looked up at him, surprised. Clearly this Khalil knew something more of the world than his gold-chasing father and beast of a brother. A bitter pang of sadness shot through me, for he would never see me as anything better than a slave girl. But I was lost to the good, gentle people of this world. The best I could ever hope for now was to serve them their food and scrub their dirty plates. "I'm something of an exception," I answered with lowered eyes.

"I see," he replied. "In that case, we are cousins." He smiled at me and as the corners of his eyes crinkled up, my fear of him was calmed. I saw clearly now that his pleasing face and refined manner were the gifts of his mother, while his nimble mind resembled his father's. But more than either of his parents, he seemed to possess that rare quality of charm which evokes the delight and affection of others. One might indeed have concluded that he was born under the most favorable of stars.

IN THE DAYS following Khalil's homecoming, relatives began to arrive from outside the city. All of the servants had been put to work scrubbing the house, preparing the garden, setting out cushions and tables, and washing the floors and walls of the courtyard.

On the afternoon of the party, the road leading up to the villa was decked with lanterns, and the house and gardens were adorned with lilies and roses. The courtyard was made festive with lamps placed behind colored glass, so as to give off enchanting blue and green light. As was the custom, the men gathered in the back garden, while the women's party was held in the in the central courtyard. All of the slaves and servants were ordered to make sure that the flow of food and drink was generous and unceasing. By nightfall, I was spent from the long days of hard work, and in my exhaustion, the long-awaited evening seemed as unreal as a beautiful dream.

The night sky was a deep blue, and a bright yellow half-moon hung over the gathering like a welcoming lamp. The guests moving through the scented rooms of the house in their finest gowns and robes, their delight at the endless stream of delicacies, the cries of greeting, of reunion, of amusing stories set against the gentle notes of the oud, all came together to transform the gardens and courtyards into a vision of paradise.

I observed Khalil as he moved among the guests, and wherever he went, he was given a prince's welcome. Family and friends alike embraced and kissed him, giving thanks to Allah for his safe return. Omar Alharazi stood at Khalil's side, beaming with pride as men of learning and influence inquired about his plans for the future. Several Ulama approached him, offering to take him under their wing so that he might continue his religious studies. Another group, esteemed experts in mathematics and philosophy, suggested that Khalil attend lectures at the *Dar al Hikma*. "New texts are constantly being discovered and translated," I heard one of them say. "If you join us, you'll have the chance to immerse yourself in the writings of Persia, India, and ancient Greece. Many of us take up the works where the great masters stopped, so that we students soon overtake our teachers."

Khalil bowed respectfully. "It would be an honor to join such respected disciples of Aristotle and Brahmagupta. I promise to visit the Dar al Hikma as soon as my father allows me to leave the house again." At this, everyone laughed, and one of the scholars slapped Omar Alharazi on the back saying, "Your son is both intelligent and diplomatic. His words are touched with honey, so that others not only respect him, but also love him."

In the courtyard, Lady Nur received her guests like a queen. Mothers of eligible daughters made inquiries regarding his marriage prospects, but Lady Nur tactfully fended them off. "Khalil has not even hinted that he's ready to marry," I heard her tell Lady Fatima, the wife of a palace clerk with two teenage daughters. "Years may pass before I hold a grandson in my arms," she predicted with a sigh.

"But Nur, he is a young man; surely he's not oblivious to the beautiful women of Baghdad!"

"Sons never share their feelings about women with their mothers. I have no doubt that a day will come when Khalil, like all men, will be struck by the arrows of love. A mother can only wait patiently for that day."

In the days after the party, Khalil began to attend lectures at the Dar al Hikma, and the house saw many new and learned guests. The weeks passed, and to my great relief, Khalil had no interest in using me as his brother did. In spite of his affection for Zahiya, he rarely entered the kitchen. When I did see him, he was usually in the company of his friends, reclining on mats and pillows under the shade trees in the garden.

Sometimes when I was sent to bring a clandestine flask of the wine that Omar Alharazi kept in a far corner of the storeroom, I would come upon them puzzling over a mathematics problem, and then defending their results in the language of numbers. Other times I found them speaking of such subjects as the nature of God, or the meaning of what they called "a good life." They enjoyed holding orderly discussions, in which one man would state a premise, and another would then show him where his premise held a contradiction. I would try to make myself busy in the garden, so as to catch snatches of their conversation, for their talk was like a secret tongue, which endowed them with the power to speak of things that are hidden to the eye.

"Aristotle distinguishes between actual and potential infinity," I heard Khalil explain to his friends one day, "but he concludes that ultimately, all infinity can only exist as a potential. In *Metaphysics*, he writes, 'Infinity is not a permanent actuality, but consists in a process of coming to be, like time and the number of time.'"

"But if God is infinite, can He too be seen to consist in a process?" his friend had retorted. I had never heard language like this before and I could barely understand what they were saying. How could they speak of infinity when they couldn't agree on what it meant?

If the discussion continued into the afternoon, they would turn in the direction of Mecca and break for prayers. The noise of their talk would be stilled, so that only the rustling of the trees could be heard. I would enter the garden quietly, setting platters of dried figs and sesame cakes on small tables beside them. Sometimes, I would stop and gaze at them a moment before returning to the kitchen; for it seemed that no life could be finer than theirs.

AT KHALIL'S REQUEST, Omar Alharazi commissioned the building of a chess table, crafted of smooth white and black marble. When it was ready, four workmen were needed to haul it into the men's courtyard. From then on, Khalil and his father would meet there each day after the late afternoon prayers. Zahiya would send me to take them a pot of mint tea, and I would come upon them seated opposite each other, heads bent in concentration, while the soft glow of early evening settled slowly over the courtyard.

As I served their tea, the chessboard seemed to call out to me. I would often linger for a moment, just to see if the players would do as I would have. I discerned that their abilities were equal, but where Khalil was clever and aggressive, Omar Alharazi was patient and subtle. If Khalil eased his concentration for even a second, he was likely to lose the game to his father. In time, as I came to know their styles of playing, those moments when I would glance at the chess table became a highlight of my day, a brief moment when the dull drudgery of my labor was illuminated by a puzzle. After covertly examining the game board, I would carry its image in my mind, mulling over what each player had to do in order to achieve a checkmate, or alternatively, to induce a stalemate. I soon found that I could work out the possibilities in my mind, even as I went about my duties.

One day, while surveying the situation on the chess table, I calculated that in the course of several moves, Khalil would be trapped in a checkmate and lose the game, yet he himself didn't perceive it. As he moved to pick up his knight, ignoring the trap that was forming around him, I couldn't help but shake my head as if to say, *You don't want to do that!* By a strange stroke of fate, Khalil raised his eyes to me at that precise moment. He made no sign that acknowledged what he had seen, yet he withdrew his hand from the knight, and returned his gaze to the board. Flustered, I spun around and left the courtyard in great haste, as if caught in the midst of an unseemly act.

I FELT MYSELF weakening; I was losing the memory of who I once was and who I once wanted to be. On cold winter nights, the foul grease of the evening meal still clinging to my skin, I would walk out to the far end of the garden and gaze at the distant lights of the city. I envisioned young girls dressing in beautiful robes and going off to wedding parties and celebrations, where musicians played sweet music and others appraised them with an eye to their eligible brothers and cousins.

There had been many nights when even the decision to live seemed like the pathetic insistence of an ant about to be ground into the dust; for my death wouldn't trouble anyone, and I didn't believe the hell of sinners to be any worse than what I was enduring in life. I imagined myself collecting a few small crystals of the rat poison that Salim sprinkled among the sacks of the storeroom. It would be an agonizing death, but also a quick one; more than once I had stood and watched how the rats convulsed, froze into stiffness, and then collapse on the floor in matter of seconds.

One night, as I sat pondering what might await me after death, I was startled by the sound of light footsteps. "Who's there?" a voice called out, and I recognized, with great alarm, that it belonged to Khalil. The night was foggy and moonless, and I wondered if I could run back to my room without him seeing me.

"It's me, Khalil," the voice said. "Who's that?" He stared through the darkness. "Shafiqa?" he asked incredulously. "What are you doing out here?"

"I . . . I was about to go in. I didn't expect to meet anyone."

"Neither did I."

"Good night, sir," I murmured, and turned to leave.

"No," he called softly. "Wait. Please don't go. I'm restless; maybe your company will calm me."

"Forgive me, sir. I have to go now," I insisted as firmly as I could, for though he had not given me reason to fear him, I could never know when he too might fall upon me and use me as his brother did. "There are others more suited for your company than I."

"That is true. I have no shortage of companions. But I can't speak my mind with them. Better an intelligent slave."

"Then I'm definitely not the company you're looking for," I replied as I began to move toward the house.

"Better a slave who's familiar with the game of chess."

I halted, not quite believing that he was referring to me. "You know nothing about me."

"I know enough to sense that you can be trusted. Please Shafiqa; I want nothing more than to talk to someone, someone who can hear my troubles and consider them without passing judgment."

"Troubles?" I repeated. "I didn't think you knew the meaning of the word." But as soon as those words left my mouth, I regretted them; I had seen Karim smack a slave and hurl him to the ground for speaking disrespectfully.

But Khalil was not about to beat me. "Ah, Shafiqa," he sighed, "a slave's life is so simple. What can you know of despair? During the day, when I am surrounded by friends and family, I put on a mask and hide my true feelings. But when I am alone, all that I keep hidden presses down on me like a grindstone." Khalil gazed up at the dark skies, and then continued sadly. "The past months have been nothing but suffering!"

I stifled the urge to laugh out loud. For it seemed preposterous to me that someone as fortunate as Khalil could speak with such pain. "You seem like a person of integrity," he continued, "a person with whom one can speak freely, without fear of treachery. If I confide in you, can I trust that you'll never speak of what I tell you to anyone else?"

"It isn't fitting for a man to make his confessions to a slave."

"The night is dark; I can't see your face, and you can't see mine. We'll speak not as a slave and a master, but as two equal souls. Will you at least hear me, and then share your thoughts about what I tell you?"

I glanced anxiously toward the house, wondering if this talk wasn't a lead up to whatever he really wanted. "I'll ask nothing else from you," he added, as if reading my thoughts. He sat down on a step, and motioned for me to sit beside him, but I remained standing in place. "On my journey to Baghdad," he began in a tremulous voice, "I stopped in the city of Basra where I stayed in the home of a distant cousin of my father's. The master of the house, Wa'il Ibn Yasin, is a well-known scholar and teacher of *Hanafi* jurisprudence. Students from far and wide come to his door to partake of his teachings. His family treated me like a son. For weeks they fed me and put me up in their best guest room. Ibn Yasin has two sons and they were as brothers to me. But there was also a daughter." Khalil sighed, as if her image had appeared before him. "A girl of outstanding spirit and beauty. The first time I encountered her, she was sitting in the garden with her mother, and I could see nothing more than her eyes. I was told that her engagement to the son of the Mufti had been negotiated over many long months, with the intent that it would enhance Ibn Yasin's name in the city's mosques. Plans were being made for a great wedding, which is set to take place when the Mufti's son returns from his travels in the West."

I could hardly believe that Khalil was speaking of such matters to me. The way he was revealing his most private thoughts threw me into confusion, and I was unsure how, given my station as a lowly slave, I ought to respond. "Though she usually wore a veil, I soon caught a glimpse of her face, and against all good sense, I found myself drawn to her as the moth is drawn to the flame. At first I kept my love for her hidden. Any show of interest would have been a violation of Ibn Yasin's hospitality. Yet she somehow sensed my feelings, and let me know that in spite of her betrothal, she was prepared to meet with me in private. Through intricate manipulations, we were able to find times and places to be alone, and we soon realized that our souls were as harmonious as the harp and the flute." I couldn't help but gasp in shock; how could one as clever as Khalil act so foolishly?

"And yet, we are separated, doomed to live out our lives apart from each other. Even here in my father's house, I think of her constantly. The longing in my heart is like a prison sentence. There is no one in the entire universe more miserable than I."

His voice fell silent, and I understood that he was waiting for me to say something in response. "Sir," I ventured hesitantly, "you've traveled far and met men from all walks of life. You must be aware that the life you live is a fortunate one."

"But without her, all that I have means nothing."

"There are other women. Just pick whoever else pleases you."

"No other woman compares with her."

I shifted and glanced anxiously in the direction of the house. "I have to go."

"Is that it then? You have nothing more to say?"

My nerves were frayed with weariness, and I wanted only to be done with this strange conversation. "All right. If you really are interested in what I have to say," I snapped, "then it is this: a man of your learning should be able to see beyond his own private concerns. He must realize that his place in this world is not that of a little ant, but of. . .of a cat. . .who can do as he wishes with the entire anthill."

He turned away in contempt. "How stupid of me to expect words of wisdom from a kitchen slave," he muttered to himself, but loud enough for me to hear.

And then something turned in me, such that I was suddenly incensed by his childish arrogance. "Do you think I was always a slave?" I retorted in a voice that I had almost forgotten was mine. "I was once a respectable girl, with a father who cared for me. I was once engaged. I too dreamed of marriage and a happy life. If it is misery that intrigues you, just look at me, wasting my life away in a stranger's kitchen."

For a moment he was silent. "Where is your father now?"

The darkness around us was thick and as black as the bitterness that pervaded my soul. "He's dead," I replied flatly. "Murdered. After it happened, I disguised myself as a boy and ran away. Before long, I got into trouble, and somehow found myself a slave in the market. At first I thought that I would find a way to escape. But I see now that I could never survive on my own. And so I remain here . . ." My voice trailed off into the night air. I had told him far too much.

The only the sound was that of the night insects, whose loud chirping seem to give the night the odd quality of a dream. "Allah has set a difficult fate for you," I heard him say quietly. "Yet He is merciful. You must pray that He will lead you back to your rightful path."

These few words of kindness, uttered as they were, almost took my breath away. "You're a kind person, Khalil," I whispered, choking on the tears that burned in my throat. "I'm sorry that I can't be of more help to you." He was silent for a moment, and I regretted now that I had spoken harshly to him.

"But you have helped," he answered. "You've held up a mirror and forced me to look at it. I was right to confide in you. Your words are not only honest, they are also wise. *Insha'Allah*, we'll soon have an opportunity to speak again."

We parted then, and as I started back to the house, I trembled, not with fear but with a strange inner elation. For the encounter with Khalil had somehow reminded me that the girl called Shafiqa was a mere imposter and that the person I used to be had not died.

BUT THE ELATION quickly turned to despair. For days I nurtured a vain hope that now that Khalil had seen a hint of who I really was, he would try to help me in some way. But the days passed, and though I sometimes saw him reading in the garden, or making his way down to the bath house, he barely acknowledged my presence. I scolded myself for my childish dreams of his rescuing me the way a prince rescues a princess. For he was master and I was a slave, and there was no reason to believe that he would trouble himself for me.

For this reason, it came as something as a shock when one morning, while Zahiya was out by the ovens, he slipped into the kitchen and whispered, "Meet me later tonight in the same place we spoke last time. Come when Zahiya has gone to bed." All that day I thought of nothing but what he wanted to say to me. Though I hoped he would tell me of a foolproof plan for my escape, I imagined that I would in fact have to hear more about his pining for the girl in Basra.

The night was cold, and I wrapped myself in a heavy shawl before making my way to the back corner of the garden. This time, I found him waiting for me. Unlike our first meeting, the moon was full, and I could see his face without difficulty. "Finally," he remarked as he set two cushions on the cold earth. "I almost thought you'd forgotten."

"I wanted to be certain that Zahiya was asleep before I left."

"Good. That was wise. We need to exercise good sense and caution."

"It was you who asked to meet."

"Yes. You see, I've given a lot of thought to our previous conversation, and there's something that's troubling me."

I smiled bitterly, for the little I had told him contained more horror than the book of Job. "And what might that be?"

"You told me that your father was murdered. Why didn't you go to the Qadi, so that justice could be done?"

"That wasn't possible."

"Why not?"

I paused for a moment before answering him, wary of uttering the words that could somehow incriminate me. "It was the Qadi's son himself who was the murderer."

"Then there was all the more reason to at least pay you compensation. That's the way these matters are settled."

"I couldn't go to him."

"But why not?"

I shook my head. "I've already told you too much."

"Shafiqa," he said gently, "I want to help you." He paused thoughtfully. "What of the Jews of your town? Couldn't you turn to them?"

"No. Nobody can help me. I've considered my situation a thousand times over and still I can't see the possibility of a life any better than the one I have here."

"Please Shafiqa, tell me what happened. I've trusted you with my greatest secret. Can't you trust me with yours?"

I looked out at the flickering lights of the city. How long it had been since anyone had spoken to me with such concern? How many nights had I come out to this garden, alone in the world without a single person who cared what had happened to me? His attention was like a warm sun, endowed with the power to release water from the coldest of snows. And so, after swearing him to secrecy, I recalled the story of my father's murder, and of the murder that I myself committed.

As I spoke, his eyes grew wide with astonishment. "But you should have gone to the authorities," he exclaimed. "Once they understood that you killed in self-defense, they wouldn't have condemned you."

I laughed bitterly. "You're naïve, Khalil. These people would never tolerate a Jew that murdered a Muslim. To confess would have been a death sentence."

"But Islam demands justice for the peoples of God," he insisted, "and certainly for the Jews."

"Perhaps, but I've learned that real life has little to do with the noble words of prophets and holy men. Real life has its own set of rules, rules that are stronger than beautiful words."

Khalil opened his mouth to speak, but found that he had nothing to offer me. Again, I had silenced him, sullying his beautiful image of the world with my ugly story. The look of sorry helplessness in his eyes made me regret everything I had told him, and I knew that no matter how brilliant or how privileged he seemed to me, he would do nothing to help me.

THE DREAM OF ending my life hadn't faded. Rather, it was an argument that seemed to grow stronger and more convincing with each passing day. In my daydreams, I imagined hiding a kitchen knife in the pocket of my robe, and then thrusting it into Karim's neck. And then, as I watched him choke and die, I would pull it from his body and plunge it straight into my own heart. I had used a knife in this way once before, and I was so mad with despair that I knew I could do it again.

Yet even as I played out the scene in my mind, I was troubled by all that remained open and unsettled. It pained me now that I had never properly parted from Shafiqa. The notion that I had abandoned my fiancé without so much as a message gave me no peace. Even the way I had disappeared from Hassan in the marketplace was like an unfinished tale eternally waiting for its end.

But the thing that troubled me most was that on the very morning of his death, my father had promised me a conversation. He had promised to tell me of Antigone because she had put him in mind of me. What did he want to tell me about her? The more I thought about that last talk with him, the more I felt that fate had cheated me out of even this modest thing. I sometimes found myself dreaming about that conversation. I saw the book on my father's desk, and heard his voice as he spoke of it, but I could never make out his words.

In the passing of the days, a plan took shape in my mind; a plan that would give me an answer, a conclusion, a sense that a question had been answered and closed. And it would leave me free to end my miserable life.

KHALIL AND HIS friends were reclining on thick cushions set under the shading branches of the date palms. A new youth, one whom I had never seen before, was speaking, one arm supporting his head, the other gesturing in the air. "Al Khuwarazmi has already shown that an unknown variable can be revealed by simply performing a transfer of terms, thereby eliminating the negative quantities, and then balancing the positive qualities which remain. He has called the first step Al-jabr, and the second, Al-muqabala. I'll show you how it works: first we—" He stopped short, because everyone had turned to where I was standing. Khalil rose and came to me. "What is it?" he asked.

"I need to speak with you," I whispered.

"Tonight," he whispered back. "Late. In the garden." As I walked away, I heard the laughter of his friends, and was ashamed for what they were saying. I was certain that Khalil would later reprimand me for speaking with him in public.

Yet when I found him that night, a cup of wine in hand, it was he who apologized to me. "I hope you were able to ignore my friends' rudeness. They're all fine people, but when they gather in a group they're like children." He held the cup to his nose, inhaled the scent of the wine, and took a sip. "We haven't spoken in a long time, but I haven't forgotten what you said to me on that first night, and how your sharp words brought me to my senses. Is there something you want to ask of me?"

Though I knew my request would sound odd to him, his willing tone made me bold. "Yes. It's something that I want very badly to resolve." I gazed up at him and groped for words. "I . . . have you ever heard of a Greek book called *Antigone*?"

He gave his head a puzzled shake. "That's it? That's what you want to ask?"

"That is all. Have you heard of it? The book, *Antigone*? Try to remember. Maybe you've heard the name."

"*Antigone*," he repeated slowly. "No. It's not familiar to me."

"The author's name is Sophocles."

He shook his head. "No. Did he write anything else?" He frowned quizzically. "How do *you* know of him?"

"My father read many languages, including Greek. *Antigone* was on my father's desk on the day he died." As I spoke, I pictured with perfect clarity the leather-bound volume as it lay on the desk. "He said that it was an ancient drama, a masterpiece. We . . . we planned to discuss it."

"Perhaps you have the name wrong, or your memory fails you."

"Impossible. That is the name. I've held it in my mind for many months; there is no mistake."

He stroked his beard and began to think aloud, as if to himself. "If this *Antigone* is as great as your father said, than perhaps someone has translated it." My heart quickened, because this was exactly what I hoped to hear. "Every week, when I go to the Dar al Hikma, I see an army of translators all working to bring the knowledge of Greece to light." He brooded for a minute, and then his face brightened. "I have an idea. I'll simply ask the translators if they know of the book. If it is really that worthy, it's inconceivable that they haven't heard of it."

"My father would have loved such a place," I said sadly. "He loved to read the books of the Greeks and Romans. He often said that if not for their writings about medicine, the work of the physician would be no different than that of a gardener."

Khallil laughed in appreciation, and then sighed as he caught my eye. "She visits me every night."

Though he said nothing more, I knew he was speaking of the girl in Basra. "Then you must tell her to leave."

"I do. But she refuses."

"Then you must thank God for the distance between you."

In truth, I had no patience to listen to Khalil's longings. In the days that followed, I thought of nothing but how he would go to the Dar al Hikma and find *Antigone*. The notion that I might soon discover its secrets swept all my thoughts of ending my life from my mind.

But when several days later he asked to speak with me, I learned that my hopes had been in vain. "Yesterday I spoke with Yihye Suliman. He is the most respected translator in the Dar al Hichma. He said that he has heard of this Sophocles, but that his works have been deemed undesirable for translation."

"What? How can that be? Tell me everything, exactly as it happened."

Khalil went on to describe how he had asked Yihye Suliman if he knew of the name of Sophocles. "I remembered that you described it as an ancient drama, but as soon as I mentioned it, he scowled as if I had said something distasteful, and said that if that is the case, then the work has not been translated, nor will it be in the future."

"But why?"

"He said that the literature of the Greeks is of no interest. Even though some scholars deem it permissible, or even desirable, to study their medicine and rhetoric, there's no need for a Muslim to study the pagan works of their culture. He told me that the scholars will not translate the pagan writings of the Greeks, because they have nothing to offer."

"He speaks foolishly," I replied, my scorn masking my great dismay. "My father said that *Antigone* was a great work."

"So what if he said? Who was your father? Was he of our Ulama? Was he even a rabbi? And what do *you* know of the Greeks? You're nothing but a slave girl! Do you dare to question the wisdom of great scholars?"

"He so wanted for me to know it," I whispered, but it came out hoarse.

"Shafiqa," he said, as if in apology, "I have tried."

In my disappointment I forgot to thank him; I merely gazed into the dark sky, wondering if there was any place in the universe where I might find *Antigone* again.

SOON AFTER, THE month of Ramadan fell, and I didn't see Khalil again for many days. Like the rest of the Alharazi household, he spent his days resting and his nights feasting, while Zahiya and I, the only non-Muslims in the house, prepared the evening meal behind the closed doors of the kitchen.

The days were growing longer. When I awoke each day, the air was warm with the scent of the flowering trees, and a hot, gold light shone down on me as I ground grain for the day's bread. Even after the holiday finally ended, the family continued their habit of retiring to their bedchambers in the afternoons, and the windows were left open all night so as to catch the evening breezes. "Wouldn't it be nice to have a break from this kitchen?" I remarked dreamily to Zahiya one morning.

"Break? What break are you talking about? *Eid al Adha* is coming. This house will soon be bursting with guests, and you know what that means." I did indeed. It seemed as if the Alharazi family lived from celebration to celebration, from festival to festival.

"I didn't know that the Muslims are blessed with so many holidays," I said to Khalil a few nights later. We had not planned to meet; rather, it happened by coincidence, not unlike our first encounter. "What is this Eid al Adha that everyone is speaking of?"

"You don't know?" he asked incredulously.

"I am not an expert in the festivals of the Muslims."

"But the story of Eid al Adha concerns someone with whom you must be familiar."

"Who?"

"It has to do with Ibrahim, our father, and yours. Ibrahim was the first man to believe in one God, but in spite of his faith, Allah wanted to test him. He told Ibrahim to take his son, Ismail and sacrifice him like an animal on an altar. Ibrahim bound up Ismail and prepared to kill him. But then, at the very last second, right before Ibrahim was about to plunge his knife into Ismail, an angel appeared, and showed him a ram that was standing nearby. Ibrahim understood that Allah meant for him to unbind Ismail and sacrifice the ram instead."

I stared at him blankly. "But Khalil, it wasn't Ismail that Abraham almost sacrificed. It was Isaac!"

He shook his head and smiled. "Were you there to see it?"

"I didn't have to see it! The story is written, black on white, in the Torah. Jews have told it that way for thousands of years."

"And among the Arabs, the story of Ismail has been passed down. The Qur'an claims that the Jews have changed and distorted much of their Holy Book. One of the distortions involves the identity of the son that Ibrahim sacrificed."

"But . . . that's outrageous! Everyone knows that the Qur'an was written long after the Torah."

"The Qur'an is eternal. It is the written word of God. And still the Jews believe that their Torah is the word of God. I must admit, I have given much thought to this problem."

"And have you an answer?" I asked sardonically.

"I have; the answer is simply that there is no answer. How can one argue matters that belong to the realm of faith?" His voice rose, and I could see that he felt passionately about the problem, and had indeed, as he claimed, given it much thought. "Those who argue about which version is the truth have ignored what's most obvious. Even if we don't agree about the details, the faith of believers, generation upon generation, cannot be denied. Perhaps the story happened as the Muslims believe it did. Or perhaps the story that the Jews tell is the correct one. In any case, it no longer matters."

I wanted to explain why his version was wrong and mine was right, but I was not so foolish as to challenge the beliefs of my master's son. "So the reason for the festival is to remember Abraham's sacrifice," I suggested, hoping to bring the matter to a close.

"It is a celebration of Allah's unfailing wisdom and mercy."

How could I disagree with such a notion? How could anyone? Nonetheless, I was troubled by the way he dismissed the problem as nothing more than two brothers quarreling over petty details. He must have read the indignation in my face, for he continued, "I haven't angered you, I hope."

"What you have told me seems very strange, as if you've deliberately mixed up the details of the story."

He laughed, ever true to his good nature. "Then let's cease this futile talk while we're still friends."

Again he confused me, speaking not as if he were the fortunate son of a wealthy merchant, but one of my girlfriends in Sura. "Friends? What strange mood has come over you tonight? Have you forgotten that I am a slave in your father's house? If I were a free woman, it would be inconceivable that you and I speak a word to each other! I would appear before you veiled, in the company of my father or husband."

"And yet my heart goes out in friendship to you." He smiled. "Who knows why? Perhaps friendship is like love, a matter which has little to do with logic. But I can't deny it. You are as a friend to me, Shafiqa, and I wish for your well-being as much as for any other of my friends."

"You seem to have a preference for what is unfitting," I remarked.

"I have a preference for what my heart tells me, and it tells me that you are not what you seem."

"Well you are mistaken, Khalil," I answered sharply, furious that for all his good will, he refrained from doing anything to end my slavery. "Look at me, dressed in these slave robes, scrubbing pots day and night in your mother's kitchen. I am exactly what I seem. If it was in my power to be otherwise, rest assured that I would not be here." I bid him good night and quickly took leave of him. I saw now that Khalil and his fine words were as a poison to me. If I ingested them, they would torment me and drive me to great despair.

IN THE DAYS that followed, Zahiya and I barely left the kitchen. It was customary that on the morning before the festival, lambs were slaughtered in honor of the holiday, and then served at the feast. Yet this dish was only the centerpiece of the meal, and an astounding number of accompanying dishes had to be prepared as well. Servants were sent to help us, but nonetheless, we worked from dawn to dusk.

On the day of the great feast, Lila and Amal came into the kitchen accompanied by a girl I had never seen before. I had grown used to a constant stream of family members and guests who took it upon themselves to sample the dishes and offer advice. But when I saw the girl who had come in with them, my hands stopped working and I had to tell myself to refrain from staring. She had a delicate oval face, shimmering dark hair, and green eyes that sparkled as if she had just heard something that amused her. Her gown was tied with a green sash at the hip, the same shade as her eyes, and her bearing was that of a princess.

"This is Samira, my father's cousin's daughter," Amal told me proudly, as if some of Samira's radiance might enhance her own plainness. She arrived this morning with her brothers. From Basra."

"And where are your parents?" Zahiya asked. "It has been so long since they've honored us with a visit."

"Unfortunately, they won't be coming. My father had to stay behind to tend to some business, and since Grandmother fell ill, my mother scarcely leaves her bedside."

"Samira's father is among the most respected Ulama in the city," Amal informed me proudly. "The Mufti of Basra has asked for Samira's hand in marriage to his son."

Something about that sounded familiar, but it took me a moment to remember where I had heard it. And then suddenly, I knew. I looked away, trying to conceal my alarm. Was it possible that this Samira was the very girl whose memory still tormented Khalil?

"Here." Lila snatched a walnut cookie from the tray that sat cooling on the table. "Try this."

"Yes." She nodded after taking a delicate bite. "The texture is perfect. Last month we were at the wedding of the two richest families in Basra. The deserts were extravagant, but they don't even come close to this!" Zahyia bowed with pleasure.

"Perhaps Zahiya will cook for your wedding," Lila suggested with a wink.

"My wedding is many months away," she replied breezily. "The groom has extended his stay in the Hijaz."

At that very moment, Khalil strode into the kitchen followed by two young men. I watched his face carefully, yet he and Samira seemed casually oblivious to each other. "So this is where everyone's hiding," he joked, and then turned to Zahiya. "Idris and Fawwaz have asked to go riding. Can you spare a few refreshments?"

"You won't find anything here." Zahiya laughed, and everyone laughed along.

"Why is it that men always seek out the kitchen when they're least wanted?" Samira asked in a tone that invited even as it scolded. I gazed at her in admiration; clearly she was one of those girls whose clever talk allows her to attain whatever her heart desires. Yet I perceived that no one but me had understood the double-sided nature of her words. Or rather, no one but me and Khalil, who replied, "And why do the women always run to the kitchen when they want the men to find them?"

"Kahlil is always welcome in my kitchen," Zahiya declared as she handed him a sack full of fruits and cakes.

"God preserve you, my dear Zahiya," Kahlil blessed her. Did Samira's eye linger on Khalil for a second longer as the men turned and walked out to the stables? If it did, I failed to see it. The performance that I had just witnessed astonished me; perhaps I had only dreamed that Khalil had told me of his love for her.

Later, when I went to the girls' room to collect the empty plates, the three of them were in the midst of a lively discussion. An ebony makeup box lay on the table, its array of jars and creams reminding me of the way my own make-up table once looked. "But Samira, how can you say that?" Lila was saying. "You've never even met him."

"My dear cousins," Samira replied, as she selected a vial of perfume from the box, removed its delicate lid, and with its thin glass rod, applied the fragrance to her wrists. "The girl who is granted the chance to meet her fiancé before her wedding is lucky. Most of us must rely on the whims of our parents! However, it is possible to find out a great many things without even laying eyes on the boy." Lila and Amal stared adoringly at Samira, as impressed by her womanly confidence as I was.

"Oh Samira, you're so clever when it comes to boys. Teach us everything you know," Amal pleaded, and I too was eager to hear what she had to say, and so I busied myself by picking up and folding the sashes and undergarments that were scattered around the room.

Samira loosened her head scarf, shook out her hair, and ran her fingers through the long tresses. "I'll let you in on these matters, but only because you're family." Lila and Amal waited breathlessly for her to begin, but Samira, who was in no hurry, picked up Lila's pearl-studded comb from the dressing table, pinned up her hair, regarded herself in the looking glass on the wall, and then, as if unsatisfied, withdrew the comb, allowing her hair to cascade down her back. Only then did she turn to face her audience.

"The first thing," she began, "is to appraise the parents. You must investigate: are they high-born or newly wealthy? If high-born, what is their family history? But that's only the first stage. You must then consider, are their features harmonious and fair, or are they pronounced and homely? Are they intelligent? Merely clever? Or are they fools? Is their success in life due to their own efforts, or was it handed to them on a platter of gold? Are they among the pious, or are they hypocrites who profess piety while sinning behind doors?"

The girls chuckled softly, hanging on her every word. "Only once you've verified these things," she continued, "is it time to turn your attention to the boy. Is he the eldest in his family? If so, he is bound to be a leader of others. Is he the youngest? Expect a spoiled, soft boy, who will forever try to prove his worthiness. Are there many servants in his house? If there are, it's likely that the boy will be lazy, and possibly slow-witted, for a boy who has had to do nothing for himself will view even the most elementary tasks with distaste. However, if the servants are few, it's likely that his mind has learned to be inventive, and he has acquired a taste for challenge."

Never before had I known a girl who knew so much about the world and how it worked. Watching her was as entertaining as hearing a clever poet recite his poems, or a gifted storyteller tell an intriguing tale. My heart went out to Khalil; in all likelihood he would never find a woman whose qualities surpassed Samira's.

THE FESTIVITIES IN the Alharazi home were to take place over the next four days. On the afternoon before the first night of the Eid, most of the family and their guests either went to pray in the mosque or performed their prayers quietly in their rooms. Suddenly, the house was empty and quiet, and Zahiya and I took advantage of the lull to collapse onto our beds and massage our aching feet. Without this respite, the two of us would no doubt have fallen asleep that evening, even as we waited on the guests.

As usual, the women's party took place in the central courtyard, while the men celebrated in the back garden. I, along with two other servant girls, was assigned to wait on the women. All night long I ran back and forth from the kitchen to the courtyard, while the Alharazi women and their guests showed off their fine clothes, ate from the sumptuous dishes we had prepared, and entertained each other with amusing and outrageous stories. Later in the night, when the moon rose high in the sky, the musicians came to perform for the women. Their entrance was greeted with applause and cheering, and when the music began, the languid mood of the courtyard was charged with fresh excitement as the women got to their feet and joined in.

As they sang and danced, they formed a circle. One of Lady Suraya's elderly aunts broke into the center and began a song in praise of Allah, his prophet Muhammad, and happy festivals like this one. The musicians fell into time with her singing, while the women clapped their hands and joined her in the chorus. The song went on for several verses, and when she was done, everyone kissed her and complimented her on her voice, still lovely despite her age.

And then, before the musicians could start up again, Samira moved into the center of the circle and began a song of her own. The song she sang was also well-known, but in contrast to the previous one, hers was a song of love and the longings of the heart. As her voice rose and fell in harmony with the music, I watched the faces of Samira's audience, and in their entrhalled expressions I saw that her singing was giving voice to their deepest and most hidden desires. The older women's eyes flashed with the fire of ancient memories, while the young girls seemed to be envisioning a moment of passion so intense that the glow of its heat would smolder until their last day. Any man that saw Samira's performance would surely have fallen in love with her.

As the song was coming to its close, Lady Suraya sent me to replenish the pitchers of drink. Leaving the courtyard, I came upon Khalil. He passed me silently and disappeared into the darkness, but from his ecstatic expression I knew that he had witnessed Samira's song.

I didn't see him again until the early hours of the morning, when even the most tireless of the revelers had finally retired to their chambers. Zahiya and I worked into the night, scrubbing pots, washing dishes, and spooning the remaining food into storage vessels. When her complaints about her sore feet and her aching back began to give me a headache, I told her that I would finish the work myself and sent her to bed.

I was alone, certain that everyone in the house had gone to sleep when Khalil came into the kitchen. His face glistened with sweat, and his eyes shone with bliss. "Did you see her tonight?" he asked in a low voice.

"Of course."

"Is she not magnificent?"

"She is betrothed to another man," I whispered. "You must stop this madness."

"Don't worry, Shafiqa. I'm not going to do anything foolish." I regarded him skeptically, for he appeared as elated as a madman, and I realized that he had drunk from his father's forbidden stash of wine. He glanced at the stacks of unwashed pots. "But what of you? You must be tired."

"You're kind as usual, Khalil," I replied wearily, "but you know that I have no choice but to clean up what is left of your celebrations. Have you forgotten that I am a slave in this house?"

"Festivals are always a lot of work, but soon this will all be over, and everything will return to its usual pace."

"Festival or not, my life consists of nothing but hard labor," I complained, no longer caring that my tone was harsh.

He frowned. "You're tired now. You forget that there are advantages to living in this house. You're well-treated here, and lack for nothing."

"I am not well-treated," I said in a low, shaky voice, half-hoping that he wouldn't understand my meaning.

Khalil shifted and looked away, and at that moment I understood that he knew, that everyone knew. I looked down at the floor, wishing that I could disappear from his sight. As if from far away, I heard him say, "Shafiqa, listen to me. I wish more than anything that I could help you, that I could somehow make your life here easier. But if I say even a word to Karim, it will all be worse. Karim despises me, and no matter what I say, he'll do just the opposite."

"Is my fate nothing more than to gratify others?"

"There's only one person in the world who can answer that."

"Tell me who he is," I whispered hoarsely.

"It is you, Shafiqa. Only you can answer that."

"Me? I scarcely know my own name anymore."

He leaned toward me and whispered, "I know that you didn't come into this house by choice. But the walls around this estate are unguarded. No one watches over your comings and goings...and still you remain here."

"But what can I do? Where else can I go?"

He looked at me silently for a minute. "Do you know Shafiqa, you remind me of another Jew who was once a slave."

"And who would that be?"

"I am thinking of Yusef. Yusef in the Holy Book. Just like you, he was sold into slavery. He too was used cruelly; he too suffered. And he too was a dreamer. He paid dearly for his dreams, but in the end, he triumphed over all the forces that tried to defeat him."

I shook my head. "No. Yusef was honorable and brave. I am pitiful...and weak."

"You conceal your true character. But I have seen it, and it is neither pitiful nor weak."

I stared down at the cold stone floor. My shoulders trembled like thin leaves in a winter wind, and I feared that if he said another word I would fall at his feet, wailing like a woman in mourning.

"I must go now," he said gently. "And you need to get some sleep."

I could not look at him, could not bid him goodnight; I couldn't even thank him for his kindness. I heard the light tread of his footsteps on the stone floor. "Khalil," I suddenly called softly after him. He spun around. "Be careful," I whispered into the darkness.

It was the hottest hour of the day, and most of the family had retired to their chambers. Under the palm trees in the central courtyard, Amal and a younger cousin, Aziz, were in the midst of a game of *Tabula*. Lila reclined on pillows nearby, absently fingering the beads of her necklace. I was collecting their dirty cups and plates when Lila called me to her side. "Amal is certain that she'll finally win at Tabula today," she said. "What do you say, Shafiqa?"

I hated when Lila spoke to me as if I were a friend of hers when, in fact, I had no choice but to do her bidding. But I had learned, in my long months of servitude in her home, to flatter and humor her. "I say that if she considers refraining from hasty decisions, she may have a chance. Of course, a bit of luck always helps too."

With her index finger, Lila gestured for me to bend down to her. "Shafiqa," she whispered, "you just reminded me. I said that I would play the winner, but I need my lucky ring—you know the one. It's silver, with a big tiger-eye stone in the middle. It's in my jewelry box, at the back of the cupboard in my bedchamber. Go quickly and get it for me."

"I can't just go into your room and open your cupboard," I whispered back. "If your mother sees me going through your things, she'll think I'm trying to steal something!"

"Silly girl! You worry like an old woman," she said with a laugh. "My mother is resting, and so is everyone else. In any case, Samira's in there. She'll be your witness if there is any trouble."

Cursing her under my breath, I put the cups on a table and went to Lila's chamber in the women's courtyard. Lila was sharing her quarters with Samira, and from the state of the room, I could tell that the chambermaids had not yet been in to tidy up. White nightdresses lay abandoned on the floor, and the mattresses and pillows were strewn with the previous day's robes, tunics, and sashes. I crossed the room nervously, for Samira was nowhere to be seen. With a quick glance behind me, I opened the clothes cupboard and rummaged through the piles of silky leggings, tunics, robes, and undergarments. Soon my fingers brushed against the smooth wood of the jewel box. Its fine gold clasp was tricky, but I had once owned one just like it, so I knew exactly how to open it.

The ring was buried under a pile of gold and silver bracelets. Just as I was slipping it into the pocket of my tunic, I heard footsteps approaching. In a panic, I stepped into the cupboard and pulled the door shut, but I couldn't close it all the way. A narrow crack of light shone through, so that I could just make out the unmade bed.

It was Samira, probably about to take a nap. She stood before the mirror and pulled off her headscarf in a slow, beguiling gesture. Anxious but puzzled, I saw her eyes dart nervously around the room, and then, as if unable to make up her mind, she went first toward the cupboard, then to the mirror to fix her hair, and finally to the bed, where she loosened the drawstring of her pants and let them fall to the floor.

I was about to emerge from hiding and invent some explanation when suddenly Khalil came into the bedchamber and bolted the door. Without a word, he crossed the room and approached Samira. My tongue dried in my mouth; I had to bite it so as not to let out a scream. He moved to sit beside her. I dared not breathe.

Astounded, I watched Khalil as he took Samira's hand in his own and uttered, *"I am in love. I love in spite of this weakness, and I weaken because of your love. Tell me, what do I do?"* I covered my mouth in astonishment; his warm tone sounded like a recitation, and the words floated on the air like soft music. Could it be that he was reciting love poetry?

"I am patient with the one I love without misgivings," I heard her reply. *"Distance has increased my love. There is a saying about me and what they say is true; 'A burnt heart has no cure.'"* What was this? Was she too familiar with the poem? Or was it another?

Khalil must have recognized it, for he responded, *"This love nested and lives within my breast whilst I still reach out for you. My moon, tell me, why did you leave me?"*

As I waited for the next verse, I saw Samira run her fingers down the length of his arm, her gold bracelets jingling softly, and then lay languidly back. *"Be merry, enjoy and take advantage of the carelessness of the spy,"* she answered in a tone of such invitation that I gasped in shock.

What was Samira doing? Her recklessness was unfathomable. I wanted to break out, to make them stop before things went any further, but my limbs were as stiff as sticks. *"Oh child of the gazelle of joy!"* Khalil responded. *"Let us resume the love which yesterday flowed between us."*

"Light of my eyes," she cried softly, *"I pick your rose and surrender as a lover. You are my true yearning."* Hearing these words, Khalil fell upon her. Astounded, I turned back into the darkness of the cupboard.

When I looked again, Samira was drawing her robe up over knees and thighs, and higher still. My knees buckled under me; I felt as thought I might faint. I looked away, and then, as if compelled by a demon, I looked again. He lay over her now, and for a brief moment I caught sight of his hands, moving on her flesh with the silent ravenousness of a fire slowly devouring a dry log. Their bodies appeared to me as two dragonflies, joined together and locked in a silent, dance-like struggle. I closed my eyes and commanded my shaking limbs to be still. *They're insane*, I cried in my mind, for if they were caught, the consequences would be terrible.

Through the narrow crack in the door, I could see the smooth flex of the muscles of his back, and the long curve of his body over

hers. And then I caught a glimpse of Samira's face. Her cool, graceful demeanor had abandoned her for something far stronger, which
she was powerless to withstand. Her face was weirdly contorted, as if
she were being pulled, the way the sea's undertow pulls shells to its
soft floor. I turned away in disbelief, sinking again into the darkness
of the cupboard, when suddenly a sharp groan pierced the room. Its
animal rasp chilled me, for I had heard such a sound once before, on
the night that I lay trapped beneath the weight of a bestial stranger.
A wave of nausea passed over me as the memory surged through my
brain. And then all was silent. I peered out and saw him whispering
into her ear. *Now what?* I wondered, terrified for them.

Khalil left first. Samira checked the basin for water and found
it empty. When she left the room to call a servant, I emerged from
the closet and ran out into the courtyard. My limbs were cramped
and aching, and my head hurt from staring. But there was no time
to waste. I clasped the ring tightly in my hand and ran back to Lila,
trying to think of an excuse for why I had taken so long.

I WAS AFRAID for Khalil, afraid for Samira, afraid of what might
happen to a girl who did as she pleased with no thought to the consequences. But the thing that troubled me most of all was the strangeness of what I had seen: Samria's eyes, closed, but not from pain. Her
mouth open, but not to scream. The undeniable fact that Samira
had *invited* the very act which I knew to be the most repugnant and
terrible of all.

That night was to be the last of the celebrations, but I dreaded
having to look upon Samira and Khalil. I complained of a headache
and asked Lady Nur that she allow me to retire early. Angel of mercy
that she was, she told two servants to take my place and released me
from my evening chores. I fell into my bed, my head pounding and
my mind numb.

Early the next morning I was awakened by Zahiya poking me in
the ribs and yelping, "You've slept enough! There's plenty to do and
I can't do it alone." The festival was officially over, but the house
was still full of guests. As I scrubbed the piles of dirty pots and bowls
that Zahiya had left for me from the night before, I could think of
nothing but the scene I had witnessed the day before. I feared that

one glance at Samira would reveal what I knew, and as for Khalil, I doubted that I could ever look him in the eye again. Who would have thought the beautiful Samira was little better than a harlot, and that clever, refined Khalil was such a fool? Who would have imagined that such well-born people could behave so dishonorably? It was enough to make one see the entire world with crooked eyes.

In the middle of the morning Lila burst into the kitchen. "Has anyone seen Samira?" she demanded.

"I haven't seen her at all today." Zahiya shrugged.

"And you, Shafiqa? Have you seen her?" I shook my head and looked away.

By the end of the day, the only remaining guests were Samira and her brothers, who planned to set out on their long journey back to Basra the following morning. The knowledge that Samira would soon be gone was a great relief to me, and when I retired that evening my sleep was sounder than it had been for many days. The night air was warm and sweet, and as I closed my eyes I could almost imagine that I was back in my garden in Sura.

I dreamed peacefully until I was awakened by a heart-stopping scream. The cries of cursing pierced my window, followed by the unmistakable blows of a fistfight. I crawled under my sheet, and tried to shut out all that I knew, and all that was yet to be.

"You son of a dog!" The cry echoed through the courtyard.

"No! Idris, no!" I heard Samira scream, and then the loud clatter of a clay pot shattering on stone.

"Your days are numbered, you stupid slut. You'll pay dearly for your whoring."

"Stop!" I recognized Khalil's voice, and sat up in my bed. "Idris! Fawwaz! Let me explain. Please. Stop and listen to me!"

"You! Shut your mouth, you snake. How could you partake of our hospitality, live in our home, and all the while disgrace our sister?"

"But you don't understand! I love her."

"Love her! Ha! Maybe you would like to explain that to the Mufti of Basra! You scheming bastard! We'll kill her with our own hands, and then we'll come for you."

By now the entire house must have been awake, but no one dared enter the courtyard. I lay curled under my sheet, not daring to move. Finally Omar Alharazi appeared. "Silence!" he cried in a booming voice. "I understand that some serious accusations have been made."

"Accusations? We saw it with our own eyes!" Idris cried, hoarse with outrage.

"Khalil!" Omar Alharazi addressed his son sternly. "Is there any truth to their claims?" I didn't hear his reply, to which Omar Alharazi responded, "I see. Idris, Fawwaz, I will deal with my son with all the severity the situation demands. But first, I want to make myself clear. There will be no more violence in my home. Tomorrow you both will ride to Basra to summon your father. Have him come here, and I will entrust Samira to him, and only him. What has happened is very grave, but you will not take it upon yourselves to dispense justice while you are guests in my home! And now," he ordered, "you will all return to your rooms, where you shall remain until you depart at first light tomorrow morning."

Heavy footsteps rang out and faded away. But even when all was quiet I could not calm my pounding heart. I lay awake, trying to make sense of Khalil and Samira's folly. Khalil was well aware of what could happen, and Samira had knowingly brought all of this on herself. And for what? To hear Khalil's groans as he lay over her? Finally, before the stars began to fade from the sky, I drifted into sleep.

I don't know how much time passed before I opened my eyes to see Khalil, kneeling at the side of my bed. His neck was ringed with black bruise marks, and a jagged line of blood was drying across his lower lip. I uttered a short, shrill cry, and Khalil clamped a hand over my mouth. He was about to say something when I moved his hand and whispered, "I heard everything."

"I have to leave now," he whispered back, "but I have several things to say to you. Will you walk me out to the back garden?" I got out of bed, threw on a housedress, and together we went out into the dark morning.

"Where will you go?" I asked him, my throat tight with pity for him.

"To *Al-Sindh*, to my mother's people. I'll probably have to stay there for some time. If Idris and Fawwaz find me, they will not be merciful."

I shuddered but tried to keep my voice steady. "And what of Samira?"

He looked away. "God will judge us, both me and her."

"You're leaving her to face her brothers alone."

He shook his head. "What fools we were. We . . . we forgot ourselves. And now, there's only one possible resolution."

"No!"

"Yes. We have ruined them. They will never hold their heads high, until—. Oh Shafiqa! It can't be any other way."

"Does she deserve to die?"

"How can you ask such a thing?"

"You said you loved her!"

"What can I do?" Khalil asked, tears forming in his eyes. "I'll never love anyone as I love her. But to remain together could only mean death for us both. Idris and Fawwaz won't rest until she's dead." He put his face in his hands and wept bitter, hopeless tears, and I saw that, in truth, Khalil was a coward.

And yet my heart went out to him; it ached for everything that he was about to lose. "In time their anger will pass," I said. "Even if they punish her, they won't dare to kill her."

"But they will," he said. "If there is one thing I know, it's that she is as good as dead." He wiped his eyes. "If I stay here, I won't be able to leave my home without fearing for my life, and I cannot live like a prisoner." He raised his eyes and rubbed his face vigorously. "I have to leave now, before they wake up. Promise me that you'll make her last days as comfortable as possible."

I looked up at his bruised face and recalled the way he smiled that first day I saw him, his eyes crinkling at the corners, as if the entire world were smiling back at him. "I will Khalil. I'll do whatever I can," I promised as I wiped the tears from my own eyes.

"May God protect you, Shafiqa. May He reward your goodness, and help you to return to your true path."

His words were as a bolt of lightning that reaches out to whatever stands tallest to meet it, and like one struck by lightning, I couldn't speak. I could only reach out and clasp his hand, as one soul reaches out to another in the darkness.

THE NEXT DAY, a somber mood pervaded the Alharazi home, as if Samira's presence were a poison, and life could not return to normal until she was cast out. Omar Alharazi called me to his office and instructed me to bring Samira her meals. He also asked that I accompany her to the servants' bathhouse. "When her father arrives, he must find her well-cared for. God only knows what awaits her when she leaves this house." Normally, a servant, and not a slave, would have been sent to attend to Samira. The fact that her care had been given over to me was a sign of the depths to which she had sunk.

Karim appeared in the doorway of the office and folded his arms smugly across his chest. "So after his dirty deeds, Khalil stole away like a thief in the night."

"Your brother made a terrible error," his father replied sadly, "and his exile is his punishment. But he will return one day, and, *insha'Allah*, he'll claim his rightful place. In the meantime, we must all remember him in our prayers."

"Because he's my brother, I will pray for his safety," Karim replied, "but it's obvious that his fate hasn't just descended on him by accident. Praise be to Allah, who blesses the pious and punishes the sinners." *Indeed*, I thought to myself, *may he give the sinners all that they deserve.*

Lila, Amal, and Lady Suraya were no more compassionate. Lady Suraya ordered Samira to move her things out of her daughter's chamber and into a tiny room in a corner of the courtyard that was normally used to store brooms and rags. And later that morning, as I passed through the women's quarters, I heard Lila say to Amal "I can't believe that scheming whore. Did you see her singing at the party the other night? You could tell that she's shameless."

"I can't wait for her father to come and take her away," Amal grimaced, holding her nose. "It's like having a rat in the house."

I too felt little sympathy for Samira. Hadn't she brought this upon herself? I had seen the entire story unfold, and had, in fact, imagined that it might conclude as it had. As I crossed the courtyard to her chamber, I resented that I had been sent to wait on such a despicable girl. But when I opened the door to her room and saw her curled on a worn straw mattress, I could not help but gasp with shock. Her beautiful dark hair was matted and tangled, and her robe was dirty with mud and blood stains. I could not see her face, except for one blackened eye. As I looked into the blank stare of that black-

ened eye, contempt drained out of me, leaving only pity. I put the
tray down and went to her side. Instinctively, I reached out to stroke
her damp hair. "I've been sent to accompany you to the bathhouse
in the back garden," I told her. But Samira shook her head and motioned for me to go.

Later in the day, when I brought her a tray of leftover meat and
rice, I found her exactly as I had left her. "You need to eat," I told
her, "or you'll have no strength for the journey home." I knelt down
and took her hand in my own. I remained like that for a long while,
and still she said nothing, but when I rose to leave, she called to
me in a voice so scorched it almost made me jump out of my skin.
"Shafiqa. Where is Khalil?"

"He's gone. Fled to his mother's family."

She broke out in a loud wail. "Ay, ay, ay, ay, I'll never see him
again!"

"I spoke with him before he left."

"What did he say?"

"He asked me to help you."

"Ay, ay, ay," she cried as she rocked herself back and forth. I was
afraid for her, afraid that in her grief and fear she would sink into
madness. And so I went to her again and embraced her. "You must
be strong, Samira," I heard myself say. "Soon your father will come
and take you home." But she fell back into the mattress and turned
away.

When the sun began to set, I came to her again. She was sitting up, and I saw that she had eaten some of the meat and rice.
"Omar Alharazi asked that I accompany you to the bathhouse," I
told her, "so that you will be fit to meet your father when he comes.
We should go now; night is falling, and everyone has gone inside."

She shook her head fearfully. "I can't. My brothers will see me
and kill me with blows."

"But they've left, Samira. Don't you remember? Omar Alharazi
has sent them to Basra to get your father. They've been gone for
hours."

"What if they've only pretended to leave? What if they're lying in
wait for me out in the garden?"

"I saw them ride off, and they wouldn't dare violate Omar Alharazi's orders."

She shook her head and laughed bitterly. "Who would have thought that a kitchen slave would prove to be the noblest soul in this household?"

She walked with small, painful steps, leaning on my arm as if she could not walk alone. I caught sight of the servants whispering as we passed their quarters, for there could be no better proof of her downfall than this. As we approached the bathhouse, Samira glanced at the plain, shabby-looking structure with the despair of one who has come to the ends of the earth. I feared that she would turn back, but she readied herself and started down the path that led to the cracked wooden door.

Unlike the attendants at the baths in Sura, I averted my eyes as Samira disrobed. Yet for some reason, she wanted me to see her. "Look at this, Shafiqa," she demanded. "Look at what those animals did to me."

Her body was a map of brown and purple with bruises. It occurred to me that she was, in fact, lucky that they had broken no bones. "They'll fade soon; nothing will remain of them," I told her, trying to mask my horror.

I held her hand as she stepped down into the crudely dug immersion pool, which was only half filled. In the many months of my life as a slave, I had grown used to bathing in the cold, shallow water, but Samira stood in the knee deep water like a lost little girl.

Nevertheless the bath seemed to refresh her. I helped her to change into a fresh robe and combed out her hair. Back in her room, I spied her cosmetic box lying in a corner of the dusty room. "I remember seeing this box on the day you arrived here," I said, as I picked it up off the floor. "Your creams and perfumes made me green with envy."

"Give it to me," she said quietly. "You have no cause to envy me now." She lifted the elaborately carved lid, examined the contents, and selected a glass vial of perfume. She held it up to the lamp, turning it this way and that in the light, and then held it out to me. "Take this, Shafiqa. I want you to have it. You're the only one in this house who's shown me any kindness."

I looked down at the vial and laughed. "I have no use for perfumes."

"I suppose you don't," she agreed. "What can a slave do with things that are beautiful and useless? But take it anyway; I want you to have it."

The frail glass felt almost weightless in my hand. There was a time when I owned many like it, when I could choose from a shelf laden with little bottles like this one, without a thought for their worth. I pulled out the cork, inhaled its fragrance of soft jasmine, and murmured, "May Allah watch over you, and grant you His protection." And then, perhaps because I wanted to give her something in exchange, I said, "Khalil occasionally visited the kitchen. He sometimes spoke freely with me."

"What did you talk about?"

"He adores you. From the day he left Basra he's thought of nothing but you."

These words were like a dam that opened, releasing a flood of tears. "Oh Shafiqa," she sobbed, "I would give the world for him, but I made a terrible mistake. I don't want to die. I'll suffer for all eternity. Who can help me now? My brothers will kill me like a dog."

"You mustn't think the worst." I tried to comfort her. "They won't kill you. Your father will come for you, and by the time you get home, their anger will have passed."

"It will never pass!" she wailed. "Even if he spares me, they won't rest. They'll search everywhere, even if it takes years. They'll hunt me down until they finish me. I've ruined them, and there will be no forgiveness. My life is finished."

"Go to sleep, Samira," I whispered as I rose from her side, for I had no more strength to listen to her.

THE COURTYARD WAS dark and eerily empty. Zahiya was out by the water basin, piling the day's pots and dishes for me to wash. As usual she was singing to herself, "*I searched for you high and low, until I came upon your footsteps in the sand.* . . Shafiqa," she called out. "Come in here and wash up. With you attending to that whore, I have this whole kitchen on my back."

I knelt down by the pile of dirty pots. Normally this was the hardest time of day for me, when I was overcome with exhaustion and my life seemed at its most worthless. But tonight, a strange feeling of lightness had come over me, as though I had tapped into a hidden reserve of spirit. And then, as she handed me the wash rag, an astounding idea came upon me. "You go to bed," I told Zahiya. "I'll finish up the rest."

"Allah preserve you, my daughter," she murmured, and in a flash she was gone. As I knelt there over the basin, I envisioned it all. How Samira would dress herself as a boy. How she would scale the garden wall in the middle of the night and travel to a place where she would begin a new life. It had been easy enough for Khalil. What was to stop her from doing the same?

When I was done with the dishes, I lit a small lamp and made my way to Samira's room. "Wake up," I whispered as I shook her. "Listen to me. I've thought of a plan."

She sat up sleepily. "What? What are you talking about?"

I gripped her shoulders tightly and made her look me in the eyes. "You must flee."

She sank back and waved her hand as if shooing me away. "Leave me alone. I want to sleep."

"No. Listen to me. Forget that I am slave and just hear me. You can escape your brothers and your father, and whatever awaits you in Basra. What you must do is cut your hair . . . and . . . and put on the clothes of a man. Arm yourself . . . yes, with a dagger, even a kitchen knife will do. And pack a sack of food for the way, and then—"

"Are you mad?" She yawned. "Cut my hair? Wear the clothes of a man? I wouldn't last an hour!"

"No Samira! You're wrong. You could flee as easily as Khalil has. In the guise of a boy, you would walk the roads fearlessly, and you would meet other travelers. They would befriend you, and share their provisions with you, and you could travel far, far from Baghdad, until you came to a place where no one knows you. Your wits are sharp, Samira. It would be nothing for you to play at being a boy. I know it's possible."

"Shafiqa," she sighed, "you are good-hearted, but you are also ignorant. I cannot walk the roads alone. I cannot live as a traveler lives. I'm used to servants and finery, cooked food and soft beds. I am like a pampered bird that cannot fly. And even if I attempted escape, the roads are crawling with scum and swindlers. I would barely be able to speak for fear of betraying who I am."

"You're bewitched by your own fears!" I whispered. "You say that your brothers will kill you. Isn't it better to disguise yourself and flee? What fate could be worse than the one that awaits you?"

She shook her head and again her eyes filled with tears. "No. It cannot be. Without my family, I'm nothing!"

"That's not true," I cried. "Samira, can you not see yourself? You know how to use your charm like a weapon. The same way you won Khalil's heart, the whole world could be yours if you wished it!"

"Go back to the kitchen, Shafiqa," she barked hoarsely. "You're nothing but an ignorant slave. You can't help me. No one can help me."

I rose slowly and left her, but as I crossed the courtyard, her taunt resounded in my brain. *An ignorant slave*, she had called me. But those were just words, empty insults, devoid of all truth and meaning. I? An ignorant slave? It sounded like a joke. As though I were waking from a nightmare, a fountain of mysterious joy rose in me; I wanted to sing and laugh out loud. All my fear of the world was falling away, and suddenly, just like that, there was no reason for me to remain in the house of Omar Alharazi for even one more day.

The hour was late, and the house was as still as a graveyard. I went to my room and took the blanket from my bed. Then I crossed the men's courtyard and headed for Khalil's chamber. Agile as a cat, I crept to the clothes cupboard and silently took out a light shirt, a heavy woolen tunic, one pair of leggings, a thick sash, a man's cap, a boy's cap, and a pair of men's boots. I returned to the kitchen, where I filled a water flask and collected whatever food I could find: figs, dates, nuts, a leftover loaf of bread, and a large wedge of goat cheese. I took three clean rags to use when I next bled, and then, standing before the assortment of knives hanging on the wall, I selected a small, sharp dagger.

As I did all of this, my thoughts were racing, but my mind was sharp and clear. I was thinking of the day I arrived. How my wrist was tied to a wagon and how I was lead by the arm into the kitchen. How my clothes were taken from me and in their place I was given the clothes of a slave. I ran to the storeroom and dug my hand down behind the sack of beans. My fingers brushed the rough wool of my bag, exactly where I had hidden it on that first day. Back in the kitchen I stuffed everything I had taken into my bag, and packed Samira's vial of perfume deep at the bottom.

I dashed back to the storeroom, where I swiftly removed my slave's garments. I tore off my headscarf and wound it tightly around my chest so that it was as flat as a man's. Then I put on Khalil's pants and tunic, and then fixed these in place with the sash. I guided my feet into his socks and his boots. And then, with a trembling hand, I gathered up my hair and took the knife in my hand.

With one sharp stroke, the long, dark locks fell to the ground. I should have regarded them with sadness, but instead, I felt the lightness of a snake that sheds its skin, or a butterfly, emerging from its cocoon. As I donned the cap, my head felt as unencumbered as a boy's, and it seemed to me that I had somehow *become* a boy, with a boy's fearlessness and thirst for adventure.

I left the home of Omar Alharazi in the dark hour just before dawn. Khalil had spoken the truth; the walls of the garden were easily scaled. As I strode through the dewy fields, I tried to fathom why I had waited so long for this morning.

KNOWLEDGE

In the midst of one of my of midnight conversations with Khalil, we happened upon the subject of travel. "The most important attribute in a traveler is caution," I insisted. "To walk the roads is to invite a thousand sorts of danger."

"One thousand?" He laughed. "Maybe in the realm of the imagination. But a traveler who lets caution be his guide may as well remain in the safety of his own home."

"Here in your garden, you're fearless. But I heard you telling Karim that wherever you traveled, your dagger was close at hand. Obviously your fears refused to remain in the realm of the imagination."

Khalil shook his head. "We're speaking of two different premises. Yours is that the roads are so dangerous that they're not worth the risk, while I say that the joys of travel far exceed the terrors of the imagination. When I was on the roads, it wasn't fear that guided me, but a sort of faith, a sense that I could confront whatever might come my way." I thought then of my own brief journey, trying to envision what it would be like to enjoy such confidence.

"You know Shafiqa," he remarked suddenly, "I once heard Almakrizi, the geographer, speak on the subject. He had just finished telling one story, and was about to begin another, when someone asked him: 'If you were to advise a man about to set out on a long journey, what would you tell him?'

"Almakrizi considered the question and replied, 'I would tell him three things: first, he must always bear in mind that when one is far from all that is familiar to him, things are not always what they seem; a man who seems a friend may actually be a foe, and likewise, the man that we call foe may in time prove to be a valuable friend. Secondly, I would tell any traveler that no matter how much gold and treasure he seeks, the greatest gift we can hope for is opportunity. For is opportunity not like a key to a hidden door, whose existence we've never suspected? If the traveler truly seeks to enhance his knowledge of the world, then he must teach himself to recognize opportunity. And finally, I would advise him that of all the danger and villainy that he may encounter, his greatest enemy will be the fear that he himself has cultivated. For what can be worse than the torment perpetrated by our own minds, and if we do indeed have reason to fear, of what use can that fear be to us? For none of our fears will save us from the fate that Allah has written for us.'"

The memory of this conversation came upon me as I traveled north along the Tigris River. Perhaps it sounds too improbable to be believed: a girl disguised as a boy, setting out alone, her only provisions a ragged bag filled with food, her only possession a vial of perfume, and her only protection the kitchen knife in her bag and her wits. And yet the journey involved nothing more complicated than putting one foot in front of the other. In my time as a traveler, I came to perceive that the incredible, the miraculous, the utterly unfathomable often unfold quietly, without commotion, without spectacle.

Several weeks before my departure, I was granted an opportunity to see, with my own eyes, how the earth might appear if I were a bird flying over the land. Omar Alharazi had called me to his office. He was meeting with two of his merchants who were preparing a long trip to the markets of the east. I recall that he had been to the baths that morning, and the air in the room carried a hint of rose water. Dressed in his immaculate robes, his beard and moustache neatly trimmed, he appeared as fine as a prince.

He sent me to the storeroom to retrieve a jar of his furtive wine, but when I returned with the jar, he and his guests were nowhere to be seen. I set the wine and goblets down, and as I rose, my eyes fell upon a detailed drawing of a landscape, lying unfurled on the table.

For a few brief moments, I surveyed the expanse of rivers, mountains, roads, and cities, in much the same way that God might look down on us. I identified the thick blue line as the Tigris River, and surmised that parallel to it, sketched in red ink, was her sister, the Euphrates. As I marveled at this view, which made the great and mighty seem small and easily negotiated, I recalled my father saying that if one were to follow the Tigris River far north, one would reach the city of Mosul. And from there, one could continue through the mountains to the town of Tiflis, where his father's brother, Hannan-ya Bar-Ashi, had long ago followed in the path of a Karaite woman.

A twinge of excitement pulsed through my heart as I traced the line of the Tigris northward with my finger. I could scarcely decipher the Arabic words that lined the river, but I made out that one of them was Mosul, and that from there, the way to Tiflis was easily reached.

Now, as I moved northward, I tried to recall that map with its promise of wells and markets and townspeople who would show me the roads leading through the mountains.

From the moment I stepped out of Omar Alharazi's garden into the dark fields, fear accompanied me like a surly companion who will not allow a moment's peace. As I walked the dusty roads in the hot sun, there were moments when I called myself a fool for leaving a place where I enjoyed a soft bed in a clean room, where food was plentiful and I slept through the night without fear. Like a child, I had been duped by an insult; a meaningless remark by a doomed woman had led me to abandon all I had. Now I was forced to suffer the consequences of that mad moment of misplaced courage. It seemed to me then that slavery was sweet, and freedom bitter.

But, left as I was with nothing in the world to lose, I decided to be brave. *What can be worse than the torment perpetrated by our own minds*, Almakrizi had said, *and if we do indeed have reason to fear, of what use can that fear be to us?* Where I had once hidden myself from others, I would now seek their company. Where I used to think only of the harm people might do me, I would now think about what help they could offer. And instead of groaning about the loss of high walls, cooked food, clean clothes, and a soft bed, I would remind myself that for a traveler, safety and comfort were rare privileges.

At the end of each day, when the sun began its descent, I would find a cluster of trees or bushes and open my blanket under the stars. The first few nights I barely slept. Every rustle of leaves in the hot wind and every call of the night animals through the darkness reminded me of the terrible night I had awakened to find Kubani breathing down my neck. But when one is on the road, rest is as essential as food and water, and I knew that if I could not trick myself into sleep, I would never reach my destination. And so I willed myself to look upon my life coldly, as a prospect no more certain than a wager, and of no more consequence than that of a fly. Somehow these thoughts calmed me so that I could finally fall asleep.

THE ROAD THAT runs northward from Baghdad is well-traveled. Wagons and caravans, laden with every kind of foodstuffs and luxuries, make their way from the city markets to the Caliph's palaces in Samara and back. High officials in fancy coaches share the way with artisans, merchants, officers returning from the provinces, as well as farmers from the villages that lie along the banks of the Tigris. As they passed me in the road, I was often taken for a local boy. Wagon drivers would slow their horses and ask me how long it would take them to reach Samara, or how far they were from Baghdad. I learned that rather than plead ignorance, it was best to toss off a guess in the rough dialect of the villagers.

On the fourth day of my journey, I came upon a group of musicians who had been invited to perform at a banquet within the palace walls. They asked me about the distance to the nearest town, and I was about to invent a reply when I noticed the face of the youngest, a boy of my own age with a drum strapped over his shoulder. Something about his kind eyes and charming smile reminded me of Khalil. "I don't know," I admitted. "I've never been north of Baghdad." I walked alongside them, and we soon fell into a conversation of the type that travelers have, about the conditions of the road, the heat of the sun, the location of public wells, and the ways of the local villagers. When they stopped for their evening meal, they shared their provisions and invited me to pass the night with them.

Though I traveled with them for three days, they never suspected my disguise. I saw that my boy's garb granted me a freedom I had never even imagined. The world was opening itself to me, unfurling at my feet like a carpet and inviting me to tread easily upon it.

THOUGH ONLY A week had passed since leaving the house of Omar Alharazi, I was quickly taking on the appearance of a seasoned traveler. My clothes were brown with dirt, and my skin became tough and dry. Mud and dust clung to me like a veil, and my legs were spotted with small cuts and bruises. My feet soon got used to Khalil's heavy boots, and I learned to ignore the soreness in my legs. As a kitchen slave, I had acquired a womanly layer of flesh, but now I felt my body to be taking on a new leanness, growing stronger and harder with each day on the road.

I had long finished the food I had taken with me, and now had to manage with whatever I found in my path, for once one passes the Caliph's palaces at Samara, the landscape changes its face. Suddenly, the horizon promises nothing but vast, desolate deserts, and only a thin ribbon of arable earth hugs the river as if clinging to it for life. The villages along this dusty road are few and know little of the prosperity and refinement of their southern sisters. The people are generally all of one clan, and their homes are mere mud huts, because they allot the best plots of land to their crops.

After several days, the food I gleaned from orchards and fields could no longer satisfy my hunger. Whenever I went to the river's edge, I would watch the fish swimming by and think how I might grab one from the water and strike it on the head. Yet if I was to catch a fish, I had little idea of how I might start a fire. I had seen Hassan do so a few times with the two sharp stones he carried with him in a small pouch. But I had no such stones, and even if I did, I wouldn't have known how to use them.

I once heard Khalil mention to a friend how in the course of his travels, he would buy strands of salted meat which stayed edible for long periods. As I lay under the stars that night, hunger gnawing at my shrinking frame, I remembered the vial of perfume that still lay at the bottom of my bag. Along these roads it was indeed useless, unless I could find someone who wanted it badly enough.

The next day, I came upon one of the small villages that lie between the road and the river. It consisted of little more than a few scattered mud huts, and the only people in sight were a group of peasants gathered around an old camel by the side of the road. As I approached them, their gaping gazes fell upon me as if I were the most curious creature their God-forsaken town had ever seen. Suddenly, I longed for the throngs of Baghdad, who looked upon any traveler, no matter how odd his appearance, with cheerful indifference. But here in this lonely spot, I knew that shyness would only arouse their evil instincts. Better to be bold and indignant, to tell blatant lies with conviction. "*As-salaam alaykum*," I called out. "Could you good men tell me where a traveler can get some provisions?"

The men seemed both suspicious and amused. They eyed me skeptically, but I held their stares until finally one of them spoke. "You're a little young to be traveling the highway on your own, son."

"I'm not alone. My father sent me. He's waiting up the road."

"Eh," he grunted as the others looked on skeptically. "You've just missed the market. The merchants won't be back till next week. But if you go to Fahed, he'll sell you what you need. Ahmed!" he barked to one of the younger men in the group. "Take this boy to Fahed."

One of the younger men stepped away from the group and motioned for me to follow. To my eyes, still used to the wealth and finery of Omar Alharazi's villa, the village huts looked pitiable. Ahmed halted before a particularly shoddy dwelling and called out. A short, heavyset man with one thick eyebrow running low over his eyes appeared in the doorway. "Eh," he replied in the same grunting intonation I had heard before, sounding like a greeting and an answer and a question all at once.

"Help this boy," Ahmed commanded. "Get him what he needs." I followed him inside, and as my eyes adjusted to the dark interior, I saw that the room was lined with half-empty sacks and clay vessels. A dirty and torn curtain hung half-open over a doorway to a second room, where I could just make out the moving figure of a woman.

"And what would that be?" Fahed scowled as he looked me over. From the corner of my eye I saw the woman fasten her veil across her face and then open the curtain a little. I reached into my bag and dug out the vial of perfume.

"This vial contains perfume of the highest quality, which comes all the way from India," I told him. "It is worth good money in the market of Baghdad, but I'm willing to part with it for several days worth of salted meat."

The curtain moved and the woman slid out. Her dark eyes, peering over the rim of her veil, were alert and curious. Fahed took the vial in his thick hand and eyed it suspiciously, and I feared that his rough grasp would shatter it. He brought it to his nose, sniffed, and made a face. "No thanks, kid," he barked, handing it back. "We have no need of such luxuries in this town. That stuff is for spoiled city princesses, but our women wouldn't know what to do with it."

I was about to put the vial back in my bag when the woman spoke up. "Wait. Let me see that."

I moved to show it to her, but Fahed raised his arm. "I said we have no use for such things," he growled. "And who told you to come out here? Didn't I tell you to move the beans into the storeroom?" The woman glared angrily, but turned and retreated behind the curtain. "My sister wants to be a fancy lady," he said with a laugh. "Your best bet would be to try to sell that stuff in Baghdad. Maybe some official will want it for his whore."

"Fahed, are you in there?" a voice called from outside. He looked up and then ran out the door. I too wished to leave, but I felt something grab hold of my sleeve. I turned and saw the veiled woman. "Let me see," she whispered. Hesitantly, I handed the vial to her. She removed the small cork stopper and closed her eyes as she held the perfume to her nose. "Ah," she sighed. "The scent of heaven."

"It is," I agreed, "but it looks like your brother disapproves."

"My brother is a stupid ignoramus. Ever since our father died, he thinks that he can treat me like his daughter." I looked out uneasily. Fahed was examining the blade of his companion's knife. "Listen," she whispered. "I'll prepare a sack of meat and cheese. Come back in an hour, and you'll find it behind the bush underneath the window. Leave the perfume in its place." I signaled my agreement with a nod.

"Hey!" Fahed burst in. "Weren't you just leaving?" As I walked out to the road, I deliberated about what to do next. I was wary of provoking Fahed's anger, and I could have easily moved on and tried my luck at the next village. But my heart went out to his sister, stuck in a dreary village with a tyrannical brother. I reckoned that she would be true to her word, and so I sat down behind some bushes by the road, and waited a short while until sunset.

When I found my way back, only the dimmest of lights shone from the village windows. As I neared Fahed's hut, my heart was pounding, and I imagined how any of the men I had seen earlier might suddenly jump out at me. I knelt down under the window and moved my hand behind the bush, where my fingers met the rough cloth of a sack; true to her word, Fahed's sister had given me a good amount of dried meat, cheese, and even some freshly baked bread. I hurriedly put the vial in place of the provisions, and then stole away in the darkness, not stopping to eat until I could no longer see the flickering lights of the village.

But I well knew that the food would not last long, and I had no idea how many days it would take to reach Mosul. A peasant atop a donkey promised that in only ten days I would arrive at the city gates. But a camel driver at a roadside well swore that I would not reach my destination for at least two months. The great difference in these estimates gave me cause for concern, and I began to limit my daily portion of meat to a minimum. The villages were growing fewer, with greater distances between them. As I followed the road that runs alongside the water, I never lost sight of the desert, yellow and burning and threatening to overtake the river, which, like me, resolutely continued its path.

One morning, several days after my encounter with Fahed and his sister, I heard a voice call out, "*As-salaam alaykum*." I turned and saw a gray-bearded wagon driver, obviously a local villager, approaching from behind. Two long black keys hung around his wrinkled neck. "Where are you headed, my son?"

"Far from here."

"You look like you could use a few coins. It would be worth your while to help me out."

I stopped and waited for him to catch up to me. "What sort of help?"

"I'm taking these up to the Mar Yuhanon monastery," he replied, pointing to two large chests in the back of the wagon. "I could use another pair of hands, in case I run into trouble with the load. If you can spare a few days, I'll pay you ten dinars."

He spoke a Syriac tongue, so similar to the Aramaic we spoke at home that I well understood him. I had occasionally heard Syriac spoken at Omar Alharazi's gatherings, when Christian scholars and officials were among the guests, and I knew that if I could just mimic his odd pronunciation and word endings, he would regard me as one of his own. I glanced at his horse, and then at the wooden chests. If I were to agree to his offer, I would earn not only the ten dinars, but also a ride in the wagon and a share in whatever provisions he had brought with him. "Where is this monastery?" I asked.

"Mar Yuhanon? I reckon it's about five days up the road. If you're headed north, you'd do well to ride with me. It'll get you that much closer to wherever you're going."

I shrugged as if the offer meant little to me one way or the other. "I could do it for twenty."

His eyes narrowed. "Twelve."

"Eighteen."

"What's your name, boy?"

"Yusef," I answered, remembering how Khalil had likened my story to Yusef's.

"Listen, Yusef. My name is Habib. If you were from around here, you would know that, but it doesn't matter. I see that you're a good boy. I've been riding these roads for forty years but I'm an old man now, and these trips take the juice out of me. I agreed to do this one job as a favor to Rabban Basilius. The way I see it, a favor to Rabban Basilius is as good as a favor to God Himself. But the best we can hope for from those monks is a handful of rusty coins. So you see, my son, I can't pay you any more than fifteen dinars."

Though I imagined he was lying, I congratulated myself on my raising my fee and grunted my agreement, just like a village boy.

He broke into a wide grin. "Get up here on the wagon."

I climbed aboard. From my new vantage point, I was as comfortable as a prince. Instead of walking over hard mud and stones, I sat atop an old cushion, my feet sprawled out lazily in front of me. "What's in the chests?" I asked my new companion.

"What's in the chests?" he cried. "Ha! If you knew old Teodosiyos, you wouldn't be asking that question."

"But I don't know him."

"Of course you don't; he's dead two years now. Where are you from, boy?"

"My parents are from Baghdad. But I've been on the road for months."

"What are they? Christians?"

"Uh, yes. Yes they are."

Habib broke into another grin and slapped his knee. "I knew it! I can always pick out the Christians; I could tell that there's something decent about you."

I smiled uneasily. "What were you saying about the chests?"

"Books!" he cried. "Teodosiyos had a library of three hundred. His daughter Tabitha told me herself, and she was the one who counted them after he was dead and gone. Her husband wanted to keep them; he said he likes the way they look sitting on the shelf. But Tabitha wouldn't hear of it. She told me, 'Mar Yuhanon was the only place where my father found any peace in this life. If anyone deserves to get the books, it's those monks.' I told her I'd be happy to do this job for old Teodosiyos. See, I've got the keys to the chests right here," and he held out the string around his neck so that the two keys clapped against each other.

Joining Habib proved to be a wise decision, for I saw now that the way to Mosul was much farther than I imagined. Forty years of traveling the roads that link the Christian villages of the North with the cities of the South had made him an expert in the precise location of wells and the best spots to stop for the night. Just as I hoped, his wife had packed him plenty of provisions: barley flour, dried traveler's cheese, apples, dates, smoked meat, and date beer.

I took care to maintain low tones and a boyish demeanor, but Habib turned out to belong to that category of person who enjoys the sound of his own voice, and so he barely noticed what I said, let alone how I said it. As we drove he told me stories of the road and bragged about his exploits, vividly describing what he would do to any bandit stupid enough to try to ambush his wagon, and recounting the long-standing feuds between the various clans and villages.

Once he had secured my assistance, Habib treated me as a trusted friend, and seemed to care little about what circumstances had brought me, a young boy as it were, to travel the roads. Though I sat at his side and shared both his meals and his campsite for seven days, he did not discover my secret. Even when my days of uncleanliness arrived, making it necessary to stuff thick cloths into the seat of my pants, he did not discern that he was traveling alongside a woman.

ON THE SIXTH day of our journey, Habib brought the horse to a halt and stopped at a crossroads by an edifice of two large rocks placed one on top of the other. "This place marks the spot where the Tigris splits in two," he explained. "It's like two brothers—one decides to go west, the other goes east. If we keep to the left, we'll end up in Mosul. But Mar Yuhanon is to the east, towards Irbil." We were heading into green, hilly terrain, and as the roads grew steeper, the horse slowed his pace. Later in the day, the river split again, and again, and each time Habib steered the horse along the smaller stream.

We drove along the empty roads until finally, after several hours, Habib pointed to a cluster of buildings nestled in the rocky hills. He broke into a wide grin as if sighting a familiar friend. "There she is, mighty as a mountain!" We began the climb up a barely visible wagon path. The horse was laboring harder now, and several times we had to jump off the wagon to lighten his load.

But I was enthralled by the sight of the monastery up ahead, for it was unlike anything I had ever seen. High stone walls seemed to rise, as if by unnatural force, from the rocky hillside, creating an enclosed fortress that not even an army could penetrate. And the bare hills that surrounded it were pierced with mysterious cave-like holes. "That's where the monks like to go," Habib explained, "when they want to be alone."

The path brought us to a heavy wooden door, decorated with a picture that seemed to combine the ancient symbol of the Tree of Life and a Christian cross. Habib brought the horse to a halt and slapped me heavily on the back. "Why don't you get out and pull that cord over there," he said, pointing to a rope hanging from an iron bell. I tugged on the rope and a weak din resulted. He slapped his knee and bellowed, "Harder, boy!" so I pulled with abandon and produced a clanging that must have been heard all the way to Baghdad.

"Have you ever been inside a monastery, Yusef?" he asked while we waited for someone to appear.

"Uh, no. Never."

"Well, you'll have your chance now. It's a strange life those monks live. Some are brought here when they're still boys, and that's the last you hear of them." We waited for some minutes before a small window in the door opened and a man's face peered through. "Habib! Wait a minute, I'm coming out."

He was dressed in the simple garments of the monks I had seen in the markets of Sura, with a linen cloak belted at the waist with a piece of rope. But unlike those impoverished, unkempt travelers, his robes were clean and his beard was neatly trimmed. "Habib, my friend," he cried and kissed him on both cheeks. "*Shlama lookh*. We've been awaiting this delivery for weeks. How did your horse manage to navigate the hill with such heavy cargo?"

Habib knocked on the wooden chest. "Praise be to God, this animal has proved his worth again."

The monk laughed and glanced at me. "I see you've brought an assistant."

"This," he said glancing in my direction, "is Yusef, a fine young man from the city. The poor boy's been listening to my gabbing for seven days now. I found him on the road and offered him a ride. Now he's going to haul your books. You just tell him where you want them. I would do it myself, if it weren't for my back."

"Yusef is it?" he asked cheerfully. "Well it's a good thing you're here. Most of us are out in the vineyards today. I'm Elias." He instructed us to drive around to the rear, where he opened a gate, guided us to a small stable, climbed up on the wagon, and pried open one of the chests. "What treasure!" he exclaimed. "Monk Gibreel will be ecstatic." He handed me two heavy volumes and then pointed down a stone path. "Follow along until you reach the library. When you get there, just put the books on Monk Gibreel's table in front of the scriptorium—it's just to the right of the entrance."

The volumes were big and heavy, and I could barely manage two at a time. I feared that my efforts would appear suspicious, but neither man seemed to notice my struggles. Habib busied himself with feeding his horse, while Monk Elias stood by the open chest, excited anew at the sight of each book he laid eyes on. "Finally!" he would exclaim. "Our own copy of such-and-such," and then he would open the volume, only to look up and spot another book that claimed his attention.

The monastery grounds were a maze of buildings linked by stone pathways lined with cultivated shrubs and trees, but I would not have found the library if not for a pair of monks, deep in conversation who, without my having to ask, pointed me to a nearby building with gracefully arched windows. Clasping the books tightly, I tapped on the door with my foot.

"I was told to put these on Monk Gibreel's table," I explained breathlessly to the monk who answered my knock. He put a finger to his lips, ushered me in and pointed to the designated spot. I put the books down carefully and shook out my arms. It was late afternoon and the room was quiet and dark. If not for the warm beams of sunlight streaming through the windows, I wouldn't have been able to see at all.

The heavy scent of leather and parchment pervaded the air, and for a moment, I was put in mind of the *beit midrash* in Sura, where men pored over the holy books at all hours of the day and night. The place was empty except for two monks, silently bent over a large volume. Across the room, at the back, I noticed another, smaller room, where a third monk sat working at a table in the corner. Two manuscripts lay open on his desk, and his right hand held a pen, but instead of writing, his gaze turned upward, as if pursuing an elusive thought.

When I returned to the wagon, three young monks were loading the books onto a small wagon. They insisted that they could complete the job alone, and Habib and I were invited to take a meal in the dining hall.

THE MONK'S LUNCH hour was long over, so Habib and I sat alone at the long, narrow dining table. The fare—flat bread, goat cheese, and freshly cut vegetables—was so simple that I could only conclude that the cook was either sick or very lazy. Habib was happy to sample the monastery's beer, but I drank only water. Just as we were finishing the last of the bread and cheese, Monk Elias came in and sat down beside Habib.

"Forgive me for leaving you to dine alone, but the hour for afternoon prayers was upon us. In the meantime, I've spoken with Rabban Basilius, and he's asked if you need to stay the night."

"Oh no, sir," Habib replied. "I have to get on to Irbil, the sooner the better."

"And what about you, Yusef? Do you need a bed for the night? Our rooms are modest, but we can offer you a warm meal, and an opportunity to worship in our humble company."

Habib grinned. "You men of God see a monk in every youth that enters your gates, but Yusef is only here to earn a few coins. Aren't you, Yusef?"

"Is that so?" Monk Elias remarked before I could reply. "If that's the case, we just might be able to help each other. I mentioned before that this is the week of our grape harvest. We've taken on some local boys, but I'm sure we could well use another pair of hands. We pay only a modest wage, just ten dinars a day, but most of the boys are happy to help Mar Yuhanon."

A modest wage. These words were as a seed planted in fertile soil. Why had the notion of earning a wage not occurred to me before? As a boy, finding work would be easy, and with money in my purse, I could easily continue on my own. I would hire a wagon driver and buy my own provisions. Then, when I arrived in Tiflis with a small fortune, it would be all the easier to find a worthy groom. And all I would have to do was pick some grapes.

It did not occur to me then that I was of the wrong sex—and the wrong faith—to be joining a bunch of Christian boys in the fields. At that moment, those facts were as minor details, irrelevant trifles that could be overcome as easily as a mild headache. "I'd be glad to stay and help," I told him eagerly.

"Excellent. Monk Nabil will be glad to have you."

"Ha!" Habib remarked, amused by this development. "It looks as though I've brought you a Trojan horse."

"Trojan horse? How can you say such a thing! He's just a boy looking for work." Monk Elias rose from his place and smiled. "And now, if you wait here a minute, I'll see about a small tip for your efforts. Yusef, you wait here for me. When I return I'll show you to the workmen's quarters."

"Now you can pay me my portion," I reminded him once Monk Elias was out of sight.

He laughed slyly. "Are you not aware that monks take a vow of poverty? Under the circumstances, I think we can delay your payment until we meet again!"

"We had an agreement," I hissed, wary of raising my voice and provoking a loud argument.

"What agreement?" Habib sneered. "Why don't you tell him your troubles?" He pointed to Monk Elias, who was fast approaching, his fist holding part of what should have been my wages.

"Here you go," Monk Elias chimed as he placed three silver coins in Habib's hand. "Make sure to convey our blessings to Teodosiyos's daughter."

"Always a pleasure to help Mar Yuhanon," Habib replied, and then, glancing in my direction he added, "God be with you, Yusef."

"Scheming scoundrel," I muttered under my breath. But while Habib was considered a friend in this place, I was a mere stranger. To accuse him of theft would only make me look like a conniving beggar. Why was it my fate to always be the victim of cheats and criminals?

"Allow me to welcome you to our community of brothers," Monk Elias declared in his cheery tone. "Come with me and I'll show you to the vineyards." I followed him out the back gate and along the path that traversed the monastery walls. Now, having thoughtlessly taken on the role of Yusef the Christian boy, there was no time to reflect on my own stupidity.

He led me to the top of a hillside planted with long rows of vines, the green grapes sparkling in the late afternoon sun. Young men and boys were scattered throughout, some cutting the grapes and tossing them into straw baskets, others gathering up the baskets and loading them onto wagons. The vineyard stretched all the way to the bottom of the hill. Far in the distance, I could see a small stream cutting its way across the valley.

"Come," he said. "You can leave your things in the tent and start working right away. You don't have to worry about theft; all of these boys are from good Christian families." I smiled weakly as he led me to a giant tent that had been raised over a floor of straw mats, travelers' bags, and blankets. "Put your bag in a corner," he instructed me, "and we'll go find Monk Nidal."

But my thoughts were not with Monk Nidal, or my new employment, or even the fact that I was now regarded as a Christian. I could think of nothing except that that this night, I would have to make my bed amongst a multitude of men.

My father, had he been able to see me, would have turned in his grave. In his wildest dreams, he could not have imagined his daughter—who had once found a brief hour of work in the garden oppressive—standing under the hot sun, dressed in the clothes of a man, her hands covered with cuts and blisters, her legs bruised and stained with grape juice. And as for my spending the night under a tent full of village boys, if he hadn't been dead already, it would have killed him.

During the day, the men were hard-working and deferential. While in the presence of the monks, they labored diligently, speaking in quiet, respectful tones, and volunteering for the most menial of tasks. But at night, after they had built fires and drunk the beer they brewed from barley, they would grow rowdy and their polite demeanor would give way to coarse talk and crude jokes. At first, the vulgar descriptions of village girls and tales of encounters with traveling whores mortified me, and I thanked heaven for the cover of the darkness that concealed my blushing face.

I worked in a constant state of foreboding, dreading that someone would notice the smallness of my hands, or the smoothness of my face, or hear a note in my voice that gave reason for suspicion. But trickiest of all was the boys' ritual of going down to the river for a swim at the end of each work day. The moment that Monk Nidal called for everyone to hand in their knives, the boys would dash through the vineyards, yelping as they crossed the rocky slopes like a pack of wild dogs. When they reached the river's edge, they would strip off their robes and hurl themselves into the cold water.

The first time I witnessed this ritual, I ducked low among the vines, praying that no one would notice me and invite me to join in. When their shouts faded to a distant hum, I took my basket and sought out the nearest wagon. Monk Nidal was still working together with two of the young men who were loading up the last of the baskets. They seemed somehow different from the others; not older, but more serious. Both wore linen garments, similar to those of the monks.

"Don't you want to go for a swim with the others?" the taller one asked me.

"No, I'm just getting over a head cold," I said, thinking fast. "What about you?"

The two exchanged glances. "Estefan and I are not village boys."

Clearly, I had said something wrong. "Oh no, of course not. Are you monks?"

Again they glanced at each other, and then at me. "Not yet; right now we're just novices," the one called Estefan replied.

"Ah." I nodded, as if this clarified everything.

The shorter one smiled kindly, as one smiles to a simple child. His eyes conveyed an expression of sadness, perhaps because of their slightly downturned shape, and said, "My name is Shimun, and this is Estefan. What is your name, my brother?"

"I amYusef."

"I must say, Yusef, it looks like you don't know much about monastic life."

"Well...no. I don't. This is the first time I've ever been inside a monastery."

"There! Do you see?" Shimun said to Estefan. "A Christian boy who has never even been inside a monastery!" He regarded me critically. "How is it that you know so little about your own religion?"

I had to think of something fast, a believable explanation that would close the subject and prevent further questions. "Well... what happened was that my father died when I was very young, and then my mother remarried a Muslim."

The two of them gazed at me worriedly, but I continued, "And, of course, he insisted that we be raised as Muslims, and so my mother abandoned her Christian ways. That's the reason that I know so little." I was quite pleased with my story, invented in the space of a moment, but the looks of dismay on their faces told me that I had only made things worse.

"That's terrible!" Shimun shook his head. "You shouldn't accept this...this forced ignorance. You should learn the teachings of your true religion!"

"Yet the fact that Yusef has come to us is evidence that he is not ignorant of his origins," Estefan reminded him.

I looked on helplessly, afraid to say anything further for fear of upsetting them more than I already had. Luckily, our exchange was halted by the sound of a bell, which I learned was the means of calling everyone to dinner.

I followed my new companions up to the well that stood behind the dining hall, where I finally had an opportunity to wash the dust from my face and scrub the grape juice from my arms. By the time we were done washing, the boys who had been to the river were already seated at the end of the long table, their wet hair glistening in the lamplight. Dinner was little better than lunch: fresh vegetables, yogurt, flat bread, and boiled eggs, a far cry from the sumptuous meat and rice dishes I had prepared in the Alharazi kitchen. Could it be, I wondered unhappily, that this was all they ever ate?

Once the meal was over, the boys left quickly. In the dining hall, they had restrained themselves, speaking quietly and keeping conversation to a minimum, but once outside, they reverted back to their natural habits of bawdy laughter and shameless boasting. They teased and baited each other, falling over one another with mock blows and challenges to each other's honor. I followed behind, pondering the troubling notion that I would soon have to sleep alongside them.

But by the time I reached the tent, their mood had grown calmer. Some of the boys lay down to sleep immediately, while others remained outside, drinking beer and playing backgammon in the moonlight. Someone produced an oud and began to pick out a familiar tune. In the darkness of the tent, I somehow found my bag, pulled out my blanket and settled into a far corner. The strangers who lay beside me were already sleeping, but in another corner someone was telling a story about the spirits of monks long dead, who often returned in the night to haunt the monastery.

I closed my eyes and tried to ignore where I was. *What would happen if they found me out?* I dared not think about it. Instead, I opened my ears to the melancholy sound of the oud. The player was not of the quality that was invited to play in the villas of Baghdad, but he had a lightness of touch that drew out a mournful music, whose quivering tones seemed to float on the night air like a soft wind. It was this music that coaxed me into sleep.

I woke before the dawn's first light. All around me were sleeping men, yet in their peaceful state, mouths half-open, hair falling over their eyes, their blankets drawn up around them against the morning cold, they seemed as innocent as children.

I rose quietly and hurried down the rocky slope to the river. Here in the hills, the air carried an autumn chill, but I knew that both privacy and the warmth of the bath house were luxuries that would not be mine for a long time. I followed the river's edge until I found a place where the bushes grew densely, causing the water to collect into a shallow pool. Closing my mind to the danger, the disgrace, and the threat of discovery, I stripped off the filthy garments that I had worn since leaving Baghdad, and stepped into the cold waters.

No one suspected me. Perhaps it was because men seldom appraise their peers with the sharp and critical eye of their sisters. Or perhaps my short hair and flat chest gave them no reason to wonder. But whatever the reason, I saw that as long as I put on a simple and carefree demeanor like their own, it was possible to fool them all.

A few days after my arrival, I noticed several of the men packing up and taking their leave. "It looks like it's time to move on," I remarked to Estefan, as we sharpened our knives.

"But you can't leave us yet," he replied. "The harvest isn't finished; on the contrary, Monk Nidal says we'll need several more days."

"So why are people packing up?"

He put down his knife, shook out the joints of his right hand, and shot me a disapproving glance. "They're going back to their villages for the Sabbath. Everyone who leaves will be back early Monday morning."

"Ah." I laughed sheepishly. "The Sabbath."

"Dear God, are you really so ignorant? Well, tomorrow you'll finally have a chance to worship with us. On Sundays, all are invited to hear the holy *Quarbana* in the church."

I tried to appear pleased, but I was thinking of how I used to go to the synagogue with my father on the holy days. I had understood little of the Hebrew prayers, and though I enjoyed dressing in finery and meeting my girlfriends in the women's courtyard, the long hours inside were tedious. Now, faced with the prospect of sitting through the prayers of the Christians, I wondered how I might politely decline. "Does everyone attend?" I asked, hoping that by volunteering for some important task, I could miss the service.

"Everyone," he assured me. "Even the cook."

And so, on Sunday morning I found myself in the monastery church, standing as one with the same men and boys who labored beside me in the vineyard and slept alongside me at night. The interior of the building was stark and simple. Woven mats covered the stone floor, and there were no benches or chairs. The front and rear walls were bare, but large, colorful images were painted on the sides of the room. The wall on the right depicted a young lightly-bearded man, who seemed to be speaking, and directly under him, two scribes, presumably recording his words onto a piece of parchment. The heads of all three figures were encircled by bright halos. The second painting, on the opposite wall, was of a young woman, her hands raised as if in prayer. In her lap was a sweet-looking infant. Both the woman's and the baby's heads were also encircled with halos. Glancing about, I was reminded that the images depicted a story familiar to everyone under this roof but me.

A group of monks dressed in festive white robes with embroidered belts and scarves gathered around the white marble altar at the front of the church. The leader was dressed most colorfully of all, with a special hooded cloak. A white cloth, embroidered with a complex pattern of blue crosses and delicate flowers, lay across the altar. While everyone around me settled into a state of quiet reflection, I surveyed the various objects set out on the cloth. There was a long white candle fixed in a brass holder, and beside it, a second group of candles. A plain white cloth was draped over some object, covering it completely. Beside this stood a ceramic vase, from which wisps of fragrant smoke were floating up. But the object that distressed me most was a single wooden cross, set upright in the center of the altar. I glanced back at the doorway, but lacked the courage to leave, so I returned my attention to the pictures painted on the walls. I guessed that the young man with the halo was supposed to be Isho, the Jew the Christians claim was the Messiah. I knew this because Anna, the apothecary's wife in Sura had once told me about the festival in honor of his birth. And the woman with the baby on the opposite wall? She must have been Isho's mother. Anna had told me something about her that at the time had struck me as very strange, and I strained my memory to recall what it was.

One of the monks stepped up to a high, narrow pulpit and began a chant. His voice was clear and pleasant, and if I closed my eyes and didn't listen too carefully to the words, I could almost imagine that I was back in the synagogue in Sura. Yet whenever I opened my eyes, I was reminded that I was not surrounded by friends and neighbors, but in a church, amongst men who believed that the Messiah had already come to earth.

I turned again to the picture of Isho. If what Anna had told me was true, and Isho really was a Jew, than I was not alone here among the Christians. As I stared at his long, earnest face, it seemed that he could have easily been one of the young Jewish men of Sura, perhaps even a scholar. Suddenly I was overcome with a loneliness so strong that I was moved to speak to him in my heart: *If you really were a Jew, how is it that your likeness is hanging on the walls of a church? Why do the Christians claim that you are the one who was born to redeem the world? Was it your fault that this has happened, or was it the fault of others, so enthralled with whatever words you spoke that they called you their savior?*

Now the monk was speaking of Mother Maryam. Yes. That had been the name that Anna had mentioned. But what else had she said? And who was the other woman they sang of, the one they called "the Holy Virgin?" I turned to the woman on the wall, the only other female present beside myself. I gazed at her picture and suddenly recalled what Anna had told me about her. *Maryam*, I addressed her, *you must have once been a modest and God-fearing Jewish girl. Who invented that crazy story about you? Was it a young man of your village, someone you once disappointed in love? Or were you so enamored of your own virginity that you continued to insist on it, even after you had given birth to a son? And if you were indeed foolish enough to make such a claim, why did anyone else believe you?*

I felt uneasy now. The air in the church was cold, and the singing and prayers seemed to drag on without end. I was vaguely aware of various rituals and ceremonies taking place at the altar. The words of the prayers seemed to repeat themselves, and I soon stopped following them. But when the head monk called out, "Truly, truly I say to you, unless you eat the Body of the Son of Man, and drink his Blood, you have no life in yourselves. He who eats of My Body and drinks of My Blood has eternal life; I will raise him at the last day," I could not restrain a grimace.

And then, finally, the service was over. The monks were approaching the altar, where they each received a morsel of bread. I followed them, eager for something to eat, but Shimun put a hand on my shoulder and said, "Only those who have taken on the Christian faith with all their heart may receive the *Quarbana*. But don't worry; if you do choose to return to your faith, you'll be welcomed with open arms."

I nodded, looking into his downturned eyes as if I well knew what he was talking about. "I'd like to speak with you, Yusef. Will you join me for a walk after lunch?"

A walk with Shimun was far preferable to watching the men arm wrestle and play Tabula. "With pleasure," I told him.

"Good. I've been thinking about your predicament, and there are some things that I want to discuss with you."

"Do you know who you really are, Yusuf?" We were hiking the rocky path that circled the outer walls of the monastery. The day had turned gray and windy, and Shimun had lent me one of his cloaks, such that walking side by side, we looked as natural as any two novice monks. Though the question was a troubling one, Shimun's philosophical tone told me that he suspected nothing.

I tilted my head innocently. "What do you mean?"

"Are you a Christian? Are you a Muslim?"

"I...I was born to Christians," I stammered, "and so...that's what I am."

"Yes. But assuming you were baptized, do you feel yourself to be a Christian in your soul?" Before I had time to compose an answer, he added, "Do you even believe in God?"

"Of course! Of course I believe in God."

"That's good to hear; if you believe in God, there's always hope of salvation."

We continued along the path that overlooked the low hills and valleys that surrounded Mar Yuhanon. Juniper, oak and poplar trees grew amongst clusters of ancient rocks and long, green grasses that danced furiously in the wind. After some time, we came upon a large rock that seemed to rise up over all the others. Shimun climbed atop it while I surveyed the wide view. Far in the distance, I could make out the buildings of a small village.

"Look." I pointed. "Neighbors."

He glanced out and nodded. "Come and sit down." I wrapped the cloak around me tightly and climbed up to sit at his side. "Those neighbors are my village, the place where I was born, and where my parents and brothers all live."

"Your village?" I laughed incredulously. "But it's so close...you can go home to your family whenever you wish."

"No." He shook his head and frowned. "A monk serves God in solitude. And in any case, I haven't seen any of them for three years."

"Three years? Why?"

He sighed and looked out at the village with his sad eyes. "It's a terrible story. But I want you to hear it. It may change the way you think about God and Jesus."

I nodded as though I was interested in such a change.

"You see, my family, the Ibn Tawfiq clan, breeds horses," he continued. "For generations, we've been known in this valley for our stables. But my father and uncles weren't content to merely provide for our needs. They wanted to be rich. Even now, they're always on the lookout for a gullible customer, one who can't tell an old mare from a young steed, and who doesn't know how to appraise the stride of a horse. If they succeed in duping such a customer, they mock him for many months afterward. And yet, in spite of their ignoble practices, my family stood firm in our Christianity. For one hundred and fifty years we resisted the temptation to join the majority of our neighbors who converted to Islam." I shifted uncomfortably; clearly he was thinking of my "mother" who had not resisted the temptation.

"I can still remember my grandfather saying, 'We will pay the *jizya* tax even if it comes to half of our income, but we will not leave our holy faith.' What a man he was! Full of honor and principle. Not like the pleasure-loving, gold-digging sons he raised." Shimun examined the dried twig in his hand, then drew a knife from the pouch on his belt and began to strip off the outer layer.

"How did it happen?" I asked.

"Three years ago, a new tax collector was appointed to our district. He paid us a visit and said that the governor had raised the *jizya* tax, and that he would be back to collect the entire amount at the end of the month. My father and his brothers panicked. Normally, we paid the tax in portions, spread over the space of the entire year. To pay the entire sum on such short notice would be impossible. When they protested, he reminded them that if our family abandoned Christ and converted, we would be exempt from the tax."

I was familiar with the *jizya* and the difficulties it caused. In Sura, there were enough prosperous Jews to pay the taxes of the poorer ones. I remembered how each year, the heads of the community would come to our door asking my father for a contribution.

"My father and his brothers cast off their faith as if it were an old rag," Shimun continued scornfully. "I well remember their foolish words: 'The Muslims and Christians pray to the same God. What difference does it make if we say that Isho is His son or that Muhammad is His prophet?' For my mother though, it was the end of the world. She begged my father to remain in the community of the faithful, even if it meant hard times for our family.

"But what does that matter now? I've told you this story because I've been thinking about you. Soon the harvest will be over. The village boys will return to their homes, and your work here will be finished. But when I look at you, Yusef, I see a soul that is lost. You're like a traveler with no final destination, no welcoming home at the end of your journey."

"I . . . I am seeking my fate," I answered.

"But look, Yusef, look what has happened. You were wandering the roads and your fate brought you here. Isn't that a sign? It's as if God Himself has led you here, so that you can return to the path of Christian grace."

My mind was racing, trying to think of a way out of this strange turn of conversation. "Do you understand my meaning?" he continued. "You don't have to leave, at least not yet. Just think, Yusef; you've finally met the faith of your fathers here. You've begun to experience the Christian way of living. What I mean to say is that maybe you should consider staying on at Mar Yuhanon. We welcome travelers, men who want to retreat from the world in order to find the spirit of God within. They stay for weeks or months, and while they're here, they pray together with us, and take on productive work for the monastery. Eventually some move on, but others remain, and even join us. Please, Yusef, will you think about it?"

I glanced out at the little village with a new longing for a simple life, where I could be a regular girl and not have to suffer these impossible conversations. "Shimun, I can't. I'm not suited for it."

"It may seem that way, but still, please consider the idea. Just imagine—passing from a state of ignorance and ignominy to a state of Christian grace. How can you dismiss such a privilege so casually?"

"I'll think about it," I told him with a sigh.

The sky had turned dark gray, and a light rain had begun to fall. Shimun looked out over the hills in the direction of the village. Then he grasped the twig in his hands and snapped it into two sticks of unequal length. I watched as he placed the short one over the longer, so that they made a small cross, and then picked a long piece of weed, which he wound deftly around the twigs until they were fastened together. "Do you see this?" he asked, holding up his creation. "This is the symbol of our faith. It is humble, but it is true. And it doesn't require gold or precious stones to beautify it; it is beautiful in itself."

He handed the cross he had constructed to me. "You take it, Yusef. And when you look at it, remember that the power of our Savior is not in his pride, but in his humility. We must all work to emulate him."

Incredibly, my deception seemed to be taking on a life of its own. What would Shimun think if he knew that my destiny was not a monk's cell in Mar Yuhanon, but a marriage bed in far away Tiflis? He was smiling at me now, pleased with his small success. He jumped off the rock and motioned for me to follow him. "Shall we return?" he suggested. "It's almost time for prayers." The mention of the prayers brought on the depressing thought of having to endure another session in the church. Feeling as guilty as any imposter, I held out the little wooden cross to him, but he shook his head. "You keep it, Yusef. If nothing else, it will be a reminder of your true faith."

By THE END of the week, the rows of vines that covered the hillside had been picked bare of their fruit. On the afternoon that the last rows of grapes had been cut from their vines, Monk Nidal came down to the tent and gave each man a small pouch containing his wages. I tied the pouch to the inside of my robes, as many of the others did, and made arrangements to leave the next morning with a group of men who were heading toward Mosul.

In those final days of the harvest, Shimun's idea of staying on at Mar Yuhanon amused me to no end. What would they think, I wondered, if they could see me as I appeared in my father's house, my long hair fixed in a pearl-studded comb, my girl's limbs clothed in soft fabrics, and the curve of my breasts (now pressed against my chest like flatbreads) undeniably present under my robes? I found myself indulging in these ponderings often, for in the course of the long hours of work in the vineyards, I had discovered that it was possible to enjoy the company of men.

I had learned to work easily alongside them during the day and rest peacefully among them at night. For the first time in my life, my gaze was drawn to the hard line of a jaw, the contours of angular shoulders, the delicate hair of the arms, or the long muscles of a leg. In the mornings, when they rose from their blankets, some in nightshirts, but many without, I had always looked away, so as not to blush and stammer. Yet now, on these last mornings, my eyes would seek out the very sight that I had taken pains to avoid.

The most confusing hour of all was late at night, when my mind could run free. It was then that my new way of looking at the men would flood my brain with imaginings. Though I had tried to banish it from memory, my thoughts would return to that terrible night when I woke to feel the weight of another's body forcing itself into my own, and those horrible moments where I had functioned as a receptacle for Karim's animal desires. As much as I wished to forget everything, there was always a stubborn curiosity that nonetheless tried to remember, *what was it like?* I began to wonder if perhaps, in spite of everything, I might be capable of willingly uniting with a husband. In those final days of the harvest, I found myself trying to conjure up an image of the young and handsome groom that my father's uncle would find for me when I reached Tiflis.

AND THEN, ON the night before I was to leave Mar Yuhanon forever, I overheard a conversation that was to change everything. The bell had rung, calling the men to the evening meal. As I joined the line for the wash basin, I found myself standing behind three senior monks. They were in the midst of an animated conversation, and I couldn't help but overhear them. "Sophocles was the greatest of the Greek playwrights," one was saying as he scrubbed his hands. "Aristotle himself calls his *Oedeipus the King* the perfect tragedy."

"Yet Plato chose to use Aristophanes, not Sophocles, as a speaker in *The Symposium*," one of his companions replied, and then turned to the third and asked, "What do you say, Emavus?"

"The two cannot be compared; one wrote comedy, the other trag-edy," the third answered. "But now that Teodosiyos has bequeathed us his collection of Greek dramas, we can read both Sophocles' tril-ogy and Aristophanes, and judge for ourselves."

The three continued their conversation as they walked away, but I remained by the well, breathless and stunned. Sophocles was here. And that meant she was here. *Antigone* was here at Mar Yuhanon. It was as startling as seeing a ghost before me, or as meeting a familiar face in a foreign town. Who would have believed that here, in the midst of these strange men with their strange beliefs, I might find something of my old, lost life. A sudden, desperate longing came over me like a fever. For fear that someone would notice, I left my place in line and ran out into the dark night.

The moon was half-hidden and pale, but I managed to follow the path toward the flickering light that shone through the library windows. It took all of my strength to pull open the heavy wooden door, and once inside, the stifled air, sweet with the scent of parch-ment and leather, made me dizzy. I gazed into the darkened rooms, my eyes burning with dream-like rapture. A single lamp illuminated the librarian's table, and I could barely make out the form of a monk, sitting before an open text.

"*Shlama lookh,*" he greeted me softly. "Who's there?" I peered into the darkness, trying to identify the speaker's features. I saw that he was gray-bearded, with the sharp blue eyes that one sometimes sees in the descendants of the Romans.

"*Shlamaa,*" I answered him. "I am Yusef."

"Yusef? We have no monks by that name."

"I arrived with Habib last week; I helped him to deliver the books from Teodosiyos."

"Ah." He nodded. "In that case, I must greet you as the bearer of great treasure!" He studied me, as if trying to discern my face in the dim light.

"You're Monk Gibreel," I said excitedly, for he was the very one who could help me find what I was looking for.

"Indeed. But the library is closed now. I'm merely waiting for Monk Anton to conclude his work." I followed his glance across the library and into the smaller room in the back. At the desk in the far corner, a lone monk was bent over a text. I remembered him, for he sat in the same bent posture, in the same pose of deep concentration that he had on the afternoon I arrived at Mar Yuhanon. "Why have you come to the library at this hour?"

I looked into the light of the candle. Why had I come? I no longer knew. My mind was whirling in confusion, as if lost in a place that was both strange and familiar. "I have a question, sir," I managed to say.

"If you've come here at the dinner hour it must be of great importance."

"I . . . it is about something that I want very much to know."

"And what is it that the young bearer of great treasure must know at precisely this moment?"

I drew a shaky breath. "Does this library have a copy of *Antigone*? Written by Sophocles?"

"*Antigone*?" he repeated, and then pondered a minute. "Yes. It seems to me that I saw that name among the new books that you helped to deliver. If it is *Antigone* you seek, then you've no one to thank but yourself, and Teodosiyos, of course." He gazed quizzically at me. "How do you know of this book? Do you read Greek, my son? I believe that it hasn't been translated."

I avoided his question, which at that moment seemed utterly trivial, and asked, "May I see it?"

"I'm afraid not. *Antigone* was one of several books that we had to send to the repair room."

"The repair room?"

"Yes. The book arrived in very poor condition. If anyone tries to read it in its present condition, the bindings could fall apart."

As my heart had soared at Antigone's presence, it fell with the news of her absence. "When will it be back?"

"Oh, it will take several weeks, I think. Perhaps even longer. There are many books awaiting repair, and I expect that Monk Ipni has put *Antigone* at the end of the queue, so to speak." My face must have betrayed my dismay, for he added, "But one never knows. If you're still here next week, come back and check if it has returned."

A wave of despair broke over me. I mumbled a blessing and went out into the night. The winds were blowing stronger now, and they chilled the warm tears that welled in my eyes. *"Let's see if you can read the title,"* my father had challenged me. And though the writing was strange, and the letters combined to form a word that sounded like none I had ever heard, I had read out her name. *"A day will come when you'll recall this conversation. . . "* The words echoed in my mind now, and as I recalled the day they were spoken, I was filled with a longing so powerful that I no longer knew what to do with myself.

Behind the library walls, I fell to the ground and wept. I would never have imagined that a person could be as lost as I was at that moment. I saw my father's face before me, as he sat at his work table in his study, but when I opened my eyes there was only the cold, damp earth and the trees against a black sky. I lay that way for a long while, until finally, I picked myself up and walked in the direction of the church.

The monks were at evening prayers, and I could hear their low voices singing in unison. I sat down on a bench outside the building, drew my cloak around me, and tried to think. The winds rustled through the trees, and the night smelled of rain. I wished I could leave this lonely, cold place. Yet I knew now that I couldn't leave. Not yet.

What I had to do now would be harder than anything I had ever taken upon myself. It would require stronger will, greater courage and a sharper mind than anything I had ever done. But I knew, as well as one can know but a few things in this life, that I had no choice.

When the prayers were over and the monks left the church for their chambers, I spotted Shimun amongst the novices, donning his hood as he went into the cold night. I rose from the bench and ran to him. His companion, another novice, waited by his side, but Shimun urged him to go ahead. "I've given some thought to what you said," I told him gravely. "What do I need to do in order to stay at Mar Yuhanon a little longer?"

I HAD NEVER been what people call a liar, but now, seated before Rabban Basilius himself, I felt myself to be as lowly as any conniving trickster. I looked up at the wooden cross, set high on the wall behind him, and then quickly averted my gaze. The room was stark and simple, furnished only with a work table, some low stools, and a bookshelf filled with a few leather volumes and numerous parchment scrolls.

Shimun had spoken with Monk Elias, asking him to arrange this meeting. While the men were taking down the tent and counting out their wages, Monk Elias showed me to Rabban Basilius' office in a far corner of the monk's dormitory. I had never been inside the monks' living quarters, and as I passed through the arched entrance to the central courtyard, a chill of foreboding passed through me. For if all went well, this courtyard with its somber corridors of monk's dwellings would soon be my home.

We entered an office where a small, clear-eyed man of about sixty, with a balding head and a clipped, pointed beard sat behind a simple wooden desk. He motioned for me to take a seat on the stool opposite him. "I am Rabban Basilius, the *Hegumenos* of Mar Yuhanon," he said in a clear, soft voice. "And you must be Yusef."

I bowed politely, trying to ignore the pounding of my heart. All morning I had been composing answers to the questions this man might put to me. I had ready responses for my family name, my mother's family name, my stepfather's name, my city, my father's profession, and my extended family's whereabouts. But Rabban Basilius didn't ask about these details. Instead, he broke out into a lecture. "What is the nature of Divine Love?" he began.

I shifted in my seat. When he remained silent, I wondered if I was meant to suggest an answer, but he soon offered his own reply. "It is the love that is inside of you. It's the way that you feel the presence of God in your very soul. And what is the way toward discerning that presence?" he continued, as if reflecting on the question himself. This time I waited for him to provide the reply. "It is to follow in the path of Christ, to shun all that is fleeting and worthless in this world, to find inner peace through humility, simplicity, and loving kindness to all men. You see, Yusef, human beings can never share in the knowledge of the Divine Mysteries. The Trinity and the Incarnation, the Cross and the Redemption, the Resurrection and the Second Coming, the Church as the Bride of Christ, Mary, the Mother of God, all of these must remain veiled from our understanding." I was trying to follow him, hanging on to familiar phrases about Christ and Mary, but nothing else that he said made sense to me.

"The most perfect life on earth," he continued, "is that of a man who obeys the injunction to do penance, for as it is written, the Kingdom of Heaven is nigh." He paused for a moment, leaving his words hanging in the air. "Of course, there have been many interpretations regarding the subject of penance. We all know of the holy hermits, who have not only renounced worldly concerns, but gone as far as to enact the most severe forms of asceticism, such as living in caves or trees, binding rope round their bodies, severe fasting. We've all heard of the zeal of the Stylites who make their home atop high columns, or the famous sleepless monks of Studion, who keep an unceasing round of prayer and psalm-singing day and night. But here at Mar Yuhanon, we refrain from such extreme practices. We are content to take upon ourselves the teachings of St. Anthony, St. Pachomius, and of course St. Basil, renouncing the world, and immersing ourselves in prayer, contemplation and moderate fasting. We believe that by following their teachings, we too will reach the kingdom of heaven."

Though I tried to keep an interested expression, doubts were arising in me, doubts that made me regret that I hadn't left the monastery along with everyone else. But then Rabban Basilius turned his attention to me. "Monk Elias has told me about your circumstances. I understand that you've been helping out with our grape harvest. Allow me to thank you, in the name of all who will benefit from your labors." I smiled sheepishly, and he continued, "I understand that you are Christian-born, but your parents and siblings are now practicing Muslims."

"Yes, sir," I replied, trying to summon up the fictitious details I had prepared for this moment.

"That is truly distressing. These are such difficult times. Each month I hear new stories of Christians who have exchanged their faith for a fist full of gold or a titled position. I hear of Christian leaders deserting the very people who need their example, of Christian communities disintegrating. Of our churches falling into disrepair, of the poor who turn to the Church only to be sent away in disgrace. And that is why when a young man such as you comes to our threshold, we welcome the opportunity to show him our way of life. I believe that given the chance to learn about the deeds and teachings of Christ, to study his words and partake in our prayers, you will have the spiritual means with which to return to your true faith." He smiled like a father, beaming at a son who has come home. "Yusef, you are welcome here. Please partake in our hospitality, and know that we expect nothing material in return."

I bowed my head in acknowledgment, and then said, "May God bless you, and this house."

"While you reside here, you must try to take a part in our way of life. Of course, you will not be able to partake in the spiritual joys of the Holy *Quarbana* or Confession. Until you are re-baptized and chrismated, you will not be considered a true Christian. But sometime in the weeks after Christmas, Bishop Hanna will be visiting us, and that could be a perfect opportunity to welcome you back into the Church. In the meantime, attend our prayers and celebrate our festivals with us. Take up work that will benefit this house, and make an earnest effort to learn and study as much as possible. The life of a monk is not an easy one, yet for those who seek it, the rewards are great. A man can choose any one of a thousand lives, but truly, there is no gladness like that of he who has devoted his life to emulating the ways of our Savior."

"I'll do whatever I can, sir."

"Of course, we'll help you on your way. Monk Elias will instruct you in our daily routine, and inform you about our way of life. Do you know how to read, Yusef?"

"My father taught me a little."

"Well then, we shall see about some further instruction. When a man knows how to read and write, a thousand horizons open before him, and he is able to do work that glorifies that name of God." He glanced at the parchment scrolls on his shelf. "Are you familiar with the story of the scholar, Ibn Ishak?"

I had heard this name, both in my father's house, and also on the tongues of the scholars who visited the home of Omar Alharazi. "I have heard the name," I replied, "but not the story."

"Then allow me to tell it to you now. Ibn Ishak is not only a scholar but a doctor of medicine. It once happened that the Caliph Al-Mutawakil asked him to concoct a poison, which was to be administered to an enemy. When Ibn Ishak refused, the Caliph offered him a rich reward. Ibn Ishak blessed him for his generosity, but refused to make the potion. The Caliph was furious, and in his anger, he threatened that if Ibn Ishak refused the request, he would throw him into the royal prison for a year. The Caliph gave him a full week to think on his request, but still, Ibn Ishak refused. When Ibn Ishak was brought before him, the Caliph said, 'If you insist on refusing to comply with my orders, I will have no choice but to have you put to death.'

"To which Ibn Ishak replied, 'I have skill only in what is beneficial, and have studied naught else.'

"'Worshiper of Christ,' the Caliph cried. 'What is it that prevents you from obeying my wishes?' And Ibn Ishak replied, 'Two things: my religion and my profession. My religion decrees that we should do good even to our enemies, and how much more to our friends. And my profession is instituted for the benefit of humanity and limited to their relief and cure.'

"And so you see Yusef," he concluded, "a man who is learned brings honor upon all who share his faith. I will arrange for you to be schooled in reading and writing. But in the meantime, I urge you to attend our study groups, so as to better familiarize yourself with the Scriptures." He gazed at me quizzically. "Your face is gentle, almost like that of Christ himself."

I shifted uncomfortably, for I knew exactly what was disturbing him. "I . . . I am only fourteen years of age, sir," I offered as an explanation, and then added, "I'll do my best."

Rabban Basilius nodded approvingly. "We can ask no more from any man."

Monk Elias led me across the inner courtyard of the monk's dormitory. "In some monasteries men share their lodgings," he told me as he unlocked the door to the room that was to be mine, "but Mar Yuhanon, the holy man for whom this house is named, believed that solitude is essential for any man who seeks the presence of God within."

The room was narrow and dark. A worn straw mattress and a blanket of rough wool lay strewn on the floor. The stone walls gave off a damp and musty smell, but when Monk Elias opened the window shutter, a gust of cold, fresh air flooded the room and a wide vista of the rocky hills came into view. "That's much better," he said as he wiped the dust from his hands, and then, eyeing my robes as if for the first time asked, "Do you have any other garments with you?"

Though another set of Khalil's pants and tunic was still packed deep in my bag, I thought it best to save these for whatever misadventures lay ahead, and so I shook my head in reply.

"Then I will arrange for fresh clothes for you. The days are getting colder, and most of us have put on our heavier robes. As yet, you're not permitted to wear the cloak of a novice, but I'm sure that something suitable can be found."

The jangle of shepherd's bells floated in through the window. "Do shepherds bring their flocks here?" I asked him

"Only our own Monk Tuma. He takes the sheep out to the caves on the north side of the hills. It is said that the work of a shepherd is conducive to reflection and penance because when a man is alone with nature, he feels the presence of God most clearly. All of us, each man here, has chosen to live apart from the world of men, so that we may better know God. It is difficult at times, but abstinence and the fortification of the spirit soon make the life of society appear hollow and frivolous. I believe that in time, you too will come to see the world outside with new eyes."

HAS ANYONE SUFFERED for the sake of a book the way that I suffered for *Antigone*? My decision to stay on at Mar Yuhanon had been rash, and now I was paying dearly for that rashness.

Rashmo, Sootoro, Lilyo, Saphro, Tlath Sho'in, Sheth Sho'in, Tsha Shho'in. These were the names of the seven daily prayer sessions. I tried to make a show of learning the chants and songs, but once everyone had taken their place and the service began, I found it difficult to stay awake. This was not only because of the repetitive lull of the chanting, but also because, as a resident of the monastery, I was expected to rise in the middle of the night to join the monks in a final set of prayers

Nonetheless, anything repeated seven times a day will eventually sink into one's brain, and I quickly learned at which places in the service to enact the sign of a cross, when to bow my head in private prayer, and when to recite the lines:

"We believe in one Lord, Jesus Christ,
the only Son of God,
eternally begotten of the Father,
God from God, Light from Light,
true God from true God,
begotten, not made,
of one Being with the Father."

In my first days at Mar Yuhanon, I tried to make sense of the religion of the Christians; what were its commandments, what acts were forbidden, and what was allowed. There were many confusing paradoxes. I knew, for example, that unlike the Jews, Christians were permitted to eat anything at all. Yet the monks abstained from eating meat. They celebrated their Sabbath faithfully, but thought nothing of profaning it by lighting fires and cooking. They revered the Jewish prophets, but seemed to disdain the Jews.

Even more puzzling though, was the way they expressed their piety. True, the monks took on a great many limitations, but where were their laws concerning behavior? How could one know what found favor in God's eyes, and what did not? And how could they consider their way of life to be a search for perfection, when they refrained from marriage and fathering children? Amongst the Jews, a man who remained unmarried was considered a luckless misfit.

Monk Elias suggested that I attend the group Bible readings led by the same monk Emavus who had been partially responsible for my staying on in the monastery. Each afternoon monks and novices would crowd into a small room off the dormitory courtyard and listen while someone read a chosen passage from their holy books, which they called the *Peshitta*. Monk Emavus would then discuss the passage, yet these readings only added to my confusion. If Isho was, as the Christians claimed, a Jew, then the stories they told about him were obviously mere invention. For what Jew would speak so vehemently against the teachings of his own faith? How, I wondered, could these men, serious—earnest, some of them quite intelligent—really believe these tales?

I pondered the question, both in church and while I toiled at the tasks assigned to me by Monk Elias. "Each of us," he had explained that first day, "from the newest novice to Rabban Basilius himself, is required to contribute to the running of the monastery. What labors can you do, Yusef?"

"I can cook, sir," I told him. "And I know how to weave at the loom."

"Cooking and weaving? That is very good. Most of the men prefer outdoor work to the domestic tasks." I was assigned to help Monk Sarkis prepare the midday meal in the mornings, and to work alongside Monk Yakub at the loom in the afternoons.

I soon saw that I had been fortunate, for just as I had suspected, meals at Mar Yuhanon required very little effort. While the Alharazi family loved delicacies that took hours of preparation, the monks preferred their food to be as simple as possible. They were happy to eat whatever vegetables were growing in their garden, and the main staple of their diet was yogurt, made from the milk of the sheep and goats kept by the solitude-seeking monastery shepherds. Though the barley and wheat had to be ground each day into flour, other monks were assigned this task, so that all we had to do was mix the dough and bake the bread.

Work at the weaving loom was more demanding. Not because there were complicated designs to copy, but because Monk Yakub had taken upon himself to make as many blankets as possible to be distributed among the poor at the festival of Christmas, which was fast approaching. Though I tried to appear as slow and clumsy as a boy, he praised my neat, swift work from the first day. But my success at these tasks gave me no pleasure. On the contrary, I became restless, scolding myself for wasting time on a fruitless quest when I should have been on my way to Tiflis.

More useful were my reading lessons. A young monk by the name of Andraouis was assigned the task of teaching me. I asked him to teach me to read Greek, the language of Sophocles, but he refused, explaining that his primary task was to instruct me in Syriac. "You're very ambitious," he remarked approvingly. "Perhaps when you've mastered reading in your own language we'll see about progressing to the alphabet of the Greeks."

Each afternoon, we would meet in a small room at the back of the church, where he would teach me the Syriac letters. Once I was familiar with the alphabet, he would bring me prayer scrolls filled with small cramped script, which he asked me to read aloud. These lessons were not unlike the instruction my father had given me, but when Monk Andraouis placed a pen in my hand and told me to copy out passages onto a sheet of parchment, I could not help but smile because I, a mere girl, was mimicking the labors of a scribe.

Nonetheless, I could soon read through an entire prayer scroll and copy it without mistakes. Monk Andraouis was impressed with my progress. "You're reading extraordinarily well," he remarked after two weeks had passed, "and your calligraphy is also quite pleasing. I would say that you have an aptitude for learning."

"Then I'm ready to learn Greek?" I asked excitedly.

The next day he began to teach me the language of Sophocles.

The days were growing short and far colder than any I could remember in Sura. The monks took to retiring early, for as soon as the sun set, the winds would sweep over the hills and through the dormitory walls, and the darkness would send each man far into himself. I began to wear a second, heavier cloak over my lighter one, a habit that made movement cumbersome but nonetheless kept me warm and helped my disguise. For three weeks I went to prayers, attended study sessions, made yogurt in the kitchen, wove blankets at the loom, and learned to read. All of these labors had but one purpose, and every few days I would return to the library in the hope that *Antigone* had returned.

My eyes would adjust to the soft, dusty beams of sunlight that fell on the reading tables, and the scent of parchment and leather would fill me with a strange pleasure. Some men worked alone, while others gathered in groups of two or three, hovering over the texts that lay open in front of them. I soon came to recognize some of the faces: the three youthful men who occupied the table under the window that faced the garden, the two grim faced scholars who shared a long scroll filled with tiny Roman letters, and several other, lone monks, who would stare up into space, as though lost in thought. The second room at the back of the library was reserved for the translators. They would sit for long hours at their tables, a dusty, yellowing text open on one side, and a sheet of fresh parchment on the other. And I would see the monk called Anton, bent over his table beneath the far window that looked over the hills.

Antigone was here, as near as a hovering spirit, yet it was as though we were separated by an unbridgeable river. How would I ever learn Antigone's story, I wondered, when I still had to obtain the book, read the Greek words, and understand their meaning? Even my home in Sura seemed closer.

At my request, Monk Gibreel would check if *Antigone* was among the books that Monk Ipni had brought him. As the days passed, and *Antigone* did not appear, my excitement turned to exasperation.

"Perhaps I could help Monk Ipni in his workshop," I suggested one day.

But Monk Gibreel frowned and shook his head. "Monk Ipni gets anxious if anyone so much as enters the repair room. He is like a physician, tending to the pages as if they're his patients."

Two monks approached the desk, and as Monk Gibreel turned his attention to them, my head swirled with a despair that almost made me cry. I moved off to one of the tables and plunked myself down. The idea of enduring more days of prayer, piety, and deception was becoming unbearable. A well-used volume of the *Peshitta* lay on the open on the desk. Almost as a reflex from my sessions with Monk Andraouis, my eyes moved over the text.

Blessed are the poor in spirit,
for theirs is the kingdom of heaven.
Blessed are the meek,
for they shall possess the earth.

I paused. Reading had always seemed to me a tedious activity, like chopping vegetables or washing dishes. But somehow, these lines seemed to draw me in and promise something more.

Blessed are they who mourn,
for they shall be comforted.
Blessed are they who hunger and thirst for justice,
for they shall be satisfied.
Blessed are the merciful,
for they shall obtain mercy.
Blessed are the clean of heart,
for they shall see God.
Blessed are the peacemakers,
for they shall be called children of God.
Blessed are they who suffer persecution for justice' sake,
for theirs is the kingdom of heaven.

I read the passage again, and then again, and then closed my eyes, as if to hold its beautiful lines in my mind. Just as I had once wished for fine robes and sparking jewelry, I now yearned to possess this passage. Who, I wondered for the first time, was the man who wrote these lines, lines that spoke not of heroes or kings, but of the meek, the peacemakers, those who suffer persecution? Though I could scarcely imagine him, reading his words made me feel as if he were speaking to me.

I looked up from the book; all around me, monks were sitting in stillness, their minds given over to the writing before them. I had grown used to this placid scene, but now, rather than appearing dull, it seemed to pulse with endeavor. The quiet of the library was not lifeless, but rich and deep, a core of silent activity punctuated by the inspired rhythm of pens scratching on parchment. Suddenly I was struck with an idea. I rose and approached Monk Gibreel's table. "Yes?" he inquired, as though he expected me to ask about *Antigone* again.

"I want to . . . to write something," I told him, the words sounding thick and awkward coming from my voice.

I half-feared that he would question me and demand to know what a mere girl could possibly want with instruments of writing. But instead, he opened a drawer, took out a torn piece of parchment, and handed me a pen and a vial of ink. "Be careful," he warned. "Make sure not to spill it."

Just as Monk Andraouis had shown me, I filled the pen with ink, positioned it in my hand and began to painstakingly copy out the passage. And as I shaped each letter, I realized that words, which I had always used carelessly and without forethought, could actually be held and examined in the mind like singular gems. For like gems, each had a weight, a shape, a texture that might be purposely selected for a particular use, much as a cook selects a specific spice to enhance a stew or pot of jam.

When I had copied out the entire passage, I rolled it up as if it were a treasure. Now that it bore the beautiful words, the flawed piece of parchment had been made beautiful in itself. I ran to the church, where I found Shimun emerging from noontime prayers. He read what I had copied, and nodded in recognition. "Isho's Sermon on the Mount."

"You're familiar with it?"

Shimun broke into a good-natured chuckle. "It's one of the best known passages in the *Peshitta*."

"It is beautiful; as beautiful as the finest verse."

He smiled at my description. "Indeed it is."

That evening, as I stood with the monks in prayer, I looked at the picture of Isho on the wall with new eyes. Had anyone else ever written such words about mourning and suffering and those who hunger and thirst for justice?

With my new way of seeing Isho came a new way of seeing the men of Mar Yuhanan. Who, if not they, were the meek, the merciful, the clean of heart?

"Allow me to explain how our system works," Monk Gibreel told me the next time I asked him if *Antigone* had been returned. "He motioned for me to follow him behind his table and into the room where the library's books were kept. The heavy smell of must and old leather rose from the long wooden shelves, and when he held up the lamp to what must have been hundreds of volumes, I could only gasp with wonder.

But it was not the books that Monk Gibreel meant to show me. Rather, he led me to a small table, on which a half-finished book lay open. "This," he explained, "is the library ledger. Every book that this library acquires is inscribed here. It's arranged in alphabetical order, according to the book titles. You see, each page is divided into three columns, and there is a page for each letter." He pointed to the first column at the far right of the page. "In this column, we record the name of the acquisition. And in this next one, I write the name of the author. The third column tells us the book's language."

I read the top line on the page: *De Dialectica, Augustine, Latin.* It still amazed and delighted me that I could decipher what were once meaningless pictures. Glancing down the page, I saw that many of the books were in Greek and Latin, but there were also many titles in Syriac and Arabic. "Now, why don't you check if *Antigone* has been recorded." As I scanned down the page, I pictured the words that I wanted to see: *Antigone, Sophocles,* and then in the third column: *Greek.*

My eye ran down the pages like a hungry man looking for a morsel of food. But alas, *Antigone* was not there. "It isn't here," I told him.

"Not yet. But as you can see, there's enough in this library to occupy you in the meantime."

His words put me in a dark mood. I was beginning to wonder if I could endure much more time at Mar Yuhanon. Not wanting to return to the dull tasks awaiting me in the kitchen, I wandered

listlessly back into the reading room, and then into the translators'
room.

A stack of books was piled on one of the tables. Instinctively, as
I had once done when I saw new books in my father's study, I attempted to read the titles. *The Republic*. I managed to make out the
Greek letters in the title of the first book. I lifted the heavy book off
the top of the pile so as to read the next title. The letters were Syriac,
but the title, *Categoriae*, was in Latin. I lifted it a little, trying to
make out what came next.

"If one truly wants to acquire knowledge, one must overcome all
tendencies toward bashfulness." Startled, I looked up. It was Anton,
the monk who always sat at the far table by the window. Because he
usually sat with his head bent over his books, I had never seen his
face. He was about forty years of age, with an oval-shaped, balding
head and studious, intelligent eyes. His expression seemed to betray
a focused intensity, as if all he saw required scrutiny and analysis.

"Excuse me," I mumbled. "I was curious about which texts are
going to be translated."

He smiled and shook his head. "Oh, I think there's more to it
than that. You've been here seven times in the last month. Obviously
you're searching for something."

"Why do you insist?" I asked, returning the smile.

"No man enters the domain of a monastery unless he's searching for something. No man enters the library unless his mind has
become restless from the search."

There was something in his manner, sharp, forthright and provoking, that both confused me and compelled me to think clearly. In
those short few seconds, I understood that if anyone in all the world
could help me, it was he. "Well, yes," I admitted. "I was looking for
something...for an ancient Greek drama. It's called *Antigone*."

"*Antigone*," he repeated. "Who wrote it?"

"A man by the name of Sophocles."

"Sophocles. Yes. One of the geniuses of Athens." He glanced at
Monk Gibreel's table. "Does this library own a copy?"

"It does, but it's being repaired," I replied, and then added, "I'm
hoping to read it, even though I'll don't think I'll understand a word."

"You have not yet mastered Greek."

"Not yet."

He nodded to himself and then looked up at me. "Then I suppose you'll have to learn it as we read."

I could feel my heart leaping with joy. Finding this man had truly been a miracle. "Sir, you're too kind," I protested weakly. "You mustn't interrupt your work for such a diversion."

"Oh, it will be a diversion," he said, chuckling, "but I can see that you are a true student, and to guide a true student is to walk in the path of God."

I gazed at him dumbly, barely believing that he might be referring to me. "Did Isho say that?"

"No, the words are my own. It isn't every day that I meet someone who longs to learn."

This miraculous conversation had taken me entirely by surprise, yet it had a strange quality of rightness, as if all had been predestined to unfold in precisely this way. "If we are to study together," he continued, "I must know your name. Mine is Anton."

The weight of my deception was pressing down on me, but now that all the lies I had told were proving justified, I was not about to ruin everything. "I am Yusef."

"*Antigone* should be back in the library soon. But in the meantime, perhaps you ought to study some of the other works of the period. Have you read any philosophy?"

"Philosophy?" I stammered. "I've never really had the—"

"Well, I recommend you correct that deficiency as soon as possible. To walk down the road of life without knowing the wisdom of ancient Greece is to embrace ignorance."

"There are many who lack that knowledge."

"And they are all the poorer for it. Now you have a chance to familiarize yourself with writings that are like rays of light in the darkness of this world."

I scarcely knew what to answer him. The thought of me sitting at a scholar's table was as odd as my working at the blacksmith's oven or the stonemason's bench. If my father was looking down on me, he must have been laughing.

After that first encounter with Anton, my despair fell away, and I again found the will to endure long hours of dull prayer and tedious work. I could not quite believe my good fortune, for it seemed that after many months of abandoning me to evil and hardship, God had finally remembered me. That night, as I lay on my bed of straw, I envisioned my father, as wise and good-humored as he had been on the morning of our last conversation. Now that I understood what it meant to read, I knew that I would meet him again when I finally heard Antigone's words.

The next day, on my way to the kitchen after morning prayers, I heard a voice call out, "Yusef. Wait." When I saw that it was Monk Anton, I was filled with a strange new gladness.

"Yesterday afternoon I went to the repair room," he began in his direct manner of speaking. "Monk Ipni knows the book, but he's busy with a collection of early Church writings from *Mar Elia* in Mosul, and so he won't have time to work on it until sometime after Christmas."

"After Christmas?" I cried. "Then it will be months!"

"Yes. But that might be for the best; now you'll have the time to study some works of philosophy. Familiarity with Greek philosophy can only enhance the reading of Greek drama."

I shook my head. "Philosophy isn't for me; I'm not a scholar."

"Nonsense!" he cut in. "On the contrary, your mind yearns to learn, just as a dry plant craves water."

This sentence, spoken with such conviction, struck me as a strange joke. "You speak with such confidence," I remarked, "but you barely know me."

For a moment he considered my response. And then he abruptly moved toward a clump of white and yellow winter wildflowers growing amongst the grasses in the yard. "Come here a minute. I want to show you something." He bent down, picked a flower and held it out to me. "What do you think when you see this flower?"

I stared at him blankly. "That it's . . . a flower."

"Of course, but what else do you think?" I shrugged and shook my head, hoping he would answer for me. "Here. Hold it in your hand. Look at it. Just look at it. Now what do you feel?"

"It's . . . pretty."

"Yes, yes," he said impatiently, "but what else do you feel? What do you feel in your soul?"

"I . . . I don't know what you mean."

"I mean the simplest of feelings. What do you feel when you see the intricate design of this flower?" He looked up and I followed his gaze as his eyes darted around the yard. "Or of that tree? Of the hills and the valleys? What do they evoke in you? What do you feel about the world that God has created?"

His expression both scared and captivated me. It was as if he were asking me to join him on a journey, and part of me wanted to follow him. And then, as I gazed at the flower in my hand, a memory appeared.

I was perhaps no more than four years old. Shafiqa had taken me for a walk on the road that ran along the river. It was early spring, just before the celebration of Passover. After some time, we came upon a spot I knew well, where a slope of wild grasses stretched down to the river. But on this day I was met with an astounding sight: the entire field had bloomed into a garden of white and yellow wildflowers, many of them almost as tall as I was. My mouth dropped open in wonder, and I squealed with delight as I ran, my feet weightless and my arms open wide, into the high grasses. I turned the flower in my hand, and murmured, "I am amazed."

"Exactly. You are amazed. You are full of awe at this world. And that, my son, is precisely what Aristotle felt. He writes that the moment of wonder is the spark that causes us to ask why things are as they are. It was the very thing that led him to ask the questions of philosophy. You too are capable of feeling the same wonder. And that is the proof that you do indeed have a philosophic mind."

I opened my mouth to oppose him, but had no answer. Under my heavy cloaks, I was trembling. Part of me wanted to turn away from him, to ignore what he was trying to show me. And yet a powerful urge, that same urge *to know* that Eve couldn't suppress in the Garden of Eden, had opened within me. I wanted to follow him; I wanted to know all that those who have a philosophic mind can know. Did he perceive what I was feeling at that moment? I didn't speak of it, yet the gentleness in his tone told me that he did. "Come to the library tomorrow afternoon, and I will introduce you to some people that you ought to meet."

The first texts that Monk Anton set before me were painstaking to read, and impossible to understand. But at the close of the day, in the falling winter light, I would sit at his table in the corner of the library, and he would explain all that had perplexed me. And like a man who discovers the power of wine, I came to crave the moment of mystery, and its unraveling, and the sudden clarity that lit up my mind like lightning.

What is the world? Thales said that all is water. Anaximenes said that all is air. Aneximandros said that all is the infinite matter of *apeiron*. But Heracletos saw differently. He knew that things are never what they seem. For him, all is fire, and the true nature of the world lies in the eternal fury of the flames.

It is not peace, nor tranquility, nor patient yielding that describes this world. Rather, it is movement and change, contrast and conflict. For is it not so that each thing holds the seeds of its opposite? Just as day follows night, just as calm must come after a storm, just as a man eats, only to know hunger again, so we cannot know a thing without perceiving its opposite.

Heracletos understood this. He saw that in this ceaseless struggle, there is harmony, hidden, mysterious, and potent, in which a thing partakes in a never-ending dance with its mirror image.

If the only certainty is change, then the nature of the world is the struggle. There is no justice; justice exists only in the outcome of things. There is no peace in this world. All is war.

Socrates would go down to the marketplace, and when he would come upon the respected men of Athens, he would ask them, in front of everyone:

What is piety?

What is bravery?

What is knowledge?

What is modesty?

What is wisdom?

The men would try to answer Socrates' questions, but he would respond by challenging them to explain further, and the men didn't notice how with each question he drew them further into the trap of their own words.

"Admit your ignorance!" Socrates would say. "Admit that you don't really know. Recognize that you are but a man, constricted by your faculties, humbled by your failure."

"But why? Why did Socrates want to humiliate the men of Athens?" I asked Monk Anton, unable to fathom a why a man with a neck so long would want to stick it out.

"Do I perceive a flicker of curiosity in that lazy brain of yours?" he taunted me, and he sent me back to the books.

"PLATO IS NOT for the young," Monk Anton warned me as we sat in his corner in the library one rainy afternoon. The sky outside was so dark that even though Monk Gibreel had lit all the lamps, we could see little more than shadows.

"What do you mean?" I asked him.

"I mean that it takes a man many, many years to understand that all he thinks is real in this world is only an illusion."

"An illusion? Are those your thoughts or Plato's?"

"Alas, though many have suspected that this world is an illusion, it is he who posed the notion for philosophical inquiry."

"Isn't that similar to when we read about vanity of vanities, in Ecclesiastes?" I asked, thinking of a recent study group session.

He reflected on this and nodded. "An interesting comparison, but Plato was saying something else. He believed that all that we can really know in this life stems from a recollection of the ideas we once knew in our souls."

"We once knew? When did we once know?"

"Before we were born. According to Plato, we once knew the true and absolute nature of everything in this world: beauty, justice, love, and also tragedy and death. But after our birth, we forget all of this knowledge. All that remains is our vague, shadow-like recollections of what our souls once discerned clearly. Our lives are as a dream; we can never really know the true and essential nature of anything and so we must suffice with imitations."

In my lessons with Monk Anton, he often encouraged me to express my opinions about the ideas we read. At first I was reluctant, for I didn't relish the notion of showing my ignorance, but he refused to leave me in peace. "Have we not agreed that bashfulness is an impediment to learning?" he scolded me. "Centuries of scholars, young men just like you have read these passages and struggled to understand their meaning. They've read these same words that you're reading now, and then questioned them and formulated thoughts of their own. You see, Yusef, when you ask a question, you join a family of scholars, a family that stretches from the ancient Greeks through the ages, all the way to our own scholars of the Church."

And so, though it was against my nature, I allowed myself to speak somewhat freely. "Your Plato sounds like the madmen one sees begging in the markets. This world isn't a shadow; it's real. As real as the pen you hold in your hand. As real as the rain that will fall on your head if you step outside."

He frowned at me, clearly displeased. "You speak like a peasant. Have you no depth? Can you perceive nothing but that which is plainly visible to the eye?"

I looked down at the yellowing book before us. "I have my thoughts," I said quietly. "But they have nothing to do with the words of men long dead."

"That," he replied gravely, "is a very foolish thing to say. Would you allow your mind to close, so that you can continue to wallow in your ignorance? Would you be like the lovers of sights and sounds that Plato speaks of?" His face grimaced in the pained expression of one who expects more. "Let me ask you this: Do you know why Plato mocks the lovers of sight and sounds?"

I shook my head. "I didn't understand that part either."

"Yes. The concept is a difficult one. Now listen carefully: You remember that we spoke of Plato's theory of essential and ideal forms."

I nodded, for we had spent a long afternoon discussing its relation to the Christian notion of this world and the next.

"When Plato considered the men and women of Athens, he perceived that there were two types of people. The first type, whom he called the lovers of sight and sound, are the majority. They're people who love what they perceive to be aesthetic, beautiful, and fine. Yet they're unable to see that these things are a mere illusion, a meager imitation of the ideal of beauty. Plato mocks these people. He compares their lives to a dream, where imitation takes the place of the real."

"He is arrogant," I remarked. "What about the second type, the minority who don't fall into that category?"

"The others are a small remainder, a chosen few, the philosophers who love only the truth, and they alone are capable of recognizing true beauty. They know to distinguish the *genuine* idea from objects that merely *participate* in the idea. Where others live in a dream, they're wide awake. Where others have only opinions, they have knowledge."

"What do you mean by 'only opinions?'"

He considered my question for a moment, and then reached for his satchel. "Allow me to suggest an example." He untied the satchel and drew out a red apple, one of those recently harvested from the monastery orchards. "Here." He handed it to me and grinned. "Take a bite."

Hesitantly, for it seemed to have no connection with the lesson, I took the apple in my hand and bit into it.

"How do you like it? Is it sweet?"

"Yes." I grinned back at him.

"But how do you know that it's truly sweet? Perhaps another young scholar would bite into this apple and pronounce it sour."

"Perhaps. But I say that it's sweet."

"And so that is your opinion. And do you know why you call it sweet?"

"I'm sure you can tell me."

"Plato would say that it's because there was a time when your soul knew what sweetness was. But when you were born and your soul was joined to your body, you forgot that singular, essential knowledge of sweetness. All you can do now is recognize that your apple partakes in the idea of sweetness."

I glanced at the apple quizzically and then took another bite; nothing about its taste seemed to be an imitation of some mysterious ideal. "Give it some thought," he suggested. "New ideas must be contemplated over time."

"Even so, without your explanations, I wouldn't understand a word of it."

"Nonsense!" he exclaimed. "You are completely capable of understanding, if you only open your mind to new ways of thinking." We sat in silence for several minutes, so that the only sound was that of the rain, its soft, uneven rhythm filling me with a sudden sadness. Monk Anton too seemed to sink into his innermost thoughts, until suddenly, he closed the book that lay open before us, and turned to face me. "The first time I read Plato's ideas about the ideal forms and their imitations, I was astonished. It was as if he was somehow addressing the very questions that had been troubling me for a long time."

I blinked in surprise, for never before had he spoken of himself in this way. "Do you mean to say that you wondered if this world was real even *before* you read Plato?"

"Well, no. I mean, not exactly. You see Yusef, all of us, that is, every man who has decided to take on the life of a monk, arrives at this decision after a period of much reflection and struggle. This path that we've chosen is in fact a quest of sorts."

"But isn't joining a monastery and becoming a monk the end of the quest?"

"I once thought so, but now I know that it's only the first step on a long road." He looked away from me, and stared at the flickering light of the lamp. "My decision to come to Mar Yuhanon was probably the most difficult I ever made. It's one thing to leave the world of the common man when you're young and have no bonds that tie you to a place or person. But once one has made a life for oneself, it's not at all simple to leave it." He sighed and turned to me again. "You are young; I don't expect you to grasp my meaning. But perhaps if I tell you of my own experience, you'll better understand the nature of a monk's quest."

I nodded, fascinated and wary of interrupting him. "For three generations," he began, "my family has run an inn for wayfarers. The inn lies on the road that leads to Aleppo and Antioch, and then on to the sea. Though it is nothing but a lone building on the highway, the rooms are always occupied. In my youth, I spent long days and nights seeing to the guests, supervising the staff, and taking care of whatever needed repair. After my father fell ill, I also took on the task of managing our accounts. Eventually I married a woman, the daughter of a devout family from Nisibin. Four children were born to us, and my responsibilities multiplied."

My eyes opened wide with amazement; I could scarcely imagine that Monk Anton had ever lived anywhere but Mar Yuhanon. "You were married?"

"Oh yes. My life was pleasant, and I lacked for nothing. But within, I was unhappy. I would observe the guests that stopped at the inn, each one of them in the midst of a journey. There were the soldiers with their polished weapons and smart uniforms, pulling me aside to inquire about the way to the nearest brothel. There were merchants, counting out their coins by candlelight, and dreaming of ways to increase their fortunes. There were officials and tax collectors, stuffing themselves with food and wine, even as they plotted and schemed against one another. At night, when they ate and drank and sang and laughed with their companions it seemed that their lives offered endless pleasures. But in the gray mornings, when I saw them rise early and continue on their way, I would wonder about the object of these journeys. What awaited them at their destinations? For the officials, more intrigue and scheming. For the merchants, another pile of gold. And for the soldiers, a battle that might be their last. I came to see the journeys of men as little better than the designs of ants, using all of their strength to accomplish some small and meaningless feat. The more I thought about these men, the greater my sense of restlessness became.

"I began to take long, solitary walks, during which my mind burned with those questions that seem to have no answer. What is our purpose in this life? Does my time on earth have no meaning but to live out my days in complacency? What does God want from us? How does He want us to live? For years these questions echoed in my mind. Plato would have said that I was no longer content to live among the lovers of sight and sounds." He grinned, and the appearance of Plato in his story made me smile as well.

"One day," he continued, "a traveling monk arrived at the inn, asking for nothing more than a bowl of soup. Naturally we took no money for the meal we served him. While he ate, I was sitting in my office, counting up the day's earnings. But I could see him through my door, offering a prayer for every dish we set before him. All of a sudden, counting the coins seemed trivial and devoid of true meaning. I felt compelled to speak with him.

"He told me that he was journeying to the Mar Sabba monastery in the Judean dessert. His father had died, leaving him livestock and fruitful orchards, but he had given his share of the inheritance to his brothers, and set out to emulate Isho, renouncing all material possessions and earthly desires. I sat with him for hours while he spoke of the nobility of the spirit and of the joy of living a life of truth.

"The monk left a powerful impression on me, and even long after we parted, I continued to ponder all he had told me. My wife, Yulia, had always been more pious than I. Two of her brothers attended the great School of Nisibin, and the family has produced several priests and bishops. When I told her of this man, she was certain that he was a traveling saint, sent by God to give me strength and inspiration. Months passed and my life at the inn grew more and more oppressive to me. I was tired of waiting on guests; I wanted to be free of the petty concerns of men. The only life that seemed worthy was one that would allow me to seek a path to God.

"One dark night, after the children had gone to sleep, I told Yulia of all that had been weighing on me. She listened solemnly, and when I was done, she urged me to do as the traveling monk: to leave my home and devote my life to God."

"She actually told you to leave her?" I asked, incredulous.

"She understood. I believe that God Himself blessed me with such a spouse. My mother was less sympathetic, but there was little she could do, for I had made up my mind. At first I thought to seek out a desert monastery, but a traveling bishop told me about Mar Yuhanon. He described Rabban Basilius, and the daily life of the monks, and also this library, and convinced me to make the journey here. Three years ago, I took my vows. I sent word to Yulia that Mar Yuhanon was now my home, and she and the children returned to Nisibin."

He fell silent. The rain too had ceased, and the only sound was that of heavy drops falling from the trees onto the wet earth.

EACH SUNDAY AFTER morning prayers, Rabban Basilius would address the monks, giving a talk so dull that my thoughts would drift away as soon as he began. Though he often began with a story from the Scriptures, or the writings of the Church Fathers, he would soon take up the subject that most troubled the monks of Mar Yuhanon, which as far as I could tell, involved a disagreement about the nature of Christ. I would glance at the pictures of Isho and Maryam, and wonder what they would have made of it all. *Here we are, you and I, the only Jews among the Christians. I know why I am masquerading as something that I'm not, but how did it happen to you?*

"In recent months," Rabban Basilius began, "we've been reviewing some of the writings of our Church Fathers. Today we will read from the homilies of St. John Chrysostom." Though the monks were looking up at him with rapt attention, I was unable to suppress a yawn. "Now the meaning of the name Chrysostom is 'golden-mouthed.' St. John's insight, his straightforwardness, and his rhetorical splendor no doubt earned him this title. Though his words did not always find favor in the eyes of the clergy, St. John was nonetheless proclaimed one of the Four Doctors of the Church."

He went on about St. John, and I let my thoughts wander far back to my last few weeks in Sura, when Shafiqa and I were busy embroidering sheets for my wedding trousseau. I was recalling the design we had chosen, a pattern of red roses with green leaves, when I heard Rabban Basilius say, ". . . so that we may understand the true nature of the Jews." My ears opened wide. I had read enough of the writings of the Christians to know the strange things they thought about Jews. "They are a people who have not only rejected the holy teachings of Christ, but in spite of the punishment God has inflicted on them, still refuse to see the evil of their ways. Let us read from the sermons delivered by St. John in Antioch, almost 500 years ago."

Now it was I who was listening to his every word.

He began to read: *Nothing is more miserable than those people who never failed to attack their own salvation. When there was need to observe the Law, they trampled it under foot. Now that the Law has ceased to bind, they obstinately strive to observe it. What could be more pitiable than those who provoke God not only by transgressing the Law but also by keeping it? On this account, Stephen said: "You stiff-necked and uncircumcised in heart, you always resist the Holy Spirit," not only by transgressing the Law but also by wishing to observe it at the wrong time.*

But what is the source of this hardness? It comes from gluttony and drunkenness. Who says so? Moses himself. "Israel ate and was filled and the darling grew fat and frisky." When brute animals feed from a full manger, they grow plump and become more obstinate and hard to hold in check; they endure neither the yoke, the reins, nor the hand of the charioteer. Just so the Jewish people were driven by their drunkenness and plumpness to the ultimate evil; they kicked about, they failed to accept the yoke of Christ, nor did they pull the plow of his teaching. Another prophet hinted at this when he said: "Israel is as obstinate as a stubborn heifer." And still another called the Jews "an untamed calf."

Although such beasts are unfit for work, they are fit for killing. And this is what happened to the Jews: while they were making themselves unfit for work, they grew fit for slaughter. This is why Christ said: 'But as for these my enemies, who did not want me to be king over them, bring them here and slay them.'" This last sentence made me gasp aloud, but most of the men standing beside me were so enthralled with the sermon that they didn't notice.

Rabban Basilius looked up and addressed the room. "It is clear that the punishment that God has visited on the Jews is more than justified. But let us read what St. John says about Jerusalem: *Come now, and let me give you abundant proof that the temple will not be rebuilt and that the Jews will not return to their former way of life. In this way you will come to a clearer understanding of what the Apostles taught, and the Jews will be all the more convicted of acting in a godless way. As witness, I shall produce not an angel, not an archangel, but the very Master of the whole world, our Lord Jesus Christ. When he came into Jerusalem and saw the temple, he said: 'Jerusalem will be trodden down by many nations, until the times of many nations be fulfilled.'"*

I could stand it no longer. I turned and, pushing my way along the back wall, I ran out to the empty yard. My hand trembled as I dug deep into the pocket of my cloak, pulled out the cross that Shimun had given me, cast it to the ground and then stomped it into the mud.

My mind was burning with confusion. I thought now of the monks, Shimun, Nidal, Elias, and Rabban Basilius. Though they had taken me in and given me work, food, and shelter, I saw now that they had only acted kindly because they believed me to be one of their own. Had they known my true identity, they would have surely sent me away and locked their doors. But I was not about to give them that pleasure. I would pack a bag and leave tomorrow, even if it meant giving up the chance to hear *Antigone*. For the rest of the day, I remained in my room, reviewing my old plan: I would go to Tiflis, I would find my father's uncle, and he would find me a husband.

When Monk Elias saw that I failed to appear at evening prayers, he came looking for me. I wanted to say that I was feeling sick. And truly, the mere thought of hearing again about their so-called Christian love and righteousness made me nauseous. Yet, if I was going to flee, I knew it was best not to arouse suspicion, and so I followed him back to the church.

It was difficult for me to even look at the faces of Isho and Maryam now, for they appeared to me as nothing more than graven images. From the back of the room, I spotted Monk Anton, kneeling in prayer. This sight, above all others, filled me with dismay. After all I had learned of his love of truth and wisdom, the very fact that he belonged to this hateful religion seemed to me a betrayal, not only of me, but of himself as well. At one point his eye caught my own and he motioned that he wanted to speak to me. But I was no longer sure that I wanted to speak to him.

When prayers were over, he quickly sought me out. "Yusef," he exclaimed. "Monk Elias told me that you were feeling unwell this afternoon, and so I made sure to mention you in my prayers. It was nothing serious, I hope."

His eyes were full of sympathy, and his tone of concern convinced me that were I to tell him the real reason for my "illness," he would dismiss Raban Basilius's ugly words as mere nonsense. I decided to restrain my anger and hear what he wanted to say. "Just a headache," I replied. "I've already forgotten it."

"Praise God," he murmured, and then, grasping my arm with the exuberance of a boy, he continued, "I've set aside *The Republic* for you. I want you to read *The Allegory of the Cave*. I believe that once you study it, many of Plato's ideas will be clearer to you."

"*The Allegory of the Cave?*" I repeated, for in spite of the confusion that still stirred in my mind, I was intrigued by the mysterious title. I imagined myself back in the library, sitting amongst the translators and scholars, a broad shaft of sunlight falling on my table, where a book of Plato's writings lay open before me. "Actually," I admitted, "I'm looking forward to reading more of Plato."

He broke into a wide smile. "Good. I'll be waiting for you." He walked away, but I remained in place, amazed by my own words.

I DISLIKED MONK Anton's ideas about truth, and so it was heartening to learn that Aristotle too had disagreed with his teacher, Plato. And indeed, once I became acquainted with Aristotle, I preferred his ideas to Plato's. *We can be certain of only two things in this life*, Aristotle had said. *Time will pass, and things will change.* These words were a great comfort to me and, in the days that followed, I recalled them often.

Plato believed the things of this world to be as meaningless as last fall's dead leaves. For him, the truth was only in the eternal. But Aristotle saw it all differently. He claimed that the logic of existence was change itself. For it is through change that the potency of every living thing becomes an actuality. The hen is the ultimate fate of the newborn hatchling. The towering palm fronds emerge from the heart of the date seed. And is the design of a man not concealed in the soul of the infant?

"Potency becomes actuality," I repeated slowly, as if uncovering a secret.

"Precisely," Monk Anton replied. "Aristotle even coined a term for the process: *entelechy*. It means 'the final form.' You see, Aristotle believed that each thing is always developing toward a singular goal, as if it has but one desire: to realize its ultimate essence. Every living thing, plant or animal, given the right conditions, will eventually become what it must become. In this way, it achieves its true potential."

The idea intrigued me, and I pondered it carefully. "And so according to Aristotle each living thing has its own unique entelechy?"

"Not exactly. The idea is that all members of a species share a common entelechy. The entelechy for a caterpillar is to become a butterfly. The entelechy for the calf is to become a cow. And the entelechy for our species, humans, is to study. Aristotle claimed that it is only in study and contemplation that we can realize our essence."

Monk Anton returned his attention to the text he was translating, but I was not satisfied. I looked at him quizzically, and he, with his sharp senses, put down his pen and sighed. "Yes, Yusef, what is it?"

"I've given the matter some thought," I told him with a self-assurance that surprised me.

"Yes?"

"I can't agree with Aristotle's description of entelechy."

"And why is that?" he asked, amused.

"Because even if study is in fact the most noble of pursuits, it's clear that not everyone is suited to it. Isn't it possible that for some there is an entelechy of a different sort, one that has nothing to do with study? Maybe each man develops toward his own *unique* destiny, toward an essence that exists only in his own singular soul."

"Oh no!" Monk Anton shook his head as he chuckled. "What a novel idea you have come up with! But Aristotle would not have approved. He would say that you've failed to understand his meaning. You see, Aristotle was not concerned with the individual. He considered all things according to their species. And a life of philosophizing led him to conclude that study is the entelechy of all mankind. Naturally, not all men are suited to its rigors, yet even you must admit that study represents the best of human endeavor." He paused a moment, and then added, "And the Church has agreed with him in this respect. Just think, Yusef. What is a man's life but an imperfect, temporary thing? He's born into sin, and then dammed to live a life filled with toil and suffering. Unless, that is, he manages to rise above the ugliness of this world, and devote himself to Isho in an exalted life of prayer and study. Can you not see how this is so?"

He gazed at me, waiting patiently for me to agree with him. But my gaze had moved outside the window, to the rolling expanse of the rocky hills. This view had often saddened me with its emptiness, but now, as thoughts flew through my head like heady birds, the vast spaces seemed as inviting as the field of wild flowers I had seen as a child.

IN THE DAYS leading up to Christmas, I had been excused from both prayers and study meetings, so as to help Monk Yakub weave blankets for the poor. But once Christmas had passed, there was no reason that I not join the novices in the drafty study room, our thin mats a pitiful defense against the freezing stone floor.

I wondered how much longer I would have to endure this miserable life I was leading. Winter in the hills was far colder than any I had ever experienced. Even the extra cloaks and blankets that Monk Elias had given me were a poor match for the merciless chill that pervaded all the buildings of Mar Yuhanon. At night in my meager bed, I remembered the warm sun and pleasant breezes that blew through our garden in the winter, and I pined for Sura as one longs for a lost paradise.

"Today," Monk Emavus began, "I want us to review some writings on the subject of the monastic vows. We'll begin with a text written fifty years ago by Theodore of Studium: *Do not acquire any of this world's goods, nor hoard up privately for yourself to the value of one*

piece of silver. Do not have any choice or costly garment, except for priest-
ly functions. But follow the Fathers in being shod and clad in humility."

How wonderful, I was thinking, it would be to go again to the
bathhouse in Sura, and bask in the warm light of the lamps as the
bath attendants combed out my hair and scrubbed my skin.

"Depart not from the rules and canons of the Fathers, especially of the
Holy Rabban Basil; but whatever you do or say, be as one who has his
witness in the Holy Scriptures, or in the custom of the Fathers, so as not
to transgress the commandments of God."

A few of the novices shifted on their mats. I well knew, as did
everyone else, that Monk Emavus would soon speak about chastity.
I found the subject troubling not only because of my own defiled
state, but also because it always left me feeling that I was somehow
endowed with the power to wreck havoc on the defenseless inhabit-
ants of Mar Yuhanon. Sometimes, when I was overcome with boredom, I would entertain myself with deliberations on which discovery
would be most alarming: that I was a woman, or that I was a Jew.

"And on the subject of chastity, Theodore instructs us thus: *Do*
not join in brotherhood or close relation with secular persons, seeing that
you have fled from the world and from marriage. Do not sit at a feast
with women, except with your mother according to the flesh, and your
sister, or possibly with others in case of necessity, as the Holy Fathers
enjoin."

I drifted into daydreams, until I was jolted back to reality by
Monk Emavus's somber voice. "Who among us has not struggled
with impure thoughts?" The novices avoided each other's eyes. I
too looked away. "My brothers, confession and repentance are the
means by which a Christian renews the purity of his baptism," he
concluded. "When you next sit in confession, I urge you to recall the
moments of your own human weakness."

At prayers that evening, I counted all the things I could confess.
Surely there was no penance for the sins I had committed against
the Christians. But what truly weighed heavily on me was that I had
abandoned my own faith. Week after week, I now desecrated the
Sabbath. I had failed to mark and keep Passover, Shavuot, Yom Kippur, and Succoth. Although I had not eaten meat in months, I had
disregarded the Jewish dietary laws. And worst of all, I had pretended
to be a Christian, traced the sign of the cross over my body, and knelt
in prayer before the church altar. Surely these sins were punishable

by death, and the fact that I was still alive meant only that I would meet a more terrible end.

That night, when I bolted my door and took off my cap, I felt how my hair had begun to creep down my neck. I took care to trim it off, making sure to scatter the cuttings out the window. I had not bathed in three weeks, and I could barely stand the touch of my own skin. Still, I dared not go down to the river. Living at Mar Yuhanon had taught me patience and I willed myself to wait for a rain storm, when the monks would close their doors and bolt their shutters tight.

The following Sunday the sky was dark and heavy, and the winds were cold and full of rainy mist. Though the notion of going out was not an inviting one, the yearning to bathe overpowered all.

As I walked down the wet hillside to the hidden spot on the river bank, the rain grew stronger, beating down on my cap in cold, heavy drops. I disrobed quickly and forced myself to enter the rushing water.

The cold was so sharp that for a few seconds I couldn't breathe. I combed my fingers through my hair so as to wash out the dirt and sweat, and tried to scrub the grime from my limbs. The touch of my own flesh was odd and foreign to me. Uneasily, I moved my hand over my body, and was filled with a powerful sense of disgrace. What would happen if one of the monks spotted me now? I dared not even imagine it. When Monk Anton and I sat in the library speaking of Aristotle and Plato, I felt as if I were a soul without weight, a mind without body. How distressing it was to be reminded now that under my cloaks and cap hid the ignoble form of a woman. Gales of wind rushed over the surface of the water, making me shudder and shut my eyes in pain.

Back in my room, I peeled off my wet clothes and put on my second tunic, the only dry garment I had. But even after I crawled under my wool blankets and curled into a tight ball, I couldn't stop shaking. I had no strength to stand at prayers that night, but later, when the sky grew black, I forced myself to put on my robe and go out to the kitchen.

The dining hall was empty. The monks were in the midst of the long period of fasting that the Christians call Lent, so that most of the men ate nothing all day except for a brief meal after the evening prayers, but when I told Monk Sarkis that I wasn't well, he sat me down and served me a steaming bowl of lentil stew.

When the first men began to come in from prayers, I gulped down the last of the stew and headed for the door. But as I was making my way against the stream of men, I heard Monk Anton call out to me, "Yusef! There you are! I've been looking for you all day." He moved toward me, and before I could answer him, he put a hand on my shoulder and exclaimed, "Good news! Sophocles's *Antigone* is back in the library, and Monk Gibreel is holding it in reserve for me. We'll begin tomorrow."

That night should have been one of my happiest at Mar Yuhanon, but instead I was plagued with fits of coughing. When the monks rose for prayers, I stayed in bed, too ill to move. Visions of my father haunted the room; he was talking to me, explaining something, but I couldn't hear him. I stretched out my hand to touch him, but he was always just beyond my grasp. Finally, when a thin white light had already slipped through the shutters, I fell into a deep and dreamless sleep.

When I woke, the sun had risen over the hills, flooding the valleys outside my window with golden light. I forced myself to rise, drink some hot tea in the empty dining hall, and then head for work at the looms, where Monk Yakub informed me that Monk Anton had left a message that I was to meet him in front of the library following afternoon prayers.

Finally, I had a reason to praise God, for He was about to fulfill the hopes of long weeks of deception and hardship. As I stood in prayer amongst the monks, chanting their now familiar songs of praise, I envisioned myself with Monk Anton, sitting in his remote corner of the library, he reading to himself from the Greek and painstakingly translating each passage for me, while I sat with closed eyes, transported to my father's study.

But as I neared the library, I was surprised to see that several monks had gathered where we were to meet. Apparently Monk Anton thought to turn our reading of *Antigone* into a group study session. Monk Hurmiz and Hiba, the novice whom I had often seen alongside the translators in the library were there, as were the monks Emavus, Narsai, and Babai, the same three men whom I had heard speaking of Sophocles on the night before I meant to leave Mar Yuhanon. "Yusef, you're here," Monk Anton greeted me. "Look what an esteemed group your book has attracted." But he quickly turned his attention to the rest, who were in the midst of a heated discussion. "I say we use the empty room beside Rabban Basilius's office," he proposed.

"I say we use the library itself; after all, we are going to be reading——"

"No, we'll make too much noise. The dining hall would be better."

"The dining hall? That's the worst place for a reading!"

After several minutes of such argument, Monk Anton's suggestion eventually won over the others, and we all made our way to the empty room in the dormitory courtyard. Though the air in the room was cold, warm sunbeams streamed onto the floor, filling the room with pleasant light. Once we had each settled on our mats, Monk Anton opened the faded leather volume on a reading stand before him, looked around at us and declared, "This is a fine gathering."

"Indeed," Monk Emavus replied. "Let's hope that the illustrious Sophocles will prove worthy of an afternoon's work."

"Oh, there's little doubt of that," Monk Babai said. "I, for one, am intrigued by the fact that both Plato and Aristotle praise Sophocles in their writings."

"Before we begin I'd like to thank Monk Anton," Monk Nasrai said, "for suggesting this reading."

Monk Anton glanced at me. "Your thanks are due to Yusef. He is the one who inspired me to undertake it at all." All eyes turned toward me, and I saw their expressions of surprise, but I said nothing and merely nodded with humility. "Shall we begin, then? Monk Hurmiz and I have agreed that I'll read from the original Greek, and then he'll then translate, so as to compensate for differences in our proficiency." I thought of my father then. I closed my eyes and tried to evoke his presence as if he too sat among us, nodding with satisfaction as I fulfilled his wish that I know Antigone's story.

Monk Anton read out the first lines. Though I didn't understand a word, I could feel the rhythm of the ancient language resounding with weight and power. Monk Hurmiz closed his eyes and nodded, as though the words were flowing over his mind like a slow stream of water. And then, in a low but stirring voice, he translated:

O sister! Ismene dear, dear sister Ismene!
You know how heavy the hand of God is upon us...

ANTIGONE AND HER sister Ismene live in the palace of their uncle, Creon, king of Thebes. They are orphans, and their warrior brothers, Etocles and Polynices have died in battle. But while Etocles fought for King Creon, Polynices joined the enemy, and fate willed that the two fight a hand-to-hand battle, in which each killed the other. Now the war is over, and peace has come, and Antigone is engaged to marry Creon's son Hæmon.

King Creon decrees that Etocles be given a hero's burial, with full honors of state, while Polynices corpse will be left to rot ignominiously in the fields. Creon will suffer no disobedience. Anyone who attempts to bury the body of Polynices will be put to death by stoning.

Ismene complies with the wishes of the king, but Antigone will not consent. She can't bear the thought of the vultures feasting on her brother's unburied corpse, even though the slightest violation of Creon's orders means the risk of death. She goes to the field where Polynices's corpse lies, digs at the ground with her bare hands, and buries him.

The first night, she goes unnoticed, but the king's guards find Polynice's body and shake off the dirt, so that it's once again exposed to the sky. The next night, Antigone goes out to the field again. She brings a bronze urn, so as to make a ceremonial offering. But this time she's spotted by the guards, seized, and brought to the palace. Creon is furious that Antigone has dared to contradict his decree. But Antigone's refusal to admit her wrongdoing angers him more. Antigone is not afraid. She insists that she has obeyed the laws of the gods and she will bear any punishment, even death.

Antigone's obstinacy is a mystery to Creon; it's obvious to all that a traitor should be denied the honors that are the right of a loyal soldier. He is not happy to punish Antigone, for she is his niece and future daughter-in-law; yet to forgo the death sentence would make a mockery of his own words and invite the scorn of his subjects.

Creon orders that Antigone be sealed in cave. But then the prophet Teresias appears, claiming that the gods demand that he pardon Antigone immediately. He warns Creon that if he refuses, his son Hæmon will die. After Teresias takes his leave, Creon sees his own folly, and is frightened. He goes to out to the field himself to retrieve the corpse of Polynices and save Antigone. But he is too late. He and his son Hæmon open the cave, only to find that Antigone has hanged herself. Devastated, Hæmon kills himself by leaning on his sword. When Creon's wife Euridice hears of her son's death, she too kills herself. The house of Creon has been destroyed.

At the close of the play, Creon says: *I am nothing. I have no life. Lead me away...*

And the chorus answers him: *Of happiness the crown and chiefest part is wisdom, and to hold the gods in awe. This is the law that, seeing the stricken heart of pride brought down, we learn when we are old.*

MONK HURMIZ'S VOICE fell silent. A profound hush hung in the air, as if the power of speech had abandoned us all.

"This play is a masterpiece." Monk Emavus broke the quiet of the room like a stone cast upon a pool of still water. "Even if Sophocles had no knowledge of the Almighty, he must have felt his presence within his soul."

"Indeed," agreed Monk Hurmiz. "It's almost as if he had a Christian sensibility. Antigone's capacity for suffering recalls the sufferings of Our Lord."

"As does her choice," remarked Hiba, "again and again, of duty and obedience to the gods, even at the price of her own life. What a noble figure she is."

Monk Anton nodded. "Yes, but what do you make of Creon?"

"Creon?" Hiba frowned. "He's a mere villain. History is full of men whose craving for power leads them into the abyss. Did the Greeks not consider pride to be the worst of all sins?"

"What is it about Creon that interests you?" Babai asked.

"Well, if we consider the play in terms of good and evil, then we can find several places where Creon is given a chance to take back his words and forgive Antigone. Yet each time, he insists that he cannot."

"Perhaps we can liken him to Pharaoh, refusing that Moses take the Children of Israel out of Egypt," Monk Emavus suggested.

Monk Anton nodded. "Exactly. Creon disdains the will of the gods. In this way, he knowingly chooses to do evil."

"He chooses, or God makes him choose?" Monk Nasrai asked cryptically.

Monk Hurmiz rolled his eyes. "Sophocles was a pagan. What did he know of a God in Heaven?"

"He may not have known a God in Heaven, but he knew right from wrong," Monk Nasrai replied. "Obviously the notion of man endowed with the power of moral choice was not unfamiliar to the pagans."

"Nasrai, you raise a question that didn't exist at the times when Sophocles lived," Monk Hurmiz reminded him. "His gods had neither the power nor the infinite knowledge of the Almighty. After all, Sophocles was not present at the Council of Ephesus, when Augustine's predestination won out against the notion of Pelagian free will."

I followed their talk with rapt attention, for the play had evoked fountains of wisdom in their minds. My father would surely have wanted to hear their impressions, and so I tried to feel his presence again, but like the lifting of an ephemeral morning mist, I was suddenly aware that that he was no longer with me. All at once I was overcome with loneliness, for I knew then that he was finally and irrevocably gone.

"And that is why we must all ask ourselves," Monk Nasrai was saying, "can we too claim the humility and self-sacrifice of Antigone? Or are we weak and spineless, like Ismene? The answer is only conjecture until the moment of truth exposes us. Only when we are truly tested is the strength of our faith revealed."

The others nodded in thoughtful agreement, but my thoughts remained with Antigone; try as I did to admire her righteousness, her story troubled me, and the more I pondered it, the more I thought her a fool. True, she had suffered, but her life was about to take a turn for the better. She was about to marry, to begin a life as wife to a prince, and yet she had turned her back on this happy fate. And for what? To die alone in a cave!

Surely I had earned the right to judge her, for I too had been tested. But unlike the noble Antigone, when *my* moment of truth came, I had left my father lying in a pool of his own blood. The memory of it was the harshest of punishments, a curse more terrible than being sealed in a cave.

WHILE CAUGHT UP in the story of Antigone, I was able to forget my illness, but as soon as the reading ended and the discussion began to grow dull, I felt the heat of sickness rising in my bones. When I could no longer sit with them, I rose from my mat, protesting that I was unwell, and went directly to bed. Night fell, and I drifted in and out of sleep, tossing on my bed of straw, both sweating and trembling with cold. Visions of my father passed through my dreams, but instead of greeting him with longing, I cried out to him, *Why did you have me dress as a man, and masquerade as a Christian, just so I could read that cursed book? It's nothing but a foolish tale of a foolish girl! Surely you don't approve of her. We both know that if I had stayed to bury you it would have been the end of me.*

My father said nothing but merely stared back, as if disappointed. Well, he could be disappointed if he wanted. His last conversation with me had only led me into folly. And now, when I was sick as a stray dog with no one to care for me, I would be lucky to survive this madness.

The next morning, my head was swimming. My bones ached with fever, and each gust of fresh air from my window brought on a new fit of coughing. When I failed to show up in the kitchen, Monk Sarkis came to my room with a cup of hyssop tea. He had some basic knowledge of medicines, most of it learned in the kitchen of his grandmother, and it was he who usually took on the task of administering to anyone in the monastery who fell ill.

My eyes fluttered open. I wanted to sit up, to thank him and apologize for leaving him alone in the kitchen, but I could barely lift my head. "Don't spend your strength," he told me. "You need rest. Perhaps we should send word to Ibn Bahlul."

In spite of my delirious state, the name set my heart pounding with alarm. Ibn Bahlul was an esteemed physician from Irbil who was called in whenever a monk's condition grew dire. More than once, I had helped Monk Sarkis carry food and drink to the chamber of a sick man, only to come upon the physician leaning over the bed of a patient, opening his robes and moving his hands carefully over his bare chest. "No," I whispered hoarsely. "There's no need."

I tried to sleep after he left, but the mortifying notion of Ibn Bahlul examining me, most likely in the presence of Monk Elias, compelled me to remain vigilant. Visions of the brothers, their faces twisted in shock and fury, kept my every bone in a state of alertness.

The next evening, Monk Elias came in the company of Rabban Basilius. The Hegumenos of Mar Yuhanon knelt by my bed and put his hand on my forehead. Through my hazy vision, I could barely make out their worried faces and whispered words. "God preserve you, Yusef," Rabban Basilius told me. "If your condition hasn't improved by tomorrow, we'll send for Ibn Bahlul." He frowned as if considering a problem, and glanced at Monk Elias. "The fast of Holy Friday is upon us. We may have to call in a Jewish physician."

I tried to shake my head, but Monk Elias smiled kindly. "We've called on Avraham Halevi before; rest assured that in matters of medicine, he is entirely competent."

A wave of dread washed over me. *I'm doomed*, I thought, but there was no way to avert what was going to happen. All that remained was to watch my fall into ignominy unfold.

A night and day of near oblivion passed before my door opened and Monk Elias led an unfamiliar man dressed in the turban of a Jew into my room. My bones felt as heavy as iron rods. Even at this fateful moment, I wanted nothing more than to sleep.

I recall it all only as the vaguest of memories. How Avraham Halevi greeted me in a kindly voice, how he asked my name and how I answered him in a delirious mumble: Rahel. How he glanced at Monk Elias, no doubt puzzled by the notion that an inhabitant of Mar Yuhanon bore the name of a Jewish matriarch.

"And your father's name?" he continued, staring at me.

"Yair," I whispered, as though yearning to reveal it. "Yair ben Shmuel."

He said nothing but proceeded to open the belt of my robe, and raise my tunic above my leggings, to encounter the head scarf that bound my chest. And then the dry warmth of his hand as he loosened the knot that held the scarf in place and slipped it under the scarf, over my faintly beating heart.

Oh, the humiliation! The savage shame of exposure! It's difficult to recall the look of surprise on Avraham Halevi's face, and the stare of profound confusion on Monk Elias's. As if in a dream I heard Abraham Halevi ask, "Are you aware that this monk is a woman... and I think, quite possibly, a Jew?"

"He's what?" Monk Elias whispered, as if certain he hadn't heard properly. "What did you say?"

The physician gently eased the scarf downward, as if to offer proof of his discovery. Monk Elias merely gasped, open-mouthed and wide-eyed, and then abruptly turned his gaze from the offending sight. Did he look again, his hand clasped over his mouth, his eyes wide with horror? Perhaps time has made the memory more dramatic. On the other hand, it is possible that this is exactly what I saw.

Time must have passed, but I couldn't have said if it had been hours or days. Occasionally, my delirium was pierced by the sound of footsteps at my bedside and low voices. I would open my eyes to find Monk Sarkis at my bedside, urging me to drink a cup of hyssop tea, or trying to feed me some cooked barley or lentils. Now, when word must have spread through Mar Yuhanon that I was an imposter, he was the only one to show me the charity that the Christians prize. And if I finally overcame the illness that might have killed me, it is entirely thanks to his efforts. For one afternoon, I woke as one who's struggled through a violent storm. Though my chest ached from coughing and my clothes were damp with sweat, the fever had passed. My head felt light and cool, and when I touched my hair my fingers were met not with a cap but with short, matted hair.

I felt myself to be as lowly as a criminal, caught in a foolish crime. Most people endure their judgment day only after death, but I would have to suffer for my sins while still a girl. And there was no doubt in my mind that the punishment would be terrible; the monks could not tolerate a woman in their midst, and they detested Jews.

I had almost succeeded in frightening myself into a stupor when Rabban Basilius entered my chamber, accompanied by Monk Elias. I sat up, pulling my blanket close around me.

The two sat down on the low stools that someone had placed by my bedside, and regarded me, not in the heat of anger, but rather as foreign and distasteful presence in their midst. "Miss Rahel," Rabban

Basilius addressed me in the stern tone he often used when reading the scriptures. "The time has come for us to have a little talk."

I nodded soberly. "The deception that you have worked on the trusting men of this house is treacherous indeed. You've taken advantage of our good will, and made a mockery of our way of life. Were you in good health, we would have asked you to leave Mar Yuhanon at once. Yet I could not, in good conscience, send a sick girl into the wilderness. Against the counsel of others, I insisted that you remain until your health improves. However, I have given orders that no one except for Monk Sarkis and Monk Elias are to enter your room."

He paused, staring at me with unmasked fascination. "You see Miss Rahel, I look at you and I see not a liar or a swindler, but a confused child. Though you've shown us little more than cunning and duplicity, I believe that it's not for me to punish you, but to help you." Though I could not meet his eye, I nodded again.

"In any case, I'm pleased to inform you that the matter has been settled. Avraham Halevi, the physician who attended you, has kindly agreed to bring your case before the elders of the Jewish community of Mosul. I assume that they'll deal with you as befits your troubling behavior. In two days, Halevi will return, and you'll be turned over to his guardianship."

"God bless you, sir. I . . . I . . . I'm sorry," I stammered.

"That is good to hear. You have much to be sorry for." Without waiting for any response, Rabban Basilius rose and left the room. Monk Elias shook his head in reproach and followed close behind. With a sigh I sank back into my bed. The whole affair had been strangely uneventful; rather than condemn me as a sinner headed toward the bonfires of Hell, they seemed to regard me as no worse than a nuisance.

And now, in his kindness, Rabban Basilius was going to put me in the hands of a good and righteous Jew who would possibly help me to find a groom. I would go with him to Mosul, where he would take me to the town rabbis. Hopefully they would select someone as worthy as the man my father chose for me, for in spite of everything, I wanted to believe that I was still a worthy bride. Worthy, that is, except for my secret flaw. Surely it was possible to conceal that flaw; among the girls of Sura, stories were whispered about girls who didn't bleed on their wedding nights, though there could be no doubt of their virginity.

Excitedly, I rose from my sickbed and went to the window. I unhooked the heavy clasp and pushed open the shutters, so that the wide horizon of the valley lay before me. The day was cool, and the leaves on the trees fluttered in the cold breezes, but the sun was shining, lighting up the fields below with a warm light. I could hear distant sounds of sheep bells, and sure enough, a flock soon wandered into view, with their shepherd, Monk Tuma, prodding them on.

My father had selected a promising young scholar for me, but would the rabbis of Mosul do the same? I might have to settle for one of the lesser scholars. Or, I reflected unhappily, a boy who was not a scholar at all. For they would not see me not as the daughter of the physician, Yair Ben Shmuel. All they would know of me was that I had disguised myself as a boy and gone to live among the Christians at Mar Yuhanon. And if they knew only this, perhaps they would see me as a girl suitable only for a man whose strange, unsavory history matched my own—a queer old bachelor, for example, or the village fool.

I looked out at the empty hills, watching the flock plod across the valley. And then I heard the voice of Monk Tuma, just below my window, arguing with a wayward sheep. "Come on, Fatma, we're disturbing the monks! Move on and join the rest." The sheep bleated back loudly, as if insisting, *I'll come when I'm ready*. Yet she must have known that in fact, she had no say in the matter.

I am that sheep, I thought, with the astonishment of one waking from a dream. Rabban Basilius and Avraham Halevi would settle my fate. All that was required of me was to do whatever they decided was best.

I ENVISIONED AVRAHAM Halevi as he came before the rabbis. After swearing them to strict secrecy, he would describe how he went to Mar Yuhanon to examine a sick boy, and how he had discovered that unbeknown to the unsuspecting monks, the Christian boy was, in fact, a Jewish girl. No doubt the rabbis of Mosul would be appalled, and perhaps wonder if I were insane. In a few days time, when he brought me back with him to Mosul, I would have to explain myself to these men, to suffer their incredulous gaze and answer their every question. And doubtless there would be a moment when they would ask, respectfully, with lowered eyes, if I was still a virgin. How would I answer them? To pretend to be a virgin was to risk being caught in a lie, but if I told them the truth, my value as a bride would be far lower.

These were my thoughts when the door to my room opened abruptly. It was Monk Elias, who seemed to avail himself of every opportunity to visit me. I thought to feign exhaustion, but I saw that Monk Anton was with him. "In spite of Rabban Basilius's explicit instructions, Monk Anton insists on seeing you." I sat up slowly, for of all the men of Mar Yuhanon, it was towards him that I felt the most remorse. Now, as he regarded me as one regards an unmasked criminal, I could barely find the courage to face him.

"It appears you're feeling better this morning," Monk Elias remarked. "I hope you're aware that when Halevi returns, you'll be leaving the premises with him."

Monk Anton said nothing. I knew that he would remain silent until he had composed precisely what he wanted to say. But Monk Elias had no such reticence. "The tranquility of this house has been shaken by your deviousness. Shimun, Estefan, Monk Nidal, Monk Yakub, Monk Gibreel, and particularly Monk Anton here, are terribly distraught. And the notion that I'm the one responsible for this dreadful error gives me no peace."

He had begun quietly, but now, incited by his own words, his tone grew louder and angrier. "I wanted only to extend the hand of kindness to a fellow Christian, as you claimed to be, to offer you shelter and guidance. But you deceived me, as you proceeded to deceive Rabban Basilius, and all the upright men of this house. Shame on you! You're no better than Eve, leading Adam to his downfall in the Garden of Eden. You are as cunning as Delilah, leading Samson to his capture and death. You are as stupid as Lot's wife, who could not master her urge to see that which was forbidden to her, and you are as Godless as the Israelite women, dancing before the golden calf. But God above sees all, and you will pay dearly for your lies."

"I . . . I want to—"

"I must agree with all that Monk Elias has said." The voice that cut me off, haughty and hard, was Monk Anton's. I looked up sharply. "But where he sees in you the treachery of Delilah and the guile of Eve, your behavior reminds me of that of a common thief. You disguised yourself in order to know what you could not by any other means. I have given of my time, my effort, and my good will to a mere girl, a mere Jewish girl! Rahel is your name? Well Rahel, you have tricked me into giving what was never yours to have!"

His words stung me like a slap. I thought of those afternoons when we would sit in the corner of the library, reading from books that were like rays of light in the darkness. How was it possible that he now looked upon those afternoons with regret and considered me a villain? For without knowing me, he had perceived within me things so concealed that I myself scarcely recognized them.

I looked up at him now, not cowering but steady, and spoke words that only he, of all the men of Mar Yuhanon, could fathom. "My name and clothes may have been a deception, but the delight that I came to take in your books was real. If you could only ignore all that is...external, you would realize that when we spoke of those books, I revealed more of my true nature than any woman's dress could tell you."

He remained stonily silent. I glanced at Monk Elias, frowning with contempt. His expression angered me, and provoked me to speak more freely than I would have normally dared. "And if it is the truth you would want, let me ask you this: In this house, you speak of pity, of kindness, of forgiveness, and you indeed have an endless supply of these, but only for people exactly like yourselves. What of kindness to a stranger? What about forgiveness for those who don't share your faith?" I looked into their indignant faces. "It's no secret that your Isho was, as I am, a Jew. And as for Maryam," I laughed tersely, "she was, as I am, a Jewish woman. Can you not find it in your heart to offer your compassion and charity to a flesh and blood daughter of the Jews?"

Monk Anton shook his head, as if to say that I was hopelessly ignorant. "We've heard enough from you," Monk Elias muttered. "What stupidity!" He spun around and left the room. Monk Anton looked at me with a pity reserved for the mad and followed him out.

I sank back into my bed feeling strangely satisfied. How good it was to say the things that I had held inside for so long. It was as refreshing as a splash of cold water on a hot summer afternoon, and as invigorating as rising from a good night's sleep. *No!* I suddenly thought to myself. *I will not go with Avraham Halevi. I'll leave this place before he arrives. I'll start out for Tiflis, and find Hannanya Bar-Ashi, and he will secure the best possible groom for me.*

Though I still lay in my sickbed, I imagined myself again, not as a sheep, but rather, as a dreaming bird. *Tonight*, I said to myself, *I will leave tonight. I'll pack a bag this very night, and steal out the monastery gates.*

I must have drifted back to sleep, for I woke to find Monk Anton sitting by my bedside. "Rabban Basilius has given strict orders that no one enter your room," he said with a defiant grin.

"And yet you're here," I replied, sitting up and rubbing my eyes.

He was looking at me as if trying to comprehend the fact that Yusef the boy and Rahel the girl were the same person. "Rahel," he began, his tone unusually gentle, "this strange turn of events has thrown me into a terrible confusion. I was very upset when I came here earlier. . .and I said some things that I now regret. This morning you posed a difficult question: how can a Christian venerate Maryam, yet ignore the teachings of her son? I've given much thought to your harsh words, and I am ashamed to say that there is truth in them." I gazed at him in wonder, for I knew how difficult it was for him to admit such a thing. "However," he continued, "that is not all that I've come to say. I called you a thief this morning; that was thoughtless and arrogant of me, and I want to ask your forgiveness. Any man who claims to know which of us deserves to acquire knowledge sins against God, for only He determines our true destinies." His eyes, sober and solemn, caught mine. "Will you accept my apology?"

Tears sprang to my eyes. A lump of gratitude formed in my throat, so that for a moment I couldn't speak. "Thank you," I managed to reply. "You've lifted a terrible burden from my heart."

"I couldn't let you leave without telling you that." And now, as a last request, would you share your story with me?"

"If I did, you wouldn't believe even half of it."

"Oh, but I would, Rahel. You're a remarkable girl."

Maybe it was the kindness in his tone, and maybe it was nothing more than the way he was looking at me. How long had it been since anyone had looked at me and seen something true? For the truth, I have found, is far more potent than any drug in a physician's cabinet. I burst into tears and would not be calmed. All the while he sat by my side, patient and undaunted.

When I was able to speak again, I told him much of what had happened to me. I recounted the story of my flight from Sura, and my time as a slave in the home of Omar Alharazi, and of how I came with Habib to Mar Yuhanon, and I told him the reason why, against all good sense, I had taken on the life of a monk and stayed. "But now I see that it has all been for nothing. *Antigone* is just a book, like any other. I thought that I would find my father between its pages, but I found only the story of a foolish girl who dies for nothing." I shook my head as though marveling at my own folly. "It is I who has been tricked."

"Why tricked? How so?"

"How, you ask? Do you think I would ever have *chosen* to stay in this place, the only woman in a house where women are unwelcome, the only Jew in a house of Christians, eating dull food, sleeping on straw, enduring the cold, and spending long days in endless prayer? I thought that if I could only know *Antigone*, I would find something important there, some message from my father that I might take with me and keep. But my longings have only led me on a journey of suffering!"

"Yes. I can see how it's been difficult for you." He paused and then added, "But as for your father, I think he gave you an invaluable gift."

"A gift? What gift? Can you see a message for me in *Antigone*?"

"No. Not a message. Antigone's tale shares nothing with the pleasant life you led in Sura, and your father would never have dreamt what was to happen to you. But just think, Rahel, your father managed to convey to you that the wisdom found between the pages of a book is worth your most earnest efforts. And in this, was he not teaching you that to seek knowledge is a valuable endeavor? Was he not urging you to allow your own thoughts to commune with the thoughts of others? As much as he would have you married and living amongst the Jews, he wanted you to keep a small window in your soul through which you might meet the world. And you took that with you. You carried it on your journey, and that journey led you here, to the library at Mar Yuhanon. If you value any of the knowledge you have acquired, know that in compelling you to search for

Antigone, your father has indeed given you a gift, and it is yours to keep for as long as you live. You are like... like King Saul, who went looking for his lost donkey, and found a kingdom."

His talk rendered me speechless. I closed my eyes, and silent tears began to fall from them again.

"Yes. You have understood. And now I want to confess something to you. I have long imagined a student, a young man who is intelligent, spirited, and questioning. I imagined that I would take that student and teach him, train him in the reading of ancient texts, and help him to bring his own mind to those writings. I envisioned a student who would seek that knowledge with an open heart, and come away in gratitude. And then, one day, I found that student. He appeared in the library, as if sent by God." He nodded as if to himself, and then added softly, "It's been quite a surprise to find that student was a woman."

"I'm so sorry," I whispered.

"There is no need to apologize. You are who you are. And what you are is a student of rare ability. You have not only studied the ideas of Plato and Aristotle, you have struggled with them, argued with them, and speculated on how to improve them." He sighed a regretful sigh. "But now you will return to your rightful path. God willing, you will have sons, and they will inherit their mother's abilities."

"God willing," I repeated.

"I heard that Halevi will soon return to take you to Mosul."

"Yes. It's all been arranged," I admitted hesitantly.

"And you're not pleased with the arrangements?"

"The rabbis of Mosul won't approve of the time I've spent at Mar Yuhanon."

He nodded, and I could see that he understood my meaning. "You must consider your future carefully; circumstance has left you in an unusual situation."

I stared at him blankly. "Circumstance has left me nothing but misery."

For a moment he said nothing, but his eyes took on a faraway look, and I knew that he was thinking of his own life. "You are very young, and what I am going to tell you may sound odd, but I'll say it nonetheless. Listening to your story has put me in mind of the time when I was living with my family. The period before I decided to devote my life to God was a very difficult one. I was, shall we say, restless. I would go for long walks in the hills trying to imagine how it would be to be free."

"But you were free."

"No. I mean truly free. Free of my responsibilities, my obligations. Free of my life." He had spoken as if to himself, but now he looked at me. "Rahel, you are master of your fate. You can go anywhere, do anything, without having to answer to any man. Not even a queen has such freedom."

"Freedom? What do you mean?"

"You speak of marriage," he continued, "and it is most understandable that you do. But when a woman marries, she places all of her dreams, her desires, every detail of her life in the hands of her husband. She does this willingly, because she has no choice. But you—you're all alone in the world; perhaps that seems a curse, but it has nonetheless given you the possibility of choice."

"What choice?"

We sat in silence for a moment, but the silence was tremulous and volatile, as if lightning were about to strike the black skies over the valley. I sat up, fitful and trembling, while Anton turned inward, grasping for the right words. "God has seen fit to grant you...opportunities. Situations that you might encounter were you indeed a man."

"But I am not a man, and all of my time here has been nothing but an act. I was only playing a part."

"Yes. And you played it most successfully. But you were not merely an actress. You were also a dramatist of sorts. You are the author of the character that you created. And if that character was born and bred in your own soul, then you must share in its essential traits."

I was about to answer him, to tell him that those traits which are natural in a man are foreign and strange in a woman, when we heard the sound of footsteps crossing the courtyard. As if a spell had been broken, we shifted postures and changed the tone of our conversation. "I've decided not to go with Avraham Halevi to Mosul," I told him, for I could not bear to mislead him anymore, and I knew now that he would keep my secret. "I'm going to leave Mar Yuhanon tonight."

"All alone? Where will you go?"

"My father has an uncle in Tiflis. I'm going to travel there and find him."

"Tiflis?" he exclaimed. "That is very, very far. Do you even know this man?"

"I've never met him. But I know his name, and I'll find him. Hopefully he'll take me in and seek out the best possible husband for me."

"I see," he replied, but he seemed troubled by my plans. "The city of Tiflis lies many weeks to the north. To get there you'll have to cross steep mountain passes. The roads are poor, and towns are few and far between." He shook his head again as if thinking aloud. "The journey is too difficult to make alone. You'll have to join a caravan."

At that moment, Monk Sarkis knocked on the door to my room and let himself in. I glanced at the tray he carried and saw a bowl of barley stew, an egg, two slices of bread, and a piece of date cake, left over from the meal marking the end of the Fast of Ninveh. Monk Anton rose and excused himself. Monk Sarkis stared after him as he went out.

"It seems my appetite is returning," I said. "I feel as though I haven't eaten in days. Could you possibly bring me something more?"

"Praise God you are indeed recovering," he said with a smile. "God willing you'll be back on your feet very soon." He glanced at my bare head, and then looked down, suddenly bashful. "You know, while we thought you a boy, the men liked you very much. You had all the qualities of a righteous and God-fearing youth."

He left quickly, but returned several minutes later carrying a tray that held two more eggs, some radishes and carrots, half a loaf of bread, and another piece of date cake. "I hear that you'll soon be looking for a groom." He smiled shyly as he placed the tray by my bed. "God willing this will fatten you up. Good night, Miss Rahel. Sleep well," he called as he closed the door to my room.

I needed to sleep, but my mind was raging. I rose from my bed, went to the window, and released the latch of the heavy wooden shutters. Though the night sky was black, a gust of fresh air blew into the room, and I welcomed it, closing my eyes and taking in deep, exuberant breaths. Soon I would be out there, where nothing was certain. But I would find a way to get to Tiflis. I would find Hannanya Bar-Ashi and his Karaite wife. I would pretend that I was still a virgin—after masquerading as a boy, the role of virgin would be child's play—and I would marry the finest and most promising young man he could find for me.

With this happy thought in mind, I lifted my mattress and pulled out Shafiqa's bag. I hadn't touched it since the day I moved into my room, and I was relieved to find the clothes I wore on the day I arrived, still folded exactly as I had left them. As I felt around inside for the knife, something small and hard grazed my fingertips and then disappeared. Curious, I moved my fingers gingerly along the bottom of the bag, and sure enough, they came upon a small hole between the bag's inner lining and the outer cloth. I dug my finger inside, tearing into its lining until they grasped the mystery object. When I drew out my hand it held a gold ring, set with a brilliant green emerald.

For a moment, I could only stare in astonishment, for I recognized it immediately. It was the ring that Hassan's father had given to me at the inn in Baghdad, in reward for caring for his son's fractured leg. I was certain that I had left the ring on the table with Hassan's father. So how could it possibly be here with me now?

Perplexed, I tried to retrace what had happened that afternoon in Baghdad. Hassan and I had gone to buy saffron in the market. And then, before we set out, Hassan's father had come running after me, clutching my bag. "You've forgotten this," he had cried. "Take care not to let it out of your sight again!" So that was it! He must have slipped the ring into my bag before returning it. I turned the little ring over in my palm; like a secret treasure, it had been in my possession all along. And then, as I pondered my plans, an outrageous idea began to take shape.

Freedom. Choice. Monk Anton's words burned in my mind. They gave rise to things I had never dared to think. And now, with the little ring nestled in my hand, the world was expanding before my very eyes.

ALL NIGHT I lay awake, waiting for that early hour of the morning when everyone at Mar Yuhanon lay asleep in their beds. As I thought over my final conversation with Monk Anton, I was sorry that I hadn't parted from him properly. Yet I wanted nothing more than to be outside the monastery walls, and on my way to Tiflis.

When the dark sky over the hills began to fade to gray, I removed my monk's clothing, wound my headscarf about my chest, put on the tunic and robe that I had worn the day I came to Mar Yuhanon, and set my boy's cap on my head. The blanket from my home in Sura lay at the bottom of my bag, and on top of it I packed the extra food that Monk Sarkis had brought me. The water flask was stiff with dryness, but still fit for use. I slipped my feet into Khalil's boots, and I was ready. Just then, I heard a soft knock on my door. I froze, and watched it slowly open.

It was Monk Anton, a large traveler's satchel strapped across his shoulder. "I've brought some things for you," he said. I watched as he took the bag from his shoulder, untied it, and took out two stones for starting fires, a rope, three skins of wine, and a pouch of sunflower seeds. "This bag is fit for a traveler," he told me. "Give me that sack of yours." I handed him Shafiqa's bag, and watched as he transferred the food, the blanket, the knife, and then the sack itself to the bag he had brought.

I was about to try to thank him, to shower on him all of the blessings that I knew, but then he stuck his hand in the pocket of his robe and pulled out a rolled parchment. "This," he said solemnly, "is most important of all." He unrolled the parchment to reveal a finely drawn map. "It shows most of the roads and towns between Baghdad and Damascus. You see we are here," he explained, pointing to an illustration of the monastery, "and this is the road to Mosul."

"But you may need this one day."

"You will need it more. Now listen carefully. My family's inn stands three days from Mosul on the road leading west to Damascus. Even though it means straying from your plans, you must go to the inn. The place has been in my father's family for four generations but now, since my father's death, my mother oversees all. Tell her that I've sent you, and she'll provide you with good maps of all the roads leading north. My brothers, Daoud and Leo, will advise you about the best route to take on your journey to Tiflis. Promise me that you will go to her. Without good maps and guidance, you may never reach your destination."

I took the map from him gratefully. "I'll go to the inn," I promised. "What is your mother's name?"

"Luna. Her name is Luna. If you get lost, ask for the way to Luna's Inn, on the road between Mosul and Nisibin. You'll meet my family: Daoud, and Leo, and my sisters Olivia and Marsa." He grinned enigmatically, as he often did when he was thinking his private thoughts.

"Why do you smile?"

"They'll treat you well, but don't try to deceive them. They've seen far more of the world than the gullible monks of Mar Yuhanon. Tell them only the truth. Answer their questions faithfully, and they will take you in and treat you as one of their own."

"They sound very different from their pious brother."

"I suspect they would do poorly in a monastery."

I gazed at him quizzically. "Rabban Basilius will be furious if he finds out that you've assisted me."

"Indeed." He grinned again. "Perhaps I have a little bit of Antigone in me." He was regarding me now as if still incredulous, and still puzzled. And then, in a moment of clarity, I understood the magnitude of my debt to him.

I should have fallen at his feet, as one falls at the feet of an emperor who has given you the most dazzling of gifts, and embraced him, as one embraces a true friend. But I knew that he disliked spectacle and emotion. And so I told him, as if replying to the words he had spoken at my bedside the night before, "If I have found a kingdom, then it was you who led me there."

He nodded the slightest of nods. He seemed to be looking beyond my boy's cap and man's robes into my eyes, as if they might hold the key to what was, for him, an elusive riddle. "May God keep you and protect you, Rahel," he blessed me. He took my hands in his, and held them tightly. Then he turned and left. From my doorway, I watched as he crossed the courtyard and walked out in the direction of the church. When he was gone from view, I strapped his satchel over my shoulder, passed through the low beams of the doorway, and closed the door behind me.

Silently, I made my way down to the well by the front gates, where I filled my flask. Then I lifted the heavy iron latch and stepped out.

The road that wound through the hills was long and empty, but the spring rains must have stirred something in the earth, for the rocky fields had blossomed into a sea of white and yellow wildflowers.

FREEDOM

The sky above me turned gray, and the winter winds made the wild bushes sway as though in a dance. Soon, fat drops of rain were running down the sides of my face and washing the grime and dust from my skin. I was cold and wet, yet I was as jubilant as an escaped prisoner, for I had freed myself from two masters: the monks of Mar Yuhanon and the Jews of Mosul. The fear I once felt on the roads had fallen away, and the lightness of my step made me feel like if I only wanted, I could fly.

For the first time in many months, my plans were clear and certain; I would go to Tiflis, I would find Hannanya Bar-Ashi, and together we would select a husband for me. The very thought of the boys I would find there delighted me, for the long months spent in the company of men had somehow calmed my dread of the marriage bed, and my anxiety about having to play a virgin was mixed with a secret curiosity that was unseemly for the role. Would my future husband be tall and thin, like Shimun, or fair, like Monk Nidal? Heavyset with big, wide eyes, like Monk Sarkis, or perhaps, by some mysterious trick of ancestry, blue-eyed like Monk Gibreel? In my choice of husband, I would not be fussy. My sole requirements were that his face be fine and that his mind be sharp.

Now, with the small green treasure at the bottom of my bag, I was a wealthy woman. I could easily afford a seat in a caravan, where I could travel like a queen. But as I walked down the road that first morning, there was something about the idea that troubled me. Maybe it was nothing more than Monk Anton's strange words that echoed in my mind like a fly that won't go away. *Freedom,* he had said. And *choice*. As if he were speaking to one of the village boys who came to work in the vineyards.

And yet there was truth in it. Here I was on a highway between two towns, with no one in the world to care if I lived or died. Or if I walked or traveled in a caravan or rode on horseback as I had with Hassan. As I recalled the sensation of sailing across a green field atop a racing horse, a rush of joy surged though me, flooding me with a longing that I could feel in my blood. A girl has no use for freedom or for choice, but the thought of riding a horse once more enthralled me, and the little ring in my bag made me fanciful and reckless.

THERE WERE FEW people about that morning, for the sky had carried a warning of certain rain, and most, unlike me, did not relish the thought of getting wet. I walked for several hours in the light but steady drizzle without meeting a soul, until I was passed by a boy on a donkey pulling a wagon. An old man and woman were sitting in the back of the cart, huddling beneath a blanket they held over their heads. As they passed I greeted them, and they waved back at me. After a minute or two the wagon came to a stop, and the driver turned and called out, "Good day, my brother. Can I offer you a ride? My grandparents can't stand to see you out in the rain like a stray cat." He must have been about fifteen or sixteen years of age, with a ruddy face and a crooked-toothed smile.

"Allah preserve you," I replied. "But I prefer to walk."

"As you like," he said, shaking his head as one marvels at the bizarre behavior of hermits, and continued down the road. But soon the rain came down stronger, and as my robe grew cold and heavy, I regretted not taking the ride. When, a short while later, I spotted the three of them crouched in the shelter of a cave by the side of the road, I accepted their invitation to join them.

They had built a small fire, and a blackened pot sat at the cave's opening, collecting the thin stream of water that ran down from the roof. As I sat myself down, the three of them stared at me. "Where's your father, boy?" the old man asked.

"He's dead," I told them, in a tone that sounded, to me, oddly matter of fact. "I'm on my own."

"It's a hard life, alone on the road," the old woman remarked.

"*Insha'Allah*, I'll reach my destination."

"We are all headed toward one destination, whether we wish it or not," the old man remarked, "and our journey is in the hands of Allah."

"Praise be to Allah, the fulfiller of destinies," the old woman added, pointing to the sky. "Where are you going, my son?"

I knew that I had to be careful now, for if anyone knew that I had a valuable ring in my bag, I would be as a welcoming beacon to tricksters and thieves. "In the village up ahead, there's a Christian dealer in horses who owes us a large sum of money. My father sent me to procure a horse in payment of the debt."

"Eh!" The woman spat on the ground. "You want to get a horse out of that Christ-worshiper, Ibn Tawfiq?" the old woman asked.

"He owes us," I replied, trying to keep my tone even, for I knew that they were speaking of Shimun's father. I was surprised that in spite of his conversion, he was still considered a Christian.

"My son, don't go to Ibn Tawfiq," the old man said gravely. "He's a scoundrel, a thief, and a villain." He bent in close to me, as if to share a secret. "Some time ago, a cousin of my mother's was looking to buy a horse. He's a good man, but also a fool. Ibn Tawfiq managed to trick him into buying a sick mare, and the horse died a month afterward. We took him before the Qadi, but that son of a snake claimed that my cousin fed the horse moldy oats. That scoundrel must have paid the Qadi well; he wasted no time in ruling against us." He shook his head in resignation. "Ah well, we should leave it to Allah to dispense justice. But as for you, he'll take one look at your smooth face and see a gullible boy"

I grinned slyly. "The better to fool him."

He smiled broadly. "A jackal in the skin of a lamb. But are you a match for him?"

"Is it not easier to deceive the arrogant than the humble?" I replied. The three of them broke out into hearty laughter.

"You speak like a scholar!" the old man cried. "God help you in your mission. After we drink our tea, I'll tell you something more about Ibn Tawfiq."

I nodded eagerly, but the old man was in no hurry. He opened his bag, drew out a small sack of mixed herbs, brought the leaves to his nose and inhaled deeply. "Aziz, bring the water," he ordered his grandson. The boy stuck a long arm out of the cave and retrieved the pot, now filled to the brim with rain, while the grandmother set out four clay cups. The old man submerged the leaves in the pot, and steam rose up, filling the cave with the sharp smell of the herbs. After several minutes of slow stirring, he poured the green tea while his wife brought out a sack filled with date cakes, similar to those Monk Sarkis had prepared for the Christmas feast.

"What were you going to say about Ibn Tawfiq?" Aziz asked excitedly.

The old man rapped him on the head. "Not while we're enjoying our tea, you donkey."

Only after the entire pot of tea had been consumed, and the old woman was washing the cups in the drizzle, did the old man reveal what he knew. "Ibn Tawfiq is a thief and a villain," he began, "and us locals know it. He can't trick us, so he tries to sell his tired old horses to any stranger he can cheat. But he and his brothers all ride handsome steeds with long strides." He thrust out his chest as if imitating the proud posture of a rich man. "Good strong horses bred from the seed of Najib. Have you heard of Najib?"

I shook my head. "Najib's father rode in the Caliph's cavalry," Aziz explained. "Ibn Tawfiq bribed an officer to sell him a foal, and now he breeds Najib's offspring for the sons of governors and rich merchants."

The old man put a hand on my shoulder and drew me closer. "When you go to Ibn Tawfiq, refuse any horse that he tries to sell you. Stand firm and tell him that you'll accept nothing but a descendant of Najib."

"Najib. I'll remember. He won't cheat me," I assured him.

The old man seemed pleased with me. I supposed he was envisioning how I would repay Ibn Tawfiq's treachery. "Ride on with us," he told me, "and I'll show you the road to the village. When you get there, look for the largest villa on the hillside; that scoundrel built it with money stolen from honest men."

By the time he drew the wagon to a halt and pointed me in the direction of the village, the rain had stopped, and the hazy traces of a rainbow had opened over the treetops. I watched as the wagon disappeared into the horizon of the road, and then, after scanning the bushes along the side of the road so as to make sure that I was alone, I retrieved the ring from my bag and slid it onto my middle finger. It was a man's ring, so large that it could easily have slid off. I held it up to the sky, delighting in the way its deep green glimmered in the sunlight.

It occurred to me that I could have used my ring to secure a ride to Tiflis, and perhaps this is exactly what I would have done had I still been the naïve, virtuous girl that I once was in Sura. Yet if that virtuous girl were to meet me as I walked down the muddy road to the village, she surely wouldn't have recognized me. I am not speaking only of my boy's cap and dusty cloak, for there was something else, a certain inner quality that cast its light through to my outer demeanor. Or perhaps it was nothing more than a new resolve in my step.

THE STENCH OF the horses grew stronger as I made my way up to the gate of Ibn Tawfiq's estate, but this only served to heighten my determination. I pulled on the bell rope, and a servant soon appeared. "You'll have to wait," he said with a contemptuous glance at my mud splattered clothing. "The master is with a very important personage this afternoon. It could take a while."

"I've come to buy a horse," I told him. "For my master."

"And who might that be?"

"Omar Alharazi, the silk merchant from Baghdad. He insisted that I come here, to Ibn Tawfiq's stables, in order to buy a horse from the seed of Najim."

I tried to appear as earnest as possible, but the doubt in his expression made me wonder if he suspected my lies. "Come with me," he said after a long moment. I followed him down a stone path that led around the back of the property to a vine-covered porch. I guessed, by the finely crafted mosaic floor and the polished copper table, that this was where Ibn Tawfiq entertained his customers. The porch looked out over an expansive walled yard, where several horses were grazing contentedly. "Please make yourself comfortable. You can watch the horses while you wait." He glanced again at my robe and asked, "Whom may I say is here?"

"Yusef is my name," I told him. I sat myself down on a cushion and looked out at the yard below. Two men were examining the hooves of a beautiful black horse. I assumed that the older one was Ibn Tawfiq, and the younger, dressed in riding boots and a cloak of deep purple, was the important customer. I watched as he mounted the horse with an agility that appeared effortless, and rode him around the yard. After circling several times, he brought the horse back to the center and guided him through a series of sharp, sudden turns.

The horseman's skill troubled me, and a fear came over me that I would soon be exposed for the imposter that I was. But when I looked out at the horses grazing in the damp grass, I willed myself to not to lose heart. Soon the servant returned with a pot of tea and a bowl of apples. He glanced up at the wooden lattice windows that looked into the house, and following his gaze, I saw that a veiled woman was watching us. Though her eyes were on me for no longer than a second, I guessed, judging by their downward turn that she was Shimun's mother.

I had thought to keep my connection to Shimun a secret, but it suddenly occurred to me that if this woman knew that I had been a friend of her son's, she might want to help me in some way. "Tell the lady of the house that I want to speak with her," I whispered to the servant. "Tell her that...that I've been to Mar Yuhanon." The servant stared at me, confused, so I whispered again, "It's important. Tell her now!"

I prayed that he would give my message to her, and in a matter of seconds, she slipped out and sat down beside me, her sad eyes hungry for news of her son. "He is well," I told her. "I've seen him, and he is well."

She clasped my hands tightly and held my eyes in an anxious gaze. "When were you at Mar Yuhanon?"

"Not three days ago."

"God bless you, my son. Has he received his monk's mantle?"

"He'll take his vows in the coming year."

She closed her eyes and crossed herself, not slowly like the monks, but with a swift, almost imperceptible movement. "You've brought me great joy," she told me. "May Christ watch over you." Again she took my hands in her own and squeezed them tightly, as if I myself had carried some small part of Shimun with me. After a long moment, she released them and wiped the tears that had filled her eyes. "But what is your business here, my son? Surely you haven't come to see me."

"I've come to buy a horse," I told her. "Shimun told me of your family's stables."

She sighed and looked out over the yard. "He loved the horses. He would spend long hours grooming and feeding them. And each evening, before sunset, he would take Jabar, his favorite, out for a long ride in the fields." She eyed my traveler's bag. "Do you need a place to stay the night?"

"You are very generous," I replied, "but I want to head on to Mosul before nightfall."

She nodded, and paused a moment before asking, "Forgive me my son, but have you the means to pay for a horse?"

"I have this," I replied, holding out my hand so that she could see the stone on my finger. A fleeting expression of distaste crossed her face, and I recalled how Shimun distrusted all marks of material wealth. "Yes." She nodded, as if she was well-acquainted with expensive jewels. "My husband will be prepared to make a worthy exchange for it. But you must bargain hard. Insist on the best of his horses." She paused thoughtfully. "What sort of horse do you want?"

"I need a horse that is strong enough for long days of travel, but calm in temperament. I've heard," I added, "that some of your horses are descendants of the esteemed Najim. I was advised to seek out them out."

She shook her head. "Najim's seed has been watered down with too much mating. The new generation has inherited his impatience, but not his ability." I nodded, wondering how in the world I would select the right horse, when she leaned over and whispered, "Jamila. Only Jamila. Look for the reddish-brown horse in the last stall on the right. She is sure-footed and very swift, with a good long stride and strong legs. My husband will not want to part with her, but he has a weakness for gems, and for this stone, he will be prepared to part with her." Just then we heard the sound of footsteps on the stair, and before I could thank her, she was gone.

A short while later a tall, broad-faced man with round, protruding eyes and thick graying moustache entered the porch. "The son of the Vazir has just bought one of my finest stallions," he boasted, and then looked me over with a long, appraising stare. "Are you here on behalf of your master?"

"Yes. Exactly. I'm here on behalf of Omar Alharazi from Baghdad."

He frowned, and thick wrinkles formed just under the line of his turban. Unlike his ascetic son, he carried great weight on his large frame, and spoke in a smooth, deep voice. "All the way from Baghdad?"

"Your name is known, even there."

"Hmm. But his is not familiar. And how does he know of my stables?"

"Omar Alaharizi has many experienced horsemen among his friends, men who know every horse in the Caliph's stables. They speak of the famous horse breeder of this village who deals in the finest of animals," I replied, amazed at the way it all rolled so easily off my tongue. "My master sent with me this ring, one of his most treasured possessions, and has given me leave to exchange it, but only for your best horse."

Still frowning, he eyed the jewel. "Let me see." I slid the ring off my slim, grimy finger. "An emerald," he remarked. "Perfect for the hand of a man." He held it up to the sun, examining it from all sides.

"My master bought it in Baghdad, but it comes from India," I told him.

"An emerald from India! Allah be praised," he murmured, turning the ring this way and that. "Where is its marking? Ah, here it is. Forgive me, but one can never be too careful when it comes to gold. There's plenty of painted bronze in the markets of Baghdad. But what about the stone?"

"Sir, Omar Alharazi is an honorable man," I snapped, assuming the appropriate air of insult. "He would never sully his own name by cheating in business. And just look at this gem; see how vivid the color is. How clean and brilliant. But if you're not interested, give it back and I'll find another dealer."

"Oh no. No, no, no." He smiled. "The last thing I thought to do is insult your master." He held the stone up again, squinted, and nodded as if to himself. "Yes. Of course the stone is genuine." He returned the ring to me and extended his arm graciously. "Come. Let's go to the stables. I invite you to observe my horses at your leisure, until you find the one that will best please your master."

IN MY FORMER life as a pampered only daughter, I had little use for the art of negotiation. How then was I able to assume precisely the right expression of distaste and boredom as I walked slowly past the horses in Ibn Tawfiq's stables? Had it been possible for me to linger at the stalls of those beautiful animals, I would have been happy to buy any one of them. Each seemed more promising and desirable than the next, and I could easily have been one of those fools from Ibn Tawfiq's stories. Nevertheless, I moved quickly past the animals, my nose in the air, barely looking right or left, until I reached the last stall on the right, where a sturdy looking, reddish-brown horse was swatting at flies with her tail. I gave her only the briefest of glances before waving my hand with a dismissive gesture and breezily remarking, "No. There's nothing here that would please my master."

Ibn Tawfiq's face twitched with dismay. "Nothing at all? But these horses are as fine as you'll find anywhere, in any stable." I shrugged and shook my head.

"It can't be. Please, look again." He frowned and tried another approach. "What sort of man is your master?"

"Oh, he's the most noble of men," I replied, stressing the word noble. "But if anyone tries to cheat him, he gets furious and swears vengeance."

He smiled impatiently, as one smiles at a child. "I have no doubt of that, but I ask with regard to his preference of horse."

"Ah. Of course. Well, Omar Alharazi is a cautious man. Ever since he was thrown to the ground by a wild horse and broke his hip, he refuses to ride any animal that is not calm by nature."

"I see. Then allow me to show you Abal. Her grandfather was from the seed of Najim, one of the most superior horses in the Caliph's cavalry. Yet she herself is even-tempered." As we approached a stall in the middle of the row, the horse, a handsome gray mare with shining eyes, thrust out her neck in greeting. "Isn't she beautiful? Abal is the princess of the stable."

I put on a stern, doubting expression. "She looks fine enough, but she's gray, and my master believes that gray horses bring bad luck."

"Bad luck?" He shook his head quizzically. "Well, who am I to question the preferences of a customer?" He crossed to a stall father down on the opposite side. "Allow me to present Kadar, a horse of outstanding qualities."

I shook my head and bit my lip. "My master insists on a mare."

"Yusef, sir," he said employing a fawning tone, "I am prepared to make your master a most attractive offer. I ask you to do me the honor of viewing the horses for a second time."

"As you wish," I replied curtly, "though I don't think I'll see anything this time that I missed the last." With an even more pronounced air of boredom, I passed through the long row of horses again, and then, as if some particular feature had caught my eye, I paused at Jamila's stall, where I allowed my expression to betray the slightest hint of interest. "What can you tell me about this one?"

A shadow of uneasiness clouded Ibn Taqfiq's face. "Oh, that's Jamilla. A good horse. But a little slow-witted. I wouldn't offer her to a customer."

I clapped my hands loudly in the air. Jamila looked up sharply, as if seeking the source of the sound. "Her wits seem sharp enough to me."

"Any animal will respond to noise. What matters is how she reacts to commands."

I brought my hand to my mouth and pretended to yawn, so that the ring would again be in full view. "If you don't mind, I'd like to take her out for a ride."

His gaze followed my hand. "Eh . . . yes. With pleasure. I recommend that you do, so that you see for yourself that she is without distinction." He called for a groom to outfit Jamila with a saddle. As she was led from her stall, I was pleased to note a distinct alertness in her stride.

Ibn Tawfiq showed me to the yard. When Jamila was finally brought out, saddled and bridled, a thrill of anticipation seared through my limbs. With a surprising agility, I climbed atop her, and though I had not sat on a horse for over a year, all the sensations of riding awoke in me. I gave a light kick to her flank, and she broke into a trot that was but a hint of greater speed and power, stored up like an arrow at a taut bow. *Yes*, I wanted to cry out. *This is exactly how I imagined it!*

But when I brought her back to the stables, I shook my head decisively. "As you said, she is a little slow-witted. If I were purchasing her for my own use, she might be good enough, but I fear that my master would not be pleased." I held out my hand and gazed at the stone. "The ring is, after all, of great value."

I climbed down from Jamila and made a show of dusting off my pants so as to calm my racing heart. "Allow me to make your master an offer," he said, his merchant's wiles playing in his tone. "Because he is such a discerning man, I'll make him a special gift of a saddle and a pair of rider's pants. That way your master can tell his friends in Baghdad that it's worthwhile to do business with me."

I glanced again at the ring, biting my lip as if making a momentous decision, and replied, a little too quickly, "Agreed."

But he was too pleased to notice. He bowed ceremoniously and declared, "Splendid. I'll instruct my groom to prepare her. And now, to celebrate our trade, please allow me to serve you a meal from my own kitchen." This invitation, I knew, was as important to closing our agreement as a signature on a contract, and I was glad to accept. He led me back up to the porch, and showed me to a terrace laid out with fine carpets and cushions set around a low table. Soon a servant came in carrying a basin of water and a soft towel, a faint reminder of the luxury I once took for granted. After we had both washed our hands, he asked me to excuse him.

As I looked out at the grazing horses, a feeling of such elation rose in me that I had to clasp my hands together tightly so as to contain the urge to sing out as women do at weddings. There were so many reasons for fate to deny me this horse, yet by wits alone I had conquered them all.

Ibn Tawfiq soon returned carrying a tray filled with steaming dishes. "My wife is as clairvoyant as a fortune teller. While we were in the stables, she prepared a meal for you." He set down plates piled with roasted lamb, stuffed vegetables, freshly baked bread, and a flask of wine. The sight of such expertly prepared fare almost brought tears of joy to my eyes. How many months had it been since I had eaten such a meal? And how many months since I had been served one? With a wink, he poured me a cup of wine. While he heaped my plate with food, I looked up at the latticed window, and saw Shimun's mother, smiling as if she had prepared the meal for her own son. "A saddle and a pair of riding pants!" Ibn Tawfiq declared. "Your master has sent a seasoned trader in the garb of a youth."

"Seasoned trader? I'll be lucky if he doesn't send me back to my village after such a deal."

He shook his head as he refilled my cup. "You'll soon see, my son, it is Jamila who is the real treasure."

A servant came in carrying a pair of riding pants. They were of the best quality, sewn from strong material, with close, tight stitches, exactly the sort that Khalil and Karim wore when they went out riding. He handed them to me, and I held them to my waist. "Hopefully, your master is a larger man than you." Ibn Tawfiq chuckled.

"He'll be satisfied with these," I replied, stuffing the pants into my bag. "How long do you estimate it will take me to ride to Mosul?"

"Mosul? Didn't you say your master lives in Baghdad?"

"Ah, yes...but he plans to meet me in Mosul in the coming days."

I hoped he wouldn't notice the quivering tone of my voice, but Ibn Tawfiq merely glanced up at the sky and replied, "If you get a start this afternoon, you can ride up to the river. In the morning, cross the river, and you'll be in Mosul by the end of the day."

When I had eaten what seemed like enough food for a week, I followed him down to the yard where Jamila had been outfitted with a leather bridle and a woolen saddle, the stirrups dangling down from her sides. "Your horse," he declared grandly. "My groom has prepared a bag of crushed barley for her. Feed her a little of it after she's taken her fill of grasses. And now," he said with a barely concealed anticipation, "if you please, may I have my ring?" I slid the jewel from my finger and he took it greedily, the thrill of possession enlivening his face as he forced it onto his pinky. Then he daintily held out his fat fingers and admired the stone.

I stepped up into the stirrup, swung my leg over the horse as coolly as the son of the Vazir, and took the reins in my hands. "May Allah watch over you, and your esteemed master," Ibn Tawfiq murmured, still gazing at his own hand.

"And may He grant you continued health and prosperity," I replied. The groom opened the gate and directed me to the road below. I rode Jamila carefully down the hill, too absorbed in guiding her to rejoice. But once we had reached the road out of the village and the way opened before me, I whispered in her ear, "We'll be good friends, you and I," and then kicked my boot firmly against her flank.

As if she herself had long waited for this moment, she gave her mane a stiff shake, and then broke into a run. I clutched the reins and clasped my legs tight against her, and as I rode I sang out, as loud and joyful as women at a wedding.

But I did not sing for long. Soon after I set out, dark clouds overtook whatever light was left of the day. I no longer welcomed the idea of traveling in the cold rains, but welcome or not, it was soon raining, and I was soon drenched. I slowed Jamila to a trot, scanning the terrain along the road for some form of shelter. The land was mostly flat and treeless, but eventually I came upon a small forest of trees, their wet leaves quivering in the winds. I led the horse under the thick green branches, drew my damp blanket from my bag, and settled under the largest of the trees.

Before the sky darkened into night, I collected the driest twigs I could find and using the stones that Anton gave me, I managed to light a small fire. I fed Jamila some of the crushed barley, and then wrapped myself in my blanket at the base of the tree and fell asleep.

I woke at daybreak to the sight of Jamila sleeping, a sight so improbable that I was certain I was still dreaming. But when she opened her eyes, gave herself a rousing shake, the thought of riding her again rushed through my veins like strong wine.

After finishing the last of the provisions from Mar Yuhanon, we started on the road to Mosul. I was traveling alone again, but somehow, everything was different. It was as though this gray sky, these damp paths, this fragrant forest was not a dark trap, but a home in which I could move easily and without fear.

Later in the morning, I arrived at a town by a river's edge. I consulted Anton's map, and it told me that I had reached one of the many daughters of the Tigris. A crowd of people, most of them local families with children, stood at the shore, watching as a barge paddled towards them. I dismounted my horse, and as the barge pulled up to the waterside dock, I approached a young man who was traveling with his veiled wife, each of them holding a child in their arms. "*Shlama lookh*," I said. "What does the boatman charge for the crossing?"

The man shifted the child from one arm to the other and replied, "Old Zafrani? He takes one dinar from each passenger, unless he doesn't like the looks of you—in which case he takes two." I must have appeared alarmed, for he laughed good-naturedly, and added, "I'm joking of course." I smiled, feigning amusement, but I was thinking that if I didn't want to swim across the Tigris, I would have to offer a flask of wine as payment. The young man glanced at the flask as I pulled it from my bag. "Have you no money, my brother?"

I shook my head. "I'll offer this instead."

Soon the boat arrived and the boatmen greeted many of the passengers as if they were old friends. When it came my turn to pay, I showed him the flask, but before I had a chance to offer it, the man handed the boatman several coins, put a hand on my shoulder and said, "I'm paying this boy's fare as well."

"Sir," I said. "I won't be able to—" but he put a finger to his lips. "One day, if Allah is willing, you too will pay the fare of a youth."

May I one day have the means to be as generous, I thought in my heart. When the ferry reached the western shore, I asked my new friend to point me towards Mosul, and then started off at a moderate pace, so as not to tire Jamila.

The way was bustling with wagons and caravans traveling in both directions, and Anton's map suggested why. I could surmise, for example, that the merchants and caravans going east were headed for the cities of Tabriz, Hamadan and beyond, while those going west were on their way to Damascus or the sea coast. I marveled that the little map had the power to grant its owner the knowledge of an experienced traveler; truly it was as wondrous as a genie.

The map also told me that the empty, rock-strewn expanse across the river from Mosul was in fact the ancient ruin of Ninveh, where God sent the prophet Jonah to warn of impending doom. Just a few weeks before my departure, all of Mar Yuhanon had observed a three-day fast as if they themselves had been saved by Jonah's prophecy.

Soon afterward, we came upon another, wider daughter of the Tigris, which could only be crossed by a barge similar to the one I had ridden earlier. I had no coins for the ride across the river, but as a gesture of welcome to the merchants who brought business to the city, the governor provided the crossing for free. I broke from the crowds streaming into the town, and led Jamila to a shady spot near the gates where I consulted the map again. To my dismay, I saw now that the road north stopped short at the parchment's edge, at a place called Dahuk. From there, my map-genie would fall silent and I would have to continue without him. Or I could do as Anton had urged me, and travel to his family's inn on the road leading westward out of Mosul. It would be a long detour, but I saw now that to travel the roads without a map was to render oneself a blind beggar, prey to the whims of every scoundrel and rogue on the way.

After allowing Jamila to finish the remains of the half-eaten apple she found in the street, I followed the crowd through the gate and into the marketplace. I searched the stalls for merchants who might trade their wares for a flask of wine, but I had to be careful. Although many Muslims happily take wine in secret, it is forbidden to sell it to them. And so I opened my ears for the sound of the Syriac that the Christians speak.

The first stall I approached sold blocks of dried goat cheese. When I told the merchant that my wine came from the vineyards of Mar Yuhanon, he added a flask of yogurt to my purchase. I asked him to point me to a baker who would trade bread for wine, and he showed me to the town ovens where a cheerful woman eagerly counted out four loaves of fresh bread in exchange for a flask.

Just across from the ovens, I saw a group of four young men filling their water flasks at a well. As sometimes happens with groups of friends, they all looked alike, for they were about the same height, with their belts casually tied in the same lose manner about their hips, with the same loud laugh, and the same lanky shuffle. "Let's get some wine for the way. We have at least four days' ride to Nisibin. Luka will catch us hares and gazelles and we'll have a feast every night."

"Me? Speak for yourself, you imbecile. I'll catch you a rabbit if you trap me a wild pig."

"You couldn't trap a wild pig if it walked right up to you and handed you a rope."

"And you couldn't catch a sleeping goat!"

I supposed, by their dress and manner of speech, that they were students from the School of Nisibin, an institution that the some of the monks of Mar Yuhanon had attended and often recalled fondly.

They were of my own age, and it occurred to me that I might join them as a traveling companion by simply offering to share my flask of wine. But I was wary of passing myself off as one of them. It had been one thing to fool the pious and contemplative monks, but I well knew the merciless scrutiny to which boys—and girls—subject one another.

And so I set out on the road to Nisibin alone, thinking of how good it would be to live a more truthful existence, one in which I would not have to deceive everyone I met. For three days and two nights I traveled alone, undisturbed by those I passed. I slept under twinkling spring stars and a comforting yellow moon. Each morning I allowed Jamila to eat from the oats and graze on the green grasses as the fresh smells of wildflowers wafted in the morning sun. When she had eaten her fill, we set out on the road, my eyes constantly scanning the horizon for a sign of the inn.

AND THEN, ON the evening of the third day when the sky was a deep darkening blue, I spotted a flash of yellow lights in the distance. Jamila was reluctant to navigate the thorny path in the darkness, but as we neared the lights, I could hear shouts and laughter ringing out across the fields, and I so goaded her on until I could see a large traveler's inn, half-illuminated in the moonlight.

As we approached, I tied a scarf around my head, so as to appear a good and modest girl. I moved slowly, feeling the day's ride in my aching bones, until we arrived at a pair of large iron gates. A burning torch hung on each gate pillar, and a burly sentry stood on guard, the knife in his belt flashing in the flickering light. "*Ramsho tobo,*" he greeted me as he looked me over quizzically, and then stood aside so that I could lead Jamila into the large courtyard behind him.

The courtyard looked like a stable, with perhaps thirty horses, camels, and donkeys occupying the stalls that encircled it. It was almost empty of people, except for a few men tending to their animals, and three wagon drivers standing by a well in the center, discussing road conditions on the roads going east. A trill of high-pitched laughter rang out. I looked up and saw two women passing through a half-open corridor on a second floor above the stalls. I watched as they descended the stairs, the animated chime of their talk floating on the night breeze, and then disappeared under an arched doorway across the courtyard.

The sounds and smells of the animals excited Jamila. I found her an empty stall between another mare and a donkey. From across the courtyard I spotted two boys of about twelve or thirteen, watching me and whispering. Something in their grinning faces reminded me of Anton, and I guessed that they were his nephews. They pointed to the arched doorway through which the women had passed and said, in the same dry Syriac spoken at Mar Yuhanon, "Right in there."

As I opened the door a gust of warm, pungent air blew over me, and I gazed about, bewildered by what seemed to be a carnival. The room swirled with shouting and laughter. Copper lamps cast a warm orange glow and the scent of spiced meat filled the air. Serving men and women carrying trays of steaming dishes moved amongst tables laden with beer and wine. And at a table in the far corner of the room, a handsome older woman was counting out coins and writing into a ledger. Her hair, fixed in a thick braid, was long and black, as if refusing to grow old. Without anyone having to tell me, I knew that she was Luna.

Suddenly, as if from nowhere, a serving man, carrying a pitcher in one hand and a tray in the other, swung by and called out "Dinner?" I stared after him, for he was truly a younger and rougher version of Anton. I opened my mouth to reply, but before I could say anything he handed the pitcher to a table of camel drivers, grabbed my arm and led me to a table in a dark corner, one of the last available places in the room. "I'm Daoud," he told me. "Sit here. I'll be back soon with some food. Musa had to go to Damascus for his niece's wedding, so there may not be anything in the way of entertainment tonight, but the stew came out very well, and I can bring you a cup of good wine." I nodded, more out of amazement than agreement, and he was gone.

Wearily, I sat back against the wall, and listened to the loud hum. I realized that the quiet, serious talk I had envisioned with Luna would have to wait, for this was no place for the quiet and the serious, and besides, I was too weary to tell anything properly. Daoud soon returned with a cup of wine and a bowl of meat stew, the second hot meal to be set before me that week. Never had a dish looked so appealing to me, and I could barely restrain myself from devouring it. But I remembered that I had no money, and that it would be best to first explain who I was and why I had come.

A table of soldiers was calling to him from across the room, and he was about to go to them when I put a hand on his arm. "Wait. I...I need to tell you something."

He glanced across the room, and then down at me. "Now? Why don't you have something to eat first?"

"Daoud, listen. My name is Rahel. I...I've brought word from Anton."

"Anton!" he cried out, slapping his thigh loudly. "Where did you see him?"

"At Mar Yuhanon."

"You were at Mar Yuhanon?" he exclaimed. "Praise be to God! Did you speak with him for long?"

"He was my—er, yes. We saw each other almost daily."

Daoud was rendered speechless, but only for a moment. "Mother! Leo!" he called across the room. "Come over here." The woman with the long dark braid rose from her chair with surprising vigor and made her way across the room, greeting guests and instructing serving girls as she went. Behind her followed a man younger than Daoud, but unmistakably another of Anton's brothers. "This is—"

"I am Rahel," I cut in. "Rahel Bat Yair," I repeated as I stood up, my tongue heavy with the forgotten feel of my real name.

"She's seen Anton! At Mar Yuhanon!"

I expected that this news would have her embracing me in teary excitement, but instead, she merely appraised me with a cool, dark gaze. "Rahel," she repeated as if pondering a riddle. She reached out to touch my short hair. "You were in disguise."

"Yes," I admitted.

"You must have a lot to tell us."

"Yes, I do."

"And was he aware that you're a woman?"

"Only at the end."

She nodded, as if none of this was surprising to her. On the contrary, it was I who was incredulous in the face of both her quick wits and her cool reaction to me. She spun around to her sons. "She'll be a fine replacement for Musa." I smiled at her, assuming that she was speaking of someone else. "Have you eaten?" she asked.

"No, I've only just—"

"Well, go ahead. I see Daoud has brought you dinner. When you're done, I invite you to share a story or two with our guests. Tell them about. . .about Anton at the monastery. Yes. Tell a story about Anton and the monks. Try to think of something amusing." I laughed good-naturedly, and was about to reply that Anton had warned me about the family sense of humor, but before I could say anything she had hurried off with Daoud following close behind. Leo, however, continued to stare at me quizzically.

"Your mother is quite a character," I remarked, trying to mask my confusion. "I would have thought that she'd be eager to hear news of her son."

"Oh, she'll want to hear everything, but only tomorrow morning when the guests have departed. Now tell me, do you have any good stories? Believe me, nobody cares if what you tell is true or clever, or even interesting. But it's best that it be. . ." he paused to find the right word, "spicy."

"Spicy? Wait a minute. . .your mother. . .she wasn't serious."

"I'm afraid she was. You see, usually Musa is here on Tuesday nights. He tells a few stories, and everyone forgets their troubles and goes to bed happy. But yesterday he left for Damascus; all day we've been trying to think of who we could use instead. Any story about Anton at the monastery will be perfect. Many of the people here tonight know Anton. They'll be excited to hear about his life as a monk."

I shook my head. "Actually, I have nothing to say about Anton to anyone but your mother."

Leo sat down beside me and put a hand on my shoulder. "I don't know if Anton told you anything about the business of running an inn, but in a place like this, we sometimes have to do things in a way which might seem, well, haphazard. We never know who is going to walk through our gates. One night it is a bunch of holy men, and the next it's a group of traveling whores. But what are we supposed to do when they show up on the same night? Or what are we supposed to do if the sons of Ibn Ishaq come in on the same night as the Alsharif family, when the grandfathers haven't spoken to each other for fifty years? Or when the *Muktasib* from the morality patrol brings his band of thugs here for a night out? If we didn't know when to smile and when to turn a blind eye, we would have been closed down long ago."

"Well, that's fine for you, here in the middle of nowhere, but you don't really think that I—"

"Look," he cut me short and made a wide sweep with his hand. "Just look around at the people in this room. Some have been traveling the roads for months. Some have crossed oceans and deserts. They arrived here at the end of a long day, weary and dreaming of the homes and people they've left. We can't cure that longing. But we can offer them a hot meal, a cup of wine, and sometimes, when we can, entertainment, good music, singing, or a tale that lifts their spirits." Though I myself was weary, I glanced around the room, noting for the first time that, like me, everyone here was in the midst of some sort of journey. "Will you help us? As Anton helped you."

"He did help me, but this—he would never have asked such a thing in return. Anton is a monk. He detests gossip and idle chatter. He would never—"

"Forgive me," he cut in, "but you have no idea how many times he himself sat in Musa's chair and assumed the role of storyteller, inventing whatever he needed to satisfy a crowd. You've only known him as a pious monk, but before that he was a master at turning misfortune into good."

He was interrupted by the opening notes of a well-known melody. We both glanced across the room and saw that a soldier had climbed atop his stool and broken into song. He sang poorly, in a range too high for his voice, yet there was something in the mood of the place that bestowed a certain license, so that foolishness and unseemly behavior were all benevolently forgiven. "All right," I told him. "For the sake of your brother, I'll think of something."

He jumped up and held out the cup of wine to me. "God bless you, Rahel. Drink this; it will give you courage." I knew that it was best to eat before drinking alcohol, but the wine was so warm and sweet that I finished the entire cup at once. "You'll be well-rewarded for this," Leo promised, and then rushed away.

DAOUD LED ME to the center of the room and showed me to Musa's chair, a high stool that raised me above most of the crowd. From my perch I watched as people gathered around, pulling up chairs, wine and beer cups in their hands. My tongue felt heavy, and the crowd before me seemed as boisterous as a yard of squealing pigs. Daoud announced that I would be taking the place of Musa, who had journeyed to his niece's wedding, and the crowd broke into loud groans and hisses. But when he explained that I, an unexpected visitor, had recently seen Anton, and that I brought fresh news of him, all eyes turned to me and a murmur of interest passed through the room. I overheard several women discussing my hair, but they soon fell silent, waiting for me to begin. I motioned for Daoud to come over and whispered in his ear, "What should I say?"

"Tell them why you came here," he suggested.

"I came here, to this inn, in order to bring word from Anton to his family," I told them, trying to steady my voice. "As you may know, Anton is at the monastery of Mar Yuhanon. That is where I met him."

"What were *you* doing at Mar Yuhanon?" a woman hollered.

"Well, I was living there too. In disguise, that is."

"In disguise? In a monastery? What were *you* looking for?" a soldier asked in a loud voice, and several of his companions laughed crudely.

"An excellent question. I was seeking an opportunity to study."

"To study what? The monks?"

"A girl could do worse," someone called out.

More comments of this nature followed, and I realized that if I was going to speak of long days of prayer, fasting, and study, my audience would chase me off stage. They glared at me indignantly, as if they already knew that my stories would be dull compared to Musa's. Their mocking distressed me, yet there was something about those glares that challenged me and filled me with an unfamiliar boldness, for they knew nothing of me. Nothing at all. I could tell them the most outrageous of tales without fear of their judgment.

I joined in their laughter and somehow, as if suddenly possessed by wicked jinn, I managed to conjure up a tale I had once overheard the grape pickers at Mar Yuhanon tell at night in the tent. "Actually," I began again, raising my voice, "I was there to help someone else. To help a nun."

"Ooooh!" cried the crowd.

"You see, I was out walking one morning, and I stopped to rest by the gates of Mar Yuhanon. I was about to move on when suddenly I spied a young nun. She was sneaking around the gates, trying to peer over the heavy stone wall, like this," and here I enacted the role of the young nun, "as if she were looking for someone. She spotted me and froze with fright, but I wished her a good day, and asked if she was in need of assistance. At that, the poor girl began to cry, and her whole story came out."

"What was her story?"

"Be quiet, Abdul. Just let her tell it."

"Well, the problem was that this nun, Mona, that was her name, didn't really want to be a nun. She told me that her father had put her in a convent because he had found her alone with a boy from her village. Nico was his name." A tremor of excitement ran through the crowd, and I felt my tongue growing looser. "Nico's father had always wanted to send him to the monks, and this seemed like a good excuse. So Nico was packed off to Mar Yuhanon." Several women in the front row shook their heads, some feeling the sorrow of the parted couple, and others in disapproval of their immodest behavior.

"The girl, I mean the nun, Mona, told me that she couldn't bear to be apart from her love, and that she wanted nothing except to see him again. And then she told me of her plan."

"Just as I always say, there is no way to separate a couple in love," an elderly woman said approvingly.

"Now the story is getting interesting!"

"Go on, girl. What was the plan?"

"Well, Mona dug into her sack and pulled out a monk's garment that she claimed that she had stolen from her brother, who was also a monk. And then she asked me if I would agree to disguise myself. As a monk!"

Gasps of shock along with gleeful giggling rose up from the crowd. "So that's why your hair is short like a boy's!"

"I would have sworn that she *is* a boy!"

"Shhh!"

"What was the plan?"

"Her plan was that we would then go into the monastery together, and hopefully no one would notice that we didn't belong. Well, I was skeptical, but the poor girl looked so wretched that I agreed to help her. I donned the garment, and together we walked through the monastery gates." Here I got up, and mimicked the cautious gait of the imposters.

"The work of the devil," someone muttered, while others shook their heads in disbelief. A camel driver gave a low whistle. Out of the corner of my eye I could see Daoud and a woman, perhaps Anton's sister, watching me, incredulous. And beside them, her face dispassionate and sober, I saw Luna give me the faintest of nods.

"Once we were inside, I tried to blend with the other monks, while she tried to look as pious as possible. And all the while, she was checking the faces of the monks, trying to find her boy. 'Ask someone where we can find Nico,' she whispered to me."

At this point I paused, as storytellers do when they hold the crowd in their palm of their hand. "Then, mustering all of my courage, I approached an elderly monk, and said to him in a low voice," (and here I made an attempt to affect a low voice) "'Have you seen Brother Nico today?'

"Luckily, this monk was so old that his eyes no longer served him well, and after taking a long, sort of squinting look at me, he pointed me in the direction of Nico's cell. I returned to Mona, and together we went to find Nico's room. It wasn't easy, with all of those rooms being exactly alike and bare as dungeons, but we soon found the place we were looking for."

"Then what happened?"

"Well, Mona knocked on the door, and Nico answered. At first, he didn't recognize her, and he looked absolutely shocked to see a nun in his quarters. But then she brought his ear to her lips and whispered, 'Nico, it's me, Mona.' Well, you can just imagine! Nico turned white, and then he turned bright red, and then finally was able to speak and he said, "Mona, my love, is it really you or am I dreaming?"

"And then what happened?" a woman cried.

"Naturally, I left them alone."

"Alone?"

"A nun in a monk's room! In the monastery! God preserve her."

"That's blasphemy. Don't those monks take vows?"

"They're not supposed to go near women, or even look at them!"

"That's true," I interjected, "but don't forget that the boy didn't really want to live as a monk. His father had put him there forcibly."

The crowd was silent for a moment, as if considering this point, and then suddenly erupted in passionate debate. "That's right," an officer pointed out. "He didn't really want to take those vows."

"Nothing can stand in the way of true love!"

"But such behavior in a monastery!"

"I say it's a beautiful story."

"And I say it's shameful. They'll go straight to Hell for what they did."

The debate continued for a while, giving me time to think about what to say next, but soon someone shouted out, "So what does all of this have to do with Anton?" which reminded everyone, including me, that Anton was the reason I was even telling this tale. I sensed that this was the place for a quick, humorous ending, something that might resolve nothing but nonetheless leave the crowd satisfied.

"Anton? Anton was the one who discovered them," I replied, shouting as if both amused and outraged. At this the crowd broke into applause and hooting and all manner of cheering. I could see Luna covering her eyes and shaking her head. Perhaps I had gone too far, but she had brought this on herself.

"What did he do?"

"He told them to extinguish the lantern when they were done."

A brief moment of confusion gave way to peals of bawdy laugher as the closing line sunk in. I descended the stool, and everyone applauded loudly. Though I scarcely recognized myself, I was filled with a strange, secret satisfaction, for I had managed to please the crowd beyond all expectations. Amidst friendly slaps on the back, Daoud stepped up, took my arm and escorted me to a table in a far corner of the room. I slumped into a chair and put my head in my hands. "That was perfect!" he said. "You're a born storyteller."

I slid my hands down my face and shook my head. "I just used the first tale that came to mind."

"No. You have a talent," he insisted. "But you must be thirsty. Wait here; I'll be right back."

He returned with a jar filled with red wine. I poured a cup and gulped it down with relish, for never had I so longed for the intoxication of drink. Luna approached my table and sat down opposite me so that now, in the light of the lanterns, I could discern her features. Though she must have been over the age of sixty, her presence was a commanding one; her face was pleasing, with dark eyes that surveyed me as if she could easily see through my false exterior. "That was very impressive," she remarked. "You have an instinct for performance."

"Perhaps, but only before an audience of strangers."

"Yes," she agreed. "That's it exactly. Nights at a wayside inn are like a carnival. People behave with abandon. Even women sometimes forget themselves and join in the revelry. But the night passes, and by the time the sun comes up, all is forgiven. No one remembers and no one cares."

"Luna," I said, feeling the heaviness of the wine dulling my senses, "I only agreed to do this for the sake of your son, Anton."

She raised a surprised eyebrow. "You must indeed have much to tell us. Tomorrow, when all of these people have left and gone, we'll have a proper talk. But surely you're tired now. Have you come alone?"

"All alone, except for Jamila."

"Your servant?"

"My horse."

"Your horse?" she repeated, shaking her head. "You rode here alone on horseback? How unusual. I look forward to hearing your story. But tonight you're our guest. My daughter Olivia will show you to a room, and tomorrow we'll receive you properly." She glanced at my traveler's sack. "Do you have a bedroll? Most of our guests travel with their own bedding."

"No, I . . . I don't."

"Then I'll ask Olivia to bring you what you need."

"Mother, can you come in here a minute?" a young woman's voice called out.

Luna sighed and rose from the table. "You must excuse me, my daughter. Sleep well, and tomorrow you'll tell me everything."

By the time I finished my wine I was faint with exhaustion, but someone had apparently been keeping an eye on me. For the instant I put my cup down, a woman of about thirty-five, with a dry smile and restless dark eyes appeared at my table. "I'm Olivia, sister to the infamous Anton," she told me. "Your story was wonderful. It's too bad that the man himself wasn't here to see your performance, though he probably would have embellished a little more with the final scene."

I could not, by any means, picture Anton standing before the crowd and "embellishing" the final scene. But at that moment, I had neither the strength nor the inclination to argue with her. "Here, I've brought you a bedroll. Come and I'll show you to a room." She helped me to my feet and led me into the moonlit courtyard. I followed her up the flight of stairs to an open corridor lined with arched doorways. She stopped before the second to last, drew a key from the pocket of her dress, turned it in the lock and pushed the door open.

Deftly, she unfurled the mattress and handed me a blanket. I expected her to take her leave, but instead she leaned against the wall, folded her arms over her chest, and remarked, "I must admit that I'm more than a little curious. How *did* you come to meet Anton?"

"Forgive me," I answered her, "but I'm afraid that I couldn't possibly tell another story right now, not even if it be the truth."

"Of course. Forgive me." She laughed as she handed me the key. "Sleep well, friend of Anton."

THOUGH I COULD hear, through the veil of sleep, the cries of travelers preparing their animals for the day's journey, I slept late that morning, and by the time I awoke, the courtyard was still and quiet. A bright shaft of sun was shining through a crack in the window shutter, casting a beam of light on a jar of water and basin, the sole objects in the room. I washed quickly, straightened the creases in my robe, and headed down to check on Jamila. Someone must have groomed and fed her, for she greeted me with a contented nuzzle, and I too felt almost as contented.

I entered the dining hall to find the room, which just a few hours earlier had rocked with song and noise, standing silent and empty. The tables and benches had been pushed to the walls, and all that remained of the night's commotion was a woman's red scarf, lying forgotten over the back of a chair. I stared at the scarf, with its fine weave of silk with cotton, and all the appalling details of my performance the night before came back to me. How could I face anyone now? How could I explain that it was not I but the wine that had gone before the crowd and told the story about the monk and the nun? I cursed myself for drinking with such abandon. For the wine had disappeared like a thief in the night, leaving me to confront Anton's family alone.

The smell of fresh bread and roasting meat was wafting across the room. I looked around to discern the source of the smell, and it was only then that I noticed a large table laid for a meal, as if a single large group was expected for lunch. Voices were coming from the direction of the kitchen, and so I crossed the room to the arched doorway.

Two women stood before a long table, their long dark braids descending from their headscarves like two playful twins. The taller of the two was clearly Olivia, but I couldn't recall who the second, shorter and stouter one might be. I noted that this kitchen was far larger than Zahiya's, and far better stocked than that of Mar Yuhanon. Yet for all of its promise, the place was a terrible mess. Sacks of wheat and barley leaned up against the shelves, the table was dusty with flour and bits of dough, squeezed lemons sat piled on the sideboard, and heaps of dirty plates and bowls were piled in the wash basin.

They stood with their backs to me, deep in conversation, kneading dough as they spoke. I was about to greet them, but I held my tongue when I realized that I was the subject of their talk. "I'm telling you, she said nothing about how she knew him. And with her short hair, it's obvious that she was in disguise."

"But that story she told, about the monk and the nun, do you think there was something to it? Maybe about her and Anton?"

"Could be. God knows those monks are only men."

At that moment, the stouter one turned around and caught sight of me. She was younger than her sister, with a rounder face and softer features, but she had the same lively dark eyes shared by all of Anton's siblings. "You must be Rahel," she said, wiping her hands on her apron. She kissed me on each cheek as if we were old friends. "I'm Marsa, better known around here as the hidden cook. I'm so sorry that I had to miss your performance last night, but I was trapped here in the kitchen as usual. Leo told me all about it, but I'd love to hear the story again from you."

I shook my head, desperate to correct the impression I must have made. "That story was just a joke . . . just an old joke, and I'm sorry for it now. It was unworthy of Anton."

The sisters eyed each other and then laughed out loud. "Your story was just fine," Olivia told me. "And as for Anton, it's all well and good that he's decided to live in righteousness and chastity, but you should know that before he went to look for God, he enjoyed stories of that sort more than any of us. He may be a monk now, but he was no saint before." She laughed the same sly, almost mocking laugh again.

"Well I'd prefer that you all forget about it."

"Forget about it?" Marsa asked. "Am I once again to suffer for my cooking?"

"Just as we do," Olivia answered her.

"The guests love my cooking!"

"The stew last night was perfect," I assured her.

"An ally at last!" Marsa ran over to put an arm around my shoulder. "Promise me you'll ignore the ignorant lack of appreciation of my cooking that goes on around here."

Olivia went out to ring a bell that announced the midday meal. When I followed Marsa out of the kitchen and into the dining hall, I was startled to see that a room full of spouses and children had appeared. "Attention, everyone," Luna called out, and the chatter came to a halt. "For those of you who missed last night's performance, this is Rahel. As you all know, she's come from Mar Yuhanon, and she's going to tell us all about what *really* goes on there."

I smiled weakly. For the first time, it occurred to me that what I had to say might be as disappointing to them as it would have been to the crowd the night before. "Rahel," Luna called, "you come and sit here, beside me." She recited a brief prayer of thanks, the longer version of which I knew well from Mar Yuhanon, and the meal began.

"Leo and I were trying to decide which part of your tale is true," Daoud called to me across the table. "We decided that none of it could be." At this, debate erupted.

"But she claims that she's seen Anton. At Mar Yuhanon."

"We still don't know what she was doing there."

"As far as I know, women aren't even allowed to set foot in a monastery."

"And no Muslim would venture inside one."

"Who said Rahel is a Muslim?"

"I'm not," I told them.

"Then you're a Christian," Leo's wife concluded, smiling at me with approval.

"Don't be ridiculous!" Luna cut in, as though disappointed by her family's slow wits. "Isn't it obvious? The name Rahel is that of a Jewess."

Now they were watching me, waiting for me to affirm her conclusion. "Luna's guessed it." I shrugged with a sheepish smile. The room fell silent, as everyone pondered this new information. One of the older boys whispered something to the little girl beside him and the toddler began to complain and yank on his mother's arm.

"Well then, how are things at Mar Yuhanon?" Leo asked, and everyone again broke out into peals of laughter.

I stared at them, baffled at the way they made light of their brother's life at the monastery. "Rahel will tell us everything," Luna declared, "after we've fed the children."

As everyone piled their plates with bread and stew, I tried to compose an explanation that would be adequate. But it was difficult to think clearly. For unlike the somber meals at Mar Yuhanon, the food was accompanied by conversation so chaotic and lively that I could scarcely follow it. One minute they were speaking of adding a new dormitory, the next they were gossiping about a guest who always complained about the wine, and suddenly they were comparing how long it might take a racehorse to get to Nisibin. Luna would listen to all that was said and then respond with her own appraisal. Each of Anton's siblings was endowed with a quick wit that resembled his own, and I wondered at how strange it must have been for him when he first came to the monastery, to take his meals in silence.

Yet I knew that even as they chatted and joked, people were watching me, stealing glances at my face and my hair as if they might hold the secret of my involvement with their brother. When the younger children had left the table and Daoud had taken upon himself to peel oranges for everyone, Luna turned to me and said: "And now Rahel, the time has come for you to tell us how it goes with Anton. Why don't you stand, so that we can all hear what you have to say."

I rose awkwardly from my chair. All around the table, keen eyes were staring at me in anticipation. For the second time in less than a day, I was compelled to tell a story. But this time, everyone expected what I said to be the truth. This, I realized, was to my advantage. I could say anything, and they would be inclined to believe me. I glanced around the table and made a quick decision to keep my story short. I tried to be eloquent, but without the help of the wine it came out nervous and uncertain. "I'm on my way to Tiflis, you see, to find my father's uncle," I began. "I'm traveling in disguise, as you can see, but I ran out of money and food. Some Christian priests I met on the way told me that I could find work at Mar Yuhanon . . . in the vineyards. During my time there, I was sent to clean the library, and that's how I met Anton. He spends a great deal of time in there, in the library, and he would sometimes speak to me of the work he was translating. He used to call me his student—as a joke, of course. He's held in very high regard there, at Mar Yuhanon. Before I left, Anton gave me a map and advised me to come here, to the inn. He said that you would help me to continue on my journey to Tiflis."

I paused for a moment and tried to gauge their reactions. Every face was regarding me with expressions that ranged from incredulous to perplexed. "He said that you would help me with advice and directions." I concluded. "And that's about all I have to tell you," I added as I sat down.

For a moment no one said anything. I worried that perhaps I had confused them, and so I rose again and added, "You see, he was concerned that the journey would be difficult. He supplied me with a good map, but it only shows the roads up to a place called Dahuk. He made me promise to ride out here from Mosul, so that you would...you might help me."

I sat down again, and for a long moment no one said anything. Finally Daoud spoke up. "You said you were a Jew," he said slowly.

"Yes," I answered, hoping that they weren't familiar with St. John's famous homilies.

"So how did you manage to convince the monks that you were a Christian?"

"Oh, that wasn't difficult," I told them brightly.

"Where are you parents?" Olivia asked.

"I'm an orphan."

"And the rest of your family? Sisters? Brothers? Aunts and uncles?"

"I have none, except for my father's uncle."

"In Tiflis," she suggested.

"In Tiflis."

A fly buzzed loudly, and one of the boys smacked his hand on the table in an effort to kill it. "I must say," Luna remarked, "that your tale is extremely unusual."

"Perhaps, but that chapter in my life is over, and now I want nothing more than to grow my hair again, and wear the robes of a woman," I replied emphatically, so as to show that I was in fact a girl like any other.

"You must be pretty, when you're a female," Daoud said with a wink.

This was met with hearty laughter on all sides. "I suppose that my transformation will have to wait until I get to Tiflis. Then, I plan to—"

My speech was cut short by the appearance of a man who had come in through the kitchen. Daoud rose from his place and went to him, and everyone took this as a sign that it was time to get back to work. The women began to clear away the dishes while the children ran in asking their mothers for sweets. Only Luna and Leo remained at the table. "You didn't mention what led you to leave your home in the first place," she remarked.

I shifted in my seat. "There are unpleasant things in my past. Things that I prefer not to speak about." Luna nodded knowingly, and I realized that I had revealed myself as a girl of loose morals. To my relief, however, both of them seemed content with this explanation.

"Tiflis. That's over the northern mountains," Leo said as though thinking aloud. "My friend Toma once led a caravan up that way. He told me that the mountain passes are steep and hard on the animals, and that the ride was dangerous and difficult." He tilted his head slightly and asked, "Do you have enough money?"

I shook my head. "None. The only thing I possess is my horse. But it's possible to survive on the roads without money. One can find food in all sorts of ways, and now that the weather is growing warmer I can sleep outside."

Leo was about to say something, but just then, Daoud called him out to help unload the vegetables that had apparently just been delivered. And so I was finally alone with Luna. She gazed at me with her cool, probing gaze. "My son doesn't take easily to other people," she remarked. "He must have thought well of you." I looked down at my hands, unsure of what to reply. "How did he respond when he discovered that his pupil was a woman?"

The hint of sarcasm in her voice when she said "pupil" was unpleasant. "He was angry at first," I told her, "but once his anger passed he forgave me."

"Were you his lover?"

I looked up in astonishment. Though her tone was even, her gaze was hard and calculating, and I realized that this was her way of trying to discern the truth. "You speak very bluntly," I answered, "but as you must know, Anton has taken a vow of chastity. He has renounced all contact with women."

"Then you would be an exception."

"Not if you consider that Anton thought me a man."

"Yes," she nodded slowly. "I believe you."

"You owe it to your son to believe me."

I wondered if I had offended her, but apparently, my words had done just the opposite. After a long moment, her face softened and she said, "Stay another night, and tomorrow we'll give you a proper map and directions to Tiflis." She rose from her place and gestured for me to the same. "We usually retire to our chambers in the afternoon, so as to be well-rested for the evening. I advise you to do the same."

But having slept most of the morning, I wasn't at all tired. Though the dining hall had emptied out, I could hear someone moving around in the kitchen. I wandered in and saw Marsa working her way through a green mound of herbs. "Rahel," she looked up and exclaimed. "I thought you'd gone back to your room."

"Oh no. I don't need any more rest. But what about you? Your mother told me that everyone goes to sleep after lunch."

"I will, right after I chop this parsley. That way I'll have less to do later."

I picked up a spare knife lying on the table. "I'll help you."

I expected her to protest, but instead she handed me a cutting board. I took some parsley from the pile and began to chop in the criss-cross way I learned from Zahiya. Marsa stared at my hands with interest. "You've worked in a kitchen, haven't you?"

"You can tell?"

"It's obvious. Where did you learn to do that?"

"I once worked in the home of a rich merchant in Baghdad."

"You were a servant?" she asked with unmasked surprise.

"I've been many things," I replied with a laugh, and though I knew she wanted me to elaborate, I steered our conversation away from the subject of myself.

THERE WAS SOMETHING amusing in the way the guests straggled in, each instructing their servants and in their own tongues and accents. Short-tempered and weary, they went off to their rooms, only to return to the dining hall a short time later as glad as children about to be spoiled by their mothers. "There'll be good music tonight," Marsa whispered as a pair of musicians, one carrying a lute, and the other a drum, sat down at one of the tables. "Whenever musicians stay with us, my mother encourages them to rehearse in here, right after we serve dinner."

But the liveliest guests of the evening were a wealthy merchant dressed in a red and gold cloak, accompanied by a party of three women, each in a light blue transparent head veil encircled by a thin gold tiara. From their bright clothes and painted faces, I guessed that they were whores. But when they entered the dining hall, Luna rose and greeted the man as if he were an old friend. "Munif, my dear. You've waited too long to visit us."

"Alas my dear Luna, I couldn't get out of Damascus," he replied grandly. "But now I'm on my way to Baghdad, and then on to Kufa and Basra and Shiraz, and any place where there are lonely men." He flashed a lecherous smile. "I'm traveling with a fine entourage."

"Yes, I see that you are. Good evening, ladies."

The women smiled at her with looks so suggestive that I had to turn away so as not to laugh. "They can sing, you know; if you allow it, they'll keep your guests entertained." But caching sight of Luna's displeased expression he added, "With their singing, of course. Only with their singing."

Marsa and I exchanged glances and made efforts to stifle our laughter. "That's very kind of you Munif," Luna replied. "But I've already arranged for musicians to play tonight. If the ladies want to sing a song or two, I'm sure the musicians would be happy to accompany them."

That night, I insisted on helping Marsa in the kitchen. I ladled the food onto trays that the serving staff, which I now saw consisted of Leo, Daoud, Olivia, and her two older daughters, brought out to the tables. Later on, just as Marsa had predicted, the musicians took the floor. They played well, but not everyone was satisfied with the slow, mournful tones of the lute. "What's with the funeral music?" a voice called out.

"We didn't come here to cry tonight," shouted a loudmouth I remembered from the night before.

The musicians exchanged worried glances, as if disappointed in the quality of the audience. Just as I was wondering what would happen next, the three whores rose from their table. Their tiaras shimmered in the soft light of the lamps, so that instead of whores, they looked like angels. One of them whispered something to the lute player, and he broke into the familiar opening of a famous love song.

It was exactly what the audience had been waiting for. People stood up, pushed their chairs to the side of the room, and began to sing along and sway to the music. They must have practiced well, for they sang in harmony, so as to give their act the quality of performance.

After breakfast the next morning, Luna invited me to see her in her rooms. The entire clan lived in a large complex, set off from the inn by a dense growth of flowering bushes. A servant girl showed me through the courtyard and into Luna's apartment. It was small and modestly furnished, but the walls were adorned with colorful tapestries, and the shelves held a collection of bowls, each fashioned in a different style. "Gifts, my dear," Luna explained when she caught me staring at them. "Each one is a gift from a guest who passed through."

Daoud was sitting at Luna's table, counting up the earnings from the night before. He looked up and nodded to me, so as not to interrupt his calculations. Luna showed me to the corner of the room and gestured for me to take a seat on one of the pillows. The servant brought two cups of herb tea and set them down on the table before us. "Last night Daoud sat with Toma, one of the local drivers who have traveled all the roads going north. He says the way is long and very difficult. In his opinion, you should sell your horse and pay a driver to take you there."

"That's not very surprising," I joked.

But Luna frowned and shook her head. "He speaks from experience, and you would do well to listen to his advice. Tell me, Rahel," she continued, "have you any money? Anything of value?"

"I have nothing."

"And your father's uncle, do you know for certain that you will find him alive and well?"

"No, but—"

"Then he might be dead."

"He might be."

"And what will you do if he is?"

"I suppose that I'll just marry a local man."

"With no relations and no money? What kind of groom will you find?"

"I . . . I don't know. I'll find—"

"You'll find whoever will have you; a girl with no dowry and no relations must take whatever she can get."

I said nothing in response to this grim prediction, for she spoke of things that I had always pushed far to the back of my mind. "And now," she continued, "allow me to make you a proposition. Marsa told me how you've been helping her in the kitchen, and more importantly, she says that you have experience as a cook. I've thought it over, and I'd like to offer you employment here at the inn. We'll pay you a decent wage, and of course your food and board. In that way you can save up for your dowry."

"Me? Work here?" I almost laughed aloud. How much lower did God want me to sink? Was it not enough that I had been a slave and lived among monks? And now He would have me cook for rogues and whores!

My expression must have betrayed my thoughts, for Daoud smiled and said, "In all fairness, you mustn't take offense; you've told us nothing of who you are or where you come from. But from what you have told us, I would think you'd be grateful for the offer. You can stay with us for as long as you like, one month, two months, even six months, however long you need."

I wanted to reply that I had never, not even in my most difficult hour, considered hiring myself out for wages. After all, I was the daughter of a respected physician. "You must consider," Leo said, as if he could hear my thoughts, "that the life of a woman with money is infinitely preferable to the life of one without. Won't it be better to ride into Tiflis a rich woman rather than a destitute one?" Though my instinct was to refuse, I willed myself to consider my situation coldly and without self-pity, and in that cold and pitiless light, I knew he was right.

"I accept the offer," I told them, grinning like a stable boy, and was immediately welcomed with a slap on the back from Daoud and a warm embrace from Luna. "And now, Rahel," she said when we drew apart, "there's something you must explain to me. How is it that a poor, orphaned Jewish girl rides so fine a horse?"

On the morning that I was to begin my employment, Luna took me aside and said, "You've chosen to be very secretive about your background Rahel, and so I can't know what you've seen of the world. In any case, there's something I suggest you bear in mind. When one works at an establishment such as ours, one can expect to meet a great many people. Some will be to your taste, others will not. But whatever you think of them, you must put aside your opinions about who is worthy and who is not. The only unwanted guests here are those who would cheat us."

I nodded, recalling the warm reception that Luna had lavished on Munif and his whores. "Ignore whatever you've been taught of respectability or morality. Morality is a luxury; it costs money, and not everyone can afford it. This place is not a monastery, where only the good and the holy may reside. In fact, you could say that it's the opposite. What passes through our doors is part of God's world, and we must welcome it, in whatever form it takes."

Thus was I swept into the ebb and flow of life at the inn. I learned the times of its waxing and waning, its frenzied mornings, its afternoons of deceptive calm, and its long fantastical nights. My day would begin at dawn, when Marsa and I would haul in the sacks of grain and baskets of vegetables that had been delivered at first light. Olivia's daughters, Paula and Anna, tended goats and fowl, and each morning after they brought us milk, eggs, and freshly slaughtered chickens, we would set to work preparing the fare to be served that evening. At noon the family gathered for the midday meal and afterward, once the dishes were washed and everyone had retired, I would saddle Jamila and ride out to the grassy fields that bordered the highway. On my return, I would find the courtyard stirring with new arrivals, and as the light faded from the sky, a fresh mix of humanity would tumble into the dining room, weary and famished.

Each evening comedies and tragedies played out before our eyes. Old-timers would meet and resume arguments sustained for thirty years. Business partnerships were forged, while others angrily broke up. Officers in the Caliph's army, their unveiled women in their arms and laps, would drink flasks of Luna's wine and in language best suited for the whorehouse, recount impossible victories over their opponents. Locals would gather in their own corner, where they would take on travelers at chess, backgammon, and tabula, while onlookers gathered around, loudly approving the clever moves and bemoaning the foolish ones. Musa soon returned from Damascus and resumed his weekly storytelling. I was presented to him as the "teller of tales in the guise of a cook," and he asked to hear my story of the monk and the nun. Though I recounted it reluctantly, it delighted him so much that he added the story to his repertoire.

I noticed that the women of the family, whether serving a meal, pouring wine, or listening to the tales of a traveler, consorted readily with the guests; that is to say, they conducted themselves as if they were men. Fascinated, I observed Anton's sisters' skill with even the coarsest of soldiers and caravan drivers, so as to learn that same lightness of demeanor. I watched the way they smiled, not indecently but as one smiles at a neighbor, and how they listened with just the right expression of curiosity to the travelers' exploits.

But the easy, forthright manner that came to me naturally when dressed as a boy seemed improper for my woman's robes. I tried to refrain from contact with the guests, for what woman wishes to offer herself—the way I had to as a slave—to the gaze of strangers? Luna noted my reticence and took me aside for a short discussion of the matter. "The women of the Jews are known for their modesty," she told me in a disapproving tone, "but among the Christians, a woman's honor comes not from avoiding others, but from how she behaves in their presence. As long as you work in this house, you must adapt your conduct to ours. When our guests want to praise your cooking, for example, you must look them in the eye and accept their compliments with grace."

And so I willed myself to converse with the diners, asking them things like where they had been and where they were headed. They never noticed the effort it cost me; on the contrary they would recount their tales of the road as though glad of the chance to speak of them. Without noticing, I became adept at conversing with strangers, so that I soon perceived that I had somehow shed my shyness, much as one sheds a heavy cloak on a spring day. And truly, I had no need of it, for nothing about the camaraderie of those encounters was lasting. I saw that an evening's tears and tempers, like its laughter

and beautiful friendships, were as ephemeral as a passing breeze, and
that most of what played out under the night skies dissolved in the
grayness of the morning.

FOR THE FIRST time since leaving Sura, I felt neither fear, nor
shame, nor anger at what I had become. The small voice in my heart
that reminded me that I should have been married by now grew softer and less insistent, until there were days, full of cooking and colorful guests and enchanting musicians, when I scarcely heard it at all.

And then one evening, I happened on a sight that stunned me,
not with its newness, but with its startling familiarity. I had gone
out behind the kitchen in order to refill the salt box. The setting
sun had cast a warm bronze glow, giving the courtyard an uncanny
radiance. It was in this light that I came upon a man at prayer, his
back to me, his face looking towards the setting sun. From the soft
syllables of Hebrew, decipherable in spite of the din from the dining
room, and the unmistakable movements of his swaying, I knew that
he was a Jew.

For a moment, I couldn't breathe. It was as though I had come
upon the ghost of my father, the orange light of dusk falling over
his shoulders as he chanted the evening prayers. This vision, utterly
absurd, yet so vivid in my memory, stirred something in me that had
long been dormant.

From the arched entrance to the kitchen, I observed him eating
alone. When he was done his lips began to move, as if he were talking to himself. Only I, of all the crowd in the room, knew that he
was in fact chanting a prayer—the prayer after meals. When he was
done I found myself moving toward his table, even though I had
no idea what I wanted to say to him. "Did you enjoy your meal?" I
stammered.

He was not old and not young, perhaps about thirty years of age,
slight of build, with a neatly trimmed beard. Though he dressed in
the style of the Muslims, something in his face made him as familiar
to me as my neighbors in Sura. He looked up at me, confused by
my sudden appearance. "I tasted only the vegetable stew, but it was
very good."

Of course! I thought to myself. He wouldn't touch any of the meat dishes. "I prepared that stew," I told him.

"My compliments," he replied politely.

"I saw you at prayer this evening, in the kitchen courtyard. For-give me, but . . . it has been many months since I've seen a Jew."

"Really? I can't imagine that I am the only one to pass through here."

I laughed nervously. "Well, there are not many, and, you see . . . I too am a Jew."

"Ah." He nodded and gave me a quizzical look. "Where are you from?"

"I am . . . we're not from this region. And I am an orphan." I paused uneasily. "Seeing you this evening has reminded me of things that I've almost forgotten."

He smiled with a sympathy that pained me, and gestured for me to sit down. "I'm Naftali Ben Yosef. What's your name, my sister? Where are you from?" he asked me again.

"Rahel," I said softly as I sat down across from him. "From the town of Sura, in Bavel." He nodded, waiting for me to say more, but my head was spinning with the sound of the word Bavel, for it is a Hebrew term used only by Jews, and I had not spoken it since the day I left home. And then, perhaps because he reminded me of the people I once knew, I told him, "My father, may he rest in peace, died two years ago. I have no other family." He was silent, and sens-ing his confusion I added, "I feared my father's enemies, and so I fled."

"You fled your home? And you have no one there at all? No one in all of Sura who could help you?"

His questions were innocent, but I suddenly lacked the means to answer him. I bit my lip and closed my eyes. When I opened them again, his expression was dark with pity. "What a hard life you must have here," he murmured, his attention caught by a table of loud young men pouring out the last of their wine.

I shrugged, trying to convey a carelessness I didn't quite feel. "The people here are good to me."

"God be praised," he replied as his eyes darted amongst the oc-cupants of the other tables. "Forgive me for speaking frankly, but it seems wrong that such a young and helpless girl is compelled to labor in a place such as this. A Jewish woman should live among her people. She should marry and devote herself to raising her children."

He was, of course, saying what anyone would have said. And in his tone of reproach, I could hear the voices of my father, and of our neighbors in Sura, and Avraham Halevi, and the rabbis of Mosul, and all the Jews in the world who would surely have told me the same thing. I could even feel the old Rahel awaking within me, shaking her head in dismay. "Do you plan to return to Sura one day?" he asked gently.

"No. My father's enemies have a long memory."

"Who are these enemies?" I bit my lip in reply. He stroked his beard thoughtfully, a gesture that I well-remembered from the men of Sura. "I myself am from Baghdad," he told me, "but my wife's brother lives in Sura. I visit him when I have business in the town. What was your father's name?"

"I...I can't tell you." Fresh tears sprang to my eyes. I looked away and murmured, "It's been a long time since I've spoken of him..."

"And what are the claims of these enemies?"

"I prefer not to say."

Again he began to stroke his beard, as though brooding over a difficult passage in the Talmud. "I want to help you, Rahel. Allow me to make a suggestion. I'll be traveling to Sura sometime in the next few months in order to collect an old debt. Is there anyone there to whom you'd like to relay a message? Someone you want to inform that all is well?"

Could I trust him? It was difficult to tell, but memories of home were flooding over me like a swelling river, and more than anyone else, I thought of Shafiqa. For I knew now that she had not been a mere servant to me, but in fact more like a sister, a mother, the most loyal of loyal friends. She had loved me and I, foolish child that I had been, had taken her love for granted. "We once employed a servant, a Muslim woman," I replied slowly. "Her name is Shafiqa. Her brother, Hannad, has a stall in the market. He sells roasted nuts and dried fruit. Find him, and he will take you to her."

"And when I meet her?"

"Say that you've spoken with me, and that I am well. Tell her that I pray that God will favor her and reward her for everything she did for me. But however she begs, do not say where you've seen me. It's best that she not know. And promise me that you won't tell another soul in Sura."

"But surely the rabbis—"

"You must tell no one. Promise me."

He nodded reluctantly. "I promise."

"Rahel, we've only just met, and I know nothing of what has befallen you, but it appears that you've strayed very far from your rightful place. It pains me to see a fine Jewish girl wasting amongst rogues and wayfarers. Please, allow me to make inquiries. A suitable groom can be found, a man of means, from a community of righteous people."

Why did I refuse him? For he was offering me the very thing I thought I wanted. Perhaps I feared the way he would tell people: *A wretched orphan, laboring as a cook in a wayfarer's inn.* "Your offer is very kind," I told him, "but I do have one living relative, an uncle of my father's who lives in the town of Tiflis. Soon, when I've saved enough money, I'll travel to him and he'll find a husband for me."

He gazed at me, troubled. "You don't have to live like this, Rahel. Please. Think again." But I closed my eyes and shook my head.

The morning after our meeting, I must have lingered a little longer than usual in my chamber, for when I came down to the kitchen, he had already set out.

THE WEEKS PASSED and the days grew longer, and the warm spring nights made the guests spirited and reluctant to retire to their rooms. The pleasant days of work in the kitchen with Marsa, the rides into the fields with Jamila each day after lunch, and the evening encounters with the guests lulled me into a life that suited me well. Every Sunday, when Luna paid me my wages, I would put them in a small cloth sack I had sewn myself, and think of the groom they would buy me one day.

One evening in late spring I was garnishing platters of chicken with ripe blackberries when Marsa pranced into the kitchen. "There's a traveler here tonight," she told me gleefully. "A real traveler, from a faraway land." She threw an arm around me and squeezed my shoulder. "Come out and have a look at him!"

Though the inn saw wayfarers of every sort, Marsa had a particular fascination for foreigners from the north and west. The lighter their skin and hair, the more they delighted her, and on those rare occasions when a merchant from the faraway cities of Venezia or Salonika arrived at the inn, she would find reasons to hover near his table. Conversation with these foreigners was impossible because they spoke no Arabic or Syriac. Yet this only served to excite her more.

It was the hour when the dining hall was full, and neither of us had time to gawk at the guests. "Don't you want to see him?" She pulled at my hand. "Come on!" Reluctantly, I left the blackberries and let her pull me to the doorway.

"Who? Where?" I asked, glancing around the room for the type she liked.

"In the corner, with Daoud at the chess table. Can you see him?"

"No."

With both hands she took my head and pointed it towards the chess table. "Are you blind? There!" I surveyed the far side of the hall, but a crowd of onlookers had gathered round to watch the game, blocking the players from view.

"I can't see anything. I have to get back to the chicken."

"I'll tend to the chicken. You go get a look at him." She grabbed a jar of water from an empty table and thrust it into my hands. "Take this so they'll let you through."

With a sigh, I maneuvered my way around the tables. As I approached the far corner, one of the men beside the chess table leaned over to whisper something to his companion, and I caught a glimpse of what had excited Marsa. For even in the half-light, I could see that his hair was the color of sand and the line of his face was clean and pleasantly formed. I couldn't make out his eyes, but there was something novel about his features that suggested that he was not from Venezia, or from the even from the lands of the Slavs. I moved in closer, so as to see him better, and the onlookers made way for me, thinking I'd come to serve the players a drink. "Marsa asked me to bring you some water," I said to Daoud.

He looked up, clearly surprised to see me out of the kitchen, and I hoped that his opponent would turn to face me as well, but he did not, for his attention was entirely absorbed in the game. And so I stood there, jar in hand, studying the board along with the crowd.

Finally, as if breaking out of a spell, he made his move. The men around him nodded in approval.

"We didn't ask for water," Daoud snapped, aggravated by his opponent's ingenuity. "Take it back and bring us some wine for after the game."

But the stranger turned to me and said in a strange, clipped Syriac, "Actually, I wouldn't mind some water now, if you could bring us two cups." It was enough for me to catch sight of his eyes. They were remarkable, a brilliant shade of green that reminded me of leaves in sunlight. I wanted to observe him a little longer, but the long months of work at the inn had taught me grace and composure. "Of course," I replied. "I'll be right back." When I returned to the kitchen Marsa accosted me, greedy for details.

"Did you see him? Did you see his eyes?" I was about to describe their color, but she went on excitedly. "Apparently he's the apprentice of the old physician Abu Talib, and they're traveling to Mosul. The old man fell asleep at the table and after the foreigner helped him to bed, he returned and headed for the chess tables." She peered across the room, almost giddy with delight. "Where do you suppose he comes from?"

"It's hard to say; he has the face of a northern barbarian."

"Of course he's a barbarian." She rolled her eyes impatiently. "But from where?"

"Maybe he's some sort of mongrel Slav," I guessed with a shrug. "He speaks Syriac, but with the strangest accent. I almost laughed out loud when he asked me to bring cups for the water."

"He wants cups? Excellent! I'll go see him up close."

She fetched two tin mugs, and then as an afterthought, filled a bowl with pistachio nuts, which, because of their exorbitant price, were reserved for special guests. "Marsa," I called as she headed for the doorway.

"What, Rahel?"

"Allow me to remind you that you are a married woman."

"Married women are allowed to look," she called back. I glanced around for the chicken platters, but they were no longer there. Someone had taken them out to be served, and the dark berries remained in the bowl, ripe and waiting.

I saw the foreigner again the next morning as he led Abu Talib, who moved with the steps of a snail, to a horse-drawn cart. As he passed by, he smiled at me in recognition, and I tried to get a last look at his unique, sharp-boned face. After all, who knew when I would see such a face again?

As it happened, I saw it not more than a month later, when I sat down to lunch one day and found him seated directly across the table from me. I recognized him instantly, and looked to see if the old doctor had returned, as well. I glanced around the table and from the way that the others were looking at him, I knew that I wasn't the only one surprised by his reappearance.

Luna rose and called for everyone's attention. "Maybe some of you remember Lucan, Abu Talib's escort. They passed through last month on their way to Abu Talib's brother's home in Mosul."

I looked to Marsa. Judging by the dreamy look on her face she remembered him well. "Abu Talib passed away a week after they arrived. Now he's on his way to seek out another apprenticeship in Fustat, but unfortunately, he's run out of money. He returned here this morning looking for work, and I told him about our plans for the old storehouse." She was speaking of a long, narrow building, once used for storage, but now standing empty. Luna had long wanted to convert it into a dormitory for servants and drivers. "We've agreed that Lucan is going to stay on with us for a while. The men of the family will lend a hand and the dormitory should be ready by the end of the summer."

Luna went on to make a quick introduction of everyone around the table. When my turn came she said "And this young lady is Rahel. She also came to us as a traveler, and we've put her to work with Marsa in the kitchen." I wanted to smile, but a sudden, almost forgotten bashfulness came over me.

"What's your name?" Leo called across the table when Luna was done. "Lucan?" Everyone laughed as the children repeated the odd-sounding word.

"Most people have no trouble with it, but for some reason Abu Talib insisted on calling me Lukas, and I didn't have the heart to keep correcting him," he replied, but we were all listening to the lilt and clip of his voice, which seemed to change familiar words into something exotically different. The children giggled behind their cupped hands, and Marsa gazed at him, enthralled.

"And where is the place that you call home?" Olivia's husband asked.

"It is a land very far from here, called *Baratiniya*."

Everyone took a moment to consider this word. Some looked as if they had heard it before, while others were puzzling over its foreignness. "Where exactly is this Baratiniya?" Leo asked.

"Well, if you were to travel to the coast, and then get on a boat and sail the whole Mediterranean until you reached *el-Andalus*, and then you turned your boat and sailed north, you would eventually reach a large island. That island is Baratiniya."

There was another long silence, as if everyone were digesting this great distance along with their food. "You've come all the way here by sea?"

"Only the last part. I couldn't afford a place on a ship, so I rode in the service of a bishop to the city of Venezia. From there, I boarded a boat to the port of Tyre."

"It must have taken months. Why did you want to undertake such a journey?" Marsa wondered aloud.

All eyes turned to hear his answer, and I felt sorry for him, subject as he was to the family's relentless interrogation. "That's an odd question for an innkeeper." He laughed. "Why does anyone want to travel? To see great cities, to observe the ways of other peoples, to—"

"And so you've come to observe us?" Leo interrupted.

"To study you," he replied, with that same grin that intrigued me in its way of concealing more than it revealed.

"Ha! Another one who wants to study." Daoud banged his hand on the table, making everyone's plate jump. "Why is it that we seem to attract those who wish to be students?"

"It's because of the highly intelligent atmosphere around here," Leo said gravely.

"Apparently," Daoud added, "we attract those who prefer study to honest work."

It was meant to be a joke directed at me, and I put on a wounded face. "As a loyal employee, I want to say that I'm offended. Beware, Lucan; you may want to leave before you begin!"

"And disappoint Luna? I'm not as heartless as that."

Everyone laughed, and Daoud slapped him on the back. "He beats me at chess, and then he sweet talks my mother. I say Lucan is quite sharp, for a foreigner."

"Just stay with us," Leo cried, "and your Syriac will be fit for the marketplace."

"Isn't it already? I spent eighteen months selling oranges in the markets of Tyre."

The conversation went on like this for some time, until finally, Leo put a hand on Lucan's shoulder and said, "Please tell us, seriously now, what is it that has brought you here from the ends of the earth?"

I thought he would respond with another joke, but his expression became serious. "The truth is that I've come to learn the secrets of medicine. My plan is to apprentice with a physician who can teach me. When I landed at Tyre I found a fruit merchant who agreed to teach me Syriac in exchange for labor. After two years with him, I thought I was ready to begin. I made the acquaintance of Abu Talib and he agreed to take me on, but now . . ."

"There are no physicians in Baratiniya?" Luna asked.

"None like you have here. There are plenty of healers, but they know nothing about real medicine. And our situation is dire; not only are we cursed with plagues and disease, but we suffer constant attacks from a race of Godless warriors. Anyone who suffers a wound at their hands is sure to die. But if we could only acquire your knowledge of medicine, I'm certain that some of our wounded could be saved."

"The peoples of the northern lands are said to be coarse and primitive," I remarked to Marsa later that night. "In Musa's tales he always describes them as clumsy and stupid. But Lucan seems just the opposite."

"Yes," she mused. "Entirely the opposite."

Like a rare spice added to an old dish, Lucan's arrival gave life at the inn a beguiling new flavor. I would see him each day at lunch when the men would ramble in, dust in their beards and dark sweat circles on their shirts. Though there was little contact between us, all of my senses were alive to his presence, and when he spoke I listened to his every word, relishing both his mistakes and his strange accent, for the rise and fall of his voice delighted me.

Lucan and Daoud took to playing a nightly chess match. Each evening, cups of beer in hand, the two would take their places at the table as a crowd of locals and guests would collect around them in expectation of great entertainment. For it soon became clear that the two were so equally matched, that when one of them won one game, the other would usually win the next. It was a running joke that until Lucan managed to win two consecutive games, he would not be permitted to continue on his travels.

In the late hours of the evening, when the kitchen had closed and the dishes were drying on the shelves, I would go out to join the crowd of onlookers. I would come upon their game at its most riveting, when the final attack is played out and the players have to sustain great mental agility and sharpness of wits. Daoud freely expressed his satisfaction or frustration. As he pondered a move, he would stroke his beard, purse his lips and then sigh in resignation. But Lucan was less transparent; he seemed to enter into a state of intense concentration, oblivious to the commotion around him, his face betraying little of his mind's activity.

I would watch the games carefully, calculating, as I had done with Khalil, the best possible series of moves. In my mind, it was I who sat across from Lucan, engaging him in a battle of wits. In those moments I would regret that I was no longer disguised as a boy, for the only instances that women were seen at the chess tables were if a husband would take on his wife, or a father his daughter.

But one night, about a month after Lucan's arrival, opportunity chose to show her fickle face. Daoud's son had fallen ill with fever, and Daoud's wife sent word to Lucan that he could not leave the boy's bedside. The air in the dining hall that night was stifling, and many of the guests had moved their mattresses up to the roofs and gone to sleep early. I emerged from the kitchen to see Lucan sitting alone at the chess table, sipping his beer and surveying the room for an opponent. I watched as he picked up a chess piece, jiggled it in his hand, and set it down again, only to pick up another.

This, I knew, would be my only chance to play against him. *Why not*, I said to myself, for I had no brother or father to forbid me. I went to his table, looked down at the board, and remarked, "It looks like you're in need of an opponent."

He smiled amicably. "So it seems, but it looks like everyone's gone off to bed."

I glanced around the room. Only two tables were occupied. At one, three traveling merchants were finishing their tea; at another, a local villager, old Abdullah, sat playing both sides of a backgammon board. This, I knew, would be my only chance to play against him. "I have a little knowledge of the game," I said softly.

He motioned for me to take a place in the chair where Daoud usually sat. "Then allow me to invite you for a match."

Even as I sat down across from him, I was amazed by my boldness, but I had set this folly in motion and, as if gripped by a devilish fascination, I had to see it through. And so I made every effort to ignore his presence. I imagined that I was back in Sura, playing an ordinary match against my father. For if I could just focus all of my attention on the board, I might be able to ignore the hair on his arms flickering gold in the dim light, and his long fingers drumming lightly on the table as he waited for me to make the opening move.

He played carelessly, making no more effort than necessary. It came as no surprise then, that in spite of my nerves, I quickly cornered his king. "What's this? You've won?" he cried out in mock dismay. "How can that be?"

I smiled in the face of his charming outburst. "If I'm not mistaken, the first rule of chess is that you must never underestimate your opponent."

"Well I'm obviously guilty of that."

"At least you admit it! But if you promise to give the next game your full attention I'll agree to a rematch, and you might repair the blow to your reputation."

"I'm in no position to refuse your terms." He grinned, and began to set up the pieces.

In the meantime, the few remaining guests assembled around our table. They had witnessed Lucan's defeat, and followed our second game closely, excitedly mocking him, and me.

"You're too earnest, like a virgin schoolboy."

"Are you really going to lose your knight to a cook?"

"If you don't watch what's happening in the corner, she'll castrate your bishop."

But in spite of their cries, he played attentively, and it was I who was vanquished. When he announced the decisive checkmate, it was with the relief of one who has been saved from ignominy.

"Give thanks to God that He's saved you from humiliation," one of the guests declared heartily.

"You've restored the honor of men everywhere," said another with a little too much relief to be a joke.

Lucan and I rose from the table, and the others wished us a good night and dispersed. I cursed them under my breath, for their comments had almost ruined our match. But as we walked out to the courtyard, he said, "You play well, Rahel. I suppose the men in these parts aren't used to women of your ability."

"The men in these parts aren't used to a woman of any ability! You see that it can be unpleasant to even try."

"Yes, and it's a real pity. I wonder if you could repeat your beginner's luck." I scarcely knew what to answer him. The notion that he wanted to play again was as thrilling as it was alarming. For he had been so near, like a rare bird that alights on your window ledge. And there had been a brief moment when I raised my eyes and caught him staring back at me.

It was difficult for me to rise the next morning, but the last thing I wanted was for Luna or Marsa to think that I needed more sleep. In the clear light of day, the events of the night before took on the dimensions of a bizarre dream. Had I actually invited Lucan to a game of chess? Had I truly sat at his table and gazed at him like a harlot?

As I descended the stairs to the kitchen, I prayed that the family had not heard about our game, and to my relief, Marsa said nothing about it, nor did Luna when she returned from the market. It seemed as though the whole episode had miraculously escaped notice.

But my relief was short-lived. At lunch that day, as Olivia was serving the soup, Leo, who loved gossip as well as any housewife, folded his arms and remarked, "Abu Fahed approached me this morning. He told me that he enjoyed himself last night even more than he did at his cousin's wedding last month."

Under the table, my leg began to tap. I stared into my plate and picked at my food.

"Why? What did he do?" Olivia asked in a way that told me that she didn't know.

"How did he put it? I think he said that our cook invited the foreigner to a game of chess!"

"You did?" Paula looked at me with wide, incredulous eyes. She turned to me, as did everyone else. "There, in front of everyone?"

I must have aroused Daoud's pity, for he shot me a sympathetic glance at me and declared, "Well I say that she's done nothing wrong. I was tending to Theo, and Lucan needed an opponent."

"I think it was very kind of Rahel to offer to replace Uncle Daoud," Paula declared. "I think she was just being nice."

"Yes," Luna agreed. "It was indeed a gesture of kindness. I looked up slowly and braved their gazes, some puzzled, some accusing, and some full of the pity that is taken on an erring child. But Luna had more to say. "Yet our guests must have wondered what lay behind that kindness. You see," her eyes narrowed on me, "we must always bear in mind how our behavior appears to others."

I studiously avoided looking at Lucan. Was he feeling regret? Humiliation? Or perhaps confusion, for it had all been entirely honorable. Only later, when the conversation moved on and the discussion was forgotten did I allow myself to steal a glance at him. He must have discerned the very movement of my eyes, for in that fleeting instant, he sent me a wink and a smile.

What can I say of that brief gesture? It was the equivalent of a thousand chess matches.

FROM THAT DAY, I became two different people. Half of me, the half that I showed the world, remained modest and honorable. But the other half reveled in the recollection of sitting across from Lucan, distracted by the lamplight flickering over his pale arms. As much as the young men in the vineyards of Mar Yuhanon had intrigued me, this was a thousand times more compelling. I tried to behave naturally, ignoring his presence, greeting him with just the right note of familiarity, and above all, keeping my eyes from his face and form, which sought my attention with the ferocity of the devil. Most of the time, I succeeded.

We had little opportunity to exchange even a word until, several weeks after the infamous chess match, Luna announced at lunch that Abbas Tahiri, a neighbor whose fields supplied us with onions and cabbages, had visited her that morning with a special request. "Tahiri is finally going to make the Great Pilgrimage," she informed us, and he's asked to board his horse, Sahir, in our stables."

"Sahir?" Leo exclaimed. "And who do you suppose is going to be the lucky one to risk his neck riding him?"

Luna turned to Lucan and smiled. "Apparently we have an experienced horseman in our midst. Lucan told me that he once rode in a cavalry. He's agreed to take on the care of Tahiri's horse." Leo slapped Lucan on the back, and Daoud raised a glass in his direction.

On a hot morning the following week, I was watering Jamila at the courtyard well when Tahiri arrived with Sahir, a black, powerful-looking stallion. As he led the agitated horse into the stable, I could only pity Lucan, charged with caring for a creature with such a wild temperament. While Luna sent one of the boys to find him, Tahiri stroked Sahir like a mother who cannot part from her son. "Sahir is the light of my eyes," I heard him say to Luna. "Please treat him as if he were your own."

"We'll treat Sahir like a prince," Luna reassured him. "I'm putting him in the hands of an able keeper." Tahiri smiled graciously, but when Luna presented Lucan, his face clouded, and he asked to speak with her alone. Luna led Tahiri to a corner near Jamila's stable. "Luna my dear," I heard him complain, "you don't mean to leave Sahir in the care of this," he glanced at Lucan and whispered, "barbarian."

"Lucan is my employee, and a skilled horseman," she replied. "I myself have seen him ride and groom the horses, and I'm very satisfied with him. Please trust me in this matter."

Tahiri frowned and fixed a scrutinizing gaze on Lucan as if searching out a flaw. But Lucan had approached the horse, and with a firm hand and a calming voice, appeared to be subduing him. I watched as Tahiri's expression softened, and a reluctant smile appeared on his lips. Finally, he whispered something to Luna, and then took a pouch of coins from his belt and handed it to her.

Later that day, as I was preparing a bowl of water for soaking dried lentils, Lucan appeared in the kitchen. Instinctively, I glanced quickly around the room so as to see who else was present. But Marsa had gone out to the back courtyard to check the progress of our homemade beer and, for the first time since our chess game, he and I were alone. "Shall I wish you luck with your new charge?" I asked him teasingly.

"My new charge is the reason that I've come looking for you," he replied. "I understand that you take your horse out riding every afternoon."

"It's no secret."

"Then do you have any objection if Sahir and I join you?"

I looked down, confounded by his request. Did he not know that for me to be seen alone with him, even in the most innocent of circumstances, was considered improper? Though he was waiting for my answer, I said nothing, hoping that my silence would tell him that his request had insulted me. Perplexed, he tried to decipher the disapproving expression on my face, until after a long moment, he seemed to finally understand. "I...I'm sorry," I heard him say. "Forgive me, Rahel."

But as he turned and started to walk away, I was filled with a regret so powerful that I no longer cared about the respect of others. The undeniable truth was that I was no longer a stranger to men. I had traveled alone in their company, heard their confessions, and slept by their side. And so why should I refuse Lucan? He was adventure itself.

"I have no objection," I called to him.

He stopped and turned around slowly. "I have no objection," I repeated.

"Are you sure?"

"Yes." He smiled, surprised but also a little triumphant. "I want to warn you though," I added, "that Jamila is capable of great speed, and when she is allowed to run freely, nothing can restrain her."

"Then I'll just have to try to match your pace," he replied solemnly, but his green eyes seemed to be laughing. We stood there for a moment, gazing at each other. Never before had I felt so bold. "I'd better go," he said finally. "We don't want to be the subject of another lunchtime conversation."

"Meet me in the stables after everyone has retired," I whispered as the noise of Marsa's shuffling footsteps sounded from the back courtyard.

He left by way of the dining hall, seconds before Marsa entered the kitchen. "The beer's almost done," she reported. "It should be ready in a few days." But I was staring into the bowl as though studying the surface of the water, for I wanted to see what the face of a reckless woman looked like.

My arrogance made a fool of me, for not only did Lucan and Sahir match our pace, they easily outran us. We rode out to the open fields where the grasses grow long and the wild flowers bloom all summer. I brought Jamila to a halt under a lone tree and released her to graze, but Sahir and his rider were not yet ready to rest. And so I sat myself down, leaned back into the gnarled tree trunk, and watched as they galloped back and forth across the grasses until Lucan rode up to me and jumped to the ground, panting with the shallow breath of a man who has well-exerted himself. "What a feisty animal," he said with satisfaction, slapping him lightly on his long neck. "As fine a horse as any I've known."

"From the way you handle him, it looks like there've been many."

"I suppose there have been. I rode in a cavalry for four years, and I can promise you that no riding lesson is more effective than doing battle while atop a horse."

Four years, riding in a cavalry! I drew my knees up to my chest and watched him as he sat down at my side. It stuck me then, in a way that almost frightened me, that behind his strangely chiseled features, and his hobbled way of speaking, he must have carried an entire world inside of him, a world where the people looked like him, spoke his language, lived differently. "Tell me about the place you come from," I said, struck with a sudden curiosity.

He gazed dreamily out at the horses, as if seeing not them, but other horses, in a place that might as well have been on the moon. "Well, if you want to imagine the island of Baratiniya, you have to think of a place that is very green and very wet." I laughed at his strange description, and he smiled, caught as he was between the picture in his mind and my disbelief. "That's how I remember it. It rains almost every day, so that the air is damp and cold, and smells of wet earth and forests. You can travel for days, and all you'll see is green hills and foggy valleys."

"But what about your summers? It doesn't rain in the summer."

"Oh, but it does. If you could see it, you would mistake our summer days for your winter ones."

This sounded so odd that I was certain he was making it up. "There is no such place!" I insisted. "You could tell me whatever you wish, and I would never know if you speak the truth or lie. And if you tell me lies, I can't know whether they are small lies, or outrageous lies, or something in between."

"Very true." He grinned. "You'll simply have to judge by what you know of me."

"Then I can only conclude that you're telling me outrageous lies and laughing at my gullibility!"

He shrugged happily. "Decide as you like."

"In that case I must ask you more questions. Tell me about life there, in Baratiniya. Is it really so primitive, as they say?"

Lucan lay back and then propped himself up on one elbow. I watched him impatiently as he considered my question. Was there nothing that came out of his mouth without first being weighed and measured? "It isn't at all primitive," he finally replied. "People there live just like people here. Of course, there are hardships; the winters are hard and very cold, and no one can enjoy the fruit of his land unless he is willing to labor for his bread. But it's not the cold and the hard work that make our life difficult. Our greatest hardship is fighting off the Viking attacks on our villages."

"Viking attacks? What are Vikings?"

"Give thanks to God that you don't know. They're a race of Godless pagans who sneak up to our shores and attack our villages. The attacks are too terrible to imagine—they slaughter everyone in their path, pillage the churches, and carry away the women and children." I gasped, horrified by what he was describing, but he merely sighed and remarked, "In a way, it is they who brought about my journey."

"These Vikings? How?"

He didn't answer. Instead, he seemed to turn inward, to a place that was very much alive in his mind. His eyes took on a far away look, and for the first time, it occurred to me somewhere in the world there had to be a girl with the same features as his, with hair like sand, and eyes like green leaves in the sunlight. No doubt such a girl was his wife, or at least his betrothed. Yet his reply was very different than what I envisioned. "I had an older brother," he said quietly. "Dunstan was his name. He too was called to serve in the King's army, but as a foot soldier. His battalion was sent to repel a Viking attack on a coastal village." His face clouded with anguish. "During the fighting Dunstan took a spear through the stomach."

"How horrible," I exclaimed. "Where were you when it happened?"

"I was guarding a village down the coast. His commander sent riders to tell me of his injury. When I finally reached Dunstan's side, I found a local medicine man casting spells." He paused and rubbed his eyes so as to wipe away a tear. "Dunstan died in agony. And when I saw him lying in the mud, covered in blood and screaming in pain, I understood that the words of a medicine man are useless. It was then, on that day, that I made the decision to seek out real knowledge, of real medicine. But I had no idea where such knowledge might be found. I made pilgrimages to the monks in their monasteries, because they're the ones who keep the keys to everything there is to know. Their answer was always the same: the best knowledge of healing was to be found in the old writings of the Greeks and Romans.

"The desire to study these writings consumed me and became my sole aim. I found a good-hearted monk to teach me to read Latin letters, with the thought that I would learn the language when I found what I was looking for. At every monastery I visited, I asked where writings on medicine could be found. Most had little to show me. The monks spoke of the vast libraries in the monasteries of Hibernia, but the Vikings have burned these libraries, and most of the knowledge they contained is lost.

"When I understood that the books I sought could not be found in Baratiniya, I despaired of ever learning anything. And then, several months later when we were camped near the Great Roman wall, one of the men was visited by his cousin, a soldier who had left the employment of our king so as to travel the world. He had gone as far as the land of the Romans, but of all his tales, what interested me most was what he told of a conversation with a Greek sailor in a tavern in the port of Naples.

"The Greek had worked on trade ships that sailed to the lands of the Muslims. He spoke about prosperous cities with splendid gardens and fountains, and markets filled with strange and delicious fruit, of beautiful veiled women who spoke with their eyes, and cultured men who had taken upon themselves to study all the ancient books they could find. He described fabulous libraries and houses of knowledge, filled with ancient writings where the wisest of scholars would congregate, but even a poor man could enter. The things that he said gave me no rest. I found it intolerable that there were men who had access to all the wisdom that mankind has amassed, while my people remain as ignorant as animals."

I listened in astonishment to all he said. Hearing him describe all that was familiar to me as if it were extraordinary and exotic was like looking into a mirror and seeing everything backwards. And I was not oblivious to his description of the beautiful veiled women who could speak with their eyes. Was I, to him, such a woman? Even though I was not veiled and spoke with my mouth? "But to travel so far," I mused, "to find yourself alone in a place where no one knows your name, or the name of your father. No knowledge is worth such a price."

"Ah Rahel," he sighed. "There was a time when I would have disagreed with you, but now I sometimes wonder. It's been three years since I left home. I've faced such trials that had I known how hard it would be, I may not have dared to start out." He lay back in the grass and brought his hands to his face. "Just learning the Syriac tongue seemed beyond my abilities."

"But you speak well; I've never met a foreigner who spoke as well as you."

"It is amazing what one can do when one has no choice."

"Yes," I agreed. "It is quite amazing." But even more amazing was the notion that inside this man's body and traveler's soul, he carried, just as I did, a gaping loss born of injustice. And like me, his loss had brought him to the threshold of learning. The idea that we could be so different and yet so similar was nothing less than astonishing.

Lucan propped himself up again, resting his head in his hand, picked a long weed, and bit on the stem. "What about you, Rahel?" He asked with his familiar grin. "Isn't the custom for a girl of your age to be married and raising a tribe of children? You're the first unmarried woman I've met who supports herself honorably. And," he added, "the first Jew I've met who lives apart from her people." I looked up sharply. "Daoud told me," he added as if in reply.

"You and Daoud have taken it upon yourselves to discuss me? What else did he tell you?"

Now it was he who looked flustered. "Well we didn't actually discuss you. He just told me a little bit about you. I mean, it's obvious that you aren't a member of the family."

For a moment I fell into a confused silence. Even though Marsa and I had often exchanged observations about Lucan, it never occurred to me that I myself might be a subject of such a conversation. But now, when he had told me so much about his life, I knew that he expected me to reveal something of mine.

"Well, now that you've indulged in speculation," I replied, "allow me to correct you. I never met the man that my father selected as my groom. You see, my father died before the wedding could take place. I never knew my mother; she died when I was born. The fact is that I have no real family." From here, I skipped over the story of my flight from Sura, the period of my slavery, and my time at Mar Yuhanon and proceeded to the present. "I was lucky enough to find honest work at the inn, and now I'm saving my wages in order to provide for my dowry."

Lucan bit on his piece of weed and considered what I had told him, a brief version of my life which, had he been more familiar with our ways, would have appeared mysteriously incomplete. But somehow, he was able to glean the truth, the singular certainty that traversed my words like a silent underground stream. "And so you were meant to lead a very different life."

"Well, yes, I suppose that's true. I haven't always had to work. My father was a physician. My life was once. . . comfortable."

Lucan jumped up as if I had just told him that the Caliph was standing behind him. "What?" he exclaimed. "Your father was a physician? Why didn't you say so?"

"I'm no longer the person I once was. What does it matter now?"

"But that's not true," he cried. "Your father must have been an extremely learned man. And you, as his daughter, you shouldn't be living the life of a simple cook, on some Godforsaken road to nowhere!"

"Yet that's exactly how things have turned out," I replied coolly. "The bitterness of it has faded; thank God that I haven't sunk to the depths that some women endure." Lucan nodded emphatically, but I wondered if he really understood. I looked out at our horses grazing contentedly in the grass, indifferent to all the suffering of this world. "We should be getting back," I told him. "Marsa will wonder what happened to me."

"It will be hard for you to leave the pleasant life you have at the inn," he remarked.

"No it won't. Not at all. As you said, my destiny is not that of a cook. My life will continue elsewhere. But what about you? Where will you go when the work on the dormitory is done?"

"To Fustat," he said purposefully.

"Why? Do you want to see the pyramids?"

The question made him laugh out loud. "The pyramids? Who cares about the pyramids! I'm going to seek out the physician Malik Ibn Abed. Have you heard of him?"

"I'm not familiar with all of the physicians in the world," I replied with a smile. "Who is he?"

"When my teacher, Abu Talib, fell ill, he was tended by the finest physician in Mosul. The family introduced me as Abu Talib's apprentice, and the man was kind enough to include me in the examination and diagnosis. When I told him about my dream of returning home with the knowledge and skills of a physician, he took it upon himself to write a letter of recommendation to his teacher, Malik Ibn Abed of Fustat. He said that when Ibn Abed read his letter, he might agree to take me on as his student." He paused and stared out gravely at the fields. "That letter is my only possession of any value."

As we reached the horses, I called out to him lightheartedly. "I say that we give Jamila and Sahir a good ride back. But now I know that it is I who'll have trouble keeping up with you."

"Ah, but you weren't a horseman in the cavalry of the king of Northumbria."

"The king of what?"

Lucan grinned and shook his head. "It doesn't matter." I watched how in one expert move he swung a leg over his horse and took up the reins. He waited for me to the same, and then asked, "Are you ready?" We set out at a gallop across the fields, and when I saw that I could match his pace, a wild jubilation rose within me.

"Shall we ride again tomorrow?" he asked me before we parted ways in the stable.

"Yes," I whispered, and though there was no one in sight, I trembled at my own boldness.

Yet riding with him was a delight which I could not forgo. I met him the next day, and the next, and the day after that. Our meetings fell into a pattern of riding until we found new pastures, and then resting under a tree or by a stream, each of us speaking of things that the other could never know, but only imagine.

I felt myself becoming as careless as a madwoman. And still I rode out with him, day after day, ignoring all the voices in my head but my own.

"HE'S COME, JUST as Musa said he would." Marsa and I looked up to see Daoud standing in the kitchen doorway, his normally relaxed demeanor stiff and anxious. "Fix a plate of sweets," he ordered. "And a pitcher of tamarind."

"What does he want now?"

"The same thing he always wants."

"That son of a dog! Are you going to sit with them?"

"Give me the food, and I'll go to them now."

I watched as she threw some cookies on a plate, grabbed some cups, and poured out half a jar of the tamarind drink we served only to our most important guests. "Whatever he says, bargain him down," she told him as she thrust the place into his hands. "Try to keep the damage to a minimum."

She looked so upset that I was reluctant to ask what was happening. I peered out of the small window that looked into the dining room. At this hour, it was empty except for Luna's table where she sat across from a heavyset man dressed in expensive robes. I couldn't make out the features of his face, only a thick black moustache, which he wore in the style of the Caliph's officials. "Who is he?"

"A scoundrel. A dog that lives off the work of others. His name is Ali Mustapha."

"Was it for his benefit that we prepared sweets the other day?"

She bit her lip and nodded. "Musa warned my mother that he would be paying us visit."

"What has he come for?"

She went to the window, watched for a minute, and then turned to me in disgust. "He's one of those brutes who thinks an establishment like ours is a hen that lays golden eggs. Criminals like him use any pretense to threaten us. Usually it's the matter of alcohol. We're not allowed to serve it to Muslims. If even one person claims that we serve alcohol to Muslims, Ali Mustapha shows up and demands to be paid for his consent."

"And if you refuse?"

"His father is the head of one of the oldest families in this region. If we don't pay, he'll run to the Muktasib and complain. Then the morality police will come and shut us down. It happened once, in my father's time, and it took us months to recover what we lost."

"Then why not just stop serving beer and wine?"

"Because if we don't, no one will stay here. There are plenty of other inns along this route who'll be happy to pay the bribe."

Everyone knows that the strong prey on the weak. Such is the way of the world. And so I put the incident out of my head, and didn't think of it again until the next morning, when Luna asked that I visit her in her rooms after lunch—exactly the hour that Lucan and I normally set out with the horses.

When everyone had gone to their rooms, I told Lucan that I had a headache and suggested that he ride without me. It was the hottest hour of the day, and the burning air hung in absolute stillness over the courtyard. I knocked gently on Luna's door, and her servant girl showed me in. The shutters were half closed, and the room was cool and dark. Luna invited me to sit on a wide, soft cushion, and offered me bowls of dates and almonds, but I was too uneasy to enjoy them. I wondered if Ali Mustapha had heard something about my flight from Sura and then told Luna, but the notion that Abu Said's murder had followed me so far seemed unlikely.

After complimenting the quality of my cooking, as well as the smooth manner in which I had joined the household, she turned to the real purpose of her invitation. "I've asked you here to speak about a very serious matter," she began. "A matter which requires the utmost discretion."

I nodded solemnly, as if to say that whatever was a serious matter for her was also a serious matter for me. "In the course of Ali Mustapha's visit yesterday, it came to my attention that you and Lucan often go riding together, without the presence of a third party."

So that was it. I almost smiled with relief that I was not about to be accused of murder. But given the grave expression on her face, I realized that the charges that Ali Mustapha had brought against me were in her opinion, equally severe.

"Yes," I replied simply, "but you have no cause for worry. We ride as . . . as brother and sister."

Her eyes narrowed, and I knew that she didn't believe me. "Perhaps you do, but all that really matters is how such behavior appears to others. I did my best to defend you to Ali Mustapha, but I can't tell you how upsetting it was for me to hear such a thing. If he has seen it, then others have as well."

"I'm sorry Luna," I said softly, and for a moment the only sound was that of a small child crying.

"Rahel," she said in a gentler tone. "Do you want to marry him? Everything can be arranged in a way that is respectable for both of you."

"You know I cannot."

"Then you have all the more reason to heed my advice. You must . . . keep yourself. Refrain from his company. It is because you have no family to protect you that you must be especially careful."

"I am not a child."

"Exactly. You are not a child. And that is why you cannot afford to make even one mistake."

The atmosphere of the room had become unbearably stifling; all of a sudden I craved light and open air. Somehow I managed to speak the words she wanted to hear and then hastily took my leave.

With scarcely a thought in my head I saddled Jamila and rode her out in the opposite direction Lucan and I normally took. Tears fell from my eyes, but I let the wind dry them as it hurled me into the dry, dusty heat of the road.

Later that night, I approached the chess table and motioned for Lucan to meet me in the storeroom. When I saw him rise from his place, I went out to the back courtyard and paced back and forth, trying to find the words that would put a wall between him and me. "Luna spoke with me today," I told him coolly, before he had a chance to say anything. "She asks that we refrain from spending time together."

He stared at me, perplexed, as though trying decipher the meaning of a riddle. "Is that what you want?"

"We can't ride together again."

I crossed my arms and locked my face into a somber, decisive frown. He studied my expression for a long moment. "As you wish," he said finally.

I bit my lip and gazed at him. And then, without warning, he took me in his arms and kissed me. "Good night, Rahel," he whispered and walked away, leaving me alone in the darkness.

HIS AUDACITY WAS nothing compared to the shocking fact of my own compliance. For none of my experience with men had prepared me for such a situation. In that long moment when I felt the soft force of his lips on mine, I had not cried out or tried to push him away. In truth, I had not even wanted him to stop. It was as though he had led me to the threshold of a secret door, behind which lurked the power to ruin me.

In the days that followed, I took care to avoid meeting him. I would go riding long after he had left, and each time in a new direction. He too refrained from speaking to me or disturbing me in any way. I should have been pleased, for it seemed that as far as everyone else was concerned, nothing at all had happened.

Yet under my cold surface, I was in torment. Try as I did to banish Lucan from my mind, the kiss remained on my lips like the aftertaste of strong wine, its heady sweetness infusing my mind with panic. For so long I had held a secret terror of a marriage bed. Yet in the space of moment, he had evoked a question that gave me no peace: *What if there was, in fact, nothing to fear?* I would never have believed it, had Lucan not, with one kiss, suggested that it all might be endurable.

Or perhaps even more than endurable. I was as miserable as Eve after she had eaten from the tree of knowledge. Like her, I could no longer return to the innocent state of not knowing. When I allowed myself to think about it, the memory of it drove me mad. To merely avoid speaking with him was not enough. I had to refrain even from looking at him.

EARLY ONE EVENING, while Marsa and I were stuffing peppers, Paula came into the kitchen looking for me. "One of the guests is asking for you," she said. It was Naftali, the Jew who had promised to look for Shafiqa. As I went out to meet him he rose and greeted me warmly. I could see that he had already washed and changed his clothes, and Paula had served him a pot of tea. "Are you free to sit and talk now?" he asked.

I glanced at the kitchen, now at its busiest hour, and hoped that Marsa would forgive me. "I can spare a few minutes."

"It's such a shame that you insist on wasting your life away at this inn," he remarked as he poured me some tea. "But we shall speak of that later on. What I've come to tell you is that I was in Sura, and I found your servant Shafiqa."

"You have?" I cried excitedly. "Where?"

"Just as you said, she was at her brother's stall in the market-place. When I told them that I'd seen you, she was overjoyed. She asked me to their home and received me with great hospitality. She wanted to know about all that's happened to you, but as you requested, I didn't reveal your whereabouts."

"God bless you," I murmured.

"Your servant is a good woman, still loyal to you and your father. She wept when she told me of how sorely he's still missed in the city. And when we spoke of you, she described how beautiful you looked in your white dress on the day that you were to meet your fiancé."

I smiled sadly and he continued. "She said that the young man and his father sent out search parties in all the surrounding towns and villages, but no one could tell them anything. To this day the people of Sura think that the earth just swallowed you whole." He paused and then added, "Shafiqa says that your father's enemies have not forgiven the murder." My heart skipped a beat; he knew. "Their eyes and ears are always opened for fresh news of you."

I put my head in my hands and groaned. "They'll be after me for the rest of my life."

"No," he said with conviction. "I can help you, Rahel. When I see you here, dressed in the garb of a servant and working yourself to the bone, I feel as if God Himself has sent me to help you return to your rightful place. The last time we met you told me that you have a relative, an uncle of your father's in the town of Tiflis, and that you want to search him out. Forgive me for saying so, but that seems like a very foolish plan. Do you have any idea how far you'll have to travel? And this uncle of your father's, have you even met him?"

It had been a long time since I had thought of that faraway, almost mythical relative. Now, when Naftali gave voice to my pathetic plan, the notion of finding him and hoping that he would secure me a groom struck me as nothing more than a childish fantasy. The truth came upon me then with utter clarity; I would never go to Tiflis. I had no idea if my father's uncle was even alive. And even if I did find him, there was no reason for me to trust him with the most important decision of my life. "I want to help you return to the path of a righteous Jewish woman," Naftali was saying, "to become a wife to a worthy man. If you'll only permit me, I can take you to a place where no one knows you. I can find you a decent husband. You'll have a home of your own in a community of God-fearing Jews."

A husband, so that I would no longer be alone in the world. *In a community of God-fearing Jews*, who would take me in as one of their own. And if I showed myself to be righteous and devout, they might even come to speak my name with respect. Respect and honor. I had once taken them for granted but now I knew them to be more valuable than gold. "Yes," I told him with a certainty that I had not known since the day of my engagement. "I would be grateful if you could help me."

His eyes lit up at my acquiescence. "Tomorrow I'm continuing on my way to the town of Aleppo. I have contacts in the community there. When I tell them about your circumstances I'm sure a groom will be found in no time. Next time I return here, God willing, it will be with an offer of marriage."

"No!" I cried, alarmed. "You mustn't say anything about my circumstances. Any groom will want to make inquiries, and my father's enemies will hear of it and know that I am alive."

"Yes," he nodded thoughtfully. "That could happen. But any groom will also need proof that you're in fact a Jew." He considered this problem for a moment, and then his face brightened. "Listen. I've met Shafiqa, and she has verified that your father was a Jew. Hopefully, that will be good enough."

"It will have to be."

"Oh!" he exclaimed suddenly, patting his belt. "I almost forgot. Here. This," he said as he withdrew a small pouch, "is from Shafiqa. She asked me to give it to you."

I took the pouch and spilled its contents into the palm of my hand. And there, flashing gold in the warm light of the lanterns was the *hamsa* pendant that Shafiqa had given me in the moments before Abu Said burst into our house and changed my life forever. The shock of seeing it again in my palm was so great that I could hardly speak. "Shafiqa told me it was once your mother's."

"Yes," I whispered. "All this time I've been without it and my fate has been abysmal. God willing, now my luck will change." I held up the chain of bright gold, feeling the finely-carved metal graze my palm. I put it back in the pouch and glanced toward the kitchen. "God bless you, Naftali. When will you be back?"

He made a brief calculation in his head and replied, "I expect in about a month's time. Hopefully, I'll bring good news for you."

"God be with you. I'll await your word."

Once I was back in the kitchen, I ran out the back courtyard, where I burst into quiet tears. I took out the necklace and held it up to the light of a lantern, entranced by the delicate shadows it cast on the courtyard walls. Never, not even in Sura, had I felt my mother's presence as strongly as I felt it at that moment. With a trembling hand, I fastened it on my neck, and swore never to take it off.

Naftali left the next morning, and with his going, I knew that my days at the inn were numbered.

I NOW LOOKED upon Naftali as an angel, come to repair all the damage that had been done and set my life right again. Finally I would be a bride, and the terrible abyss of dishonor and licentiousness that I had fallen into would be left behind. Just as the ritual bath has the power to wash away impurity, marriage would make me clean again: good and respectable in my own eyes and in the eyes of others.

Yet as the days passed, a hard pit of dread rooted in my heart. Though I tried to think only of the new life I would soon have as a married woman, I could not forget for a single moment that once married I would have to endure not just one, but an infinite number of "wedding nights." Though the act might be sanctified in the eyes of God, I would feel nothing but the black horror of being taken against my will.

Only one thing gave me reason to think that it might be otherwise. The memory of what Lucan had done remained vivid, not only in my heart, but in every part of me. I tried with all my might to banish it from my thoughts, so that I might somehow stand under the marriage canopy as though I knew nothing at all of men.

THE MUSICIANS WERE Berber tribesmen who had crossed the sea in order to perform, by royal invitation, at the court of the Caliph. Everyone hoped that Luna would find a way to elicit a "rehearsal," and when an agreement was reached, word spread quickly through all the nearby villages.

That night the dining hall was so crowded that the audience had to stand. Tables and chairs were pushed to the walls as the musicians took their places in the center of the room. As soon as the first note emerged from their instruments, an awed silence fell upon the crowd. Their mastery of the instruments approached perfection, and the guests were soon absorbed in the music, clapping their hands and singing along with the fast pieces, and then swaying, enraptured, to the rhythm of the slower ones. The minute I was done with the dishes I joined the crowd, blissfully surrendering to the flow of the music. And then, all of a sudden, I heard a soft, low whisper in my ear. "You once promised me another chess match."

The sound of his voice startled me. I couldn't see him, for he stood behind me, but I could feel the folds of his robe and the heat of the nearness of him. A shiver went through me, a raw tremor of panic and desperation. "No," I whispered firmly.

"Just one game. I've missed you, Rahel. You won't even look at me, but I see you, and I know that if not for Luna . . ."

"I can't."

"You've missed me as well. If you didn't, you would at least look me in the eye when we speak."

"I have not missed you."

"Then turn and look at me."

"No." Though his clothes fell short of touching mine, his presence behind me was maddening. I felt pinned under the weight of him, so that I could hardly breathe.

"I'm going to take a chess set up to my chamber," he whispered. "If you haven't joined me by the end of the next song, I won't disturb you again."

I felt him moving away from me, and I gasped as though struggling for air. The song ended and there was much trilling and clapping. Now there would be a slow song, perhaps even a love ballad. My heart was racing and my palms were cold with sweat. I screamed silent commands to myself: to wait, to think, to stifle the urge that would destroy me.

A new song had begun, and I stilled my frenzied mind and willed myself to listen to the singer's passionate voice. *"You grew before my eyes and my love for you grew. I am in love. I love in spite of this weakness, and I weaken because of your love. Tell me, what do I do?"* Where had I heard those lines before? All of a sudden, the image of Khalil and Samira arose in my mind. Yes. Khalil had spoken those words to her. I had heard his warm, tremulous voice recite them as I crouched in the dark of the cupboard; how beautiful they sounded now, how true, how full of fine feeling. The sweet, familiar lines overpowered me, infusing me with both the longing of that moment and the terror of this one.

Samira and Khalil had paid dearly for their recklessness, and it had always seemed to me a pitiful bargain, but now, when I myself was fitful with an impulse so foreign that I barely knew its name, I knew that one would have to be dead to ignore it. *What could be the harm?* my racing thoughts cried. *Soon you will submit, night after night, to the touch of another out of mere duty. What can happen if you submit out of your own will, your own desire?*

I glanced around as if to check if anyone might be reading my thoughts, but no one was even looking at me. They were gazing dreamily at the musicians, transported by the words of the song and the slow, haunting melody coming from the lute. As I pushed my way out to the courtyard, no one took more notice of me than they would of an annoying fly.

The courtyard was empty. A pale half-moon shone in the indigo sky, and a gentle, cooling breeze was blowing on the night air. Silently, I climbed the stairs and then glanced about nervously. *Turn back!* I screamed at myself. *You too will pay dearly.* But the words of the song echoed in my ears and drowned out my screams.

"You've come," Lucan murmured as I opened his door. The only light in the room was a dim lantern, but still I could discern the gladness in his eyes. His chamber was identical to mine, except that he had brought in a low table, and a faded, threadbare cushion. The chess board lay open on the table, and though he had in fact invited me for a game, it took me by surprise. For as I crossed the courtyard, I had not known what to expect. Would he fall upon me as Khalil had fallen upon Samira? Or would he merely kiss me again? But now that I was alone with him in his chamber, he did neither. Instead, he began to set up the pieces on the board.

I stared at him, mortified that I had perhaps misunderstood. Could he have truly invited me for nothing more than a chess game? And here I had agonized and cursed myself a thousand times. "Sit down," he said, gesturing to the only cushion in the room. "Are you ready?" I nodded uneasily. "Then we shall have a match." And then he added with a shy smile, "I've long wondered how you perform when there's no audience."

AND SO WE had a game. I was so feverish that I could barely concentrate, and not surprisingly, he quickly vanquished me. But instead of being pleased, he was disappointed. "You're holding back," he protested. "I insist that we have another game, but this time, you must be merciless." And so, with uncanny effort, I managed to forget what was to come and apply all of my attention to the contest on the board. Somehow, I was able to recall some of the ploys to weaken and entrap an opponent. Perhaps they are not known in the West, for Lucan was an easy victim. "Much better," he remarked gallantly as I cornered his king. "I suspected that you had it in you to beat me."

He turned around and reached for a small vessel. "I managed to take a little wine from the dinner table." He grinned. "Would you like a drink? I only have this one cup, so we'll have to share." Nights at the inn had taught me the power of wine. Many times I had seen irritated and overwrought travelers turn amicable after a drink. I took the cup and inhaled its warm aroma. Then I put the wine to my lips and drank deeply. When I handed it back to him, he finished the contents of the cup, in a way that told me that he too was anxious. The concert must have come to its conclusion. Outside in the corridors, I could hear the guests crooning to each other. But Lucan, it seemed, wanted nothing more than to talk.

He told me more about how people lived in that cold and far away place of his birth, and I told stories about my life in Sura. He especially wanted to hear about my father's work in treating the sick, and so I recalled stories of broken limbs made whole, of infections fought, and of diseases cured. We had spoken of these things before, and now I wondered again what would happen before this night was over.

The late hour and the flickering light of the lantern gave our conversation a quality of stark clarity. It seemed to cut away all artifice, leaving only what most essential, and led us to speak of things which usually remain locked in the soul. "You once had a good life, a family with a good name and friends who knew you well," I reflected. "How can you bear the fact that no one here knows of your family's name, or your brother's bravery, or your courage in battle?"

He shrugged. "That's the price a traveler pays, and I'm prepared to pay it."

"But all that you've seen and learned will always set you apart, even from your own family. You'll know many worlds, yet you'll scarcely be able to claim even one." I paused, trying to give words to the thing that I most wanted to ask him. "How can you bear to always be an outsider, with no one who truly cares what becomes of you?"

"I suppose that I've grown accustomed to this life, and my place in it." He fell silent for a moment and then added, "When I close my eyes at night, it isn't these barren plains I see, but the cool, comforting green of my home. You also left a home. Isn't it the same for you?"

The mention of my home at a moment such as this had the power to send me running for the shelter of my room. I only had to imagine my father's face if he could see me now, sitting in the bedchamber of a Christian from God knows where. "It does me no good to think of the home I once had."

He poured a second cup of wine and held it out to me. "Here. Let us drink to all that remains behind." I took the cup from him and drank readily. It no longer mattered to me that I might live to curse this night. The affection I felt for him at that moment overwhelmed all. He put his cup on the table and then bent over and kissed me.

Though every nerve of my body was frozen with alarm, I was relieved that the event was finally upon me. I wanted him to go on, to just do it before I changed my mind. He slid the scarf from my head, and stroked my hair, clasping me to him as if it were something he had long wanted to do, and though his hands were gentle his touch was like fire. "Have you done this before?" he whispered.

What to tell him? That I had? That I hadn't? That I hadn't meant to? I opened my eyes, and when I saw his face, his eyes alive with desire, I whispered, "Don't stop."

He moved his hand slowly over my clothes, as if I were a delicate piece of pottery that might break, but even this touch made me freeze with trepidation. *Be calm*, I told myself, *or he will lose his nerve*. I had envisioned that the act would involve quick and sharp movements, and that I would soon struggle breathlessly, the hard weight of him sinking into me. Why then was it taking so long? He kissed me again, and I felt his hand take hold of my tunic and lift it over my head, exposing my skin to cool night air. What did he see there, in the dim light of the lantern? His gaze on my naked body was almost painful, but also fascinating, for his expression was full of delight. And again, I waited for him to fall upon me, to crush me into the bed, but instead, he began again to stroke me with his fingertips, watching my reaction in the dim light of the lantern.

I closed my eyes and quivered uncontrollably, and suddenly I felt his lips on my breast, and I almost screamed out from the shock of it. And then he moved his hand down to my leggings. I stiffened in sudden recollection of how he would soon hurt me, but nonetheless, in spite of what was to come, I somehow yearned for that pain, for that horrible sensation of being ripped open; I burned for it now as if only that could cure my terror. "Do you want me to stop?" he whispered.

"I want. . ." I tried to reply, but I could not speak it. "I want. . ."

"What do you want?" he whispered, his familiar grin turning the corners of his mouth.

"I want. . ." I started for the third time, but I could not answer him. There were no words for what I wanted, and even if there were, how could I speak them? His hands held me to him, and his green eyes danced in the light of the lantern. Wordlessly, I moved my hand slowly down the length of his chest, his stomach, and then to the belt of his pants.

"Take them off." I whispered, bold as a whore, so bold I no longer knew myself. Lucan did as I said, but I could not look at him as he had gazed at me. He lay down at my side, and again I froze like a corpse, my legs shut as tightly as a sealed vessel. But with the mysterious skill of a sorcerer, he somehow knew what to do so that they would open for him. His hand, that same hand that I had seen move pieces thoughtfully over the chess board, knew the secret, wordless touch that loosened my thighs and made them sink languidly in to the softness of the bed, so that when he lay atop me, as my vile assailant had that first time, my legs miraculously parted of their own accord, and my body opened to him as readily as a flower opens to the sunlight.

WHEN IT WAS done I sprang for the wash basin, recalling Hassan's urging on that fateful night when my undoing began. Lucan watched me, amused, and then beckoned me to return to the bed, where he took me in his arms and soon fell asleep. But I, of course, had never been more awake. Truly, it had not been very bad. This was a joyous discovery for me. From the cradle of his arms I looked up at the open window, where the half moon and stars shone over us, and relived every moment of it all in my mind, until finally, sleep came to me as well.

But even more wondrous things awaited me that night. Later on, at the hour just before sunrise, I felt his hand slide like a feather along the length of me, and like a feather, arouse the most exquisite of sensations, sensations that I had not dreamt possible in a body of mere flesh and blood. It was then, in the grayest light of morning, that I learned the secret that is known by all women but never spoken. For just as the dry ground can feel the coming of the rainstorm, just as the river senses the approaching torrent of the flood, just as a gray daybreak anticipates dawn, my body responded to his touch. And when I could resist no longer, I exploded and trembled with the rapture of a bursting dam, and he covered my mouth with his hand so the low groan that sprung from my throat would not awake our neighbors. But my own sounds must have stirred him. For no sooner had my body stilled than he turned me over and had me again.

All of this came upon me as a shock and a wonder, with the hazy, fantastical quality of a dream. But the cries of the animals waking below in the courtyard brought me back to my senses. I slid away from him, rose from his bed, threw on my robe, and opened the door to his room. The long corridor was cool and still, but it would not be for long. "No one must know of this," I whispered to him before I left, because it occurred to me that the night we just had passed was the sort that often finds its way into the tales of travelers.

"No one shall," he murmured lazily. "Where are you going?"

"To my chamber. If I'm seen leaving your room it will be the end of me."

He smiled at me and whispered, "You surprised me, Rahel. Who would have thought that you have the appetite of a man?"

His words appalled me, yet I could hardly deny it; for I had consented to all of it. And I had done it not for love, like Samira, nor for money, like a whore. Why then had I done it? Invigorated by a by fresh wave of remorse, I ran to my room where I again washed myself vigorously. Outside my window, a bright orange glow was rising over the fields. Numb with confusion, I tried to banish the impossible visions of the night that kept bursting upon my mind.

By THE TIME Marsa came in, I had already started the dough for the morning bread, and set the cauldron to boil. "Where were you last night?" she asked as she swept her hair into a head scarf. "When they started singing *My Love is Dreaming of the Day*, I looked around for you, but I didn't see you anywhere."

The unsuspecting tone of her voice calmed me, and I felt like one who has narrowly missed disaster. "I wasn't feeling well, so I went up to bed."

"To bed? How could you sleep with all the noise?"

I shrugged casually. "Anyone who lives above the courtyard learns to sleep through anything."

How? I asked myself a thousand times that morning. *How could I have done it?* I must have been mad. Truly, I was an abomination. And yet, my dismay was tinged, perversely, with a small measure of self-satisfaction. For who would have thought that I had it in me to be so brave? It was as though I had cured my own soul of its sickness. I reveled in the knowledge that when the day came for me to stand under my wedding canopy, it would be without fear.

Thankfully, I didn't have to face Lucan until the midday meal. For several weeks now, the men had been forgoing breakfast in the kitchen in order to start work early, asking instead that we send out bread and jam with one of the children. But I well knew that the lunch hour would come soon enough, when he would take his place at the table and gaze smugly at me, the whore who had slept in his bed.

When I heard the men, I busied myself in the kitchen until the meal was about to begin, and then took a seat on the same side of the table as he, so that he could not look upon me. When he and Leo began to argue over how much water should be used to mix the plaster, the very sound of his voice set me trembling.

I needed to speak with him one final time. I would tell him that I had made a terrible mistake that would never happen again, and demand that he never mention it to anyone. Though I had managed to avoid all contact with him for the length of the meal, he sent me a searching glance as he passed the kitchen, and I motioned with my eyes toward the stable, hoping that he would understand my meaning.

After the lunch dishes were washed, I didn't run out to the stable as usual, but lingered to grind spices for the evening meal. I dreaded the moment that I would have to face him. I imagined that he expected I would yield to him again, for he had already proven that I could be had for a cup of wine. I tried to rehearse in my mind all I would say to him, yet nothing sounded right to me, as if words appropriate for my purpose had yet to be invented.

When I finally went out to the courtyard, he had taken his horse and gone. Quickly, I saddled Jamila and rode out to the lone tree in the field where we always met. But once alone with him, I could scarcely face him. Rather than sit by his side, I remained standing, arms folded across my chest, my gaze aloof and troubled.

"You're unhappy," he remarked with unmasked puzzlement.

"I . . . I was not myself yesterday."

He came to me and took my hands in his as if to still them. "Rahel, you are like no girl I've ever met. All morning I've been thinking about last night. I could scarcely believe it when you came to my room. Even now, it seems like a dream."

"I've dishonored myself," I said, still unable to behold his face.

"No." He shook his head vehemently. "If your feelings for me were true, then you have not dishonored yourself." I looked up at him in astonishment. His face was so solemn and sincere that I wondered if I had been entirely wrong about him. Perhaps he would not boast to the others about what he had done. Perhaps he didn't even think me a whore.

Tears came to my eyes, and he reached out to me, but I pulled away. "My religion teaches," I said in a trembling voice, "as does yours, that the only honorable union between a man and woman is in marriage, and that the only acceptable marriage is to one of the same faith. So you see, Lucan, I've betrayed everything. I have betrayed . . . all that I am."

He appeared utterly confused. "How can you speak of betrayal when—"

"It can't be, Lucan," I told him firmly, emboldened by my own disgust at myself. "We can never be together again. Please, if you care for me at all, don't tempt me with sly invitations. I am not a man, and if I only lived by my desire it would destroy me."

"Then marry me," he said. "We are right for each other Rahel—I know it. What does it matter that we weren't born into the same faith?"

All the words I had to answer him fell away. "I can't."

"Then why did you come to me last night?"

"My resolve failed me," I managed to reply. "Can you not see, Lucan? Do you not understand how wretched I am? If only I had a father, or a brother to reign me in, to keep me from . . . devastation . . . but I am alone, and I'm afraid that you'll be my ruin."

"Your ruin?" he repeated incredulously. "Is that what you think of me?"

The hurt in his tone was too much for me to bear. I rose abruptly from my place. "Forgive me," I mumbled, my voice breaking. I climbed atop Jamila, and forced myself to look upon him, to gaze one final time at the face that had led me to my undoing. His eyes stared back at me with a saddened expression that tore into me like a dagger. But I did not allow myself to cry until I was out of his sight.

IT WAS ONLY a few short weeks later that a driver arrived at the inn bearing a scroll for me. "It's from a merchant by the name of Ben Yosef," he told me, as he handed me the roll of parchment sealed with wax. The thrill of receiving a letter addressed to me was almost greater than my curiosity about the contents. The writing, like most of the correspondence my father once had with other Jews, was Aramaic but penned in Hebrew letters. So much time had passed since I had last seen Hebrew script that I feared I may have forgotten how to read it, but as soon as my eyes fell upon the black letters, they spoke to me, revealing their secrets like old friends:

Rahel—

God willing, this letter will find you healthy and well. Though I'll soon be leaving Aleppo, I've decided to write to you already, for I have some very good news. I've found you a groom. His name is Shlomo Ben Moshe, and he is thirty-four years of age. The man is, alas, a widower, with four young children. Though he toils six days a week as a cobbler, he is a righteous man, well-liked and respected in the community.

And now Rahel, when I've secured a worthy candidate for you, please allow me a small confession: When I set out to find a groom for you, my hopes were modest. As you must be aware, your status as an orphan, together with the fact that you have lived outside a community of Jews for so long, rendered the task problematic. I found it necessary to be some-what vague when describing you, attesting only to the fact that you are indeed a Jew. But to your great fortune, this man, Shlomo Ben Moshe, is desperate to find a wife to help raise his children and provide them with a proper Jewish home. When I spoke of your father's profession and explained that you are from the distinguished community of Sura, he consented to the match.

I will be leaving Aleppo sometime next week, and I expect that I'll come for you some two weeks after that. In the meantime, you must pre-pare yourself, both mentally and physically for the journey, and for the new life that will soon be yours.

God be with you,
Naftali Ben Yosef

P.S. Shlomo has asked if you are familiar with the laws of family purity. Obviously, I didn't know how to respond to this delicate question. In any case, may I suggest that on your arrival, you pay a visit to the wife of Rabbi Isaiah, who will instruct you in all you need to know.

I SHOULD HAVE been ecstatic with joy, thanking God each morning and evening for forgiving my sins and guiding me back to the path of righteousness. And yet I could not rejoice; on the contrary, with each passing day, I grew more and more fearful of Naftali's return. *Who is this man, this stranger who has agreed to make me his wife?* I would think to myself, at first with curiosity, but soon with increasing alarm. *What would he do if he were to discover that I have abandoned the most sacred laws of the Jews? That I have desecrated the Sabbath and the holy festivals? That I've failed to fast on the fast days, and I have eaten food that is forbidden to a Jew?*

And all of these were mere trifles compared to the fact of my defilement, both at the hands of others and by my own doing. For no amount of honorable behavior now could make me a virgin on my wedding night. At the end of his letter, Naftali made mention of the notion of family purity. I well knew that he was speaking of the monthly visits to the *mikveh* baths, by which a woman purifies herself for her husband. But could those waters ever wash away the impurities of the body and soul which are acquired in the bed of another man? Surely they could not.

In the dead of night, when the truth cannot hide, I would speak scornfully to myself, a harsher judge than the sternest of rabbis. *How can you think that you might be worthy of a decent man? You've already proven that you have the soul of a whore. You'll wear a mask of deceit during the day, and taint the sanctity of your own marriage bed at night.* Surely I was unfit to become the mother of any man's children.

It was not only my own unworthiness that troubled me. Though I was scarcely in a position to refuse him, I was not all certain that this Shlomo Ben Moshe would please me, for I knew nothing about his physical appearance, nor his character, nor his temperament, nor his intellect. How easily I had once been willing to put my fate in the hands of my father, and even in the hands of my father's uncle. But I was no longer a child. Now that I knew something about the world, I could no longer entrust my destiny to others.

Even as I struggled to make peace with the fact of my marriage, fleeting images of Lucan, which I had sealed like vessels of wine in a dark cellar, would burst into memory. There were moments when I heard him laughing with Daoud, and I would close my eyes and recall the hardness of his arms as he held himself over me. And when I would see him at work, or at the midday meal, I was reminded of the splendid form of his body, and my knees would collapse in silent waves of desire. Yet I did not even need to see him with my eyes in order for these thoughts to arise in me. Even as I performed the most mundane of tasks, chopping parsley, or stirring soup, I would think of the way his hands moved over me, or the slight movement of his hips, rolling like waves breaking on the shore.

Though I took great pains to avoid him, there were times when I couldn't ignore his presence. One day at lunch, Olivia teased Marsa about how irritable she had been since her husband had left for Damascus. As everyone at the table fell over themselves with laughter, I allowed myself a brief glance at Lucan. His gaze met mine and then he quickly looked away, but the entreaty in his eyes was like a bright spark that inflamed my soul.

A terrible restlessness came over me. I lost my appetite for food, and I could no longer take pleasure in music or in the company of others. My sleep too became fitful and anxious. Each night I would dream the same terrible dream in which I was led down a long, darkened hallway into a bed chamber where a strange man lay waiting for me.

And then one night as I hovered fitfully at the edge of sleep, I dreamt that I lay between two naked men whose faces I could not see. Filled with dread, I lit a lamp and held it over the first. Though I couldn't discern his face, his body was unfamiliar, as strange to me as any of the guests that passed through the inn. Terrified, I turned to the second man. And in the dim light of the lamp, I saw that it was Lucan. Every fiber of my being warmed with joy and relief at the sight of him. And in that instant, which flickered like a flame of blue fire that rises from the heat, I finally understood the riddle of Anton's words from our final conversation: my terrible fate had indeed given me the gift of choice.

I woke like one who has died and been reborn. Silently, as though enthralled by a force I could no longer oppose, I rose up and went out of my chamber. All was still and quiet, for it was that hour of the night when even the insects sleep. I moved slowly down the corridor to his room, tried the door and found it open, and, ethereal as a dancer, I slipped into his bed.

"Rahel," he whispered as he clasped me to him. "I knew you would come back." And suddenly, as though a spell had been broken, all the doubt that had tormented me fell away. I curled into him as if he himself were the only home I would ever need. As the dawn broke in the sky, he moved his fingers through my hair and spoke into my ear. "My life is neither easy nor comfortable, but I haven't known a single moment of regret. And if you stay with me, neither will you."

What he was suggesting was inconceivable; it was as fantastic and impossible as a dream. "We don't need to be married; in the eyes of God, our union will be blessed. We'll live like wandering nomads; the entire world will be ours." I closed my eyes and listened to the soft rhythm of his breath, rising and falling. "Will you come with me to Egypt?"

The words he spoke fell upon my ears like a sweet song. But how could it be done? How could a woman just go off with a man and live without the seal of marriage? I had never heard of such a thing. Yet somehow, in spite of its perverseness, I suspected that the life that Lucan was offering me was the only one that I could happily live.

IT WAS IN the very early hours of morning that I left Lucan's chamber. I prayed that no one would see me, but as I closed his door behind me, I caught sight of Marsa in the courtyard below. For a second her eyes met mine, and although the sky was still dark and the moon was only half full, I knew that she well understood what she had seen.

Now, alone with her in the kitchen, Marsa was glaring at me, waiting for me to deny everything, or at least break down into hysterical tears. But I had no desire for such a show. "He's taken advantage of you, you know," she said scornfully. "He saw that you're a helpless orphan with no one in the world to look after you. He'll use you for his pleasure until you no longer interest him, and then he'll throw you away like an old carcass!"

"He's asked me to come with him to Egypt."

"He has?" She laughed a nervous little laugh of relief, and cried, "God be praised! Then you'll marry."

"No."

"You go to his bed and you don't wish him for your husband?" She threw up her hands. "I don't understand you."

"No. I suppose you don't."

"How? How can anyone understand you?" she retorted, her voice rising in anger. "How dare you enter our house and behave as if you're in a brothel?"

Her words made me wince, but they could no longer wound me. "We tried to be discreet. Does your mother know?"

At that moment Luna herself entered the kitchen. I could tell, by the expression on her face that she had heard us. Her eyes, full of righteous fury, narrowed on me. "Oh Rahel! How could you?" She too expected me to collapse in a fit of tears. But I was past the shame, the humiliation, the tears, and the begging for forgiveness. I met her eyes and told her simply, "I have nothing to say. If you like, I'll pack up my things and leave."

Luna and Marsa exchanged distraught glances. They were torn, as it were, between the depravity of my behavior and their reluctance to lose me. "I see," Luna replied, for she was nothing if not quick-witted. "Rahel, you are not my daughter. If you were I would deal with you very differently, but thankfully, your weak character and loose morals are not my concern. Still, I'm prepared to make you an offer, the most generous offer I can make, under the circumstances. You may stay on here, in my employment, on the condition that you refrain from all contact with Lucan.

"No," I told her, strangely calm.

"What? You mean to say that . . .?"

"Lucan has asked me to leave with him. I'm going to accept his offer."

"And live as his whore?" Marsa cried "What a child you are! Do you really think that this fantasy can last? It won't be long before he gets tired of you. He'll leave you, and then where will you be? Do you really think that anyone else will treat you as well as we have? Don't

you see yourself for what you are? You're nothing but...prey...
easy prey for all of the scoundrels of this world. Good people like us,
I'm sorry to say, are few and far between."

"If he chooses to leave me, then I'll manage on my own. I
wouldn't want to remain even one day with someone who has tired
of me." Though my voice was full of purpose, I could scarcely believe
my words.

Marsa's opened her mouth in silent horror, as if I were a bizarre
species of animal, and Luna stared at me, incredulous. "Then go,"
Luna cried, pointing angrily at the doors. "Go and fend for yourself!
Leave this house and don't come back." Without another word, I ran
out the back in the direction of the storehouse where I found Lucan
mixing a vat of mud and straw.

"Marsa saw me leaving your room," I told him breathlessly. "Luna's asked me to leave immediately."

He stepped away from the vat and took my hand. "Then we'll
leave together."

I looked up at him, not quite believing how quickly things were
unfolding. "Are you sure?"

He embraced me and whispered, "We'll join the very next caravan going west."

I ran to my room, retrieved the small pouch that held my collected wages from under my mattress, and dusted off my traveler's bag.
The things that Anton had given me—the map, stones for starting
fires, a rope—were still inside, together with the knife and the blanket that I had taken from Omar Alharazi's house. I drew out Khalil's
boots and I was about to try them on when there was a soft knock on
my door. I didn't answer, but Luna pushed it open and let herself in.

"Rahel." She glanced at my open bag and shook her head as if I
were a stubborn child. "I know that I spoke harshly with you this
morning, but please understand. I only said those things out of concern for you."

She looked again at the open bag and frowned. "To leave with
Lucan is just foolishness. You're about to make a terrible mistake."
She took my two hands in her own and her solemn, clever eyes
caught mine. "Please stay. I promise you, we'll put aside this whole
incident and never mention it again. As long as you remain here with
us, you'll never lack for anything."

"Oh Luna!" I cried, embracing her as a daughter embraces her mother. "You've been so good to me, better than I deserved." I wiped my eyes and then embraced her again, for I knew that she was offering me yet another chance to live respectably. But something had turned in my mind, so that the notion of a respectable life, a notion that had once seemed the sole purpose of my journey, seemed little more than a childish dream that God had not written into my fate. It would be difficult to explain such a thing, but I felt that I owed it to her to try.

"When Anton found out about my disguise, he was angry at first. But once his anger passed he sought me out again, just as you have now. He spoke to me then of things that seemed extraordinary, even unnatural. He said that I was master of my fate, and that God had granted me a new dawn." I smiled in recollection of that night, of how we had abandoned all pretense and spoken of truths so powerful that I could still recall every word. "Of course I understood nothing. It was as if he was speaking a language I had never heard. But your son is a very wise man, and I believe I've finally come to perceive his meaning."

"It cost Anton nothing to say those things," she replied. "But you could pay a very high price for them."

"But that's exactly it! I've already lost everything. I have nothing left to lose. I'm like a pilgrim, like a destitute monk who's relinquished all, but gained the entire world."

She gazed at me with pitying eyes and moved toward the door. "My poor, foolish girl." She shook her head. "This world that you think you've gained is merciless. And as for the freedom you seek, you'll find that it's nothing but an illusion."

My last days at the inn were not easy. Olivia regarded me with the cold, proud expression she used with guests who had failed to earn her respect. Leo endeavored, under the guise of good-natured jokes, to convey that he, for one, did not feel it his place to judge me. Daoud, though clearly displeased with me, sent word to Abbas Tahiri that Jamila was for sale, and arranged for us to join a caravan heading west for Damascus in three days time.

Yet it was Marsa's sour, disapproving looks that were hardest to bear. Like her sister, she wanted little to do with me. Though we continued to work in the kitchen side by side, she took pains to avoid saying anything more than was necessary.

I understood in those last days that I had crossed an invisible line. I had exiled myself from the world of the virtuous, and that in choosing Lucan, I had chosen the way of the outcast, the heretic, and the vagabond, who may live alongside the society of the righteous, but are never welcomed into it. I should have felt sorry for abandoning the faith of my ancestors. I should have been wary of taking to the highway with a naïve, defenseless foreigner. I should have been anxious and fearful, for I was well-acquainted with the wickedness of this world. But all I felt was elation.

The caravan was set to leave at dawn with a Bedouin camel driver, Adnan, whom I knew from his regular stops at the inn. When I carried my bag down to the courtyard, travelers were already loading the camels with bags and provisions. Adnan showed Lucan and me to our camels, which were being saddled by a wiry Bedouin tribesman, whom he introduced as Tariq. I watched for a moment as he deftly packed the saddle bags. "These two fine people are friends of Daoud," Adnan told him, and held out a hand to Lucan who shook it warmly.

As I climbed atop the kneeling camel, he jerked forward, and then up and backward. I gave a little cry of surprise, and suddenly I was sitting high above the ground, looking into to the soft, orange light that was rising over the land.

Fall is the best time of year for a caravan journey. The mornings are cold and clear, and the morning's heat quickly wears itself out and then retreats like a coward. We rode from early morning until the fading light of dusk. Though there was a feeling of companionship among the travelers, much of the time passed without talk, for the steady pace of the camel and the silence of the desert made each man turn into himself.

"The desert is clean," Tariq said to Lucan as we sat one night by the fire, the deep blue of the sky enlivened by a golden moon and a thousand silvery stars. The hour was late, and the rest of the travelers had set out their mats and gone to sleep. "The cities are full of trouble and noise. The only place you can hear your own thoughts is here." His words fell on my ears like the clear tones of an oud. As we rode, I would gaze out on the hills and valleys of sand, and their emptiness somehow filled me with contentment.

On the evening of the fifth day, we came upon the ruins of an ancient city whose edifices and columns still stood as if rising out of the earth. "It's called Tadmor," Tariq told us.

Lucan stared out at the ruins from atop his camel. "Can we have a look?"

Tariq glanced up at the sun, and warned us that it would soon begin its descent. "Don't you want to ride on into the town with the others?" he asked.

"I've seen many towns," Lucan answered, "but where will I ever see a sight like this again?"

Tariq broke into a wide grin, as if with those words, Lucan had revealed himself to be a kindred spirit, and he joined us as we rode out to the wreckage of wasting ruins and fallen pillars that were strewn along the ancient roads. When we reached what once must have been the town's center, we climbed down from the camels and set out to look around on foot.

The evening winds blew sand and pebbles down the ruined streets. Lucan walked off toward the largest of the pagan temples, while Tariq and I wandered amongst the rows of broken columns. After some time, we all met again at a stone platform, flanked in each corner by a group of four columns that soared into the sky. "They say that the Romans built all this," Tariq told us.

Lucan shook his head in wonder. "Do you have any idea how far this place is from Rome?" He circled the platform slowly, gazing at the stone columns, and shook his head again. "And in Baratiniya, not one hour from my village, these same Romans built a wall that traverses the entire island."

"Where is Baratiniya?" Tariq asked.

Lucan and I exchanged glances. "At the end of the earth," Lucan told him.

Tariq shrugged, unimpressed. "It's said that the Romans were the most fearsome people who ever lived. They brought their roads and their baths and their temples to every corner of the world. But where are they now? What has become of them?" His question echoed out into the silent twilight. It rolled into the road and mingled in the dust, which rose and floated out into the endless desert. Tariq pointed to the sky. "Only Allah is eternal."

"Let's spend the night here," Lucan said.

But Tariq shook his head. "No. It isn't safe. It's best that we spend the night with the rest of the caravan. In the morning, the merchants in the town will open their stalls and you can buy provisions for the remainder of the journey."

The caravan traveled on for four more days. On the last night, Tariq came again to sit with us. "We've only known each other for a short time, but I've observed you," he said to Lucan. "I've led more than a thousand men on this journey, but I've never met anyone who carries himself as you do. Forgive me, but I must know: where is the land that you have come from? Are your people brave or cowardly? Do they live in peace, or do they have enemies? Are they blessed with full harvests, or must they toil for their bread? Are they pagans or do they worship Allah?"

Lucan answered all of Tariq's questions, and when they had spoken for some time, Tariq asked him, "And what of this girl?" Lucan looked at me and smiled wistfully. "In another time, in another place, she would be my wife."

Tariq turned to me and smiled. "Has your father granted you his blessing?"

I looked up at the heavens, with their distant, elusive stars. "My father knows all the reasons for the life I've chosen."

THE NEXT MORNING, we rode into Damascus. Anyone who's seen the splendor of Baghdad can't help feeling disappointment in any other city. And yet, there was something in the rush of noise and color that brought Baghdad to mind.

Adnan showed us to the spot just outside the market where the camel drivers gather. We asked about a caravan leaving for Egypt, but they told us that no caravan would be traveling south until the weather turned cooler. "Why don't you join a caravan that's heading to Tyre," one of them suggested. "There's one leaving this afternoon, and from there you can easily find a boat to Alexandria."

Lucan agreed immediately. He had spent time in Tyre when he arrived from Venezia, and he remembered the city well. The merchant showed us to the driver, who regarded us—a fair-haired stranger traveling with a local girl—suspiciously.

"Is this your wife?" he asked Lucan.

"Yes," he replied firmly. Skeptical, he looked us over as if such a coupling was not possible. But when Lucan reached into his purse and asked the price of the journey, he took our money and called for his man to show us to the camels.

Lucan had said that I was his wife, and this meant that we had to observe certain rules. As my husband, Lucan was regarded as my master, and I had to refrain from all contact with the other men. Yet the situation also had advantages; it was understood that we would sleep beside each other, and we could converse freely at all hours of the day.

BEFORE OUR EYES, the terrain slowly changed from that of a barren desert to green mountains and valleys. The scented air was like a salve to our throats, still parched with the dryness of the desert. We rode through forests of cedar and pine, and passed through pleasant villages with handsome stone houses and gardens abundant with fruit trees.

"If my mother could see this place she'd think she'd gone to paradise," Lucan told me one night as we lay under the stars.

I tried to conjure up an image of the woman who was Lucan's mother, perhaps an older, grayer version of Lucan himself, but I could not. "Tell me more about her," I said. "You've told me so little." Though Lucan had, in fact, told me plenty of stories about his family, his village, and his time as a soldier, I felt as if I barely knew anything about him at all. I wanted, for instance, to know the words of the songs that his mother sang to him as a child. I wanted to know how the girls of his village danced at their weddings. I wanted to know the games that the boys played on summer nights. I conjured up a vision of a village filled with fair-haired people who spoke in his strange, harsh tongue, living in a rainy land of good-natured men and pale-skinned women who thought nothing of exposing their faces to a stranger.

"I've told you much more than you've told me about yourself," he replied, a little indignantly. "I'm still waiting for you to reveal all those secrets you keep hidden from me."

As always, I remained silent. When we were living at the inn, I vowed not to share my story with anyone, and now, when I was finally able, for days at a time, to forget who I once was, I had no wish to tarnish my happiness with talk of my wretched history.

Two days later, the bright light of sea came into our view and then disappeared behind the hills. We ascended the road slowly and when we reached the summit, my eyes were met with an endless expanse of sparkling blue, rolling and shifting in the sun. From atop my camel, I stared out at it in amazement. The delicate line that separated the sea from the sky enchanted me, as if I was staring into infinity itself. *The world is indeed merciless*, I thought to myself, recalling Luna's words, *but it is also beautiful.*

As we approached the city, the afternoon breezes, heavy with smell of salt and fish, filled the air. We rode through the markets, to the place near the sea where the caravans reach their journey's end. I wanted to find a traveler's inn where we could stay the night, but Lucan said that he knew of a spot outside the city walls where we could watch the sun set over the water. As we moved through the crowded alleys and squares, I could see the blue light of the sea through the narrow gaps between the houses. We lingered a while in the port, watching sailors from a hundred lands as they called to each other across the ship's decks, while on the shore, fisherman prepared their nets for the evening's work.

We passed through the town gates, and a beggar woman, her robes torn and her hair as stiff as straw, moved toward us with an outstretched hand. Never before did I have the means to give charity, but now I dug into my bag and pulled out a shiny coin. She blessed me, and I swore that I would never forget the miserable souls of this world, for I had once been one of them.

As the sun was beginning to sink into the sea, we came upon a group of Sufis at the water's edge, clothed in coarse woolen robes, each with a wooden alms bowl hanging from his belt of rope. "They're like monks, but they're Muslims," I explained to Lucan. "They've left their families and renounced all material things so that nothing will distract them from serving God."

One of them overheard me, and came forward to meet us. "Not only do we wish to serve Allah," he corrected me in Syriac, "but we long to know Him, as one knows one's own father." He surveyed the two of us, his gaze lingering on Lucan. "Have you come to see the ruins of the old church on the hill?"

"Yes," Lucan replied. "Is it far?" The Sufi pointed to the cliffs that rose behind us where a lone decrepit structure stood overlooking the sea.

Lucan dropped a coin into the man's bowl. "God bless you," he murmured.

The Sufi bowed low. "What are your names? Tell me and I'll mention you in our prayers."

Lucan was reluctant to reply, but I knew that prayers from the mouths of holy men go directly to God. "He is Lucan," I told him, "and I am Rahel."

"The church is in poor condition," he said sorrowfully, "but Allah dwells everywhere in the universe."

A steep, narrow path led up to a crumbling edifice. Carved blocks of stone that once must have been its roof and walls lay scattered in the sand. Only the cross carved into a alcove on the rear wall betrayed that this ruin was once a church. For a long time I stood under an arch whose walls had fallen away and gazed out at the sparkling carpet of blue reaching into the copper sky.

I had paid a terrible price to reach this moment, but now that I had arrived at its threshold, a profound peace settled over me, and I perceived that even as half of me cursed God for all I had suffered, the other half might still be moved to praise Him.

That night, as we lay under the dark sky, I knew that the time had come to tell Lucan all of the secrets that I had kept from him. *Tomorrow*, I whispered to myself. *Tomorrow he will finally learn who I am.*

But later that night I awoke with a peculiar feeling of nausea. It was not the first night that I experienced such a feeling. In fact, I had felt it for several days now, and each night it seemed to grow in intensity. I rose from my bed and ran behind a tree, where I returned to the earth all we had eaten that night.

Still the nausea persisted, and so I walked a while along the cliff, taking in deep breaths of damp, salty air. Too restless to go back to sleep, I sat myself down on the warm earth and tried to recall what Elisheva, my old neighbor in Sura, had once told me about the symptoms of pregnancy. Fatigue was one, and soreness of the breasts was another. I realized, with a sense of alarm that lately I had, in fact, felt both. And try as I might, I no longer remembered how many days had passed since I last bled.

As I gazed out at the bright moon over the dark waters, I prayed, as hard as any woman ever has, that I was not carrying a child; that I was not about to feel my belly grow round and my bones grow heavy; that I would continue to travel alongside Lucan with the lightness and ease of a boy; that I was not about to lose the place inside me that was as vast as the sea and as graceful as the waves.

I must have eventually drifted off to sleep, for when I opened my eyes, the stars were disappearing, and the sky was turning gray. I started back to where Lucan slept, but as I drew closer to our bedrolls, I saw our bags strewn recklessly on the ground and emptied of their contents. And then I came upon a sight of unspeakable horror. Lucan lay facedown in a pool of blood, a knife stuck in his back.

I let out a wild shriek and fell to my knees, digging my nails into him and shaking him violently. I threw myself, weeping, into his shirt as if my tears could somehow revive him. I screamed and howled and begged, but to no avail. Lucan was dead.

As I knelt there wailing over his lifeless body, I knew that this stranger, whose language I would never know, whose face would forever remain an enigma, had revived in me the very thing I thought I had lost forever.

ENTELECHY

For two days you've lain here like a shell washed in by the waves; it can only be Allah's mercy that has finally opened your eyes."

I glanced about for the source of the voice, but there was nothing but an endless purple sky, cut with a burning streak of orange light. Waves rose and crashed nearby, washing up on the sand and then falling back. I turned my head and saw the face of the Sufi, kneeling over me, holding out a piece of bread and a flask of water. The sight of the bread opened a giant pit of hunger. He helped me to sit and stroked the damp strands of hair from my face. I devoured the bread in an instant, and then moved my hand to clutch my raging belly. "I'm carrying his child!" I cried to the waves, collapsing into the sand.

"You've found your voice. Allah has indeed taken mercy on you. Wait here and I'll try to find you something else to eat." I don't know how much time passed, but soon he was again standing over me, holding out a leg of chicken. "I came upon a family visiting the grave of a holy sheik. When I told them that I needed food for a pregnant woman, they insisted that I take from their provisions."

"He is murdered!" I wailed. "His body lies on the cliff."

The Sufi raised his eyes to the cliff and nodded. "God gives, and God takes away. That is the nature of this world."

"I wanted to drown myself in the sea. Why am I not dead?"

"God has taken mercy on you," he repeated. "Your husband is dead, but you are still alive. You must have faith that God loves you, and you must return that love by living out the fate that He has determined for you."

"Faith?" I stared at him incredulously. "I was once a Jew," I murmured, "but now I have no faith."

"But you must, even when it is most difficult. Have faith that you will endure, and your child will be born to you. Have faith that you will raise him to be a man, and that every day you will write your vision of life upon his soul."

"I told you, I have no faith," I wailed. But the Sufi sat down by my side, gently lifted me up, and made me eat. When I was done, he pulled me to my feet, and led me, shaking and delirious, through the gates of the city, past the fishing boats, down streets still warm from the departed sun, and into the neighborhood of the Jews, where candles stood on the windowsills, and the smell of cooking wafted from the courtyards. The Sufi's hands were rough but his grip was kind, and I yielded to him as a blind man yields to a stranger who promises to lead him home.

As we moved through the alleys, I discerned the strains of a sound so familiar that I thought I was dreaming. It was the sound of men chanting prayers, quiet and muffled at first, but then louder, and clear enough for me to make out Hebrew words. I followed the melody, amazed that it was exactly as I remembered. And then suddenly we were inside a narrow doorway. I waited for him to move on, but he motioned for me to climb a flight of steep stairs. I glanced up saw that we were on the threshold of a synagogue. In a panic I stood firm and shook my head, but he urged me up the narrow staircase, to the place where the righteous women pray.

THE AIR WAS stifling and the walls were damp. I would have fainted if not for a small window that let in a thin, salty breeze. The voices of the men chanting below rose up and enveloped me. I sank to the warm wooden floor and closed my eyes. As if under a spell, my lips began to whisper the words of the prayers, and I could almost believe that I was back in the synagogue in Sura, that if I only opened my eyes I would see the kind, worried faces of the women who had always known me.

But later, when the synagogue was dark and quiet, my eyes blinked open, and it was not the women of Sura I saw, but a young man. He stood over me, the moonlight casting a pale light on his puzzled face. "I'm sorry," he stammered in an Aramaic that was as familiar as a mother's embrace. "I was just about to leave when I thought I heard a noise." He stared at me and looked about anxiously. "Do you have a place to go? Is there someone I can notify who . . ." He paused and knelt down beside me. "Where are you from? What's your name?" I shook my head weakly, hoping that he would give up and go away. Instead, he put a hand on my forehead and asked, "Are you not feeling well? I'm Ezra. Ezra Ben Tzvi. What's your name?"

"Rahel," I whispered. "Please leave me."

"Leave you? Here? It's *Erev Shabbat*. I can't leave you here alone. Don't you have somewhere to go?"

I let his question hang in the air. He stood up, but could not take his eyes from me. "I won't leave you here," he said finally. "Come home with me. My wife will take care of you." Still I didn't respond, but when he grasped my arms and lifted me to my feet, I didn't resist. "You must be starving. My wife has a Shabbat meal waiting at home. Come."

He led me carefully down the stairs and out into the darkened street. I barely had the strength to walk, and I leaned heavily on him as we passed through the deserted market square and down the twisting, dark alleys to the quarter where the Jews of Tyre reside. We turned through a doorway into a courtyard, and then up some a stairs. As we entered his home, I saw, as if in a long forgotten dream, a table adorned for the Sabbath. Two candles burned, and a silver cup, fashioned with delicate silver grapes, was set beside a flask of wine. How long had it been since I last saw a table set like this one? The flickering light of the candles entranced me, so that I no longer knew where I was, or if I was even awake at all.

"Praise God you're here," the voice of a young woman rose in the pale light. She was reclining on a couch, her round, almost childlike face was framed by a housewife's kerchief. "All the other men returned home long ago; I had begun to—" She stopped abruptly in mid-sentence. "I see that you've brought a guest."

"I found this unfortunate girl in the women's section of the synagogue. She needs to eat something, and then to rest."

"But where is her family? What if they come looking for her?"

"I think she's all alone."

The woman turned again to me, taking in my damp, ragged clothes and my salty, matted hair. "Then you'll be our guest for Shabbat. I'm Bilha. What's your name?"

"Rahel," I murmured.

She took my hand and led me to the table. Ezra poured a cup of wine, and as he began to chant the blessing over the wine, the Hebrew words fell upon my ears like a forgotten lullaby. After that, everything unfolded precisely as I knew it would: a second Hebrew blessing was said over two loaves of bread, and then soup appeared at the table, and then spiced vegetables and stewed meat.

My appetite burst upon me like a thunderstorm. Before their eyes, I devoured all they put before me. But rather than give me strength, the meal left me utterly exhausted. Bilha showed me to a small room at the back of the house. She opened a bedroll and I fell upon it like a corpse into a grave.

I was standing in the doorway of the old church, looking out on the sea. Lucan was by my side, pointing at the ships on the horizon. I reached for him, but my hand found only a cold stone floor. And then in a flash of light I saw him sprawled on the earth, a knife rising from his back. I stuck my fist into my mouth to stop myself from screaming, and curled myself into a tight ball of pain.

And then suddenly it was morning. The heavy shutters of the room blocked out the light, but not the noise, and I was awakened by the sounds of animals pulling carts right under my window. A donkey brayed and I sat up abruptly. "After prayers I told everyone about the girl," a man's voice was saying. "I described her, and Shabtai said that he had seen a girl like that with a fair-haired foreigner a few days ago. They were walking through the port on their way out of the city."

"Who was he?"

"And that's not the end of it. The next morning he heard from Ahmed Sa'adi that the body of a fair-haired foreigner was found up by the old church, with a knife in his back."

"Oh my God! It must be the same man that Shabtai saw."

"It probably is. As soon as the sun goes down I'll go to the chief of police and see what I can find out."

"And what about the girl?"

"Leave her to rest; if she's the same girl that Shabtai saw with the foreigner she must have witnessed everything. That would explain why she behaves like a madwoman."

Pangs of hunger were tearing at me again. I envied Lucan, stone dead and finished with the misery of life. *To die is easy*, I thought to myself. *It's the burden of living that's unbearable.* Voices rose and fell. Soft footsteps went back and forth outside my room, and at one point, I was certain that someone had opened my door and was staring at me. But I no longer cared how I looked to others, or what they might think of me. I was like a stray dog that wants nothing but his next meal. *It's this hunger*, I cried to myself. *This hunger will make an animal of me.* Sleep was my only escape, yet each time I was about to sink into sweet oblivion, the image of Lucan lying with a knife in his back burst into my mind. The notion that I hadn't properly buried him tormented me. I thought of his mother and father, whose hearts still carried the hope of seeing him again. Strangely enough, it was this, more than any thought for myself, that brought on wave after wave of fresh tears.

"Shabbat shalom, Rahel." Bilha was standing above my bed, holding a bowl of meat soup. "You've slept half the day away. You must be very hungry."

I mumbled words of thanks as she brought a stool to my bedside. I ate as a starving man eats, desperate and trembling with gratitude. "Would you like some more?" she asked when my bowl was empty. I nodded, and she went off and returned with another portion, which I consumed at once. "You're starving," she exclaimed.

"Other than what you gave me last night, I've barely eaten in four days."

"Four days! Well, I know just how you feel." She giggled as she patted her belly, which, I now saw, was protruding in the same way as my own. "I'm pregnant. Three months. It's our first," she told me happily. "When I get hungry, I'm like a fire tearing through dry wood." I almost looked down at my own rounded stomach, but I caught myself in time.

"Do you feel well enough now to tell me where you've come from?" She spoke with the naïve confidence of the fortunate, who believe that all the troubles of the world can be resolved with kindness. "We want to help you, but you have to tell us who you are and what has happened."

I sank back into the bed. This cruel woman wanted to make me remember, when all I wanted was to forget. I felt as though I were a slave again, enduring the worst humiliations in order to eat. "Forgive me, but I prefer not to talk about it," I murmured.

"You must want to bathe," she remarked as she eyed my tattered clothes. She left the room and soon returned with a large basin, a small cotton sheet, some undergarments, and one of her own robes. I hoped that she would leave me, if only because I dreaded what she would discover if she remained. But instead she began to undress me. "Lift your arms," she commanded. With difficulty, she pulled my robe over my head, and then peeled off the stiff, salt-encrusted tunic underneath. Immediately she saw what I had hoped to conceal. "Are you—"

"Yes," I sighed.

I watched as her face clouded with horror. "Ezra told me," she said worriedly "that a man, a foreigner, was found dead on the cliff by the old church. No one knows who he is, or where he came from. But a neighbor who works down at the port said that he saw him with a young woman." She lowered her voice. "Was it you?"

I closed my eyes and nodded. "And is that foreigner the father of. . .?"

I nodded again. She put a hand over her mouth and uttered, "God have mercy!"

My throat burned, and my eyes filled with bitter tears. "I don't know what to do," I whispered. "I have. . . no one at all." I squeezed my eyes shut, and tried to wipe my face with my sleeve. "I wanted to end my life in the sea. I don't know why I'm even alive."

"I must speak with Ezra."

I shrugged weakly. "Speak with whomever you like. I can scarcely think anymore."

"I'll speak with Ezra," she murmured again, and ran from the room.

I WASHED QUICKLY and then put on the garments and combed out my hair. The Sabbath afternoon was blessedly quiet, and I easily fell into the sleep that had evaded me the night before. Later I awoke to the sound of Bilha and Ezra standing over my bed, whispering. Bilha regarded me with renewed horror and fascination, but Ezra's gaze seemed to be that of a father on an errant child. "You're looking much better," he said with satisfaction. "Tomorrow morning I'll go to consult with our rabbi, Rav Abayei. In the meantime, why don't you get up and join us for the *Seudah Shlishit* meal."

We sat down to a meal of boiled eggs, olives, beans cooked with lemon, and bread. Nothing could have tasted better to me. The food, combined with the day's rest, was like the lifting of a black cloud. After the meal, Ezra went to the shelf and took down a candle and a small box of fragrant spices. The scent of the spices must have revived something in me, for suddenly I had the strength to say what I couldn't say before. "Ezra, Bilha, please forgive me; you saved my life, and I haven't even thanked you. God bless you both, and your child that, God willing, will soon be born."

"Praise God that we were able to help you," Ezra replied modestly.

"I . . . I don't know what to do," I told them. "I come from Bavel. My father died half a year ago," I lied, looking away, "and I have no other family. I have no one at all."

"From Bavel?" Ezra asked, astonished. "How did you travel such a distance? And why?"

They leaned towards me in expectation of a shocking tale. "After my father died, I traveled to the home of my father's brother in Damascus. He was my sole remaining relative. But when I came to the place where he lived, I was told that he had died and his family had left the city."

"And was it there that you met . . ."

"Yes," I replied simply. "I had no one, you see . . ."

They continued to stare at me, waiting to hear more, but I put my head in my hands in the hope that what I had told them would suffice. Bilha put a motherly arm around me and said, "Don't worry Rahel. Tomorrow Ezra will go to ask our rabbi, Rav Abayei, for his counsel. He is very learned and very wise. I'm sure that he'll know what you should do." Ezra recited the blessings that Jews say when they bid the Sabbath goodbye and welcome in a new week. The sound of the words comforted me, and I said a small prayer in my heart thanking God that He had finally led me back to merciful Jews who lived according to the laws of the God of Israel, as I once had.

But when night came and the street below my window fell silent, sleep would not come. Visions of the beggar woman at the gates of the city pervaded my thoughts, and I saw myself standing at the town gates, holding out dirty hands to strangers as I tried to quiet an infant screaming with hunger. I imagined searching for shelter, in the wind and the rain, me and my child drenched and blue with cold.

The next morning, I forced myself to rise from my bed and help Bilha in her household tasks. I collected the ashes from the oven and swept out the rooms of the house. I accompanied her to the market where we bought green herbs and fresh meat for the midday meal. When we returned home, I mixed dough for bread and took it down to bake in the courtyard oven.

At noon, Ezra returned home from his silver workshop in the market, and after lunch, the two of them retired for a rest. I too tried to rest, but each time sleep was upon me, I heard Lucan's voice, whispering words that I couldn't understand. I saw us riding our horses up to the church on the hill, and Lucan pointing to the ships. When I opened my eyes to the four walls of the darkened room, I was filled with a despair so heavy that I could barely rise from my bed.

Later, when Ezra returned to work, Bilha and I went up to the roof to launder clothes. The view of rooftops lay before me, and beyond them, the blue vista of the sea. I walked to the edge of the roof and stared out, imagining what it would be like to end my life quickly and painlessly. To fly over the city, into that blue, and leave this life of suffering behind. "Aaay!" I heard Bilha's scream. She ran to me and pulled me back so hard I almost fell over. "What are you doing?" she screamed, white with fear.

"I can't go on," I cried.

"You have to go on. You're pregnant! Do you want the sin of murder on your soul for all eternity?"

"No," I sobbed, collapsing into her arms.

"Promise me that you won't do that again."

"I won't."

"No! I want you to swear to God. Do you swear to God that you won't do that again? Do you swear on the life of your child?"

"Bilha, I . . . cannot—"

"Swear it," she demanded. "Swear it or leave this house."

"I swear."

"On the life of your child?"

"Yes. I . . . I will do nothing that will harm him."

"Thank God," she sighed. "I can't endure a scare like that again." She led me to my room and told me that what I really needed was to rest. I sank, empty and defeated, into the thin mattress of the bedroll, listening to the sounds of the fortunate passing under my window. Heavy, silent tears streamed down my face. All I wanted was to fly out over the sea, but instead I was trapped in a tiny room, beholden to the charity of others.

I moved my hand over the rounded contours of my stomach and thought for the first time about the wretched being who was growing inside of me. What a miserable life it would have, child to an unwed mother and a dead father. Only a cursed life of hardship awaited him, for he would carry not a full ancestry in his blood, but two halves. If only Lucan had lived to see him, everything would have been different. Lucan would have given him his name, and all the enchanting peculiarities of his nature that he had brought with him from the mysterious land of his birth.

Perhaps the child had already taken on those peculiarities. Perhaps he would be endowed with the very attributes that had endeared his father to me. This notion revealed itself gradually, like a slow, silent star floating across the twilight. I perceived then that Lucan had not left me alone, and in a way, he had not left me at all. For in a few months, I would lay eyes on his child; I would look into his face, and what I would see would somehow be a vestige of what I thought I would never see again.

It would be, I saw now, as the Sufi on the beach had told me. I would endure, and my child would be born to me. I would raise him to be a man, and every day I would write all that I had learned on his soul.

I said a prayer of thanks to God for saving me when I tried to end my life, and for Bilha, who had prevented me from succeeding, and for Ezra, who had taken me in when I had nowhere in the world left to go.

BILHA AND EZRA were standing by my bed, gazing down at me with satisfaction. "You're looking better today, Rahel," Ezra said. "Much better."

"It's all thanks to you. If not for you and Bilha. . ." My voice dropped off and I merely shook my head, for with each passing day, I better understood how terrible my situation would have been if Ezra had not taken me home.

Ezra took a seat nearby me, and Bilha sat down at his side. "Rahel, something about you has touched our hearts. Maybe it's because you're in the early months of pregnancy, just like Bilha. In any case, we both want to find a way to help you."

"God preserve you," I murmured.

"This afternoon, I went to see Rav Abayei. I told him everything: how I found you in the synagogue, how the father of your child was murdered, and how you are all alone. He and I discussed what might be done to help in a way that is fitting and honorable to all of us, and we came up with a plan. You will remain here with Bilha and me for the length of your pregnancy. We will provide you with all that you need, and in return, you'll help Bilha with the running of the house."

Tears came to my eyes; I wanted to fall to my knees and kiss his feet. Thanks to his compassion, I would pass the months of pregnancy with a roof over my head and enough food to carry my child. "Yes," I whispered. "I'll do anything you need."

"We couldn't think of turning you out," Bilha told me. "No pregnant woman can manage alone."

Ezra smiled the smile of a man who has been endowed with an important task. "It won't be easy to support two women, but when a man endeavors to perform a *mitzvah*, God lends a hand."

"May He bless you and this house," I told them both solemnly.

Ezra nodded in acknowledgment, but his expression turned grave. "I understand that the father of your child was not your husband. However, if the man was in fact a Jew, I'll take it upon myself to collect a *minyan* to say *kaddish* for his soul." I looked to the floor, for I could not raise my eyes to him. "You must tell us, once and for all, Rahel: was the father of your child a Jew?"

EACH EVENING, WHEN the cool, salty breezes blew in from the sea, the women would gather in the courtyard to while away the time until the men returned from prayers. They would set their straw stools in a shady corner while the children played. There was Ezra's sister, a girl by the name of Rina who lived in the apartment below with Ezra's aging father. There was Esther, the wife of Ezra's young uncle Chaim. Though she was not more than twenty-two or twenty-three, she had already borne four children. And there was the widow Yoheved, accompanied only by her daughter, since her sons were old enough to join the men for evening prayers. From the way they looked at me, I could tell that Bilha had told them everything, and though they tried to mask their fascination, I was well aware that in their eyes, I was a grim lesson, telling proof of how low a woman could fall.

"Bilha tells us that you are pregnant as well," Yoheved said, eyeing the bulge in my belly. "How far along are you?"

"It's about three months," I murmured, for I was certain that this was something they already knew.

"Three months? Just like Bilha! You'll be giving birth about the same time."

"Maybe your babies will even be born on the same day, under the very same constellation!"

Amused, they stared unashamedly at the two of us: Bilha the respectable wife of an upright man, and I, penniless and carrying the illegitimate child of a non-Jewish foreigner.

But though my life was full of secrets and shame while Bilha's was replete with sweetness, her pregnancy was far more difficult than mine. While I found that my initial bouts of nausea and weakness soon passed, Bilha's did not, and where I soon felt my strength return, Bilha continued to suffer from constant fatigue. It came as no surprise when one morning she asked if I might take it upon myself to cook the midday meal, until she was feeling well again. Her request annoyed me, especially when I recalled how from the start, she had insisted that in her home, only she prepare the meals. But she looked so pale and weak that morning that I readily agreed.

I expected that Bilha would seek the comfort of her bed, but instead she sat with me in the kitchen, eager for company. When I served her a cup of hot water with honey and mint, her eyes lit up like a child's. "What an angel you are! Every day I thank God for sending you to us."

"But Bilha," I protested, "It's you who's saved me. Where would I be now if Ezra hadn't taken me home with him from the synagogue that first night?"

Bilha considered the question and sighed. "It's best not to dwell on such things." She raised her drink and shifted her lumbering body, trying to get comfortable in her chair. "You know Rahel, it's hard for me to imagine how a girl like you got herself into such a terrible predicament." She may have been feeling poorly, but not so poorly as to forget what appeared to be her favorite subject: the circumstances that lead to my pregnancy. When we were alone, she would often try to coax new details out of me. But lately, her questions were becoming bolder. "How did it happen, Rahel? You can confide in me. I won't breathe a word of what you say to Ezra."

"I've told you Bilha, when one has no family, one finds oneself in situations which could never occur otherwise."

"But who was he? Where was he from?"

I busied myself with the fireplace on the back porch, as if I hadn't heard her. "And he wasn't even a Jew! Oh Rahel, please tell me. I imagine that he must have been very persuasive for you to . . . I mean, I can't imagine how it happened that you, well . . . I mean if he wasn't . . ." She giggled a little to herself. "You know, I feel so sorry for you, I really do, but in a way, in a very small way, I envy you too," she confessed, hiding another girlish giggle behind her hand.

"Envy me?" I stuck my head into the kitchen. "You have no reason in the world."

"Then I'll tell you why. I married Ezra, and thank God, he's a wonderful man. But he's all I'll ever know. While you, well, you might marry someday, but no matter what happens you'll always have . . . what you remember of it."

"No one will ever want to marry me."

"Yes. That's possible," she admitted. "It could be very difficult for you to find someone decent." She sighed again to herself. "Well, whoever he was, he certainly wasn't worth it."

Even when the winter passed, and the warm spring breezes swirled through the courtyard, Bilha and I couldn't say which of us would give birth first. As our times drew near, she awaited the event with blind terror, for the women of her family, as well as Yoheved and Esther, supplied us with detailed descriptions of the great pain and suffering that awaited us. But for me, all anxiety about the birth was overshadowed by the question of what would happen after my child was born, for it seemed unlikely that Ezra would agree to support two extra people indefinitely.

Luckily, I was occupied in those last days by an event that had nothing to do with me or the pregnancy. One afternoon, when the women gathered in the shadiest corner of the courtyard, Esther announced that Rabbi Natan of Buqei'a would be passing through the city on his way to Aleppo. "He plans to stay here in the city over Shabbat," she reported. "Chaim says that he's going to teach a page of Talmud."

"Rav Natan is a great man," Bilha told us reverently. "My mother once wrote to him with a question about her inheritance, and he wrote a response that finally made peace between her and her brothers."

Yoheved put a hand on her heart. "God preserve him. My brother-in-law says that thousands write to him every year, asking for rulings about everything under the sun, even the most personal problems."

"Chaim says that Rav Natan will be teaching a section from *Seder Nashim*."

"Which one is that?" Bilha asked.

"It's the order that deals with laws related to women," I replied without thinking. The three of them turned to me in surprise.

"Do you know Hebrew?" Esther asked.

"No. I . . . I just remember the names of the books."

They exchanged puzzled glances, as if I had said something inappropriate, but though Rav Natan's lesson was only for the men,

I too anticipated his coming. In the days that followed, I found myself recalling the singular delight of mulling over a passage in a book, and then discussing my impressions with Monk Anton. Many months had passed since I had held a book, but that only sharpened my memory of how the mere act of reading could release the mind like a bird from a cage.

As the date of Rav Natan's arrival drew nearer, I imagined an extraordinary plan. What if I too could attend Rabbi Natan's talk? What if I could somehow go to the synagogue and sit amongst the men, as I had once sat amongst the men of Mar Yuhanon? The very notion was laughable, yet rather than abandon the idea, I tried to think of ways that it might be done. With my enormous belly, disguise was out of the question. But what if I could somehow be present, yet hidden from the eyes of the men? What if I could sit behind a curtain, or in a cupboard, or even under a table? Perhaps I could simply sit above in the women's gallery. What harm could come from that?

One night after Bilha had retired, I told Ezra that I needed to speak with him. Though I was wary of asking him for anything more, he seemed oddly pleased and invited me to come up to the roof where we could sit under the stars. "You're looking very well," he said warmly as I took a seat on the wooden bench beside him. "Pregnancy agrees with you."

"I've been fortunate. I seem to be exempt from the complaints that most women suffer."

"In spite of everything, you've found favor in God's eyes," he mused.

I didn't know how to reply to such a remark, so I ignored it and instead broached the matter that had circled in my mind for days. "You've already shown me so much charity and kindness, but there's something else that I want to ask of you."

"As much as half of the kingdom," he replied with a grin.

Given such magnanimous permission, I began to speak nonsense. "I admit it's a strange request, something that I'm sure no one could understand. But in the past days, I've thought of nothing else. It's almost as if I'm compelled to ask, even though I'm not at all sure that you can help me."

"You're talking in riddles, Rahel. Why not just say it plainly?"

"Yes. I will say it plainly. Would it be possible for me to attend Rabbi Natan's lecture at the synagogue? I know that it sounds strange, but maybe an arrangement could be made. I could sit at the back, behind a curtain so that my presence wouldn't distract the men. . . or I could sit above, in the women's gallery."

I couldn't see Ezra's expression, but I could hear the surprise in his voice. "But why? Why would such a thing even interest you?"

There was no way for me to tell him about the long months at Mar Yuhanon, but I still had to supply him with some sort of explanation. "It's just that. . . you see, when I was a child, my father would sometimes show me his books. . ."

"Ah," he smiled, as if discovering the key to a mystery. "So your father was a man of learning."

"Yes. Learning was a part of our household, a very important part. And even though he's long dead, I miss him terribly. I've been thinking that maybe the chance to hear the rabbi read from the holy books would be a comfort to me."

"You've told us very little of the family you came from," he said, as if this in itself were suspicious.

"I try not to trouble myself with the past."

"My own mother died before I married," he said wistfully. "I know what it is to long for a parent who's gone."

"If you do, then you must understand how comforting it could be for me to hear Rabbi Natan read from the holy books."

"It is such an odd request," he remarked, "but once again you've touched my heart. All right, Rahel. I'll make some inquiries and see what can be done."

Two nights later, Ezra invited me again to join him on the rooftop. For the first time since Lucan's death I had something to anticipate. The moon hung low over the sea, and the warm scent of salt still rose up from the alleys. Ezra had brought a small flask of *arak* with him. He offered me a sip, and I refused him with a smile. "This morning after prayers, I went to speak with Shlomo Meiri, the *shamash* of our synagogue," he began. "I told him about your request, and I was certain that he would refuse. But his reaction was just the opposite. He said that from time to time he receives similar requests from women who want to follow debates regarding various questions. And so he agreed to raise the question with Rav Abayei."

"And what did Rav Abayei say on the matter?"

"It seems that there's nothing in the *Halacha* that forbids women to hear the teachings of sages. That being the case, Rav Abayei has ruled that women are permitted to listen to the proceedings as you suggested, from the women's gallery. Shlomo is prepared to allow you to do this on the evening that Rabbi Natan is to speak, as long as you enter only after the men have all gone inside."

"Of course," I agreed. "God bless you Ezra; you've done so much for me, but this favor is the kindest of all."

He sat quietly for a minute, and then said, "There is another kindness that I've thought to take upon myself to do for you."

"Another kindness? What do you mean?"

"Rahel, I . . . I have been meaning to speak to you for some time now about a very delicate matter. You've lived under our roof for six months now, and naturally, living as we are, I've come to know you quite well. At first I feared that this arrangement would cause conflict and strife, but the truth is that you've brought a new harmony to our house. Your presence is a blessing, and . . . and in time I've grown very fond of you, so much so that I can hardly imagine our home without you. I've spoken with Rav Abayei, and he's given his approval to a desire I've carried inside for a long time." He paused, as if bracing himself, and then continued. "Rahel, would you agree to become my second wife? In this way, both you and your child will take my name, and you'll never have to worry about your well-being or his. You see, I've grown quite fond of you. I love Bilha, of course, and yet you, you're a different sort. I could see it even in the first few days."

Perhaps a wiser woman would have seen that this, more than any other outcome, would be the obvious effect of the arrangement we had entered into. I, however, was simply stunned. My thoughts were so much with Lucan that I had barely noticed what was happening in front of my eyes. I struggled to gather my thoughts, to think clearly and wisely. Marrying Ezra would indeed be a respectable resolution to my situation. He was good and kind, not of the caliber of my father, yet neither was he a fool. He was young and healthy, and could provide a comfortable life for all of us. "Say yes," he implored, "and you'll never lack for anything."

Given my circumstances, I should have fallen at his feet and promised to be a good wife to him, and I might have done just that, if not for one small but troublesome question. "What does Bilha say about the matter?"

"Bilha doesn't know of it."

"You haven't discussed this with her?"

"It's not up to her to determine how my home is run."

"Of course," I said, remembering myself. "But I'm not sure that this decision should be made without her approval, let alone her knowledge."

"Perhaps not, but ultimately it's up to the man of the house. And besides, to propose marriage to a destitute girl, a girl who's carrying another man's child, can only be considered a charitable act. I have no doubt that in time Bilha will come to understand this."

I was young then, and had no experience at all in matters relating to marriage. But I had seen enough to know that no woman, no matter how generous her nature, wants to share her husband with another. For who would ever dream of spending half of one's nights alone, left with nothing but imaginings of one's husband in the arms of a rival—a rival whom your husband has chosen because she appears to possess the very traits that you lack. If you are beautiful to him, then she is beautiful to him in a different way. If he enjoys your conversation, then he finds her conversation equally worthy. And if he seeks your opinion, he then turns to her to hear the opposite of what you said. Surely no arrangement can be more humiliating.

If I accepted Ezra's proposal, I knew that all of this, all the doubts and jealousies and bitterness of the heart, would be mine. Yet I also knew that to refuse him might be the most foolish decision I would ever make. "You've been so good to me," I told him, "and your offer is noble and generous. But I can't make this decision lightly. I'll have to think about it."

"I would have thought that a woman in your circumstances would be grateful for a proposal of marriage from an upright man." I could hear the bitterness of insulted pride in his voice, and it took all of my will to prevent myself from giving in. "What is it that makes you hesitate?"

"It's simply that..." I paused, searching for the words to explain it to him. "When I was a young girl in my father's house, whenever I imagined standing under the *hupa*, it was always as the one and only wife to my husband."

"I see," he said indignantly. "Yet several years have passed since you were a young girl, and a few unexpected things have happened. As a youth, I also imagined the woman who would be my wife. And believe me, I was not thinking of a woman who has become pregnant with the child of a barbarian!" He was silent for a moment and I too remained silent. Even though his words were hurtful, there was nothing I could say to contradict him. "Forgive me for speaking harshly," he said finally, "but there are moments when one has no choice but to speak the truth. You must realize that in spite of everything, I'm very fond of you. That's the only reason that I've made you this offer, which few men of my standing would make."

"I can scarcely think right now. Surely you don't want me to make such a serious decision while in a state of confusion. Please, let's wait until after the child is born, and then, when my mind is calmer, I'll give you my answer."

"Yes. The decision is indeed a serious one, and I can wait a little while longer. But remember Rahel, matters of the heart are like the sea." He raised a hand and moved it, as if over the surface of water. "One day the winds blow this way, but the next," he turned his hand sharply, "they've suddenly shifted."

ON THE NIGHT that Rav Natan was to speak, I went out a short while after Ezra headed for the synagogue, lingering in the town square so as to make sure that I would be the last to arrive. As the moon rose over the roofs of the city, I passed through the narrow door and tiptoed up the stairs to the women's gallery. In the main room below, all eyes turned to the figure that stood before the Holy Ark.

In appearance, Rabbi Natan put me in mind of the venerable rabbis at the academy in Sura. He spoke with an accent similar to that of people from the villages, but his voice carried the confidence and fluency of the gifted. "Our tractate begins with a ruling regarding the ways in which a woman may be acquired for marriage. The *Mishna* mentions three means: with money, with a document, or by sexual relations. Regarding money, Beit Shamai says the amount must be one dinar, or the equivalent. Beit Hillel says that it may be one *pruta*, or the equivalent. We may ask: in our day and age, how should we interpret the term 'pruta?'"

I wished then that I could once again hold a book in my hands and follow the fluid chains of letters and words. The synagogue had but precious few copies, and these were divided amongst the most worthy of the men below. Nonetheless, I tried to join my thoughts to those of the sages.

"Now Rava raises a strange question. He asks: if a man says to a woman, 'you are betrothed to half of me,' the marriage will take effect. If, on the other hand, he says to her, 'half of you is betrothed to me,' then the marriage is not valid. How are we to understand this?"

Oh, to speak of things outside the routine of everyday concerns. How I missed it all. "Now the scholar Abayye has already told us that the scriptures use the expression, 'a man takes a woman as his wife,' indicating that both husband and wife are full and complete. Yet as Rava points out, a man can, in fact, marry more than one woman. In that sense, the statement 'you are betrothed to half of me' makes sense. On the other hand, because a woman can be married to one man only, to say, 'half of you is betrothed to me' is indeed meaningless."

The words of the Talmud pierced my ears like a well-aimed arrow. *You are betrothed to half of me.* That is what my life would be, should I agree to marry Ezra. I saw now, with stark clarity, that no matter how well Ezra cared for me, the life I would live under his roof would be pitiful. It would be a life of childish jealousies, without honor, without contentment, forever condemned to compete for what other women claimed as a right.

"Of course there are some rabbis, and I myself am among them, who discourage the practice of polygamy. We feel that the spirit of a Jewish marriage can't be fully realized when there is more than one wife. I'm well aware that some of my esteemed colleagues don't agree with my views, but nonetheless, I refuse to take any part in such arrangements."

Rav Natan's words were a balm on my tormented heart. Here was a great man, a man of wisdom and learning, who was not afraid to contradict the rulings of others. For the remainder of the lecture, I could think of nothing else. Rabbi Natan's words were like a voice in a dark night, telling me that in this final struggle against fate, I simply could not yield.

THERE HAD BEEN much speculation in the courtyard as to who would give birth first. Since Bilha's belly was bigger than mine, Yoheved and Esther predicted she would soon go into labor, and that I would follow within two weeks. And indeed, when I noticed one morning that my belly was suddenly tightening up and then gradually relaxing, Bilha's mother, who had moved into the house with us, remained unimpressed, explaining that such occurrences are common in the ninth month. It was because of this opinion that, by the time Saida the midwife was called, I had all but given birth.

The pains were furious, but I bore them bravely. Each was like a wave, lifting me, twisting me like a lump of clay, and finally dropping me, battered and exhausted, a little closer to the moment of birth. Yet, in spite of what is said of childbirth, the feeling was not unbearable. Though the violence of the contractions threatened to break me in half, the pains were joyous ones, and the violence of their grip was laughable compared to the other violence I had known.

Even as I writhed in my bed, I was not oblivious to the commotion in Bilha's room across the hall. "Call Saida! Call Saida!" Bilha's mother was shrieking, for Bilha had gone into labor as well.

Ezra didn't know what to do with himself. He opened the door to my room, glanced in worriedly, then went off to check on Bilha, and then returned to my room again. After several rounds like this, he retreated to the courtyard. I heard Bilha's yelps and I prayed that God would give her the strength to endure.

"Am I going to die?" I cried to Saida, thinking of my poor mother, who didn't live to see me.

She smacked my face. "God forbid. Push harder. A little more, just a little bit more."

"I can't," I groaned.

"You can!" Saida said. "Just one more time and it's out." I pushed one more time—for Saida, for myself, for Lucan, and for my mother, who had found it in herself to make this one last inhuman exertion before she died. And then, just as my strength was entirely spent, Saida pulled the baby's head from my body.

"You have a daughter, but don't worry, God willing your next one will be a boy." Saida wiped her down roughly, but before I could tell her to handle my child more gently, she placed her in my trembling arms. A daughter! For some reason, I had never imagined, not even once, that my child would be a girl. It dismayed me, for the life of a woman is so much harder and smaller than the life of a man. Yet here she was, looking up at me, intently taking in the features of my face. Her hair was the color of sand, and her eyes were as blue as the sky.

"Look at the color of her hair," Saida whispered. "Was that the color of her father's?"

I nodded and could not keep from smiling to myself.

"What will you call her?"

I looked into her clear, blue eyes and thought again of my mother, who was named after the most noble of women—a woman who had not been born a Jew. "Ruth," I whispered.

"After someone in your family?"

I nodded. "My mother."

As I held her in my arms, scarcely believing that she was my own, I whispered a prayer of thanks to Bilha, who had prevented me from taking her life. *It doesn't really matter whether one is born male or female*, I thought with a sigh. *All that matters is that one has been born.*

I had prayed for Bilha, but God was not merciful with her, and her labor was long and difficult. For hours we all listened to her screams, and I saw that for once, fortune had been on my side. Finally the next night, Bilha's son, David, was born. Ezra was as joyful as Bilha was exhausted, and he and his parents immediately set about making preparations for the *brit*.

Bilha lay in her bed all week. I however, was back on my feet within two days. Family and neighbors all made a point of seeking me out and offering their good wishes, but I couldn't forget the terrible fact that the people who had would truly have loved my daughter were dead.

Bilha, on the other hand, received endless attention. Everyone wanted to hold her baby, fuss over her and offer an endless stream of advice. "He's still hungry," Esther insisted as Bilha tried to calm her howling son.

"But he just finished eating when Yoheved came in. He ate until he didn't want anymore."

"Maybe he needs to be changed."

"He just needs to sleep."

"No," Bilha's mother overruled them all. "You can tell from his cries that it's gas. Try holding him over your shoulder."

Ezra's sister hung special amulets on the walls of the house, protecting David and Ruth from the long hand of the evil Lilith, who causes infants to fall ill and die.

Bilha recovered slowly, but by the time the day of the brit came, she was able to rise from her bed and receive her many guests. By virtue of fathering a male child, Ezra was joyously welcomed into the community of men, and Bilha too basked in the honors that are showered upon the mothers of sons. When the time came for the ceremony, Ezra's elderly grandfather held the baby, while the women took Bilha into the kitchen. David's cries must have awakened Ruth, but no one heard her except for me.

I found her writhing like a small fish in the great sea of my bed. I took her in my arms, and gazed into her little face. I thought now of her father, and I could not help but weep myself; Bilha's son had received a prince's welcome, while my baby was as inconsequential as a stray puppy. She quickly fell asleep, and reluctantly, I put her back in my bed and went out to join in the celebration. As I passed through the kitchen, Ezra pulled me aside. "When you become my wife," he whispered, "your daughter will enjoy as much attention as my son."

IT WAS AS though the world itself had changed. The unquiet blue of the sea, the fishing boats sailing home with dawn's first light, the calls of the merchants on their way to the market, the women gossiping in the courtyard, the laundry drying on the roofs of the city, even the stars and moon at night—nothing in the world would ever be the same now that Ruth was in it. In the early mornings, I would open the shutters and hold the hamsa necklace up to the light, watching how it cast a delicate shadow over Ruth as she slept. *Look*

at her, I would whisper to Lucan, feeling his presence as if he were in the room with us. *Our daughter is as fair as you were.*

But such moments were few. With each passing day, the reality of my situation became clearer. I couldn't forget for even a single moment that it was only Ezra's generosity that allowed us to live decently. The food on the table, the small room where Ruth and I made our home, even the old clothes that Bilha gave to me were all bestowed upon me as charity, and I well knew that without him, I would have nothing. Each night when I lay down to sleep, I would see the beggar woman in my dreams, her clothes torn, her skin gray, her frail, thin arm outstretched to the mercy of strangers.

In the days after the brit, I often caught Ezra gazing at me with barely concealed impatience, his ardor so obvious that I feared Bilha would take notice, but luckily her baby claimed all of her attention, and she seemed oblivious to all else. As I watched her in her happiness, I could scarcely believe that Ezra was prepared to shatter it by informing her that she would soon have to share her husband with the orphan he had brought home, and worse, that her son would gain a sister whose father was not a Jew.

"The time has come for us to speak again," Ezra whispered to me one evening while Bilha was bathing David. "Come up to the roof tomorrow night, and we'll make our plans."

THOUGH SEVERAL WEEKS had passed since Rav Natan's departure, the people of Tyre were still talking about his visit. On the day that I was to speak with Ezra, the women's talk in the courtyard turned to the story of a Dina, a local woman who had recently sought Rav Natan's advice about how to cope with her bad-tempered husband. "Where exactly is this Buqei'a that he comes from?" Bilha interrupted the story.

"You wouldn't believe it." Rina laughed. "It's a village in the Galilee, a hole of a place where the people know nothing of books and learning. The men are all shepherds and the women work the land."

"My brother says that Buqei'a is mentioned in the Talmud," Esther cut in. "It's written that Rav Shimon Bar Yochai and his son hid from the Romans in a cave near the village for thirteen years. They lived on nothing but spring water and the fruit of a holy carob tree, and they did nothing but study Torah the whole time."

"Fine. So it's a holy place," Yocheved conceded. "But is that a reason for a great scholar to live amongst the goats and sheep? The rabbis of Bavel have begged Rav Natan to teach at the academies but he refuses them all. He studied at Sura—"

Sura! I couldn't help but smile at the mention of my home.

"—but when he had read all of the holy books in their libraries, he returned to Buqei'a. He says that the purpose of his learning was not to enhance his name, but to help others to live a life of righteousness." She crossed her arms in a knowing way. "Dina says he's wiser than all the rabbis of Bavel put together. She swears that of all of them, he's the only one who can see into a woman's heart."

And then, at that moment, I knew what I had to do. I would seek the advice of Rav Natan and let him decide everything. But there was no use in writing him as other women did, for I didn't have the time to wait for his answer. As the women continued to sing his praises, the solution took shape in my mind. I would take Ruth and set out for Buqei'a. I would find Rabbi Natan, and then I would tell him all that had happened to me.

I would reveal everything, even what was most disgraceful; for only if he heard it all would he understand what I could scarcely put into words. I would tell him to consider my story as the sages in the Talmud ponder the abnormal, the exceptional, the rare constellation that occurs but once. Surely he, of all men, would understand the meaning of all that was done to me, and of all that I had done, both out of necessity and of my own volition. Then in his great wisdom, he would advise me how best to live out the remainder of my ill-starred life.

"I CANNOT BECOME your wife."

"But of course you can. Just say yes, and all will fall into place."

"I will not be a second wife to my husband."

"Rahel, you're speaking like a child! Can't you see that if you don't marry me, you'll have no husband at all?"

"That might be true. But I still can't do it. Even Rabbi Natan is against the practice."

"Rav Natan can say whatever he likes, but he is not a destitute and unmarried mother." Though his words tore into me, I held his gaze without flinching. "Rahel," he said in a softer tone. "Come to your senses. You're making a terrible mistake. If you don't marry me, I won't be able to bear having you in my house. You'll have to leave us, and once you're on your own, you and your daughter won't last a week. If you're lucky, you'll merely be doomed to beggary. But more likely you'll be attacked and killed, just like your Goy lover."

"It is in God's hands."

"How stupid! What a child you are! Think again, Rahel. I beg you to think again."

Precisely at this moment, Bilha appeared on the roof with David in her arms. "Our son is a bottomless well," she declared happily. "He just eats and eats without filling up." She shot me a look of concern. "I hope that Ruth is getting enough, she always seems to finish so quickly."

Ezra rose and walked to the rooftop's edge. I watched his imperious, angry steps and realized that the moment had come when I could no longer stay with them. "Ezra, Bilha," I said to them softly, "It's time for Ruth and me to leave."

"Leave?" Bilha exclaimed, bewildered. "But why? Haven't we treated you well?"

"You've treated me like a queen. Each day I'll pray for you and ask God to shower all of his blessings on you both."

"But what will you do? Where will you go?"

"God is great. Who can know what's in store for me?" I looked to the sky. "Perhaps one day, I'll marry and build a home of my own," I added, avoiding Ezra's bitter glare.

"Marry?" Bilha laughed. "How can you imagine that any man will want you for a wife? One look at your child and it's obvious that her father wasn't a Jew! Everyone in Tyre knows that she is a punishment for the sins of your past!"

Though her words stung like a slap, I forced myself to swallow my anger. "You are harsh, Bilha. You know nothing of me and what I've suffered. But one thing is certain: my child is *not* my punishment. On the contrary, she is my . . . my redemption. And through her, the soul of a man who was decent and good lives on."

"You're a very foolish girl, Rahel," Ezra said coldly. "And you will live to regret your foolish choices." He got up and left us without another word.

My heart ached for Bilha. In spite of the things she said to me, I felt pity for her. "My leaving will burden you."

"Oh, Rahel," she cried, "I'm not thinking of myself, but of you. Not everyone will show you the kindness that we have. People can be very cruel."

"Yes. Some are. But others are full of good will, even for strangers. The world is full of people who are kind in their own way."

The next morning I went to a jeweler's shop in the market, where I pawned my mother's hamsa. It was painful to relinquish the only thing left of her, and I was wary of giving up the protection it is said to afford, but I owned nothing else of value, and I knew that without provisions, I could not hope to see Rav Natan. With the money, I bought a traveler's bag, a good knife with a leather sheath, a cloak of sheep's wool, a pair of heavy leggings, a woven blanket, a large flask, three loaves of bread, some traveler's cheese, and a large sack of dates. I was left with a few coins, which would, I hoped, get me to Buqei'a.

When I returned home, Bilha followed me to my room and watched, incredulous, as I packed my bag. "Don't go," she pleaded. "Stay here with me, and we'll raise our babies together."

"I can't." I took her hands in my own and caught her distraught gaze. "Bilha, I feel nothing but gratitude for you and Ezra. I'll pray each day for God to watch over you, and to grant you every blessing."

She laughed scornfully. "You'll pray for me? You're the one who's going to need God's help. You're the one who—" She was interrupted by the sound of David, crying in her bed. "He's up!" she cried, and ran off to her room.

That was the last time I was to see her. In the noon hour, when the all the city takes shelter from the day's great heat, I tied Ruth to my back, strapped my bag across my shoulder, and stepped out into the street.

I TOOK THE quiet alleys that led down to the port. The sight of the boats rocking on the water reminded me of the day Lucan and

I arrived in the city. All of a sudden, I missed him fiercely, but the weight of his daughter on my back, and the tug of her fingers on my hair cheered me and gave me the courage to walk through the city gates. As I passed the beggar woman, I stopped and put a coin in her cup. She bowed her head and recited a blessing for me, but I felt as though I had already been blessed.

As I walked along the water's edge, I soon came upon the Sufis kneeling in prayer by the sea. One of them left his companions and approached us, and I saw that it was the same man who had guided Lucan and me to the church, and then saved me, and Ruth, from withering away by the water. "All has happened as I said it would," he said with satisfaction as he gazed at Ruth.

"Yes," I said. "Every word of it."

"You have borne a son?"

"A daughter."

He smiled up at the sky. "God is great."

"God bless you, sir. If you hadn't helped me that day on the beach, who knows what would have become of me."

He bowed his head modestly. "The Jews came to your assistance?"

"They saved my life. They provided me with food and shelter so that I could pass my pregnancy in peace. But I can't stay in the city."

"Where will you go?"

"To the village of Buqei'a, in the Galilee, to ask the advice of a righteous sage."

"You must mean Rabbi Natan of Buqei'a." He nodded knowingly. "He is indeed very righteous, and very wise. But how will you get to Buqei'a? You cannot walk there with a child."

I gazed out at the shore at the rolling line where the water met the sand. "I'll find him."

"Allow me to offer you some advice: Walk along the water until you reach the town of Akka. A young man could do it in a day, but you are with a child, and so it will probably take you three. When you reach Akka, seek out the home of Sheik Ahmed, and tell him that his pupil, Ibn Nuaym, has sent you to him. He is one of our most revered teachers. Devout students and simple men alike seek the path of God under his guidance. Tell him that you are seeking Rabbi Natan of Buqei'a. He'll find transport for you."

I blessed him and set out along the shore. As I went, my eyes scanned the hills for the ruins of the old church where Lucan and I had stood looking out over the sea.

TRAVELING WITH RUTH on my back was difficult. To begin with, there was the physical burden of carrying a helpless creature. The sun poured down, and the wind raged in my face, yet my step had to stay steady and firm in order to avoid tripping. When she cried with hunger I had no choice but to stop and feed her, and the fact that it was my body that was providing her food required me to find a spot that was, if possible, both private and comfortable. And of course, once she finished her meal, she was certain, as night follows day, to dirty herself. Most of the time she was content, yet when she grew unhappy, or uncomfortable, or miserable for some unknowable reason, her screaming and crying could tie my nerves into knots.

The effort of carrying Ruth soon began to take its toll. I felt myself growing lean, and my strength waning away. It was late in the afternoon of the third day, just as I was starting to despair of ever reaching Akka that I spotted the walls of the city rising in the distance.

When I reached the town gates, I asked the beggars where I could find the house of Sheik Ahmed. "Go to the mosque," they told me, "and ask there." At the mosque, I approached a woman as she came out from prayer, and she pointed me in the direction of the market. In this way, I soon found myself standing before a high gate, closed against the noise and tumult of the town. I rang the bell, and a young Sufi dressed in a simple woolen robe opened the door. "Ibn Nuaym sent me," I told him. "I need to speak with Sheik Ahmed."

"What is your business with him?" he asked.

"I am in need of his assistance. Ibn Nuaym told me that the sheik is a holy man. He said that he can help me find transportation to the town of Buqei'a, so that I can seek an audience with Rav Natan."

The Sufi showed me inside and led me down an arched corridor to an open courtyard. In the center stood a low platform, shaded by four carob trees, where a group of Sufis sat without speaking or moving. The courtyard was lined with small cubicles. The Sufi showed me to one of them, and motioned for me to sit on the thin straw mattress on the floor. "Wait here," he told me. "Sheik Ahmed will come to speak with you." I settled myself down and fed Ruth. She soon fell asleep, but I remained vigilant, watching the Sufis sitting in stillness as the moon rose over the courtyard. After much time had passed, an elderly man appeared in the doorway.

"I am Sheik Ahmed," he said in a voice so serene that I wondered if he had just awakened from sleep. "I understand that my esteemed student, Ibn Nuaym, has sent you here." I described how Ibn Nuaym had found me on the beach, and then delivered me to the synagogue. "And he did this with no promise of reward," he said thoughtfully.

"I would have rewarded him, if I only could. But at that moment, I was in such despair that I could scarcely speak."

"Ah, but that is what made his deed worthy; by coming to your assistance he found a way to express his love of God. A Sufi's love must be pure; it need not carry any reward but itself." He gazed at me and Ruth as he stroked his long beard. "My daughter, your story pleases me; by helping you, Ibn Nuyam has progressed a little on his path. But we must see his pious deeds to their rightful end. You will sojourn with us tonight, and tomorrow, I will assist you on your way to Rabbi Natan."

The next day, the sheik himself arranged for me to join a group of his disciples who were riding to Tiberius on donkeys. One of them was traveling with his young son, and Sheik Ahmed requested that he give me the boy's donkey to ride.

The road out of the town was wide and well-traveled. We passed horse-drawn carts laden with baskets of dates and pomegranates, and wagons carrying jars of olive oil. But the orchards and olive groves soon gave way to the rocky hills and valleys of the Galilee. Cows grazed on the new spring grasses, and shepherds herded sheep and goats, their bells echoing over the mountainside. As we rode deeper into the mountains, my yearning to meet Rav Natan became more urgent. I had never shared my story in its entirety with anyone, but now, when I was finally to sit before a wise man who knew so much of the world, a man who would listen to me with compassion and not judge me harshly, I felt like a weary beggar, longing to cast off his wretched sack of scraps and rags.

After several hours of riding, we halted at a spot where a narrow path led up into the hills. "This is the way to Buqei'a," they told me. "If you start now, you should be there before sunset."

This last, final part of the journey was the most difficult. The way was dense with rocks and thorny bushes, and with Ruth on my back, I had to go slowly. The sky grew gray, and the only sounds to be heard were the winds in the grasses and the lonesome call of birds across the valleys. For a long while I saw no houses, no people, no discernable sign of human presence. It was as if I had come to the very end of the world.

And then, as the pale sun was descending into the hills, I saw a cluster of houses clinging to the hillside as if afraid of falling off. I would have liked to press on until we reached the village, but Ruth began to cry with hunger, and I had to find shelter under the branches of an olive tree to feed her. As the cold winds blew wildly around us, I prayed that we would have a roof over our heads that night. By the time Ruth was done, the moon had risen in the sky.

With a prayer in my heart, I approached the first house I saw. It was a small stone cottage, stark and foreboding in the darkening landscape, but the light of a lamp was burning in the window. I knocked at the weatherbeaten wooden door, and a peasant woman answered. "I'm looking for the Rabbi Natan," I told her.

"This is the house," she replied. She studied me for a moment, quite unsure what to make of me, and then gasped when she suddenly noticed Ruth, who had fallen asleep on my back. "Is that a child you're carrying?"

"My daughter."

"Poor thing. She must be freezing," she said, shaking her head in reproach as she opened the door to us.

The woman seated me at her table and then disappeared into one of the rooms. When she came out, she brought me a plate of bread with goat's cheese, and a cup of hot water mixed with fresh herbs and little honey. "The rabbi will see you soon. He doesn't see visitors at this hour, but when I told him that you've come with a child, he agreed to receive you. In the meantime, he asks that you refresh yourself with some food and drink."

A short while later, Rav Natan—the same Rav Natan I had seen from the women's gallery in the synagogue in Tyre—entered the kitchen. "Good evening," he said in a voice that was soft, yet weighted with presence. "My housekeeper tells me that you've come from over the hills with an infant on your back."

"I've come to see you, Rav Natan."

He nodded as if this were in no way unusual. "What is your name?"

"Rahel, sir. Rahel Bat Yair."

"Did you come here alone?"

"I am with my child."

"And no one else?"

"No one else."

"He is in good health, I hope."

"She has endured the rigors of the journey well, praise God."

I could tell from the way he was gazing at us that my haggard appearance troubled him and filled him with pity. "You must be weary," he said, "but I'm afraid that I won't be able to receive you tomorrow or the next day. If you are able, I suggest that we speak now."

Though I was aching with exhaustion, his willingness to receive me gave me fresh strength.

He led me into his study, a small, sparse room with a work table, two simple chairs, and wooden shelves set in the wall. They held a great many rolls of parchment and a good amount of books. A fire was burning in a clay oven in the corner, and behind the table, a small window was open to the dark night.

The peasant woman brought in a pillow and blanket for Ruth, and I set her down beside me.

He motioned for me to sit across from him at the table. "What is it that brings you to my doorstep?" he asked. I looked down at my fingers, thin and trembling slightly. And then, still avoiding his face, my eye was drawn to a sprig of white jasmine flowers on his desk. "Where do you come from, my daughter?" I heard him ask.

"I've come from Tyre," I answered slowly, "but I was born in Sura, in Bavel."

"From Sura," he exclaimed. "The brightest of our young men travel to Sura for the *Kallot*. I myself spent time at the yeshiva."

"Then you must know it well," I replied hopefully.

"Most of my time was spent indoors, but I do remember it as a pleasant town. Pleasant and prosperous. What would make a young girl leave such a place?" He gazed at me quizzically. "Where are your parents, child?"

This was what I had yearned for: the moment when I would tell my story from beginning to end. Yet now that it was upon me I no longer knew what to say. The hope that another person could ever understand it all seemed as wishful as a child's dream. Even if I were to recount every detail, he would not grasp the very thing that I most wanted him to know. Words, I saw now, were paltry; they could never match the truth of all I had known and endured.

I glanced at the jasmine. "Do you see those flowers on your desk?" I began slowly. "They're the color of the dress that I wore on the last day of my life at home. In Sura."

"I am listening, my daughter."

I REVEALED MY tale with care, so that his ears would hear what mine had, and his eyes would see as if through mine, and even his nose would know what mine knew. I spoke for hours, and by the time I was done, the fire in the stove had dwindled to a small, thin flame, and the sky had begun to turn gray. I spoke without knowing his thoughts, for the entire time he listened silently, and in the dim light of the fire, I could hardly make out the line of his face. Did he grimace, frown, or shed a tear for me when I spoke of all I had suffered? Did he smile or nod in relief when I described my moments of happiness? Even now, I cannot say. When I was done, he sat for a long while, his head resting on his hand as if pondering a weighty problem. Finally he looked up and said, "Anton, your esteemed teacher, told you that you are at liberty to go wherever you wish, to do as you please. And yet you have come to me."

"I came here because you are wise and compassionate to unfortunate women; because they say that you have the gift of understanding, beyond that of most men."

"I think that you've come because you knew what I would tell you, and you wanted to hear me speak it."

I shook my head, confused. "How could I possibly know what you'll tell me?"

"My daughter, you're well aware that I've listened to the tales of many men and many women. Nonetheless, the story you've just told me is one of the strangest I've ever heard. Most of us live in the world in a way that is simple; we see life from one set of eyes. You, on the other hand, have seen life out of many eyes. And your soul—it has inhabited many bodies. Yet in the face of this abundance, you've

chosen to seek out a Jew who lives in the mountains, amongst shepherds and farmers. Furthermore, you're fully aware that I can only
advise you according to the dictates of our traditions."

"And what do they say?"

"You know well what they say. They say that you must marry.
They say that the only way for you to return to the Jews is to again
become one of them, to live as a righteous Jewish woman lives, to
take upon yourself the duties and laws pertaining to the Jewish woman. All of these things you already know."

"Yes," I answered softly.

"And still you want to return."

"I can't run anymore. There is nowhere on earth left for me to
go."

"That may be true, and yet to return will be difficult."

"I can't see any other way for me to raise my child."

"Yes." He nodded thoughtfully. "It is for her sake that you want
to return. And perhaps there is a blessing in that. But you have come
to me with a set of circumstances that, shall we say, limits your op-
portunities for marriage. The men of these hills are simple, suspicious, and not always welcoming of strangers. They will see you,
a young woman with a baby, and they'll think of nothing but the
deeds you've done."

"It will be the same wherever I go."

The rabbi nodded slowly and then sat back and closed his eyes
for a long while. When he opened them, he smiled mysteriously and
said, "Something has occurred to me."

"What is it?"

"I can't say yet. But tell me, did anyone see you as you approached
my house? Did you meet anyone on the way?"

"I came after nightfall. No one saw me."

"That is good. Yes. That is very good. I will make some inquires,
and we'll see what comes of my idea. Chana, my housekeeper who
received you, lives behind this house. I'll take you to her, and you
will remain inside. Do not go out for any reason. Chana will bring
you everything you need."

Rain began to fall, stirring Ruth out of her sleep. I took her in my
arms, and Rabbi Natan led us out the back of his house and along
the muddy path to a small cottage. Chana had already started a fire,
and was rolling out dough for bread. "This girl needs to sleep," the

rabbi told her. "Fix a bed for her and the child. Say nothing of her arrival here to anyone."

All that day, the rain beat down on the roof. The air was very cold, and I made sure to keep Ruth warm as she slept beside me. I don't know how long I slept. Jasmine flowers invaded my dreams and took me back to Sura, when I stood before the mirror, clothed in a white dress, a pearl comb set in my hair.

So deep were my dreams that when Chana woke me, I was startled to find myself sleeping on a thin mattress on a frozen stone floor. "The rabbi has returned," she told me. "You must rise now and go to him. I'll mind the child."

I wrapped myself in the blanket and went out. The rain had stopped, and the air was filled with the sharp, fresh scent of mountain grasses. I found him poking at the fire, trying to revive its dying flames. "I believe I've found you a husband," he said simply as soon as we sat down.

"You have?" I asked, astounded. "So quickly?"

Rav Natan smiled. "Hear me out. I have many things to tell you. His name is Amnon, and he is my nephew. His wife died last year while giving birth to their first and only son. We urged him to remarry quickly but he refused, saying that he had no desire for a wife. You see, he too is a scholar—a scholar of great ability. While his wife was still alive, the rabbis of Tiberius approached him, offering him an appointment as head of their yeshiva. After her death, he arranged to leave the boy, Yehuda, in the care of his wife's sister, so that he could continue his work. He returns to Buqei'a every few weeks to see him.

"It appears that the Almighty Himself has arranged this match. As fate would have it, Amnon arrived last week, and has stayed on for a few days. This morning I went to his sister-in-law's house to speak with him about you. At first he didn't want to even consider the notion, but I persisted. I spoke of the advantages of remarriage, and reminded him of the words of Genesis: *It is not good for man to be alone.* We discussed the matter for a long while, and I built my argument with other passages from the Talmud and the holy books, until finally my arguments convinced him and he agreed. But the matter is a delicate one. Everything depends on how we tell your story. I had no choice, you see, but to take the liberty of omitting certain details, and inventing others in their place."

I closed my eyes. "What did you tell him?"

"My daughter, listen to me well. If you are to live in this village, we must disguise all aspects of your identity, so that no one will ever know what you have done. To this end, I told him that you are from a small town in Bavel. That while on a journey with your father, you were attacked by bandits. One of them, the father of your child, was a fair haired Turk, a renegade from the Caliph's army. Your father was killed, and you were kidnapped. They took you across highways and deserts. When you came to Akka, you finally managed to escape them. As for your child, I have explained that in the course of the journey, you were violated; she is the unfortunate result."

I opened my mouth to protest, but the rabbi put a finger to his lips and said, "If the people here should find out the truth about how you've spent these past years, they'll drive you out in disgrace. You and your child will be condemned to wander these hills as outcasts." I looked away from him, defeated, for I saw now that the truth would always have the power to silence me.

"It's not really necessary for you to meet before the wedding. Nevertheless, I have asked Amnon to come here tomorrow. I think that you'll find him more than satisfactory. My nephew is not yet thirty and is still youthful in demeanor. Before his wife died, he had a pleasant character, and I have no doubt that his good spirits will return in time. Your task will be to run his home and raise his child together with your own daughter. He is paid an adequate stipend by the community in Tiberius, and is in possession of a good house and a number of goats, a wedding present from his first wife's family. The marriage will take place next week, before Shabbat.

"It is important that the wedding take place here, in the village," he continued, "with all the women of the town at your side. They will suspect you, but if you are to marry my brother's son, they will refrain from ugly gossip, and afford you the same respect they show to all the members of my family.

"This arrangement has been made hastily, but don't think that I've made it lightly. In spite of your troubling past, and your unfortunate moments of moral weakness, I am pleased with your desire to repent and take up the life of a Jew. I believe that you feel genuine regret for what you've done, and that your repentance is sincere. As I see it, God, in His infinite wisdom, has seen fit to send Amnon a woman to whom life has taught both the importance of family and the value of learning.

"God bless you, Rav Natan," I whispered, for at that moment that was all I was able to utter, while in my heart, I offered up a prayer of infinite gratitude.

I HAD BEEN saved. God had sent a husband to me, and not just any husband but the nephew of Rav Natan of Buqei'a—a respected scholar of good character. Ruth and I would never have to beg, never have to suffer the hardships of women who have no man to speak for them. We would have a family, a village, a community of Jews, who would take us in and call us their own. The nightmare years of my life would finally come to an end.

It was only much later, when night had fallen and I lay in bed under Chana's roof that the things Rav Natan said began to trouble me. The rain started up again, light and comforting at first, but it soon gathered force and became a storm, hammering on the roof as noisily as iron nails. It woke me from my sleep, and brought on imaginings of the life I was going to have.

My husband would be off in Tiberius, studying and teaching others. And I would be here, in this lonely village, amongst strangers who would smile to my face but scorn me in their hearts. In the space of an instant, I would become the mother of another child. My days would be spent at labors no different from those I knew in the home of Omar Alharazi. And as for the man who would soon become my husband, he had been practically forced into this marriage, and would have no more feeling for me than for a servant. Considering it all now in this clear, merciless light, it seemed that fate was laughing at me again. My life would begin and end within the four walls of a cottage, and all I had done and learned and seen would be as if it never was. I rose from my bed as though waking from a nightmare, wrapped a blanket around my shoulders and went out into the black night. The wind howled and the rain poured down on my head, but a light was still burning in Rav Natan's house.

"Rav Natan," I called out as I knocked loudly at his door. "Rav Natan, I need to speak with you."

He opened the door and ushered me inside. "What is it, Rahel?" he asked. "I would have thought that you'd be sleeping soundly beside your daughter."

"I was, Rabbi. But the rain woke me. And I began to think about the plan you've devised." I paused, suddenly uncertain of what I wanted to say. "I'm not sure that I can do this. You see, I've been thinking, and what I'm thinking is that the world is vast, Rav Natan. Infinitely vast. And surely God above has led me through it all with some purpose in mind, to some end that is somehow more. . . more purposeful than. . ."

"But of course He has. He has intended you to be the mother of a new generation of righteous children. What could be more purposeful than that?"

"But is that all, Rav Natan?" I whispered tearfully. "Is that all?"

For a long moment he regarded me gravely. "Listen carefully to what I'm going to say to you now, my daughter, and mark my meaning. Are you listening?"

I nodded rapidly, trembling with cold.

"In the *Talmud Bavli*, it is said that when God created the sun and the moon to rule the heavens, the moon complained to God, saying, *Can two kings share the same crown?* And do you know, Rahel, what God answered? Do you know what God advised the moon?"

I shook my head. "God answered the moon, saying, *You must diminish thyself.* Do you hear me, Rahel? Do you perceive my meaning?"

"Diminish myself?" I felt as if he had struck me. "Have you nothing more to say to me?"

"That is all," he replied sternly. "Go back to your bed now, and get some rest. I have done all I can for you. Accept your fate gladly and gratefully. If I were you I would welcome it with both arms. Next week we will have a wedding, and the long night of your suffering will come to an end."

"A wedding! Where a man I don't even know will *acquire* me!" I cried, thinking back to the words of the Talmud. "Rav Natan, do you remember your visit to the synagogue in Tyre? I was there. I was sitting in the women's section, mute and invisible. But I heard it all. And I well remember your words."

"What words do you remember?"

"*Seder Nashim*," I said. "*Masehet Kidushin*. The Talmud speaks of three ways to acquire a wife." I held up my hand and counted on my fingers. "A ring. A contract. Sexual relations. But have you never thought that perhaps there is a fourth way?"

"And what might that be?"

"It might be love, Rav Natan. Isn't it possible that a man might acquire a wife by means of love?"

"The Talmud does not concern itself with love," he scoffed. "Love is as fleeting and changeable as the weather. It is an illusion that distracts us from what is essential. The love that you speak of is for the writings of the pagans."

"But isn't it possible that the writings of the pagans hold a small piece of wisdom between their lines?"

"You must go now," he replied sternly. "Go back to your daughter, and think about the words that God said to the moon. That is my advice to you, and you will do well to remember it."

IT WAS THE fault of the words, my words. They were weak when they should have been full of force and spirit. They failed me when I most needed them, and now, I would have to live by the words of others; words uttered long ago by sages and copied into holy books by scribes who had purified themselves before setting their pens to the paper.

Love is for the writings of the pagans, he had said. And truly, for me there would be no love; just as Creon decreed that if Antigone refused to live by his rules, she would lose all—and she had. I don't know what made me think of Antigone as I walked out into the rain, but my thoughts took me far, far from Buqei'a, to the library at Mar Yuhanon, where I would sit by the window, reading books that I would surely never see again.

And then, like a sudden flash of lightning, there came upon me a notion so bizarre that I laughed aloud in the darkness. What if I were to take a pen in my hand, and record the strange, unspeakable tale of what had happened to me? What if I were to set it all down in writing, so that my story would live on, as Antigone's did? Perhaps someone would find it one day, and read my words, and then they would know that God had once endowed me with the courage to murder my enemy, and the strength to escape my own enslavement. And He had sent me to a place where I learned that there is wisdom in the words of men long dead, even if they be pagans, and that there was once a man called Lucan from Baratiniya, and that I lay with him of my own free will, and that it was he, and no other, who was my child's father.

Yes, I whispered to myself. I would do this. I would find a scroll of parchment and inkpot, and a pen, and in the dead of night, when no one could see, I would do as Sophocles had done; I would take words and vest them with the power to reveal what cannot be seen by the eye. And when they were bashful, I would sit by the dim light of the lamp and envision them as only I knew them. In this way, the truth about my life, my real life, would be saved.

Even as I stumbled, wet and shivering through the mud, I could see it in my mind; how I would wait for the hour when the truth is ready to emerge, and how I would take the pen in my hand, and then, by the flickering light of the lamp I would write: *I, Rahel Bat Yair, was born in the city of Sura, which lies on the western bank of the river Euphrates in the land of Bavel, where the great houses of learning shine their light.*

EPILOGUE

Buqei'a, Galilee, 894

All night long Yair pored over the small, tight script. He read slowly, for the things that were revealed to him that night were as shocking as the strangest of visions and the most troubling of dreams. When he was done, he shut his eyes and put his head in his hands. He sat that way for a long while until finally, in the gray hour before dawn, Yehuda appeared at the door.

"You've read it."

"Yes."

"Are we in agreement regarding what's to be done?"

Yair shook his head slowly. "I don't know. I . . . I'm not sure. It's as if we never knew her."

"That was my first thought exactly. But in the past few days, I believe I've come to understand what happened."

"Understand?" Yair muttered bitterly. "What do you understand?"

"Imagine it: A young girl appears from out of nowhere with a baby in her arms. She's all alone, she knows no one, and after three years of unimaginable suffering, she suddenly finds herself married, the new mother of her husband's children. The rabbi has sworn her to secrecy. She can tell no one who she is and what she has endured. The loneliness of it is unbearable. And yet, in the midst of her suffering she was endowed with a gift—the mastery of writing." Yehuda paused a moment, as if to collect his thoughts.

"Go on."

"For her, the page is like a companion, a compassionate friend with whom she can speak freely. She writes her story, and then hides it away. The years pass. More children are born to her. The people of the town come to respect her and accept her as one of their own. She grows accustomed to the ways of the village, and in time, she forgets the manuscript she once hid in the wall. But if she had remembered it, she would have destroyed it, so that no one would ever know of her disgraceful past, a past of which, as we have seen, she is deeply ashamed."

"No."

"What, then?"

"I don't believe that she ever forgot the manuscript. If she truly feared its discovery she would have destroyed it herself. On the contrary, I think she wanted us to find it. She wanted the truth to survive her, so that we would learn exactly who she was. Why do you think she writes about the Greek drama? Because something in the story of the Greek girl spoke to her, something that in spite of all the differences, reminded her of herself. And like her, she too wanted to leave a record behind."

"No." Yehuda shook his head. "The Greek girl was honorable. But there are shameful things here. Things that no woman would want to live on after her."

"And still she recorded them, and called them the truth."

"The truth." Yehuda threw up his hands. "What does *that* mean? When we are young, we think the truth to be the most important thing in the world, more important than family, more important than community. Even more important than one's own honor. But what is the truth, really? Only God knows the truth. For men, the truth is just the name we give to the story that we tell ourselves."

Yair shook his head. "If we destroy the scroll we betray her."

"No Yair. The betrayal will be to allow even one other person to read this, to expose her secrets, secrets that any woman would want to take to her grave. How can you not see it? We, as her sons, have a duty to protect her name, and ours, from the indiscreet ramblings of a despondent young girl."

"I have to think about it."

"There's no time to think anymore. It must be done now. The longer we wait, the greater the chance that someone else will find it."

Yair shut his eyes for a long time and rocked back and forth, as if considering a Talmudic problem that has more than one answer, while Yehuda sat by his side, waiting for his word. After a long while Yair turned to his brother and nodded. "Bring the lamp."

Yehuda took the scroll in his hand and held it over the flame. The two of them watched as the dry parchment caught fire and then crumbled into black dust. "May her righteous soul in heaven be comforted," he whispered.

Yair wiped a tear from his eye. "May her blessed memory live on."

IN ACKNOWLEDGMENT

To Sheyna Galyan, who isn't afraid to makes decisions with her heart; to Leslie Martin, for her enthusiasm; to Monika Ittah and Rachel Quastel, my very first readers, who gave me the faith to push on; to the many people who read early drafts of this work, each of whose unique perspective shaped my thinking; to my teachers, Jonathan Papernick, Allen Hoffman, Jonathan Wilson, and Linda Zisquit, whose direction gave form and focus to what was nebulous and obscure; and to my family, near and far, whose support has made my own journey both possible and worthwhile.

I thank each of you for your time, your attention, and your good will.

—J.W.